The Royal Ghost

A MINA SCARLETTI MYSTERY

The Royal Ghost

LINDA STRATMANN

This book is dedicated to the Royal Pavilion and Museums Foundation
www.pavilionfoundation.org

First published 2016

The Mystery Press is an imprint of The History Press
The Mill, Brimscombe Port
Stroud, Gloucestershire, GL5 2QG
www.thehistorypress.co.uk

British Library Cataloguing in Publication Data.
A catalogue record for this book is available from the British Library.

ISBN 978 0 7509 6629 0

Typesetting and origination by The History Press
Printed and bound in Great Britain by TJ International Ltd.

Praise for
Mr Scarletti's Ghost:
A Mina Scarletti Mystery

'I love Linda Stratmann's writing. Her descriptions
of Brighton are so sharp and vivid you can
smell and taste the city on every page'

Peter James, international bestselling author of the DS Roy Grace series

'Linda Stratmann has provided an
indomitable heroine in Mina Scarletti'

promotingcrime.blogspot.com

'The novel is perfect for those who enjoy a
Victorian atmosphere […] it is thoughtful,
well-characterised and thought-provoking'

Historical Novel Society

'Linda Stratmann is happily feeding the
unquenchable thirst for Victorian crime fiction'

www.crimefictionlover.com

Brighton, 1871

One

Enveloped in the sweet aroma of perfumed oils, Mina Scarletti lay on warm white towels while skilled fingers smoothed away the tension in her back. Mina understood and accepted that she would never be entirely free from pain. Her spine, twisted like an angry snake, distorted the angle of her ribs and hipbone, crushed her small body and placed awkward stresses on her muscles, which gave frequent pinching reminders of a permanent insult. Islands of peace and pleasure still remained within her reach, however, when, after enjoying a herbal steam bath at Dr Daniel Hamid's popular establishment on the Brighton seafront, his sister Anna applied the 'medicated oriental shampoo' or 'massage' as it was sometimes known. After an hour's treatment, Mina felt as flat, pink and boneless as a starfish washed up on the beach, and the world outside looked a little brighter.

Anna had also, with great care and sensitivity, introduced Mina to the world of callisthenics with classes held in the bathhouse's own gymnasium. Twice a week Mina donned a light, loose assembly of chemise and bloomers, in which she worked to improve the support for her misshapen torso with the aid of stretching exercises and weights. She had even learned to hang by her hands from a bar like a circus acrobat. Mina had deliberately not mentioned this new skill to her mother, Louisa, who would have been horrified at the idea of her daughter adopting such an outrageous posture while wearing an indecent costume.

In recent weeks relaxation had come more easily to Mina, following the news that a dangerous criminal had been arrested.

Serious crime was thankfully a great rarity in Brighton, and the publication of a warning notice by the police that some unknown person was sending fruit and cakes laced with arsenic to prominent residents had sent the whole town into a ferment of terror. The word was about that the days of the Borgias had returned. Louisa had determined that she would be greatly affected by the threat of danger, and it had been Mina's exhausting duty to examine and re-examine every item of foodstuff in the house irrespective of whether it had been delivered or purchased directly from a shop. Urgent meetings had been held at the Scarletti home, to which Louisa had invited her closest friends, regaling them with the news that they were all about to be murdered and the anxiety was causing her the most terrible suffering.

Once the fiend in human form was in custody and revealed to be a middle-aged spinster with an unhealthy passion for a married doctor, Brighton could heave a municipal sigh of relief, and the search was soon on for fresher and pleasanter sensations. The latest novelty to excite residents and visitors alike was a pamphlet entitled *An Encounter* in which two fanciful ladies had described how, while engaged in a tour of the Royal Pavilion, they had seen the spectre of the late King George IV at a period of his life when he was the young pleasure-seeking Prince of Wales, and affectionately known as 'Prinny'. Some portions of their account were reputed to be of an indelicate nature – whether this was deliberate or unconscious was not apparent – and therefore wholly unfit for the perusal of the female sex. As a result, the pamphlet was selling by the hundred to ladies of all ages and walks of life, the copies being taken secretly to boudoirs to be enjoyed in private. Mina had not read *An Encounter* and had no great wish to do so. She enjoyed both stories and histories, but a work of fiction that had been dressed up to seem like fact in order to delude the impressionable she found merely annoying, not to mention dishonest.

Mina knew the difference between the real and the imaginary, since she occupied her solitary hours writing stories about ghosts and monsters. Her tales were published under a pseudonym by the Scarletti Library of Romance, a company founded by her late father, Henry. The only person privy to her secret identity was her father's business partner, Mr Greville. Her family, in so much as they took any interest in her writing, remained under the impression that she composed moral tales for children. The ghosts and monsters Mina created existed only in her mind, and while she gave them a kind of life by transferring them to paper, she knew that they would not reach out from the page and become real. She was all too aware, however, that suggestible persons of both sexes could easily persuade themselves that they had seen this or that elemental or supernatural being. In the early summer of that year Mina, with the assistance of Dr Hamid, had been instrumental in exposing the activities of a self-styled medium, Miss Eustace, who had taken Brighton by storm and extorted money from her adherents, impersonating a spirit by donning veils that glowed in the dark from the application of oil of phosphorus, and sending messages supposedly from the deceased by tapping a table leg with her foot. Mina had found the deception as transparent as the veils, but those who needed to believe had done so, gratefully, and had had their purses lightened and bank accounts severely depleted as a result. The adventure had cemented a warm friendship between Mina, Dr Hamid and his sister Anna, who often entertained her at their home or accompanied her as she limped her slow walk along the promenade. She had hoped that the public taste for the wonderful had subsided into something approaching common sense, but judging by the success of *An Encounter*, it seemed it had not.

No one had as yet introduced the subject of the supposed ghostly sighting in the Royal Pavilion in conversation with Mina, presumably to avoid stimulating her curiosity about matters no respectable woman, whether married or single, should ever contemplate. Anna Hamid, however, her hands easing away the soreness in Mina's back to almost nothing, after discussing issues relating to general healthfulness and the current news of the town, asked after some hesitation if she had read *An Encounter*.

'There have been letters denouncing it in the *Gazette*, but I have not actually read the book,' said Mina, 'and I am not sure if I would be either entertained or informed by it. If the authors had admitted from the start that it was an invention then I might find it amusing but I believe that they are quite serious about their subject. I rather thought that your brother and I had frightened away all the ghosts from Brighton.'

'That is the reason I am asking, as you know so much about these things, and I would value your opinion from a woman's point of view,' said Anna. 'I am very concerned that this book is upsetting the constitution of those who read it. Many ladies who come here for treatment have read it, and been overexcited to a dangerous degree. Some might think I would be pleased to have more patients seeking our services, but I do not want to line my purse by perfectly healthy ladies being made unwell. I wish to preserve the health of the town, and that means not only treating those who are in pain and discomfort but also maintaining the wellbeing of those who already enjoy it. Several of the patients I have seen recently complaining of attacks of agitation and nervousness have confessed to me that their symptoms began when they read the book. Certain passages I believe they found especially powerful.'

The massage done, Anna helped Mina to sit up and swathed her tiny angular form in scented linen. Anna's pale fawn cheeks were flushed, but she did not elaborate on what she had learned, and Mina knew her well enough not to enquire further. She was, like Mina, a decided spinster, although Anna, at the age of forty-eight, had chosen to be single, whereas Mina, although twenty-five and still of an age to marry and raise a family, had been told some years ago that it would be unwise for her ever to do so.

'If these susceptible ladies are afraid of encountering the Prince's ghost then surely all they need to do is stay away from those places he customarily visited when in town,' Mina suggested.

'I fear it is not the haunting that troubles them,' sighed Anna. 'Far from it; some have told me that they have actually been holding séances with the explicit design of having him appear before them.'

Mina had once seen a caricature of the late King George IV, a gourmand who had become bloated by excess, and could not imagine anyone wishing to see such an unattractive sight either living or ghostly. Had he been handsome in his youth? Was that what all the fuss was about? Or was it just the thrill of an exalted connection? A lady might forgive a great deal for royalty. 'I am sorry to hear about these foolish séances, but I suppose they are harmless enough diversions if they are not taken too seriously. Do these ladies employ professional mediums? I hope they are not being cheated any more than they deserve.'

'No, they just sit in the dark and call upon the spirits, I believe. One lady told me the Prince appeared in her parlour and took tea with her, but I think she was merely describing what she wished for, and not what actually occurred.'

'Knowing Brighton society as I do, I have no doubt of it. A story to make her friends jealous.'

Anna brought more towels and pressed their soft warmth around Mina's shoulders. 'Well, since you have not read the book, you cannot comment upon it. In fact, I would suggest for the sake of your health that you avoid it altogether. I have not read it myself and have no intention of doing so.'

In view of this strong advice, Mina decided not to pursue the subject with Anna, but she was already considering how she might use her connection to the business of publishing to make enquiries that could alleviate her friend's concerns.

Two

ina had first met Dr Daniel Hamid the previous June at a séance conducted by the celebrated spiritualist and sensation of Brighton, Miss Hilarie Eustace. Mina had attended because she was worried – quite rightly as it was to turn out – that her mother and friends were being made the victims of a charlatan whose hidden purpose was to extort large sums of money from the vulnerable bereaved. Dr Hamid, on the other hand, grieving deeply for the recent loss of his beloved Jane, his wife of twenty years, had been seeking hope and comfort in the assurances of mediums. Both hope and comfort had been cruelly wrenched from him by the discovery that he had been duped by a trickster. Furious with the heartless criminal, he had been angry most of all with himself for being so taken in, especially since he had always liked to believe that he was a rational, scientific man. He had at once thrown his energies into helping Mina expose Miss Eustace and her confederates as frauds and thieves, even taking risks that brought him close to the boundaries of what might seem appropriate for a doctor of medicine.

The deceitful Miss Eustace had demonstrated her selfless sincerity by performing her evening séances without making any charge, receiving only those rewards voluntarily given by the grateful, but it was discovered that she also offered private sittings to suitable individuals for which she charged a substantial fee. Behind closed doors, with only the medium and her dupe present, messages were passed on, supposedly from much-loved deceased relatives, which induced the victim to part with ever-increasing sums of money. Mina's determined campaign had revealed the despicable scheme before an appalled public, and the miscreants were now contemplating the fruits of their villainy at the Lewes House of Correction while awaiting trial at the next Sussex assizes.

Once her treatment was over, Mina, feeling much refreshed, went to see Dr Hamid, who had just completed an interview with a patient and was back in his office. Three years younger than Anna, he was neatly bearded, with sad dark eyes.

'I hope you are well?' he asked anxiously as Mina appeared. Each time he saw her, even on a social occasion, he would appraise her walk and posture to see if there was any change in her condition. Her unexpected visit had clearly given him cause for concern, as he was the only doctor she would trust. No one in Brighton was better acquainted than he with the presentation of scoliosis. His older sister Eliza, who had passed away that summer, had been afflicted to a far greater degree than Mina, her distorted spine creating an exaggerated twist, lifting one shoulder high while forcing the other down, pushing her neck forward so far that she was unable to raise her head. More seriously, her misshapen ribs had constricted the action of both heart and lungs. Dr Hamid and Anna had been devoted to Eliza's care, and she would have lived longer had she not become overexcited after being drawn into the medium's net of delusion.

'I am very well, thank you,' said Mina reassuringly, taking the seat that faced him across the desk, tucking a cushion under one hip to even her posture. 'Miss Hamid's massages always ease my discomfort and are a great blessing. She did, however, mention something that is causing her some disquiet. It seems that séances have come back into fashion in Brighton, and ladies are being disturbed by a publication in which two visitors to the Pavilion have claimed that they saw the ghost of the late King George. If it was not for the fact that it is upsetting people I would think it quite comical. Do you have any observations?'

Dr Hamid's relief that Mina had not come for a professional consultation evaporated rapidly. He looked decidedly uncomfortable and took some time to compose his reply. 'It is a difficult subject to discuss with any frankness, especially since you are single. I too have seen patients coming here who have been affected by this publication. All of them are ladies who have started to experience fainting fits and unusual excitement. Their family doctors assume that they are suffering from a variety of hysteria and prescribe soporific mixtures, but that merely treats the symptoms. Anna has found that steam baths and the oriental shampoo are far more beneficial in that they both calm and restore the system. But the book is an unwise publication and should never have been printed. I suspect that the authors were quite unaware of what they were writing and the effect it would have on the more sensitive reader. Some portions of the narrative can be interpreted in quite a shocking light.'

'Then you have read it?'

He tidied the already tidy pile of papers on his desk, in an effort to conceal his embarrassment. 'I – er – well – I was obliged to read it for professional reasons,' he admitted reluctantly.

Mina could not resist a smile. 'And have you suffered from fainting fits and excitement?'

He stared at her in surprise. 'No, of course not!'

'So are gentlemen immune to its effects?'

Dr Hamid was speechless for a moment. 'Apparently so.'

Mina decided to stop teasing him. 'I have been told that the ladies of Brighton are holding séances in their homes to raise the ghost of the late King. Why they might wish to do so I really can't say. It all seems very foolish and we must hope it is a fashion that will be quickly replaced by the next one.'

He nodded emphatically. 'I entertain the same hope. Brighton is a place of fashion after all, and constantly moves from one novelty to another. In a week this may all be forgotten.'

Mina agreed. In August and September it was usual for the town to be gay with noisy families in search of amusement and diversion, but with the approach of October, children returned to school, professional gentlemen came to take their leisure, and a new quieter mood began to settle. Later, in November, all would be different again, as the carriage classes began their winter season.

'I have no wish to attend such gatherings; not that I would be invited to them. After Miss Eustace's fall from grace those Brighton spiritualists who continue to believe in her – and yes I am sorry to say that there are still some who regard her as a martyr to the cause – have stamped me as a hardened unbeliever. It appears that I radiate negative influences which would ensure that any attempt to contact the spirits in my presence will fail.'

'Oh, I am done with séances,' said Dr Hamid, feelingly. 'It is a great deal of money to pay out just to learn that you are a fool.'

'Those who can never learn will remain fools all their lives,' said Mina, gently. 'Without your insight and your assistance, Miss Eustace and her henchmen would not now be facing a trial for fraud.'

'That is very kind of you to say so. We can only hope that they will remain where they can do no more harm for a very long time.'

'That is my hope too,' agreed Mina, 'however they will be free again one day, and I suspect that once they are, they will continue their lives of deception, since it is all they know, but I do not think they will dare show their faces here again. If there are people still holding séances in Brighton they are at least doing it on their own account merely for an evening's amusement and not paying others to cheat them. Let them go on and take what comfort they can until they tire of it and turn to something else. I am pleased to say that my mother will have no truck with such things again, and in any case she has plenty to distract her – my sister Enid and her twins are staying with us and they are keeping the fond grandmother happily occupied.' Mina made a significant pause. 'But just in case mother does succumb to temptation and reads *An Encounter*, what signs of upset should I look for? Fainting and excitement, you say; mother can produce them both at will when she means to have her way, without recourse to disturbing literature. Is there anything else that might give me cause for concern?'

'Imagined symptoms of illness, headaches, difficulty in sleeping, lack of appetite, overindulgence in stimulants or soporifics. The presentation can be different depending on the individual. Tight lacing can make matters very much worse. But if you should notice this in any lady you know, please do refer her to Anna, who has devised a special massage to release the harmful vapours.'

'That is very helpful, thank you.' Mina rose to depart, but did not immediately do so. 'I do have one other request.'

'Oh?' said Dr Hamid warily. He had, Mina noticed, a peculiar tone of voice which he had adopted recently at any suggestion she might make which could, if pursued, lead him into the murky waters of professional embarrassment.

'I would like to borrow your copy of *An Encounter* and study it for myself. From what I have heard booksellers might be chary of selling it to a spinster, and I would prefer it if my mother did not know I was reading it. My purpose is to learn what I can about the book, to see if it can be exposed as a mere work of the imagination.'

Dr Hamid looked understandably alarmed. 'Do you think that is wise?'

'I promise I will try very hard not to be put into a great state by it and if I am, then I already know the symptoms, and I will simply come here and enjoy a steam bath and massage which will surely set me right. In any case, I really cannot believe that *all* the ladies who have read the book suffer unpleasant consequences.'

'That is true,' he admitted. 'The ladies who derive such an unhealthy excitement are, I have observed, those with no occupation to use their natural energies, and husbands who neglect them.'

'I shall never have a husband, neglectful or otherwise, and I think I am the happier for it,' Mina declared. 'When I am not practising my callisthenics, or enjoying the sights of the town, or attending to my mother's many whims, my story writing keeps me fully occupied.'

'And what tale are you currently busy with?'

The question was intended to deflect her purpose and she smiled. 'I am writing about a little lady, one who suffers many bodily afflictions and is shunned by a society that sees only outward appearances. She has beautiful visions, because she has a good soul, and becomes surrounded by a glowing light. As a result others are at last able to see the goodness within her, and she is much loved.'

He swallowed back a sudden burst of emotion. 'Is she called Eliza?'

'She is.'

A moment passed between them in which shared sadness and fond memories mingled, as they recalled Eliza's too short yet defiantly cheerful life which had, in her last weeks, been enlivened by friendship with Mina and enjoyment of the more amusing and less bloodcurdling stories in her repertoire.

'As I am sure you know,' Mina pointed out, 'I am the last person in Brighton to be worried by a ghost story.'

'I know that you are strong-minded but believe me, it is far worse than that. There is material in the book which is quite unsuitable for a respectable single lady. I do not think,' he added cautiously, 'that you would be put into a great state by it, nevertheless, I cannot risk taking the responsibility of lending you a copy. I really am sorry.'

Mina glanced at his desk, feeling sure that a slim volume lay within her reach in a drawer. 'You are being careful of my health, which I understand and appreciate. But a lady who uncovered the secrets of an extortioner's plot can certainly obtain a book if she sets her mind to it.'

'I have no doubt of it, but it will not be from me.'

'If I can prove that the story is a fraud dressed up as history then that information could help soothe your patients.'

He wavered, but at last shook his head. 'My answer is still no, and please do not press me further. But there is one thing that I should mention. The book nowhere involves séances or mediums. It describes a vision – one for which the ladies were wholly unprepared.'

'A ghostly sighting – well there are many such stories about.'

'And have been since stories began. Brighton is rife with them. But are they no more than idle tales? I think that if ghosts did not exist at all, then people would not talk or write about them. There must be some small grain of truth in it. In fact —' he hesitated. 'I know you would not like to believe this but from time to time patients of mine have reported seeing phantoms of the deceased – those they love and sorely miss. These are intelligent people, both men and women, not disordered in their minds apart from suffering the grief of recent bereavement. Their visions are clear and convincing – the individuals appear before them as solid and real as if they stood in the same room.'

'Do these visions occur in daylight or darkness?'

'Both.'

'But only of those friends and relations who are constantly in their thoughts, not celebrated individuals unknown to them.'

'True.'

Mina paused, reflectively. 'My mother once told me that she saw my father's ghost, but I am not sure what it was she saw. She does like to embroider a tale. And you – have you experienced anything of the nature you describe?'

He uttered a little sigh of regret. 'No. I often think how pleasant it would be to sit in my parlour with Anna and have my dearest Jane and Eliza there with us, so that we might gaze on their faces again, but it has not come to pass. Perhaps some special talent is required which I do not have, and it may be that the ladies who wrote this highly unwise publication do.'

'So you think it may be genuine and not a fiction?'

'It is not, in my view, impossible.'

Mina gazed on him sadly. He had every reason to want to believe in ghosts, as did she. The passing of her dear sister Marianne ten years ago, dead of consumption at the age of twelve, was still a painful memory. So too was her father's death in the spring of last year after his long wasting illness, yet she had never sought to call their spirits to her from the heavenly beyond where they now resided, and which was surely now their natural home. Dr Hamid saw only the void in his life that had once been filled by his wife and sister, and his judgement was weakened by a keen sense of loss. She wanted to tell him that time would help heal the wound. There would be a scar, of course, and it would still hurt but it would not be so raw and open. But he had surely been told this by others, and as a fundamentally sensible man he realised it himself. Hesitantly she reached out and patted his arm, in a way that a sister might comfort a brother.

He sighed again and nodded. 'I know,' he said. 'I know.'

Three

Every day in Mina's life was a battle with the infirmity that had first become noticeable when she was fifteen. She did not, as others might have done, choose to hide from the world, but was determined to live her life to the very fullest in all ways that were both decent and possible, except those that she had been told were denied to her. By not confining herself to those restricted spheres of endeavour thought to be appropriate for women, she was able to embrace eagerly all else that the world had to offer. Some three years ago, Mina and her family had deserted the fogs and chills of London to live in Montpelier Road, Brighton, a location chosen for the invigorating air and bright sunshine, which it was hoped would restore her ailing father's health. Her older brother Edward had remained in the capital, where he helped maintain the successful publishing house founded by their father, and also to stay close by the side of the enchanting Miss Hooper, an heiress who had recently consented to be his bride.

Soon after their father's death, Mina's sister Enid, who was considered to be the beauty of the family, had deserted the house of mourning, which she had found unendurable, to marry a Mr Inskip, the dullest solicitor who ever existed, and they had made their home in London. Enid had been amusing herself by tormenting a shoal of ardent and agreeable admirers, and her impetuous acceptance of Mr Inskip, based solely on his superior financial worth, had, she soon realised, been a terrible mistake. In recent months, important business concerns had demanded her husband's presence in the far reaches of Europe and had placed a sea, a mountain pass and great tracts of barren land between them.

Enid had come to Brighton to be with her mother, accompanied by her infant twins and a nursemaid, her state of mind and health exhibiting that glowing perfection of contentment that could only be achieved by the extended absence of Mr Inskip. The boys were a source of endless delight to the doting grandmother, if not the mother, and were constantly and resolutely declared to be the image of their Scarletti grandfather. Mina did not want to contemplate the dismay that might ensue if their baby noses ever sharpened to resemble Mr Inskip's proboscis or their infant blue eyes darkened to the colour of silt.

Enid never spoke of her husband; to her he was in a sense dead, and she clearly wished him to remain so. She and her mother spent their days shopping, admiring the babies and engaging in private conversations to which Mina, as a single woman, could never be admitted.

Mina's days were largely solitary; writing or reading, exercising with the dumbbells she kept hidden in the bottom of her wardrobe, or taking in the sights and scents of the town. There were other worlds in her mind, which she could explore freely – places where ghosts and witches and demons abided, and broke out onto the pages of her books to trouble the heroes and heroines she created. Most of all Mina enjoyed the random and usually unannounced visits of her younger brother Richard, a charming rapscallion with a heart of gold, who divided his time between London and Brighton depending on where he was most able to obtain and spend money, an elusive commodity which ran rapidly though his fingers like a glistening stream.

As Mina arrived home the maidservant, Rose, was taking a laden tray into the parlour. The pile of iced fancies and a fat yellow sponge cake filled with jam told Mina at once that the visitor being entertained was her mother's friend Mrs Bettinson, whose favourite delights these were. Not that the word 'delight' was one often associated with Mrs Bettinson, a lady who gloried in her widowhood so much that her relatives obligingly died at regular intervals to afford her fresh opportunities to display her imposing bulk in an excess of jet, bombazine and crape. Above all, Mrs Bettinson relished the discovery and dissemination of gossip, and enjoyed the flavour of misery better than that of the choicest pastry.

As Mina entered the parlour, which was smokily warm from the first substantial coal fire of the season, the two ladies glanced up at her quickly and the conversation, which had been proceeding apace, abruptly stopped.

'Why Mina,' said her mother with a brightness that was too brittle to be convincing, 'we were just discussing —' there was a pause, 'the – er – healthfulness of Dr Hamid's steam baths. I trust you are refreshed?'

'Very much so,' said Mina, cheerfully. She limped to a comfortable seat and sat down, making an effort to maintain as straight a posture as possible. Mrs Bettinson frowned at her disapprovingly. 'I am at the very peak of healthfulness,' she added. Mrs Bettinson frowned harder.

Rose poured tea for Mina, and she sipped it with the contented smile that she knew their visitor deplored. A newspaper, the latest copy of the *Brighton Gazette*, was open on her mother's lap. Louisa, who had entered a profound and lengthy period of melancholy following the death of her husband, had only recently begun to emerge into the light of Brighton society in which she was rapidly becoming an acknowledged ornament. Having once declared that newspapers gave her a headache, she now devoured them for all the news of the town and its personalities, taking little interest in events that lay outside that confined circle. Her favourite study was the Local Fashionable Intelligence, which listed those gentry and other persons of note who had just arrived and which hotel they were favouring with their presence. Her thoughts seemed constantly to be occupied with how she might obtain an entrée to a more rarified social circle than the one she currently enjoyed.

At fifty-five Louisa still had a youthfully slender figure and almost unlined face, with soft pale skin and golden hair that owed nothing to artifice. Her mourning gowns, which had been sombre black for a year, were now being trimmed with white lace and mauve ribbon in preparation for her future butterfly emergence into brilliant colour. Louisa's fresh glow appeared all the more charming beside Mrs Bettinson, who occupied any room she inhabited like a great dark hill topped by a stony monument.

Mina saw that the newspaper was open at the page of correspondence, but Louisa, noticing her glance, folded it shut so quickly that had it been a book it would have made a loud snap. Mina suspected that the two had been discussing *An Encounter*, which had been the subject of much heated debate in the *Gazette* in so far as this was possible without the paper actually stating why the work was so objectionable. This led her to consider whether her mother had read the book, something that she would never admit to any member of her family. It was easy enough for Mina to avoid being drawn into the conversation, which dwelt largely on recent deaths and other terrible misfortunes, and she quickly finished her tea, declined a cake, and said she would retire to her room. Mrs Bettinson, assuming that Mina was weary and needed rest, nodded, her lip curling with grim satisfaction.

Mina went upstairs as fast as she was able, using both hands on the rail to assist her. If the amount of tea and cake was anything to judge by she had a full hour alone.

It took only moments to find a copy of *An Encounter* under her mother's pillow, and Mina took it to her room. There she sat at her writing desk, placed her special wedge-shaped cushion under one hip in order to sit up straight, and opened the book.

Four

n Encounter was a short volume numbering some forty pages. The authors were the Misses Ada and Bertha Bland, which were so obviously invented names that it scarcely seemed necessary to mention as the title page did that they had adopted pseudonyms in order to preserve their anonymity. The only information revealed about them was that they were sisters, single ladies, daughters of a respectable clergyman, and lived in London.

The cover was bound in plain brown leather and inside was a portrait, a drawing obviously copied from a painting, of the late King George IV in his princely youth. This was not the bloated gourmand he had become in later life, a man so unpopular in his latter years that he hardly ever went about in public and had even had a tunnel built from the basement rooms of the Pavilion so he could visit his stables unseen. This portrait was of a young, handsome, strongly made man, with a torrent of wavy hair and a commanding expression. How much of this portrayal was accurate and how much was flattery of the artist Mina did not know, but she could see that as depicted he might be thought quite a romantic figure, especially as he was at that period of his life Prince Regent, and therefore King of England in all but name, which was enough to make any female heart flutter.

The book had been published that same year, 1871, although there was no indication as to when it had actually been written, and neither was it stated when the events described within had taken place. There was no publisher listed, the title page simply saying that it had been printed for the authors and giving the name and address of a London printing company, Worple and Co. Mina turned to the text for possible clues.

The Misses Bland, having heard of the health-giving properties of Brighton, had, accompanied by their widowed father, made a day excursion to that popular location. Their object was to enjoy the invigorating sea air and view the gardens and the Pavilion. Once a royal residence, now an amenity of the town, this building, they had been told, was a wonderful sight to behold. None of the family had visited Brighton before, and, said the ladies, they were quite unacquainted with its history. The sisters had determined before they set out to write quite separate accounts of their adventure since they thought it would be amusing and instructive to compare them afterwards. On arrival, their father had expressed a desire to take a bracing walk in the grounds of the Pavilion. The building itself he hesitated to enter, and was content to observe only its exterior. He did not think it an entirely wholesome place, since the late King George had been known for his scandalous behaviour, which caused great grief to his parents and brought shame to the royal family. The King, said the Reverend Bland, was reputed to have lived like an oriental potentate in more ways than one. Further than this he would not say, but his warnings had inadvertently whetted his daughters' appetites to see the royal luxury promised by the domes and minarets that glistened invitingly in the sunshine.

The ladies had at last succeeded in obtaining their father's permission to enter the Pavilion by saying that there was an entertainment they would like to attend, an exhibition by a conjuror who was donating all his fees to a charity for the support of families affected by a disaster at sea. With some reservations the Reverend Bland agreed to this, and it was settled that they would all meet in one hour at the tea room. The ladies' account went on to provide some slight description of the exterior, the velvet lawns, the rookery, and the music of a military band, but their main delight was in the gleaming white Pavilion itself, the fabulously exotic spires and cupolas that made visitors feel as if they had been transported by a magic carpet to lands of the orient.

When the sisters entered the Pavilion they discovered to their disappointment that the entertainment which they had seen advertised in the newspaper would not be given until later that day, after the time appointed for their departure. They decided instead to take a tour of the building, and paid their sixpences to join a party and be guided by an attendant. The first room they saw on leaving the ticket hall was the vestibule, also known as the Hall of the Worthies. Although they thought the decorative columns and carving very fine, and could not fail to be impressed by a large statue of a handsome young soldier waving a sword – a hero of the Crimean War who had died on the battlefield – neither felt any great attraction to the display of busts depicting stern-faced gentlemen, notabilities of Brighton of whom they had never heard. As the attendant expounded at wearisome length on the many virtues and achievements of the citizens of Brighton, the Misses Bland, by mutual agreement, slipped away and explored on their own.

As they walked it seemed to them that the rooms gradually became darker and the shadows deeper. The sound of visitors' voices and the music of the band that had seeped in from outside slowly faded until they vanished altogether. The ladies suddenly realised that they were quite alone, and each commented to the other that it was very strange that no one else was about, as the day was fine and the whole building ought to be thronged with people. Supposing that they had inadvertently wandered into rooms usually denied to visitors, they decided that it would be best to find their way back to the vestibule and rejoin their party. After some further twists and turns, which confused them, they entered a room which they were sure from its dimensions and the construction and positioning of its pillars was the vestibule they sought, but it was decorated quite differently, and there were no busts, no statue, and no people. Miss Ada was becoming quite nervous by now, but her sister reassured her that they had simply lost their way, and if they walked on they would soon find the entrance again. They continued to wander, and it was in a drawing room decorated with blue wallpaper and draperies that they really became afraid. They could hear voices again, but although they were not far away they were muffled, as if invisible persons were standing in the room with them, whispering and laughing softly, and when they tried to find the people who spoke they could not. There was music, too, not of a military band, but the gentle sigh of violins and the sweet note of flutes. They heard the clatter of silverware on porcelain and the clink of glassware as if a feast was in progress, but nowhere could they discover where this entertainment was taking place. The room was all hung about with lanterns that cast a strange smoky golden light, quite unlike the gleam of gas that had lit the other portions of the house, and they realised that these beautiful old lamps were lit by oil. The sisters walked on, passing through many more rooms, one of them a long gallery decorated in the Chinese style, with deep niches occupied by life-size statues clad in gorgeous oriental robes.

In one large and magnificent room carved serpents wound themselves sinuously about decorative columns, and the walls were hung with lavishly painted Chinese scenes, the whole topped by a golden dome from which depended a lamp of glittering glass shaped like a gigantic flower and guarded by dragons. A wide recess housed a pipe organ of enormous dimensions in the form of a triumphal arch. The sisters, their feet sinking into the luxurious carpet, had been looking about them entranced by the sheer size and opulence of the room and everything in it, when a man had appeared before them with remarkable suddenness. Youthful and handsome, he was dressed very elegantly in the style of the last century. The gentleman hesitated as he saw the ladies, then bowed in a formal manner before passing them by and leaving the room. To the sisters' astonishment, when they tried the door they thought he must have come through they found it impossible to open. Not a little puzzled by this, they retraced their steps. Much later, when they compared notes, both agreed they had seen the man but while Bertha had not seen him enter the room Ada confessed that it seemed to her as if he had stepped through the wall.

Walking on, they found a drawing room decorated in deep red, resplendent with gilded mirrors, paintings and ornaments, and saw what they thought was a tableau or perhaps a play being enacted. The air was close and very hot, and before them were two figures, extremely lifelike, but moving slowly as though in a dream. The man was sumptuously dressed in a uniform with glittering accoutrements, and he was strongly built with a noble countenance and fine curling hair. The lady was reclining on a long couch which almost filled a recess that faced windows deeply curtained in rich velvet, and she was dressed in a style that had long gone out of fashion. She resembled a figure in a painting rather than a living woman, yet she moved as though alive. Her gown had a very full skirt of lustrous golden silk, with deep side draperies and a bodice and sleeves in sky blue, adorned with pink silk ribbons and bows. The bodice was very low in front, bordered with a great froth of lace revealing a white bosom that undulated like the waves of a milky sea. Most beautiful, however, was the tumbling mass of light ringleted hair that framed a face at once expressive and intelligent. With a movement of effortless grace the lady, who looked upon her swain with great affection, extended a delicate hand towards him, and he at once seized it, fell upon his knees before her and covered the hand with kisses that spoke soundlessly yet eloquently of a burning passion.

All around them the wallpaper glowed like the flames of a fire, and on it there were coiled figures of dragons and serpents, writhing in the most extraordinary manner, and exotic flowers with large fleshy petals.

The Misses Bland had by now begun to wonder if they had stumbled upon something they were not meant to see, yet the two lovers were oblivious of their presence, and gave so much of the appearance of a dumbshow that the ladies doubted that they were entirely real. They had heard of lifelike figures worked by mechanical means and thought that perhaps this was the nature of the sight before them, such things not being beyond what a royal building might contain. The male figure then started to utter great groans and sighs, and suddenly threw himself on the couch beside the lady, who, so far from trying to quell his ardour seemed actually to welcome his violent attentions. Before the sisters' horrified gaze he seized his paramour about the waist with one arm, while the other began to make free with her flowing skirts, and leaning forward, pressed his lips…

Mina shut the book.

It was some time before she dared open it again, and the scene that followed was lavished with descriptions that owed a great deal to horticulture and statuary with some military and sporting allusions. No reader would have been in any doubt as to the amorous nature of the event being alluded to, yet the words themselves were not indecent, and it was this and the innocence of the observers that must have saved the authors from prosecution. Any actual indecency was solely created by the mind of the reader.

The Misses Bland, shocked and amazed, departed the drawing room leaving the two figures in a state imitating the exhaustion of two athletes who had just run a race. Before long, they found the vestibule as they had originally encountered it, and so departed the building. By unspoken agreement the only part of their tour they mentioned to their father was the Hall of the Worthies. Neither had liked to talk freely between themselves about what they had seen, and it was only a week afterwards when they had written their individual accounts of the visit that the sisters compared their impressions. They agreed that they could not have seen actual persons but, given what their father had said about the tastes of the late King George, they felt sure that they must have seen some automata meant for his private viewing.

Later in the season the sisters once again made a trip to Brighton, and searched the Pavilion very carefully for the rooms they had seen on their earlier unaccompanied wanderings, but while they found what they thought must be the same rooms, none were decorated in the style they had previously observed. There were no large Chinese statues, no pipe organ in the large music room, and the apartment with the red wallpaper was without ornamentation or its long couch. Subtle enquiries regarding life-size figures were met by assertions that there were currently none in the Pavilion, that of the Crimean hero being too large and all the others too small. All statues were in any case quite incapable of movement. The only automaton that had recently been displayed in the Pavilion was a mechanical chess player garbed as a Turk. They were shown a poster portraying this machine, and anything less like the gentleman and lady in the red room could not be imagined. The sisters then enquired if there had been a figure or a portrait resembling the lady they had seen, and described her clothing. At this the attendant had looked surprised and directed them to a booklet that included a picture of the very lady. She was, he said, Mrs Fitzherbert, and the great love of the late King George when he had been Prince of Wales. While she had never resided in the Pavilion the Prince had provided her with a house close by and she had been a frequent visitor until he had been obliged to throw her over in order to marry a princess. Another picture in the book alerted their attention, for it was of the very man they had seen in the Red Drawing Room, King George himself, but before his excesses had made him an object of satire, when he had been a young and dashing Prince.

It was only then that the Misses Bland realised that what they had seen had not been mere automata but the ghostly figures of the Prince and his beloved, locked in the throes of their mutual passion for all eternity, sundered by cruel necessity but together again after death.

It was all nonsense of course, thought Mina, a romantic tale with more intimate detail than might be thought appropriate. As a work of fiction she had encountered far worse. Still, she had promised Dr Hamid and Anna to discover more, and decided to write a letter to Mr Greville, her father's former partner who now managed the Scarletti publishing business. She explained that this mysterious work had set everyone in Brighton talking, and asked if he knew the real identity of the authors.

The book's text did supply some useful clues as to when the sisters' visit had taken place. While military bands were a regular feature during the season, the conjuror and chess automaton were less usual entertainments that must have been advertised in the newspapers. Surely, Mina thought, she could easily discover for herself when the supposed encounter had taken place.

Mina made some notes and returned the book to her mother's room. It was probably unnecessary but she made sure that it was in exactly the same position as before. Back in her bedroom she waited for the symptoms of hysteria to overcome her, but she waited in vain.

Five

er letter written, Mina settled to completing her story about Eliza, the little lady with the twisted body who lit up the lives of all those who met her. The house was quiet, the sound of parlour gossip being too distant to invade her peaceful sanctuary. Few noises from downstairs, apart from the doorbell, or the usual clatter of excitement that announced the arrival of Richard, were loud enough to disturb her concentration. Enid's bedroom was next to her own, and as Mina worked she heard voices in the hallway, and guessed that her sister had returned from her walk. Enid's morning constitutional in the company of the nursemaid, Anderson, and the twins had become a regular event, which enabled her to display her latest adornments and invite the admiration of the town. Unlike the fate of many a matron, Enid's figure had been quickly restored to its customary trimness after the birth of her children, and she took great delight in showing off her fashion plate silhouette in tightly buttoned gowns that drew the eye to her tiny waist. Mina had no concerns that Enid might come into her room and interrupt her work. It was never explicitly stated, but Enid clearly felt awkward in contemplating Mina's distorted form, and had a horror of accidentally seeing her in a state of undress.

If Louisa was busy admiring the twins, then it was certain that Mrs Bettinson had taken her leave, as she was not fond of babies. Mina worked quietly on, but a few minutes later Rose knocked hesitantly on the door and advised Mina that her mother wished to speak to her. Such a summons never boded well and Mina reluctantly put down her pen. For a moment she wondered if her mother wanted her to inspect the twins for potential scoliosis, but as she worked her way downstairs, she passed Anderson taking her contented charges up to the nursery. Mystified, she pushed open the parlour door and found her mother frowning at the *Brighton Gazette*, which was open at the page advertising public amusements. A less amused look could not be imagined.

'You wished to speak to me, mother?' Mina hoped that she was only wanted on some trivial errand, but prepared herself for a lengthy exposition of her mother's well-worn opinions and general irritation with family, friends, society in general and herself in particular.

'It seems,' announced Louisa with a deeply offended expression, 'that we are all obliged to attend a lecture on the subject of Africa.'

'We are?' queried Mina, since this was a new and unexpected departure in Scarletti family entertainment. She was seized by a sudden fear that her wayward brother Richard was undertaking another of his wild and inevitably doomed moneymaking schemes and was about to pass himself off as an expert on the dark continent or even disguise himself as a native of that far away land, and planned to deliver a public address based on legend, newspapers and his own imagination. The potential for embarrassment was alarming. Only a few months ago he had taken to the stage of Brighton's New Oxford Theatre of Varieties in a spangled cloak, false moustache and black velvet mask, employing the worst Italian accent in the world, as the mysterious Signor Ricardo, presenting the supposed spirit medium Miss Foxton, who in actual fact was his then mistress, Nellie Gilden, a former conjuror's assistant.

Mina eased herself into a comfortable seat. This was going to be a more complicated conversation than most. 'Why this sudden interest in Africa?'

Louisa gave a little snort of a laugh. 'Oh I have no interest in it at all, only I am instructed to go by Enid. Of course *my* wishes have not been consulted, but she is very insistent about it.'

'When is the lecture to take place?'

'On Monday evening at the Town Hall. Enid saw the announcement in the newspaper and became very excited by it. She said that the subject exerts a powerful hold over her. I believe she may have attended a similar lecture in London, where it obviously affected her brain. Of course if it is of interest to society there may be a good company there, which would be some diversion at least. Mina, you must go with us, in case Enid becomes distracted. I only hope there will be no horrid pictures on display.'

Mina knew very little about Africa except that from time to time explorers went there looking for the source of the Nile, and many of them failed to return. In recent months the newspapers had been expressing grave anxiety over the fate of a Dr Livingstone who had not been heard of for some time, and no one knew if he was alive or dead. Mina wondered what the source of a river looked like, and supposing one were to discover it, what would one do with it. The subject was certainly a matter for curiosity and she was quite sure it would provide her with a rich vein of ideas for her stories.

'I really cannot imagine what Enid sees in Africa,' Louisa continued. 'She has never shown any interest in it before. Why would anyone want to visit such a place? No one of any importance lives there. So hot and uncomfortable, and I have heard that dangerous wild animals are simply allowed to roam about as they please.'

Mina picked up the newspaper, which was advertising a lecture by Mr Arthur Wallace Hope, veteran of the Crimea and noted explorer, who would be talking about his expeditions to Africa. The name had a familiar ring to it, and since Richard was far too young to pass himself off as having fought in the Crimea, it was some relief to Mina to see that this was not, after all, another of his schemes. Tickets were three shillings apiece, family tickets to admit three persons were eight shillings, and they could be purchased at Mr Smith's bookseller's shop on North Street, where copies of Mr Hope's recent volume *African Quest* would be on sale. All receipts from the lecture were to go to a special fund for the cost of mounting an expedition to find Dr Livingstone. 'It is for a good cause,' she said.

'I am not so sure of that,' said Louisa tartly. 'In fact it would have been far better for everyone if Dr Livingstone had stayed at home. First there is the cost of sending him there on a wild goose chase, and then he gets lost and we are all supposed to pay to have him brought back. What is so complicated about finding the source of a river? If they had asked my advice I would have told them to take a boat at one end and sail down it until they reached the other. But no one ever listens to me.'

Mina thought that if the answer was as simple as her mother supposed then the source of the Nile would have been found some while ago, but she knew better than to argue. 'Perhaps you could suggest that to Mr Hope on Monday? Or would you prefer not to attend?'

'Oh we must, or Enid will give me a headache with her complaints. She is already choosing her gown and bonnet. Mina, you must go at once and purchase a family ticket with reserved seats.'

Mina saw that her mother was not in fact averse to attending the lecture, but preferred to place the responsibility for their going on Enid's shoulders so she would have someone to blame if it proved to be dull or unsuitable. The idea that she or Enid should be the ones to procure the tickets seemed not to enter Louisa's head, and it was a task which she would never have entrusted to Rose. Mina said nothing. The autumnal weather was charming; the sky bright and clear, the breezes not too harsh, and the destination of a bookshop was always a pleasure. She would walk.

✳

North Street was not so very far from Mina's home in Montpelier Road. When her back was easy she liked to take gentle strolls in the sunshine and fresh clean air. She was obliged to go carefully, so as not to strain the muscles that protested against her awkward gait, the twist in her obstinate spine and tilt of her hipbone causing her to rock from side to side in a manner that made rude children point and laugh and polite adults glance at her in surprise and then quickly look away. She had been taught the importance of exercise by Anna Hamid, who said it was essential in order to counteract the hours she spent at her writing desk. Lack of activity would stiffen her, lock her fast into her awkward shape and make it harder for her to move. Idleness was her enemy. Mina was well aware that if she lived long enough, there might well come a time when she would be confined to a bath chair, and wholly reliant on another person if she wished to go out in the town, but should that fate ever come about she wanted to delay it as long as possible. She thought again of her friend Eliza Hamid, dead at fifty, her constricted lungs unable to combat an inflammation that a healthy woman would have survived.

For a devoted reader W.J. Smith's bookshop was a palace of delight. Its handsome windows were lined from their base to their height with rows of shelves displaying more books than one might have thought could possibly be assembled in the space, and the doorways were flanked with racks that towered over Mina and were filled with a wide variety of periodicals. On that day, half of one window was entirely taken up with copies of *African Quest*, nicely bound in maroon leather, the cover stamped in gold with a map of Africa. The book was priced at six shillings and like the lecture, for which there was a prominent advertisement, all proceeds were to go to the fund for the rescue of Dr Livingstone. While Mina was obliged to agree in part with her mother that the brave doctor was in a plight of his own making she nevertheless felt that this was no reason to abandon him unrescued. She was also far from convinced, as her mother was, that the exploration of Africa was an activity that would never bring rewards. Who could know what riches in terms of crops or minerals might lie at the source of the Nile, or what valuable trade routes might be opened? Dr Livingstone's work might one day add greatly to the sum of human happiness, and then he would no longer be denigrated as misguided, or branded an expensive failure, but praised and lauded as a hero. In the window, on prominent display, was a photographic portrait of the lost gentleman, staring into the camera with deep-set mournful eyes, his brow furrowed with inexpressible pain. Aged about fifty at the time the portrait was taken, he looked older. Now, after five more years in Africa, it was unlikely, thought Mina, that he would look half as well, if he was still alive, which was doubtful. Friends of Dr Livingstone frequently wrote to the newspapers expressing their confidence in his abilities and conviction that he was alive. Other reports had twice declared him dead. The only certain thing was that there had been no news of him at all for the last two years.

There was another portrait in the window, and on seeing it Mina at once understood the reason for Enid's sudden interest in Africa. Arthur Wallace Hope was an impressive figure, in the very prime of his vigorous life, tall, muscular and broad of chest, with flaring dark whiskers, the epitome of bold healthy masculinity. His expression was that of a man who had looked far over the great plains and lakes and rivers of a foreign land, faced dangers and overcome them, fought and suffered, and come through it all with credit. He was not precisely handsome, but his face inspired confidence, and his physique was as far removed from the slight form of Mr Inskip as could be imagined.

In the shop Mina asked to see the seating plan for the lecture and selected three places at the front of the hall. She was not sure if this was a wise thing to do, especially in the light of

Enid's fondness for tight lacing, but felt that had she purchased tickets near the back, she would have been endlessly castigated for her poor choice. With any luck the Lord Mayor and other town dignitaries would be present, and that would add something to her mother's evening when she became tired of listening to the speaker, which would be early in the proceedings. Mina also purchased a copy of *African Quest*. While she was there a number of ladies whose veils were drawn fully about their faces, made a creeping, diffident approach to the counter, and, leaning towards the manager in a confidential fashion, whispered their requests. Some explained that they were servants who had been sent by their mistresses on a mission, others declared that the desired purchase was not for themselves but for a friend. The manager understood their needs exactly and with no alteration in his deferential expression provided each of these shy customers with a slim volume ready-wrapped in brown paper. Mina did not have to guess which book they were purchasing, and only wished that her stories sold as well, for she would be a rich woman. The shop did stock her work, which she published under the name Robert Neil, the pseudonym her father had used for his occasional stories, and they brought in a regular income, which, in addition to the annuity left to her by her father made her financially secure if not actually wealthy.

The bookshop lay very near to the public reading room which boasted a fine collection of informative periodicals, including past copies of the *Gazette*, and Mina thought that by studying the attractions advertised in the newspaper as taking place in the Royal Pavilion, she would be able to identify if not the exact day, then the year and month at least in which the Misses Bland had paid their first visit. Fortunately the *Gazette* was a weekly rather than a daily publication, or her task would have been arduous. Slowly she worked her way back through the issues, and at last in the paper dated 6 October 1870 she saw an announcement that the automaton chess player who had created such a sensation at London's Crystal Palace had come to Brighton, and would be seen at work in the chess club room of the Royal Pavilion daily from 2 to 5pm and 8 to 10pm. Mina had never seen a chess automaton, but knew that they were machines that played chess games with anyone who wished to challenge them. How they actually worked was a mystery, but Mina thought that if the device was only a cleverly made machine and not something enclosing a hidden human operator, it would not have needed to take a three-hour rest. In the very next issue there was an announcement that Dr H.S. Lynn the famous conjuror, who had never previously visited Brighton, would be performing his 'Grande Séance de Physique et Mystères Oriental' in the Banqueting Room of the Royal Pavilion on the following Monday, the proceeds to be given to the widows and children of the drowned crewmen of HMS *Captain*, the vessel which had sunk with the loss of almost five hundred souls in the previous month. Dr Lynn promised 'a number of wondrous mysteries' never before seen in Europe, including the Japanese butterfly illusion for which he was especially noted, as well as 'top spinning extraordinary on a single thread' and the 'instantaneous growth of flowers'. The band of the Inniskilling Dragoons had also been playing very frequently in Brighton during that season. After careful study of the newspapers Mina was able to satisfy herself that Dr Lynn had only given his performance on the one occasion, and the chess automaton, after a short season in Brighton, had returned to Crystal Palace.

Mina, to her surprise, had determined an exact date. Unless there was a similar coincidence of events, the visit of the two authors of *An Encounter* had taken place a little under a year ago, on Monday, 17 October 1870.

Six

As soon as Mina returned home she was pounced upon by Enid, who, enraged at the insupportable delay caused by the reading room visit, demanded to see the tickets immediately since it would be necessary to go back to the shop at once and exchange them if they were not good enough. Fortunately they were. 'You will be so close to Mr Hope you will be able to smell the pomade on his whiskers,' Mina reassured her. Enid looked as if she was about to faint.

During the next few days Enid found it impossible to conceal her anticipation of Mr Hope's lecture. Her cheeks flushed whenever she mentioned it, which was often, and from the way they flushed when she did not mention it, Mina deduced that her sister was thinking about it. Enid's agitation and Louisa's simmering disapproval made for a very tense household, and Mina longed for a visit from Richard and his happier nonsense.

On the Monday Enid was too excited to eat, which was just as well as she was laced so tightly that anything she swallowed could never have found its way through her digestive system. Rose had helped her dress, and as this involved several changes of costume, as well as anger and tears, it was a relief to everyone when the cab finally arrived and there was no time for Enid to change her mind again.

The spacious upper room of the Town Hall was crowded with patrons. Lectures were a regular attraction there and covered subjects as diverse as religion, history, literature and geography, with the occasional dissertation on moral issues, the sanitary conditions of Brighton and the electoral disabilities of women. Serious talks on morality or religion were well attended by those eager to wear the badge of respectability. It was not therefore necessary to actually listen to the speaker, although many who sought illumination, certainty or simply improvement, did so, and declared that they had been mightily edified by the experience. Others thought that just being seen there was sufficient, and after taking the opportunity to mingle with their friends before the lecture commenced, dozed gently through the earnest address, waking only at the sound of applause. Mina had never attended these lectures but they were fully reported in the newspapers, and she had read with some amusement of the respected Brighton novelist and literary authority Mr Edward Campbell Tainsh and his denouncement of sensational literature as feverish, contemptible and unhealthy. Books, he said, should be restful, dignified and innocent. Mina, having completed her story of the little lady, had commenced a new one, in which a man was being driven mad by the torment of demons that had arisen from a life devoted to cruelty and vice. She decided not to send a presentation copy to Mr Tainsh for his review.

Enid, clutching her copy of *African Quest* as if it was a religious tract, looked keenly about as they entered the lecture room, but the imposing figure of Mr Hope had not yet appeared. The audience, Mina noticed, was composed of the usual assortment of ladies and gentlemen, with some representatives of the Brighton press, but there were appreciable numbers of young men with eager expressions, who looked ready to volunteer for perilous adventures at the smallest inducement.

Dr Hamid arrived, accompanied by Anna, a rare social engagement for them as they usually liked to stay quietly at home together after a long and busy day. Mina wondered if, following Eliza's death, they had decided to seek more entertainment outside their home, inhabited as it was by the unseen ghosts of those they had recently lost. Louisa, studying the company for friends she could greet and outshine, lighted on Mrs Peasgood and Mrs Mowbray, widowed sisters in their fifties, both of whom were plain of face and comfortably stout, and hurried to speak to them. Mrs Peasgood's late husband, a surgeon, had left her well provided for, and her elegant residence in Marine Square, which she shared with her sister, boasted a large drawing room where she often hosted musical entertainments. An invitation to one of Mrs Peasgood's soirees was a notable stamp of status and she was considered a person of influence in Brighton society. By contrast, the late Mr Mowbray's business as a wine merchant had collapsed in debt due to bad management and excessive consumption of his own stock. While Mrs Peasgood appeared thoroughly contented with her position in life, Mrs Mowbray was constantly casting her eyes at single gentlemen, like a hungry spider waiting for an unsuspecting fly to creep within her grasp. She often looked with great approval at Dr Hamid, who was not merely impervious to her attractions but unaware of her interest. The sisters, like Louisa and Mrs Bettinson, had once been members of the little circle who had attended the séances of Miss Eustace, something that none of them now cared to mention.

There was a brief pause in even Louisa's conversation and several pairs of eyes turned to the door as another friend arrived, Miss Whinstone, who did not come alone. Miss Whinstone was a highly susceptible and nervous spinster who ordinarily would never have dreamed of attending a lecture on the subject of bloodcurdling adventures in Africa. The mere idea of leaving Brighton made her feel faint, although she had once dared to visit Hove. It was she who had suffered most from the depredations of Miss Eustace, who had deluded her into believing that her deceased brother was sending her messages requiring her to meet expenses for which he felt responsible. The demands had been increasing in both size and frequency when Mina discovered what was happening and put a stop to it.

Miss Whinstone had recently astonished everyone, especially those who knew her best, by acquiring a gentleman friend, Mr Jellico, a retired schoolmaster with weak legs and a passion for acrostics. Their most recent adventures had included a walk on the West Pier, and a visit to the theatre to see a comedy by Shakespeare, and it was now widely rumoured that they were planning a day excursion to Worthing. On learning this Louisa declared that 'dear Harriet' as she called Miss Whinstone whenever she needed to prise gossip from her, had taken leave of her senses, by which she meant that she had had the effrontery to entertain an admirer when she had none. Not that Louisa envied Miss Whinstone her unsteady and grey-whiskered companion, but she would have liked the opportunity to tell him that his attentions were unwanted.

Miss Whinstone, who was usually so scant of courage, had been able, with the support of Mr Jellico and a great many glasses of water, to tell the story of her cruel deception to the Lewes magistrates, as a result of which Miss Eustace and her co-conspirators had not only been committed for trial but refused bail on the grounds that such slippery creatures would surely escape given the slenderest of chances. That evening, Miss Whinstone and her antiquated swain walked unashamedly arm-in-arm, although it was not apparent to the casual observer which of the two was supporting the other.

Still more arrivals flooded into the room, which soon became full to bursting, and through the buzzing chatter Mina could hear that a great many of those present had read or heard of Arthur Wallace Hope's adventures, and not a few carried recently purchased copies of his book, in the expectation that the author could be prevailed upon to enhance it with his signature. In front of the platform there was a table piled high with more volumes in case anyone had neglected to buy a copy, and pen, ink and blotter lay in readiness. To one side of the hall was a long table, whose contents were covered by a plain cloth.

It was being guarded in a strict but courteous fashion by a gentleman aged about sixty who wore the sombre garb of a senior servant. The platform was already supplied with a number of chairs and at the back, high on the wall, were two large furled maps and a pointing rod.

The first man to appear on the platform was an official of the Town Hall, who begged all the ticket holders to be seated, and once this was achieved, the distinguished visitors, Mr Webb the Lord Mayor, and a number of other dignitaries were announced and received polite but brief applause before taking their places. At last, the man himself, Mr Arthur Wallace Hope, appeared. Mina had wondered if Hope in the flesh might be less impressive than the Hope of his portrait but if anything the opposite was the case, as Enid's little gasp testified. A portrait could not convey stature and he was a tall man, standing some six feet in height, broad shouldered and with a confident step. He surveyed the gathering with a friendly expression before he sat down, and then the Town Hall official, his faint glory eclipsed by the glittering company, very prudently withdrew and left the remainder of the formalities to Mr Webb. The Mayor made a short address, saying what a pleasure it was to welcome such a distinguished man to Brighton, and indicated, as if Mr Hope was too modest to mention it, that after the talk copies of the book *African Quest* would be available for purchase, and the speaker would be delighted to inscribe them, as well as copies previously bought, with his signature and a suitable dedication.

Enid glowed with anticipation.

The Mayor resumed his seat and there was a breathless silence as Hope stepped forward to speak. His voice, booming from his deep chest, was everything one might have anticipated. 'Mr Lord Mayor, Aldermen, distinguished guests, ladies and gentlemen of Brighton, it is my very great honour to address you today. My journey here has been something of a pilgrimage, since one of the first visits I made on my arrival was to the Royal Pavilion, where I stood in the vestibule admiring the magnificent statue of Captain Pechell, one of the honoured sons of this town. A more valiant man and a better comrade in arms has never been known, and I confess that his likeness, showing him in an attitude of the greatest heroism as he urged his men forward, brought a tear to my eye as I recalled our service together in the Crimea and the terrible tragedy of Sebastopol that took him from us in the prime of his active youth. And yet, as I stood there, I felt that he was still with me, his spirit seemed to stand beside me as he himself had once done, and his bravery remains an inspiration to me now.

'One might think that on my return from the Crimea I would have been happy to consider my duty to my country done, but my days in the army had aroused in me a great hunger for travel, adventure, and yes I admit it, danger!' A thrill of excitement ran through the audience. 'And where can one find all three in greater abundance than in any corner of the great globe? Why, Africa! The untamed, uncharted land, whose immense size can only inspire us with wonder at what we might discover there. Surely there must be opportunities for valuable trade; furs and ivory, mines yielding gold and precious stones, if, that is, we can learn to navigate the great rivers, the courses of which have been a mystery since the time of the ancients. But I want to assure you of this,' he went on very seriously, 'we British go to Africa not as enemies or plunderers. We have no desire to conquer the land and take it for ourselves. We go in friendship, to bring honest trade to the inhabitants as well as the benefits of Christianity to their souls. However —' he paused and favoured the audience with a significant stare '— there is one evil in Africa which must be abolished – I am referring to the cruel and abominable trade in slaves. Ladies and gentlemen, do you not wonder how it is that the ivory of your piano keys and your knife handles reaches you? I will tell you. It is carried overland on the backs of slaves who are treated in the most inhumane fashion and then murdered when they are no longer able to bear their loads. It was the inspiration of Dr David Livingstone to combat this terrible practice not merely by conversion through Christian preaching but by discovering other trade routes that would pass along the rivers of Africa. With this admirable intention he proposed an expedition to open up the Zambezi. It was a monumental and ambitious task and I was at once fired with a great desire to go with him.

'When I volunteered for my first expedition to Africa in 1858 I knew nothing of what it might hold for me, I went as a young man eager for adventure. I thought it would be a fine thing indeed to chart new lands, to discover unknown civilisations, to tread paths that no white man had ever seen, and indeed it was, but I could never have known that with the elation, the achievement and the comradeship there would also be the pain and the loss, disappointment and disease, and the savage murderous attacks of slavers. I will take you now, ladies and gentlemen to the shores of the great Zambezi River!'

Hope strode to the back of the platform and unfurled the first of the maps. It illustrated the whole of the continent of Africa, and was easily large enough for the audience to see the rivers and lakes. It was not these, however, that drew the eye, but two blank areas, one to the north, labelled 'Great Desert' and another in the centre described more tantalisingly as 'Unexplored Region'. From the corner of her eye Mina saw some of the youths in the audience lean forward to gaze on the chart that held such promise of adventure, and thought how the hearts of those young men had been stirred and how they must long to go to that unknown place and unlock its mysteries.

The tales told by Mr Hope were undoubtedly thrilling, although Mina felt that some of the details had been tempered by the knowledge that there were ladies in the audience. His descriptions of the ravages of deadly disease were confined to generalisations, and the stories of his encounters with slavers ended at a point where the tragic outcome could be left to the hearer's imagination, nevertheless they were more than exciting enough for Brightonian tastes. Hope knew his audience and steered a careful path, neither boastful nor tainted by false modesty. He had done all that a man might do. He had shot and eaten elephants, hippopotami and giraffes. He had befriended great chieftains. He had suffered from mysterious fevers and the bites of poisonous insects and snakes. Twice he had almost drowned in swollen rivers, and he had once been stabbed with a spear. It was a tale of desperate privation and suffering such that it seemed impossible for any man to survive. Although the journey had added substantially to the sum of geographical and botanical knowledge, it had ultimately ended by failing in its main purpose, since the Zambezi River had been found to be not fully navigable after all, due to its cataracts and rapids. Dr Livingstone's dream of great steamers passing along the river laden with produce had vanished. The survivors of the expedition, stricken with fever and disappointed, yet bracing themselves to be ready for new challenges, had returned to the coast to recuperate and await the arrival of a new steamship with much-needed provisions. There Hope had received a message telling him of the death of his older brother, a tragedy that had necessitated his return to England to settle family business. He did not, however, forget his comrades in Africa, but worked hard to raise further funds to assist the Zambezi party. He had done so in vain, since the expedition, now denounced and even derided in the press as an expensive failure, was recalled.

'But men of courage never despair for long,' said Hope, 'rather they gather their strength and return to the fight afresh! Yes, the idea of the Zambezi as a trade route had perforce to be abandoned as impractical, but now a new object was in sight, or rather an ancient object risen to new prominence, one that has long captured the hearts and minds of men as the greatest adventure the world has to offer – discovering the source of the Nile.'

Even Louisa looked enraptured.

Seven

The ultimate source of the great river of Africa was, explained Mr Hope, a destination which offered all the allure and excitement of making a flight to the Moon and back, and was a prize that had been coveted by men of daring and enterprise for thousands of years. Even modern explorers failed to agree on where the great river rose, and it behoved those men who had the courage, spirit and dedication to answer the great question.

While his sudden and unexpected elevation to master of the family estates should have required him to reside permanently in England, he had felt the call of Africa once more, and fortunately found in his younger brother a man who was not only well able but content to manage affairs at home. The money raised for the abandoned Zambezi expedition had accordingly been employed to fund another, this one starting at Zanzibar and heading west overland to find the elusive source of the Nile.

Hope then unfurled the second map, this one showing the lake systems of East Africa as far as they had been charted. His previous exploits, he said, made him without question the obvious candidate to lead the new venture. His companions were selected with care; some were naturally men of experience, those who had travelled widely and showed that they could endure hardship, but there were others who, though lacking any specific qualification, were hungry for adventure, robust and of the right stalwart character. These latter companions, who were hardly more than boys, brought with them the promise that they could be fashioned into the hardened explorers and leaders of the future.

All preparations had been made, supplies purchased and guides engaged, but only a few weeks into their journey disaster had struck. The party had been attacked by slavers, who had assumed that the travellers were rivals for their evil trade. Both men and boys had fought bravely, but of all the Europeans, only Hope and one of his experienced men, who like himself was a veteran of the Crimea, were not killed outright, and they made a narrow escape. After surviving many dangers and privations they at last reached safety but his noble-hearted companion, exhausted and suffering from malaria, died soon afterwards. It was to his comrades in adversity, both the courageous Englishmen and their loyal African guides, that *African Quest* was dedicated.

Mina glanced at the youths who were so eager to follow the deadly path to the Nile, and saw not one whit of dismay. Their desires were plain in in their unbearded faces. Others might have perished but to them, surely, would be the glory.

Following Hope's return to England it had taken a year for him to return to full health, during which he had written his book, and he now travelled and lectured about the importance of abolishing the slave trade, opening Africa to lawful commerce, creating riverboat routes for the conveyance of goods, encouraging cultivation of the tracts of fertile land, and extending to the population the great benefits and blessings of Christianity. Whether he would ever return to Africa he did not know. Even now, Dr Livingstone was seeking the source of the Nile, which he believed flowed from Lake Tanganyika, although there were other explorers, notably the late Mr Speke, who would disagree, saying that Lake Victoria was the source. But nothing had been heard from Dr Livingstone for some time and if he was still alive he would be sorely in need of supplies. Hope reiterated that he would take not one penny piece from the lecture fee or the sale of his book, all would be dedicated to the cause of finding and relieving Dr Livingstone.

'But what conclusions can I draw from my many travels and adventures?' he went on. 'First, that we are all God's creatures wherever we may live and whatever the colour of our skin. Secondly that cruelty to one's fellow beings is a great abomination. I have witnessed the loss of so many good men; I have seen them on the field of battle, mown down by fusillades, blown to pieces or expiring from the great curse of cholera; in Africa they died from malaria or dysentery, drowned in rapids or were murdered by slavers. These deaths cannot, must not, have happened in vain. We who remain must gain from their sacrifice. We must learn courage, humility and kindness. Ask yourselves, when we contemplate these apparently senseless tragedies, what message comes to us from the Almighty? I can tell you this now, that we are all of us souls looking for salvation. We will only find it by understanding and accepting a great truth. We cannot turn away from it. It is a power that is all around us, but which many seek to deny. It is a power that has an intense focus right here in this very town. I am speaking of spiritualism.'

There was a ripple of unease in the audience. Arthur Wallace Hope looked around him at faces that had suddenly begun to frown, and his mouth curved into a knowing smile. 'Oh, I am well aware that there have been events here in the recent past that have strengthened the convictions of materialists, those who believe only in science and the things they can see and touch, and who dare to deny the existence of the soul. What a terrible hopeless life they must lead, to reject all the many proofs we have of survival after death, to have no faith! I implore you, do not be deceived by these empty and unhappy men and women. We must work together to bring them to a proper understanding, lead them away from the darkness of their bigotry and towards the light of knowledge. I see here the start of a new movement, a new church, even. Brighton, with its healing air and light, and the invigorating power of the sea can only attract beneficial forces. Nothing evil can thrive here! The greatest and most inspiring mediums will come to be nourished by the energy that exists in this blessed place. In the very near future I will be giving a talk at this same location on the revivification of spiritualism in Brighton. Tickets will be free of charge, but donations will be accepted towards the fund for the relief of Dr Livingstone. And now, my dear friends, I bring this talk to a close. You will see at the side of the hall a table with a display of some items I brought back from Africa, which I hope you will find of interest; cloth and beads which are to the Africans as paper money is to us. I will be available to inscribe your books in just a few moments, but before then I will be happy to take any questions from the floor.'

There was the usual polite hesitation that always arose in such situations as no one ever wished to be the first to speak, but finally a gentleman raised his hand.

'Mr Hope, since you believe so strongly in the world of the spirit, would you be willing to express your opinion on a certain book that has attracted a considerable amount of attention here in Brighton.'

There was a stir in the audience as a number of ladies tried unsuccessfully to look as if they had no idea to what the speaker was referring. One or two stifled an embarrassed titter, but several, with stern faces, actually rose to leave.

'Please, ladies and gentlemen,' said Hope in a placatory tone that at once commanded attention, 'I have no intention of offending anyone here. Sir, I am aware of the volume and have indeed read it. Not only that, but I can reveal to you that I have recently been privileged to meet and speak to the two authors.'

This statement aroused a babble of comment, and the sound of busily scribbling pencils in the notebooks of newspaper-men. 'Can you tell us who they really are?' called out one correspondent.

'That I cannot do since they preserve their anonymity most carefully. I was introduced to them as the Misses Bland, and did not seek to know more. But I can tell you that I found them to be modest young ladies and was utterly convinced by their assurances that they come from an extremely respectable family and have thus far led very sheltered lives. Their intention in writing the book was simply to give an honest account of their adventures and observations. In doing so, they revealed their innocence and ignorance of the world. Certain passages would appear shocking to the more knowledgeable individual, but the authors only show their pure and childlike understanding, as they wrote without really knowing what they described. But let us put aside the question of delicacy and address ourselves instead to the real importance of that extraordinary event in the Pavilion. These two young ladies actually witnessed persons of the royal court at the time when the late King George was Prince of Wales. It is a wonderful mystery! Did they perhaps witness the ghosts of the Prince and his court, in which case we must bethink ourselves how it was that these spirits appeared not as they were when they left this life, but in the full health and vigour of their youth. Or – and this has been suggested by persons more knowledgeable than I am on such matters – did the sisters actually see into a past age – see not ghosts at all, but the living? And if they did, did they do so by looking through a window in the ether that showed them the past – or did they actually step into the past themselves? These questions are of the utmost importance and must be studied by science. But I promise to speak further on this at my forthcoming talk.'

There was resounding applause, during which Mina saw her expectation that *An Encounter* would quickly lose its novelty value vanish like a phantom. There would be queues outside Mr Smith's bookshop tomorrow. Since there were no more questions from the floor, Hope bowed and left the platform to take his place at the table where copies of *African Quest* were piled. The Lord Mayor stepped forward and asked the members of the audience not to crowd too heavily about the distinguished speaker but to form queues one row at a time. Since Mina and her party were on the front row, they were called first and Enid, her eyes shining with excitement, almost ran to have her book signed. Louisa accompanied her, not, thought Mina, as unwillingly as she might have done before hearing the author speak. Mina had no wish to stand in a great crush of people so stayed back and waited for their return.

'That was an unexpected end to the lecture,' said Dr Hamid, appearing with Anna at Mina's side. 'I am glad I decided to come, as it is always advisable to keep informed as to what is upsetting my patients.'

'Will you go to his talk on spiritualism?'

'I fear it may be necessary for the same reason. I hope he will not be in town too long.'

'I know that kind of man all too well,' said Anna grimly. 'He has authority and confidence and the ability to draw people to him and make them believe what he believes. The more one warns against him the more one seems to be the person who is deluded.'

Miss Whinstone, with a very troubled expression on her face, was being led away and gently comforted by Mr Jellico.

'Poor lady, she has suffered quite enough,' said Mina. 'It will take all her determination to speak at the trial, and now she must fear a revival of the very cause that injured her.'

All around them small chattering groups were forming and none of the talk was of the River Nile.

Dr Hamid and Anna took their leave, and Mina, seeing that Enid had seized the opportunity to tell Mr Hope at great length all about her love of Africa, went to the display table to look at the items on show there. The manservant had removed the plain cover to reveal a rainbow of delights. There were rolls of cotton fabric, some in subtle shades of blue, others in golden beige, dark red and deep brown, either striped or patterned in squares. A printed card told her that the cloth was woven on hand looms and were valuable trading commodities essential for the traveller in Africa who wished to purchase food and obtain permission to pass through tribal lands. There were also glass trading beads, some strung on twisted cord, others displayed singly, cylinders in a wide variety of glowing hues, some plain but many of them banded and streaked with colour. Mina tried to imagine what a lady of Brighton would look like dressed in garments of that richly dyed cotton and wearing those beads; bright yellow like the summer sun, blue as the sky, green as parklands, red as roses. A new idea for a story occurred to her, one in which a lady put on some mysterious garments she had discovered in a curio shop and was magically transported back to the land of their origin. The possibilities for adventure were endless.

It was as she stood engrossed in thought that the gentleman servant approached her.

'Excuse me, but I presume you are Miss Scarletti?'

Mina did not have to ask how he had identified her. 'I am.'

He proffered a card. 'Mr Arthur Wallace Hope presents his compliments. He would like, with your permission, to call on you at your earliest convenience for a private conversation on a highly sensitive matter.'

Mina took the card, which was printed with Hope's London address, a handwritten note adding the name of the Royal Albion Hotel where he might be contacted in Brighton. 'This is quite surprising, of course, but if he would like to call I will be at home at eleven o'clock tomorrow morning.' Mina always carried cards advertising the Scarletti Library of Romance and she wrote her address upon one and handed it to the servant.

He accepted it with a deferential smile and withdrew. Mina's specified time was carefully chosen. Her mother and Enid would be out that morning, exploring the new arrivals at Jordan, Conroy and Co.'s fashionable emporium where Paris came to Brighton in the form of silk, fans and lace. As she gazed at the card, Mina speculated on what such a notable man might wish to discuss with her, since she was not a person of importance in the community. Why a private conversation? What was sensitive about the subject matter? Mina was left with the uncomfortable feeling that the religious, noble and philanthropic Mr Hope could actually be a very dangerous man if crossed.

Eight

Single young women would not normally be expected to receive male visitors to whom they were not related at home alone, and in the case of Mr Arthur Wallace Hope, neither did Mina wish to. She wondered if she should ask Rose to stay with her during the interview, and should Mr Hope object to this arrangement she would be obliged to inform him that the conversation could not take place under any other circumstances. Not that anyone would suspect that some impropriety might take place – that was one advantage of Mina's deformity – it was assumed that she was beyond any man's appetites.

After giving the question some careful thought, Mina dismissed the idea of appointing a chaperone. Whatever it was Mr Hope wanted to say to her it was unlikely to be either romantic or indecent and she did not want him to be inhibited in his expressions by seeing Rose standing in the corner of the parlour with her sullen stare. Rose, who was both general maidservant and personal maid to Louisa, had, despite the fact that the heavy work of the house was assigned to a charlady, a great deal to complain about, but she did so wordlessly, albeit at great volume. Mina might have ordered the maid to secrecy about the meeting with Mr Hope, but the probability of the visit being mentioned to Louisa at the earliest opportunity was close to a certainty. The best way of limiting the inevitable repercussions was for Rose to know as little about the visit as possible.

Louisa and Enid departed after breakfast, chattering with excitement, and later that morning the nursemaid, Anderson, took the twins out to bathe in the sea air, secure in their perambulator, a four-wheeled carriage like a battle wagon in miniature, with matching compartments and parasols. It was only then that Mina informed Rose that a gentleman might call to discuss a charitable donation, and she was to show him into the parlour and bring tea.

Mr Arthur Wallace Hope arrived true to the hour. As Mina entered the parlour, she found him standing to greet her with the confident posture of a man whose presence in any house bestowed upon it a great favour, and who knew it well. He reminded her of a bear at the zoo risen up on its hind legs, darkly furred, massive and threatening. As he thanked Mina for her kindness in agreeing to see him, his manner was both cordial and respectful, but there was, she saw, a sharp, cool determination lurking behind his smile. Once they were both seated, facing each other at a discreet distance, Mina said, 'I assume that the purpose of your visit is to request a donation to the fund for the relief of Dr Livingstone?'

He looked surprised. 'No, not at all, although if you wish to make a donation I can supply you with the address where it is to be sent.'

'Then I am at a loss to imagine why you have requested to see me.' Mina smiled in the way ladies did when they wished to convey that they did not understand what was being asked of them. Those who did not know her often assumed that her small tilted body was the outward sign of a deficient mind. This misapprehension was usually corrected quickly but sometimes she allowed them to go on with the error for as long as it served her purpose. It was not a mistake anyone made twice.

'I have come,' he said, as if making a grand announcement at a prize-giving, 'because I believe that it is in your power to right a terrible wrong.'

Mina was mystified, but had the strong impression that she was being offered something disguised as an honour that would ultimately prove to be quite different in nature. 'That is very flattering. To what are you referring?'

'Can you not guess? I refer of course to the pitiful plight of the spirit medium Miss Eustace, who is even now incarcerated in Lewes House of Correction, awaiting trial for crimes of which she is wholly innocent.'

Mina paused. She realised that she would have to tread very carefully with Mr Hope. As far as she was concerned Miss Eustace was a criminal who was exactly where she richly deserved to be, but it would not do to say so at this juncture. Open opposition to her visitor's wishes was not the best policy if she was to learn more of his thoughts and intentions. 'I am given to understand that that is not the lady's real name,' she said cautiously.

Hope dismissed this observation with an indulgent smile. 'Her *nom de théâtre*. Some of the most prominent and sought-after mediums choose to adopt a public name to protect their true identities so that when they are in private they can live a calm and untroubled life. Mediums, by the nature of their work, often require peace and rest after communication with the spirits, especially if a manifestation has been produced, in order to fully restore their exhausted energies.'

Rose arrived with the tea tray and an unreadable expression. After pouring the tea she stood waiting for further instructions. 'That will be all, Rose. I will ring when you are needed again,' said Mina. Rose paused only to cast a glance at Mr Hope before she retreated.

Mina sipped her tea. 'I really do not see how it may be in my power to influence Miss Eustace's situation.'

Hope cradled his teacup in his large hands, where it resembled a porcelain thimble. 'You have, have you not, attended several séances conducted by Miss Eustace?'

'I have, yes.'

'One of which, I am reliably informed, you attempted to disrupt.'

Mina saw that he was referring to an incident in which, after pretending to stumble, she had fallen against the figure of Phoebe, a radiant manifestation produced by Miss Eustace, which she had proved to her satisfaction was the medium herself clad in glowing draperies. Such was the devoted gullibility of the lady's adherents that the exposure had not, as it ought to have done, ended her career. Mina might have protested to Mr Hope that her fall was an accident, but thought it unlikely that she would convince him, and to lie would be a blunder. She remained silent.

'Despite this,' Hope went on, still maintaining his outward air of affability, 'Miss Eustace was kind enough to pay you a visit, and on that occasion she sensed that you yourself are without knowing it a powerful medium who only needed to develop your abilities, something she offered to assist you in doing, however, you rejected her generosity.'

Mina felt suddenly chilled. The incident at the séance was well known in town, but the details of Miss Eustace's visit to her home had not been broadcast. If her visitor knew so much then he had heard it from the lady herself or her associates. She could only conclude that Mr Hope was no distant admirer of the fascinating fraudster, but one of her intimates. Still she said nothing.

He drained his cup with relish and put it down. 'There followed an event,' he went on, further emboldened by Mina's reticence, 'the one at which Miss Eustace was apprehended. I will not call it a séance, since it was more of a charade, and had been deliberately and carefully designed with the sole object of entrapping Miss Eustace; an attempt to demonstrate to the world that she was a false medium. This shameless mockery was supposedly held at the behest of a new patroness, a Lady Finsbury, who made a very pretty little speech before she revealed her true colours. I must inform you that I have made careful enquiries and have established that no such person as Lady Finsbury exists.' He paused and fixed Mina with an intense and knowing stare. 'You do not seem to find that information surprising.'

Mina was not at all surprised, since the part of 'Lady Finsbury' had been performed with skill and panache by her brother Richard's then mistress, conjuror's assistant Nellie Gilden.

'I believe that you played a significant role in that disgraceful affair; in fact, I think that you devised, financed and orchestrated it. Lady Finsbury, I am convinced, was an actress hired by you in order to lure an innocent lady, one who has been a great comfort to the bereaved, into a dangerous situation. Whatever crimes were committed on that occasion, they were not perpetrated by Miss Eustace, who is the most accomplished and powerful medium in the country. As anyone with a knowledge of spiritualism would have known, such a travesty could never have resulted in a proper display of spiritualism, as it was arranged in such a manner that it could only have ended in failure. Not only that,' he went on, his voice increasing in both force and severity of tone, 'but you arranged for the event to be attended by many of the leading citizens of Brighton, as well as representatives of the press. Do you deny it?' This last was almost a shout, a challenge meant to disturb and rattle her into a confession.

Mina, unused to such treatment, was outraged that her guest thought he could use his position in society and masculine authority to intimidate her in her own home. An angry retort sprang to her lips but was stifled. She was obliged to gather all her resolve in an effort to keep her head and maintain the calmness and dignity that the situation required. 'I will neither confirm nor deny anything,' she informed him, quietly but steadily. 'You have come here to request my assistance, yet thus far have requested nothing, only raised your voice to level accusations. If that is all your message then I require you to leave now.' She made to ring for Rose, but he raised a placatory hand.

'Miss Scarletti, please, I do not mean to offend you, and I apologise if I have done so. My strong feelings on the matter ran away with me and I beg your forgiveness. All I wished to do was establish the facts, which I think I have done to my satisfaction. You need say nothing; your silence on the subject is answer enough. You must admit, however, that as regards Miss Eustace's current unpleasant situation it is very clear to any observer that all roads lead to you. Many prominent ladies and gentlemen in Brighton have described you as the person responsible, with, I am sorry to say, approval. But please, I entreat you, allow me to speak further.'

'Very well,' said Mina reluctantly, staying her hand, thankful that it was she alone who was his focus, and that neither Richard nor Dr Hamid – who had also played a part in the exposure of the fraud – had been identified as her confederates. She was also relieved that Mr Hope, having concluded that the elegant Lady Finsbury was a mere actress, had not therefore thought it necessary to make further enquiries to discover her identity.

Hope had calmed himself and now gazed on her sadly. 'Can I not persuade you to reconsider your opposition to the spirits? I have wide experience of these things and I have found that those who are the strongest mediums are often so fearful of their abilities that at first they reject the spirit world altogether until the time comes when they finally, joyfully embrace it.'

'There has been no joy for me in the spirit world as presented by mediums,' Mina replied. 'There has been upset and distress not only to myself but also to my family and my friends. Please do not mistake me. I do not deny the existence of the spirit. I attend church, I read the Bible and I pray. But some things are hidden from us during our life on earth and only become apparent after our passing. I am content to wait for that knowledge until my proper time comes.'

'But that is because you have not opened your mind to the brightness that surrounds you!' exclaimed Hope, his face lit up by emotion like that of an evangelical preacher. For a moment Mina was reminded of the expression of Miss Eustace's horrid acolyte, young Mr Clee, with his Byronic curls and mad, sea-mist eyes as he tried to draw her into the fold. 'Do you not hunger for knowledge and certainty?' Hope went on. 'Miss Eustace can lead you towards that understanding if you will only allow it.'

'Not, I think, where she is presently situated,' said Mina drily.

If he detected a tone of satire in her voice he ignored it. 'No. She is surrounded by negative influences that drain her powers. She is quite unable to manifest even the smallest apparition.'

Since Miss Eustace was presumably without her supplies of transparent draperies and phosphorised oil Mina did not find this situation surprising. She had read of mediums who claimed to be able to pass through solid walls, but decided that it would not be helpful to mention that Miss Eustace was clearly not one of their number. 'You have interviewed her I take it?'

'I have. She is in a most dejected state. She now realises that she allowed herself to fall under the influence of men who did not have her interests at heart but merely wished to exploit her undoubted abilities. They too await trial, and we may safely leave them to their fate. It is she alone who concerns me. I will be open with you, Miss Scarletti. This is what I intend to do. My first object is to see Miss Eustace acquitted of the trumped-up charges against her and, once that is achieved, I will do everything in my power to restore her to her rightful position as one of the leading spirit mediums of our day. She still has many devoted followers here in Brighton and will return in triumph. As I said in my lecture, Brighton is a focus of spiritual power and nowhere I believe is it stronger than in the Royal Pavilion. I intend to take a room there – the banqueting hall will be ideal for the purpose – to enable Miss Eustace to conduct her séances in the most favourable possible conditions.'

Mina was shocked that Miss Eustace had the effrontery to want to show her face in Brighton again, whatever the financial lure. 'Do you really think that advisable? If she must hold séances, and I certainly cannot stop her from doing so, would it not be better to try some other location, where there are no people she has cheated? There would be uproar if she came here again.' As soon as the words were out of her mouth, however, Mina understood. Miss Eustace wished to capitalise on the current excitement about the royal ghost. With her abilities she could create a sensation. 'I suppose Brighton would be very receptive to mediums at present,' she admitted.

'Exactly,' beamed Hope, 'and we will soon see what will happen to those suggestions of cheating. Blown away in a sea breeze to be replaced by the warmth of spiritual light.'

'But I still do not see what it is I am being asked to do. Supposing Miss Eustace was acquitted, which I think highly unlikely, am I expected to attend her séances? I rather think she would not permit me under any circumstances to attend a demonstration she might give, for fear that I would show her up as a humbug.'

Hope adopted his friendliest smile, one that Mina was learning to distrust. 'Since it is well known in Brighton that you were the instrument of Miss Eustace's temporary reversal, your opinion on her mediumship does carry some weight here. What I am earnestly requesting therefore is that you reconsider your position. When you have done so, and can fully appreciate your former error, I would like you to issue a statement to the press to the effect that you now accept that the lady is a genuine spirit medium.'

Mr Hope, still smiling, sat back in his chair and viewed Mina's dismay with evident satisfaction.

Nine

ina was momentarily too amazed to speak, since she had seen with her own eyes the evidence of Miss Eustace's falsity. Richard, who had been foolhardy enough to climb through the window of the medium's lodgings and search her possessions, had found trunks packed with all the paraphernalia of a conjuror, and information she had collected about the residents of Brighton to give verisimilitude to the supposed messages from beyond, material which was now in the hands of the police. The case against Miss Eustace had been made very clear before the Lewes magistrates and Mr Hope could not be ignorant of the facts. An outright refusal was the obvious response but again she bit back the instinct and stayed calm.

'I am sure you must be aware that the evidence against her is very strong.'

He shrugged. 'There may be evidence as you call it, but these things can be viewed in more ways than one, and I believe that if there proves to be a case of any sort it will not be against the lady, only the men who controlled her.'

'Mr Hope, you must know that I have experienced her trickery myself.'

He gazed on her as one might a child or a simpleton. 'Oh, I know what it is you speak of, your very tangible contact with Phoebe, a dangerous experiment that threatened the lives of you both. I have heard similar statements from so many who close their minds to the great truth. But allow me to explain. What few people appreciate is that the power of a medium is a very delicate thing – it may be well one day and drained the next, yet the public, who rarely understand these things, expect it to be always there in strength. A mere mountebank may perform his tricks at any time, since that is what they are – tricks. For the medium, on the other hand, under certain conditions, and most especially when surrounded by harsh unbelievers, the ability to commune with the spirit world may fail altogether, and yet a convincing display is still expected. On those rare occasions, the medium who does not wish to disappoint those who take such comfort from communication with the spirits, will oblige by employing non-spiritual means to produce the effects desired.'

'So you are saying that mediums do cheat?'

'I would not call it cheating.'

'I would.'

'I reiterate,' he said very patiently, 'this happens only rarely, and it is not done for the advantage of the medium, but in order to give consolation to the bereaved. And that inevitably is exactly when the accusations of fraud arise. Most of the time the apparitions seen and communications received at séances are entirely genuine. Can you not acknowledge that?'

Mina thought carefully. 'Irrespective of what I might think about Miss Eustace's abilities, or all mediums for that matter, there is an important issue which you have not addressed. Miss Eustace is not about to stand trial for fraudulent mediumship; her case is far more serious. She is accused, quite rightly in my opinion, of extorting large sums of money from an unsuspecting lady under false pretences by passing on messages supposedly from the spirit of her late brother, messages which were later proven by documentary evidence to be untrue.'

Hope shook his head emphatically. 'I do not believe that Miss Eustace is guilty of any crime. As to the spirit messages, well, we only have the word of her accuser, Miss Whinstone, as to what words actually passed. There was an arrangement that was made between the parties in good faith, and the lady completely understood its provisions, but she later discovered that it was a greater drain on her resources than anticipated. She could, had she wished, have approached Miss Eustace and asked for some variation, or even requested to cancel the arrangement by mutual agreement, but unfortunately she chose instead to try and extricate herself from her difficulty by claiming that she had been duped.'

Mina was now sufficiently annoyed by this nonsense to state her position clearly. 'That is ridiculous. I suppose it is what Miss Eustace has told you. You should know that Miss Whinstone is a friend of my family. She is a good kind lady who would never stoop to the action you have described, or indeed any dishonesty. If Miss Eustace wishes to malign her in this way then I certainly cannot offer her any support.'

Mr Hope did not appear discomfited by this. 'You may wish to reconsider. I should mention that in the forthcoming trial it will be a part of Miss Eustace's defence that her accuser did not tell the truth before the magistrates. If Miss Whinstone tells the same tale at the assizes and Miss Eustace is acquitted then your friend will be open to a charge of perjury.'

It was said calmly but it was clearly intended to shock, and it did. Mina knew that it had taken nervous Miss Whinstone all her scant courage to make a public confession to the cruel delusion in which she had been trapped, and could not imagine what additional harm this fresh ordeal would wreak on the lady's fragile constitution.

'And you believe Miss Eustace?'

'I do.'

'That is unpardonable! It is nothing short of slander!'

As Mina's anger mounted, so Hope's satisfaction increased. 'I can see you feel very strongly about what you see as an injustice to your friend. As strongly as I feel about the injustice being done to Miss Eustace. But there is something you can do to mend the situation. Miss Eustace might be persuaded out of the goodness of her heart to make some slight changes to her defence. She might, for example, decide to claim simply that she is the innocent victim of a mistake. Miss Whinstone will not therefore be shown to have deliberately lied but simply to have been confused. Under such circumstances there would be no criminal charges for her to answer.'

'How might I —?' Mina stopped. She understood it all now. She was being blackmailed.

Arthur Wallace Hope smiled at her.

She took a deep breath. Her back hurt, her shoulder hurt and her chest hurt. 'You place me in a very difficult position, since if I was to make the statement you ask for it would be a lie. Do you expect me to put my name to a lie?'

'No, Miss Scarletti, I expect you to acknowledge the truth. One day all the world will recognise it. Eyes will be opened, and the cavillers and bigots who deny the world of the spirit will finally see what is so plain and obvious to others. Their refusal to admit to the true way is a great curse on mankind. It is like the folly of the unlawful whom God punished by sending his flood, allowing only the righteous to live.'

'I cannot see that this is the same thing at all. Surely you cannot be claiming that unbelievers will be washed away by another flood?'

'It is already happening! It has happened! I have seen it with my own eyes on the battlefields of the Crimea. War is the new flood – it is God's warning to mankind! I know it may seem harsh but it was necessary, like the flood, to sweep away materialism and bring humanity to glory!'

Mina stared at him. He was noble, intelligent, and fiercely driven by the certainty that he was right. Nothing would or could ever shake him from that position. Not only that, but he had the power to convince others, and he knew it.

Mina examined the teapot while she was wondering what to say. She offered to refresh his teacup, but he declined. 'Mr Hope, you have given me a great deal to think about. I cannot give you an answer today. Would you allow me some time to consider what you have said?'

'Of course I will!'

'Please could you assure me that for the time being, Miss Eustace will not be making any accusations of perjury against Miss Whinstone, which would only distress her unnecessarily.'

'You have my promise.'

Mina poured more tea for herself, but its murky depths looked uninviting, and a few dusty leaves had escaped the strainer. She wished she did have the powers he attributed to her, then she could have divined what to do next. As she reflected on what he had said at his lecture, however, a new idea did come to her. She put the cup down. 'Perhaps it would assist me in my deliberations if you were to tell me more about your belief that the Royal Pavilion is a focus of spiritual energy. You mentioned at the lecture that you had actually met the Misses Bland, authors of *An Encounter*?'

'Yes, very recently. I found them modest and virtuous, and quite unconscious of having any powers of their own, although I am sure that they do and would take only a little development. In view of their position in life and retiring natures they do not, however, wish to undertake any séances, which I think is a great pity.'

'How did you encounter them?'

'I wrote to Mr Worple, the printer of the volume, who informed me that because of the unexpected interest in the book and the timidity of its authors, he had been advised that the ladies would not consent to meet with anyone except for a select few individuals. He was kind enough to ask them if I might be introduced and they were happy to allow it. Our meeting took place at his office in London about two weeks ago, and we had a very pleasant afternoon.'

'So if I wished to meet them I could apply to Mr Worple in the same way?'

'You might try, but in view of your opposition to spiritualism, it would be most unlikely that your application would succeed. You may not write to them directly. The ladies wish to preserve their true identity to save embarrassment to their father, who is a clergyman. They are, I might say, quite astonished at the excitement caused by their book. They wrote it for the purposes of information and had it printed at their own expense, not expecting to achieve fame and fortune. I think the supposed indecency is very much inflated. To the innocent all things are innocent.'

Mina decided that it would not be wise to reveal that she had not only read the book but also discovered the date of the Pavilion visit. Her main concern now was preventing Miss Eustace from defaming Miss Whinstone and also, if at all possible, ensuring that she never returned to ply her fraudulent trade in Brighton. Since the recent surge of interest in the Pavilion as a focus of spiritualism was solely due to *An Encounter* she thought that if she could reveal the work to be a fiction then that interest, even if it did not evaporate since such things rarely did in their entirety, would be weakened to the point where Miss Eustace was no longer able to capitalise on it.

'Very well,' she said. 'I think that I shall pay a visit to the Pavilion and see if I can feel the power of the spirits working there. You may think it strange that I have never been there, but I have lived in Brighton for less than three years, during the first of which I was helping care for my father who was an invalid, and after his death for my mother, who was deeply affected by his loss.'

'I understand, and I very much hope that when you sense the working of the spirits they will bring peace to you and your family. I will leave you now to your thoughts, but if I might be permitted to call again?'

'Of course.' She rose.

'Incidentally, I have heard tell of another medium in Brighton somewhat different from Miss Eustace but still one I should like to meet. A Miss Foxton?'

'Yes, I have seen one of her performances, but I believe she is no longer in town. If I should hear of her return I will let you know.'

At this moment, to Mina's concern she heard the front door open. Could it be her brother who was now about to discover her in close compact with a man? But chattering voices in the hallway told her it was far worse than that; her mother and Enid had returned early. Mina hoped desperately that they would hurry upstairs and she could persuade Mr Hope to leave without their seeing him, but instead they burst into the parlour, laughing, and halted in astonishment. Enid did not know whether to be delighted or furious, but Mr Hope favoured them with one of his most pleasing smiles. 'Why Miss Scarletti, these must be your charming sisters!'

Mina made the introductions, while Enid went red in the face and Louisa simpered at the blatant flattery. 'Mrs Scarletti!' Hope exclaimed as he bowed to Louisa, 'Why surely not, you are far too young to have grown daughters! But now I recognise you both as you came to my lecture and I believe I inscribed a book.' He turned the full power of his gaze onto Enid, who looked ready to melt like a jelly left in the sun.

'Oh I do hope you are not going so soon – please do stay and have some refreshment!' exclaimed Louisa.

'Yes, please do!' Enid begged. 'I should so much like to hear more about Africa!'

'Ladies, I am sorely tempted to accept your kindness, but I regret that I am already engaged for luncheon with the Lord Mayor, who expects me to regale him with my experiences in the Crimea. But I promise that we will meet again.' He supplied his card. 'I can be reached here.'

Once the visitor had gone, Enid turned upon Mina with a look of fury. 'Well, what can you mean by it? Why did he call? I can't believe he was here to see you! Was there no mistake?'

'He wished to engage my support for the publication *An Encounter*,' said Mina, which was part of the truth at least.

'He knows what I think of spirit mediums and thought that if I was to say something in favour of the book it might lend some weight to his arguments.' She decided to say nothing about Miss Eustace as that was a sore point with her mother.

'I hope you have not agreed to his wishes,' said Louisa, frowning. 'He is a man of the world and therefore we must excuse him from not thinking the book indecent, but it is quite unsuitable for the female sex.'

'I have not, but I suggested he might like to call again, something I think you would both wish for,' said Mina. 'If you like I will keep him in suspense as to my reply until you tire of his company.'

From Enid's expression Mina thought that situation would be a very long time coming.

Ten

ina decided that before she took any further action she should learn as much as she could about Arthur Wallace Hope, and so after luncheon she retired to her room to read *African Quest*. There was a brief tribute to the author in a foreword by none other than Sir Roderick Murchison, the distinguished geologist, president of the Royal Geographical Society and friend of Dr Livingstone. The editor of the *Brighton Gazette* had also, when advertising the recent lecture, published some extremely complimentary words about Mr Hope, from which Mina assumed that neither of these authors had ever had the occasion to oppose his wishes.

Arthur Wallace Hope had been born in 1830, and was the second son of Viscount Hope. Determining on a military career he had joined the 77th East Middlesex Regiment of Foot and served in the Crimea with courage and distinction. He had returned, saddened at the terrible waste of human life, to find that his father had died while he was away. Seeking a purpose and challenge not offered to him by his new status of younger brother and heir presumptive of a Viscount, he soon volunteered for his first trip to Africa. His brother's untimely death without male issue had elevated him to the family title, although he preferred to be known as plain Mr Hope.

Mina could easily see why Arthur Wallace Hope had become so convinced of spiritualism. He had been surrounded by death from an early age. Not only had he lost his father and older brother while still in his twenties, but he had witnessed young men dying on the battlefield in their thousands.

Seeking adventure in Africa he had been appalled by wars and massacres and seen his own party of gallant friends hacked to death, drowned in surging rapids or ravaged by tropical diseases. It had been impossible for him to accept that the loss of so much promising youth had been for nothing, and that those bright souls were not somewhere close by, enjoying a tranquil afterlife where he would one day meet them again.

After some thought, Mina decided that what she most needed was sensible advice, and since this was not available at home, she sent a note to Dr Hamid.

Later that day, her brother Richard arrived unannounced in time for the family to sit down together for dinner. Although not normally the best of timekeepers, his ability to put in an appearance just as food was due to be served was unwaveringly accurate. As ever he was buoyantly optimistic about a brand new business undertaking that was going to make his fortune, but predictably, was unable to provide any significant detail concerning its nature. The only certainty was that a small amount of capital would be required, which through some dreadful bad luck he was unable to lay his hands on. His brother Edward was allowing him board and lodgings at his home in London but was being a terrible bore over money. As usual, Louisa smiled indulgently at Richard, said how happy she was to help him make his way in the world, and agreed to provide what was needed.

To Mina's knowledge Richard's last three enterprises, in all of which he had failed to become rich, had been the gaming table, trying to acquire a wealthy wife, and appearing on stage with Nellie, and she dreaded to think what his next venture might be. In due course she would doubtless be burdened with the information and expected to provide an investment. The main subject of conversation, however, once the question of Richard's assured success, Mina's health, the twins' progress, Enid's new gown and Louisa's headaches had been rapidly disposed of, was the visit to their home of the renowned and heroic Arthur Wallace Hope. Both Louisa and Enid thought it obvious to the point where no discussion was required that the distinguished visitor had not wished to see Mina at all, and there had been an innocent error in which she had foolishly encouraged the great man. There, however, their opinions diverged, since Louisa, commenting that Hope must have asked to see Mrs Scarletti and not Miss, was convinced that she had been the object of his interest, whereas Enid, who had been a Miss Scarletti not so very long ago, was of another viewpoint. Enid, however, as did everyone in the house, knew better than to contradict her mother once she had arrived at a fixed opinion, and only let her opposition be known with very pointed glances at Mina and Richard.

'I suppose,' said Louisa, with a careful lightness of tone, 'that Mr Hope is not a married man? If he is then his poor wife must be very unhappy with him spending all his time travelling.'

'Oh, he has not had the time to marry, surely,' said Enid.

'He might have married while he was in Africa,' suggested Mina.

'What nonsense you talk sometimes,' said Louisa. 'There is no one in Africa for him *to* marry.'

'Unless he has a secret wife who is quite mad and he has her locked up in a tower at his castle!' giggled Enid, who seemed to find this idea quite exciting.

Once dinner was done, Mina suggested that she would like to take a refreshing walk to the seafront and asked Richard if he would go with her, to which he at once agreed. Enid and Louisa, saying they had seen the sea quite recently and did not need to see it again so soon, remained at home to examine their recent purchases and give instructions to Rose as to their care.

'Both Enid and mother are in better health than they have been for some while,' said Richard, as he walked with Mina down Montpelier Road to the inviting vista of the shining ocean. Mina leaned on Richard's arm, which reduced the awkward seesawing of her gait and therefore the strain on her muscles, and he was happy to amble slowly at her side. Brighton was glowing in its autumn beauty, the sky of that intense clear blue that seems to go on for ever, an unusually kind breeze doing no more than rustle garments and make the ribbons of ladies' bonnets flutter. 'I was careful not to mention Mr Inskip in case Enid had a relapse into melancholy. Do we know if that gentleman is alive or dead? Or perhaps he is a little of both? He never seemed to me to be perfectly alive even at the wedding.'

'Enid receives the occasional letter from him, usually to say he is very occupied with business and may not be home for some months. That always seems to cheer her.'

'And before you say it, my dear girl, it is obvious to me that Mr Arthur Wallace Hope came to see you and none other.'

'He did,' said Mina and was relieved to regale her brother with the full import of the conversation.

'The scoundrel!' exclaimed Richard. 'How dare he! I am sorry I was not here to deal with him.'

'It was a difficult interview,' Mina admitted, 'but I do think I would not have learned all that I did had there been another person present.'

'Do you want me to call him out? I would, you know.'

'No, Richard, I don't want you to do anything except watch and listen if he visits again. And not a word to mother or Enid, who would never believe me in any case.'

'What will you do about his demands?'

'I am not sure. I am only happy that the trial date has not yet been set, so I do have time to decide. The good news is that he seems not to have realised that you and Dr Hamid were part of the business, and I hope he never finds out.'

'You must speak with the good doctor, of course.'

'I have sent him a note, and will call as soon as convenient.'

'And while it might be hard on Miss Whinstone, she must be apprised of the danger to herself.'

'I agree. I cannot leave her unprepared. But she is such a nervous lady that I suspect she will beg me to comply with Mr Hope's wishes in order to spare her from prosecution.'

'Would you do that for her?'

Mina had already given this fraught matter some very serious consideration and had come to an unhappy conclusion. 'If necessary. I would not give in to blackmail on my own account but I cannot see another lady suffer for my obstinacy. Poor Miss Whinstone has endured quite enough without being threatened with a criminal charge. My thoughts are my own, of course. They will not change and I hope that those who know me will understand. But I would look like a fool to the public, and that will be hard. Still, these things are quickly forgotten.'

'If there is anything you need doing, I am your man, you have only to ask, and meanwhile, I will bend my mind to the problem.'

'Just promise me you will not break the law, and do nothing without consulting me first,' Mina pleaded.

They had reached the promenade, where a sting of salt was in the air, and the pebbled beach lay before them like so many pale brown and cream coloured eggs, streaked here and there with dark weed. In the distance was the cowbell tinkle of the last donkey rides of the day, and pleasure boats were being drawn up to take their rest out of the reach of the hungry sea. In the evening, as the sun sank, dusting the waves with rosy light, Brighton's visitors would throng to the clifftop or gather in rows along the promenade to watch the spectacle. Mina, who saw tales of horror in everything around her, thought that the crimson blush of the sea resembled blood. Supposing, she thought, it was blood, the spectral remembrance of a sea battle in which many men had lost their lives? That would make a good story. 'Ghost Blood' she would call it. Mina decided to purchase a small notebook to carry about with her so she could jot down her story ideas before they vanished.

'And now, Richard,' said Mina, as the sky gradually cooled and they strolled along the promenade past tall white hotels, 'I want to know the reason for your visit.'

'Does one need a reason to visit Brighton?' he asked with a smile.

'If it was anyone other than you I would have no need to ask. I love the smell of the sea and the air, and for entertainment I am not sure I would find more to delight me in London. But I am sure that you are not here for your health or even pleasure.'

'Now you can't deny that there has been a great deal happening here, what with poisonings and scandals, it has been in the London papers as well, and I could not wait to come here where life is so much richer in incident than London.'

'Surely living with Edward is not as dull as that?' exclaimed Mina.

'Oh but it is; he talks of nothing but work and Miss Hooper! He is in a perfect frenzy of excitement at the prospect of making that delightful maiden his bride. He wearies me on the subject incessantly. I only hope that when he is her husband at last the lady does not disappoint.'

'You do not admire her?'

'She is pretty, I admit, but tedious. They will make an admirable couple. And would you believe Edward actually suggested that I join the company as a clerk! A clerk! Imagine me sitting at a desk all day, I would dry up like an Egyptian mummy and have to be put in a museum.'

'I assume that you are here to pursue some more pleasurable and less arduous way of making your fortune. Please let me know what it is; reassure me that nothing illegal or scandalous is involved and you will not need to hide it from mother again.'

He grinned. 'Well there has been a lot of talk just lately about a certain book and the ghostly shade of old George as was, only seen when he was young and virile. Now my thought is this – if one book will make money then two will make twice as much. I did think about writing my own but somehow I can't seem to get properly started. So I thought that as you are an author you could give me some advice. Where do you get your ideas from? What do you do when the words refuse to come? Do you have to force yourself to write? It's all a mystery to me.'

'If you need to ask those questions then I would suggest book writing may not be your forte,' advised Mina.

'Perhaps not, although there are many who do not allow that to stop them. Have you read about the ghostly encounter? It might be a bit fast for you.'

'And not for you? I have been told that only mature men or married persons would not find it shocking. Mother has a copy, only she would never admit it.'

'I have read it of course. Mother likes to think that I am inno-cent of the ways of the world, but she knows the truth. All I am innocent of is ready money.' A new thought struck him. 'Tell me – how is Nellie? I haven't seen her since she was married. Is she happy with her new husband? I didn't take to him myself.'

'I believe she is content. If their marriage may be likened to a ship then he is the proud owner, but it is her hand on the wheel.'

'Well if he is ever unkind to her you must let me know at once and I will come and teach him the proper way to treat a lady. But do you see where my thoughts are tending? I might not be able to write a book but a play should be far easier. Yes, that is what I shall do!'

'It may be harder than you think,' warned Mina.

'Oh, I am sure it is very easy; after all, what is a play but people standing on a stage and talking a great deal of nonsense! I have seen enough of the theatre to know that!'

'I am not even sure if it is easy to write a bad play, but a good one will certainly require hard work and some literary ability.'

'Aha,' he exclaimed triumphantly, 'in that case you will write it, Mina!'

'I shall do nothing of the sort, and don't try to persuade me.'

'Really? Well, I should be able to dash it off in a day or two in any case, and I know exactly what the crowds will come to see. It will be the story of the Prince and Mrs Fitzherbert and their doomed love. Good or bad writing doesn't signify since there would only be a few performances and no one would know the truth until we have sold all our tickets.'

'We? Richard – I shall have nothing to do with this project in any capacity!'

'Just a little cash advance, that is all,' he pleaded. 'I have to advertise and have tickets printed and hire a room and costumes. Mother's cheque won't cover all of that if I am to make a fine show. I shall get Nellie to personate Mrs Fitzherbert, I am sure she is pining for the theatre and would jump at it.'

'Would her husband not object?'

'No, Nellie will get around that – she has her ways, you know. And I shall be the Prince of Wales. Prinny was said to be very handsome in his youth.' Richard preened himself with a satisfied pat to his chest then allowed his palm to descend to his stomach. Despite his hearty appetite he remained defiantly slender. 'I shall need padding of course. Perhaps we will get Nellie's old friend Rolly Rollason to take part; he's a good sport. I know! He could be Napoleon!'

'Do you think he will be suitable for the role? I believe Napoleon was quite a short man, and Rolly is well above six feet in height.'

'Then he will personate Napoleon on his knees. It will be a novelty. Yes, I can see it now! Prinny and Napoleon will fight with swords for the love of Mrs Fitzherbert and the honour of England! Or the love of England and the honour of Mrs Fitzherbert, whichever is more appropriate. Prinny will stab the Frenchman through the heart to the wild applause of the groundlings.'

'So it will not be a historical piece.'

'Not at all. It will be much more interesting. Then Mrs Fitzherbert will fall into the Prince's arms in an ecstasy of passion. It will be —'

'Indecent?' Mina suggested.

'Piquante.'

'Richard, you do know that the late King George was a very unpopular figure? Gormandising – drinking – running up debts – gambling – mistresses …' Mina's voice tailed off as she realised that she was cataloging her own brother's principal faults.

'Oh but I have been told that he was very well thought of in Brighton, since he brought the fashionables to town. And if not, it is high time he was rehabilitated! I would rather spend five minutes carousing with Prinny than a whole evening's dreary banquet with the Queen. I'm sure that good Prince Albert was a splendid sort, but ten years of mourning is really overdoing it.' Richard looked suddenly thoughtful. 'Did Albert ever come to the Pavilion?'

'It is possible,' said Mina grudgingly. 'Please do not personate him. Treason is still a hanging offence.'

'And of course the best place to perform my play will be in the Pavilion! I hope it will not be too expensive to hire a room. I shall go there tomorrow and find out.'

'Then I had better come with you, and make sure that you do not make any unwise arrangements with money you do not have.'

They turned back to Montpelier Road and Mina, leaning on her brother's arm, did not mind the pitying looks of passers-by as she limped by his side. There was a note waiting for her at home saying that Dr Hamid and Anna would be delighted if she joined them for a light supper that evening. Richard, Mina admitted to herself, had been right about one thing – she must warn Miss Whinstone of the threat from Mr Hope, even if the result was capitulating to his demands. Mina wrote a note to Miss Whinstone asking if she might visit her very soon.

Eleven

Dr Hamid and his sister Anna lived in a pleasant villa near the seafront, not far from their place of business. Only once had they allowed a séance to be held in their home, and it was done not at the desire of either but at the earnest request of their older sister Eliza, who had been seduced by the charm and promises of Miss Eustace and her acolyte Mr Clee into the belief that she was a medium. As Mina had later learned, adults of restricted stature were valuable allies for a spirit medium, able to appear at séances in the guise of ghostly children yet with the discipline to maintain the deception for as long as necessary. Mediums who lacked such confederates often resorted to creating the illusion themselves by crouching or kneeling, but in doing so risked an embarrassing exposure if distraught parents attempted to embrace the spirit of their dead offspring.

Mr Clee had also tried to draw Mina into Miss Eustace's fold but he had failed. A young man with a persuasive manner and the looks and address of a hero of romantic adventures, he had worked his wiles on the matrons of Brighton to considerable effect. He had initially presented himself at one of Miss Eustace's séances masquerading as a stranger and a sceptic, but had rapidly undergone a miraculous conversion to a devoted worshipper at her shrine. So ardent was Mr Clee that there had been talk all over the town that he was in love with the medium, a rumour that had saddened many a susceptible female heart before he protested that his admiration of the lady was chaste and pure. Only later had it been revealed that he was not only Miss Eustace's co-conspirator in fraud and confederate in the production of supposed spiritual effects, but her brother. Their father, Mr Benjamin Clee, was a respectable purveyor of materials and equipment for the use of conjurors, and both brother and sister were adept in that art. Mina hoped that any attempt by Mr Clee to use his skills to beguile the warders of the Lewes House of Correction where he was now securely confined would fall upon hearts made stony by long experience.

Miss Eustace had not attended the event at the Hamids' house since she had been suffering from a heavy cold, but that illness, of little consequence to a youthful person in otherwise good health, had been carried to the house on the breath of Mr Clee and found its way into Eliza's cramped and underdeveloped lungs. After her death Dr Hamid, distracted with grief, had consulted Miss Eustace in the hope of making some contact with Eliza's sprit. A simple slip had revealed to him that a message purporting to come from Eliza actually had a more earthly origin. 'Perhaps in a quite different sense it was sent by Eliza,' he had once told Mina. 'Oh I don't mean that it was actually she, but it was what I knew of my sister and what Miss Eustace did not that revealed to me how woefully I had misplaced my trust. It does not take a medium to tell me that Eliza lives on. She still, as she has always done, inspires Anna and me in our study of the spine and its diseases so that we may help others. One day Eliza and I will meet again and she will be healed in a way that I could never achieve and we will be content. But I no longer believe that I will see or speak to her before we are joined in death. I will be patient.'

With Eliza's loss the house seemed quieter. The room where she had spent her days, supported in a chair made specially for her to be able to sit and read in comfort, was as she had left it, the book she had been reading lay open at the last page she had perused, and her spectacles were where she had placed them, ready to be picked up. It was a house of double mourning, for Jane Hamid and now for Eliza, both taken to their rest far too young. But the future was there too, in photographic portraits of Dr Hamid's sons and daughter. All were engaged in study and destined for the practice of medicine, although in the case of the daughter she would need double the courage and determination of her brothers as she would have to overcome not just examinations but male opposition to women studying medicine at all, in order to achieve her desires.

The day's work done, brother and sister liked to sit together companionably and Mina often joined them. Her good health and increasing vigour were also, she knew, a part of Eliza's legacy. In the last few months she had seen, thanks to the exercises in which Anna had carefully coached her, the first positive change in her form she had known for many a year; her back and limbs were stronger and there was a curve of muscle on shoulders and upper arms that had not been noticeable before. Many would have thought such development unseemly and unwomanly, but Mina, who had her clothes specially made so that she could dress herself unaided, enjoyed her secret.

She still had to take care not to deplete her energies through incautious exertion, and that evening Mina hired a cab, delivering her note to Miss Whinstone on the way and finding a stationer still open where she was able to purchase a pocket book to record her story ideas. Once she was settled by the Hamids' fireside and the maid had brought hot cocoa and sandwiches, the conversation turned to the lecture by Arthur Wallace Hope.

'I cannot deny his bravery, and who knows but the exploration of Africa will benefit us one day, but if he is to be the champion of that indecent book then the sooner he is gone from Brighton the better,' said Anna. 'Some of my patients who attended the lecture are actually taking his words as a recommendation and reading it when they had previously determined not to.'

'I have already been invited to a séance,' added Dr Hamid with obvious distaste. 'I declined, of course.'

'I am afraid the situation is far more serious than that,' Mina confessed. Brother and sister listened to her with increasing concern as she described her conversation with Arthur Wallace Hope. 'Mother and Enid do not know the true reason for his visit, although I have told Richard, who has just arrived to stay with us. My next step will be to speak to Miss Whinstone. I don't want to frighten her, but if she is in danger then I would not want her to be unprepared for it when I could have warned her.' Dr Hamid and Anna looked at each other, and Mina could see that they saw the wisdom of her proposal. 'I fear that she will ask me to spare her by doing what Mr Hope asks, and I will have to comply. Perhaps I can find some way of meeting the demands of all parties without shaming myself. And then I will try to forget all about Miss Eustace and her kind and go back to my life as it was. I have, however, written to Mr Greville, my late father's business partner, to see if I can discover more about the book. Not only is it causing such dismay amongst the ladies of Brighton, but it is the stimulus to Miss Eustace's wishes to return here. If I can show it to be a fiction then perhaps she will be less welcome. I will let you know what he can tell me.'

Dr Hamid smiled at Mina. 'Mr Hope is a very clever, wealthy, influential and respected man. I wonder if he knows he has met his match?'

There was a knock at the front door, which caused them all some surprise since no visitor was expected, and the maid brought a letter addressed to Dr Hamid. He, assuming it to be of a medical nature, took it to his study, while Anna and Mina made the most of the remaining refreshments, but before Anna could ring for the plates to be cleared her brother returned with the opened letter in his hand and a deep frown on his face.

'This is quite extraordinary. The letter is from Mr Arthur Wallace Hope. He requests a private meeting with me at my earliest convenience.'

'Does he say what the subject of the interview might be?' asked Mina.

Dr Hamid reread the letter carefully and shook his head. 'No, he gives no indication at all. I doubt that it is a medical matter.'

Mina was thoughtful. 'Since he has spoken to Miss Eustace he most probably knows that you used to attend her séances and engaged her for private consultations. I expect she also recalls your presence at the event where she was arrested, though of course many of her circle were there as well. I think it very doubtful that Mr Hope knows the part you played in her discovery.'

'And he must never know! Fortunately, I was not asked to give evidence before the magistrates and as far as I am aware I will not be called at the trial.'

'Perhaps he believes that you might be sympathetic to her, and would be willing to act as a character witness?' suggested Anna.

'He may well be seeking out people with professional and social status for that very purpose,' agreed Mina. 'He might ask you to sign a statement attesting to your belief that Miss Eustace is genuine.'

'I shall of course do neither,' said Dr Hamid firmly.

'There is another possibility,' Mina added. 'He has been making enquiries about me and therefore might know by now that I am a patient of yours. This message comes just hours after he failed to induce me to sign the statement he wanted. Could he be trying to find out more about me – some new way of forcing my hand?'

'If so, that is deplorable, and I will show him the door at once!'

'I would prefer it if you did not,' said Mina.

Dr Hamid looked wary. 'Miss Scarletti – I know that look – what are you suggesting I do?'

'Mr Hope may be quite unaware that we are of the same mind on the subject of sprit mediums. Perhaps you might simply listen to what he has to say, and neither oppose his wishes nor agree to comply with them. Ask for more time to consider, as I did. He might reveal more to you than he has done to me.'

'As long as you don't require me to break into his hotel room and rifle through his possessions.'

'What an interesting suggestion. But no.'

'Very well. I doubt in any case that he is a man who can be put off for long. I will write to him at once and arrange to see him tomorrow.'

Twelve

Next morning, Mina received a letter from Mr Greville. A letter to her from the office of the Scarletti Library of Romance was not an unusual event and excited no comment at the breakfast table, in fact Mina's literary activities did not usually excite any comment at all in her home. Had her mother actually seen her tales of hauntings and horror there would no doubt have been unceasing comment.

Disappointingly, Mr Greville reported that he had been unable to discover anything further concerning the Misses Bland, authors of the sensational *An Encounter*. The proprietor of the printing firm, Mr Worple, was personally known to him, as there were occasional social gatherings of men in the publishing trade, and the office of Worple and Co. was not far from his own. Mr Greville had obliged Mina by finding a pretext to call on Mr Worple and mentioning to him that he was curious about the authors of the notorious book, and asking who they were. Judging by Mr Worple's reaction, this was a question the printer had been asked very many times. Nevertheless, he was more polite and communicative to a brother in the publishing trade than he might have been to a correspondent of the popular press. Mr Worple had replied that all he had been asked to do was print the book as written. He had no means of contacting the authors, since they had initially made a personal visit to his office, and thereafter the copies had been collected by a servant, who carried messages back to her employers. The servant also brought instructions when a further printing was required, and payment of his invoice, which was made in banknotes.

On their initial visit to his office, the ladies had asked, in view of the position of their father, who was a clergyman, that their identity should be protected and Mr Worple had respected their wishes. Both ladies had been veiled. They had made only one subsequent visit, some two weeks previously, when they had come to the office for an interview with the distinguished explorer Mr Arthur Wallace Hope.

The newspapers had become very exercised by the mystery concealing the true identity of the authors, and correspondents, finding Mr Worple unwilling to divulge what they thought he knew, had offered him bribes, or even sent him false messages purporting to come from the Misses Bland hoping to fool him into a revelation. From time to time articles had published with headlines such as 'Who are the Misses Bland?' or 'The Riddle of *An Encounter*'. One of the more sensational periodicals had asked the authors to visit its office promising that they could do so in the strictest confidence, and hinting that a fee might be payable. Another had offered the public a reward of £20 for information as to their identity. No one had come forward.

Frustrated newsmen eager for a story had even taken to lurking outside Mr Worple's office, hoping to see the Misses Bland arrive. Some lady customers had actually been followed back to their homes. The nuisance had been reported to Mr Worple, as a result of which he had been obliged to call the police who had dispersed the loiterers, most of whom they knew by sight, and made sure that these disgraceful incidents were not repeated.

Mr Greville closed his letter with the comment that Mr Worple, who was enjoying valuable repeat orders, was well aware that since he owned no rights over the manuscript, the authors were fully entitled to take their requirements elsewhere, and was therefore unlikely to renege on his agreement not to pry into the affairs of the Misses Bland.

Mina studied the letter wondering what, if anything, she had learned. The book had attributed authorship to two

ladies, and both Mr Hope and Mr Worple had met two ladies.
They were said to reside in London and their choice of a
London printer and the to-ing a fro-ing of a servant suggested
that this was true. All that was known about them otherwise
was what they had chosen to impart.

A second message arrived, this one from Miss Whinstone,
who said that she was at home that morning and Mina would
be very welcome to call.

'Who is writing to you, Mina?' asked her mother.

'An admirer!' said Enid, and laughed.

'Miss Whinstone, she would like me to call on her.'

'Oh?' said Louisa, puzzled. 'What can she want?'

'She doesn't say. Perhaps she was upset by Mr Hope's lecture
and would like to discuss it with me.'

'Is she going to marry that dreadful old man?' asked Enid.

'I will let you know. If she does, she might ask you to be
matron of honour.'

Enid scowled.

Miss Whinstone occupied a small but comfortably appointed
apartment in the western portion of town. She and her late and
much missed brother Archibald had once shared the accommo-
dation, and it was now marked by memories of him. His portraits
were a prominent feature, presented in carefully polished frames,
and such little honours and badges as he had been awarded in
his largely uneventful life, which had been marked by service on
local charitable committees, were proudly displayed.

Miss Whinstone greeted Mina with genuine warmth of feeling.
'Miss Scarletti, I am very happy to see you. I feel quite ashamed
of myself that I have not asked you to call on me sooner. I am so
grateful to you for rescuing me, there can really be no other word,
from the clutches of those horrid cheats. I know I shall never see

my money again, but if my unhappy story can save others who are less able to endure the loss, I shall be content.'

Miss Whinstone, once her period of mourning for her brother had drawn to its conclusion, had been wont to wear a gown of an unflattering shade of dark bronze, the reflection of the silk on her naturally pale face making her look yellow and ill. The messages she had received supposedly from her beloved Archibald through the mediumship of Miss Eustace had initially been cheering and had caused her to trim up and wear an old light green gown, a colour that matched her eyes. She was the same age as Louisa, but without her claims to beauty, nevertheless, when her face was not creased with anxiety, she was not an unhandsome woman. That morning she wore a new gown, in a warm shade of deep plum, a colour that had by some means or other transmitted itself to her hair.

Miss Whinstone showed Mina to the large room which served as both parlour and drawing room, and where she also dined. As Mina entered, Mr Jellico, who had been seated on a sofa, made some effort to rise to his feet to greet her. Mr Jellico was a gentleman of some seventy years, very sparely made, like a withered tree that looked as though it might snap in a high wind. His eyes, from behind the thick glass of his spectacles, were moist and bright, his hands misshapen, the fingers contracted like claws. His glance as he looked at Miss Whinstone was admiring, even affectionate.

'I am delighted to make your better acquaintance,' said Mr Jellico. Apart from seeing him in passing at Mr Hope's lecture, Mina had met him only when he had accompanied Miss Whinstone to take tea with her mother, and on those occasions he had merely sat silently by and listened.

'And I yours,' said Mina.

'I have been longing for the two of you to meet and converse, as Mr Jellico has been such a good friend and a great comfort to me in these difficult times,' said Miss Whinstone as her maid brought in a laden tray. 'I know I am not a very brave person, and I really did think I might faint dead away before those frightening magistrates, but Mr Jellico sat there and smiled at me, and do you know, he did make me feel a little stronger. I know the trial will be a far worse ordeal, but I am determined to bear it.'

Once the maid had distributed the refreshments and departed, Mina asked her first cautious question. 'What did you think of Mr Arthur Wallace Hope?'

'Oh I did not care for him at all,' said Miss Whinstone. 'I know some ladies find him very interesting but when he speaks about all his so-called adventures, all I can think of is how he goes about shooting things, which surely cannot be right.'

'I believe,' said Mr Jellico carefully, 'that in Africa that may be the only way to obtain food. Of course he may shoot when he is in England too. Gentlemen of his class often do.'

Miss Whinstone's mouth was set in a firm line. 'Archibald never shot anything. He didn't believe in it.'

'My family attended the lecture because of an interest in geography, as I imagine most people did,' said Mina, 'but I was not prepared for Mr Hope's comments about spiritualism.'

'Nor I,' said Miss Whinstone, feelingly, helping Mr Jellico raise a teacup to his lips. 'What a nasty surprise. And to think he is in favour of that dreadful book, something I promise you I will never read.'

Mina took as deep a breath as she could manage. 'The reason I have asked to see you is that Mr Hope called on me yesterday, and your name came up in our conversation.'

Miss Whinstone could only stare at her, and Mr Jellico almost dropped the cup.

'I am afraid that what he had to say you may find alarming, but I cannot in all conscience keep you ignorant of his thoughts and intentions.' Mina glanced at Mr Jellico, and Miss Whinstone understood her hesitation.

'Oh you may speak freely before Mr Jellico. He knows all; both the best and the worst.

Mr Jellico smiled. 'The worst of it is only that Miss Whinstone has a warm heart.' He put his cup down and prepared himself for Mina's story.

Mina described in as much detail as she could remember the conversation with Mr Hope, holding nothing back, and as anticipated her revelations were met with shock and dismay.

'Might I ask,' said Mr Jellico thoughtfully, 'was this interview entirely private? Was there no one there to witness what was said?'

'I am afraid not. He requested a private discussion on a sensitive issue but he did not reveal in advance any clue as to what he might say. Even knowing his belief in the Bland sisters, I was amazed to find him a champion of Miss Eustace, and appalled to hear what he required of me.'

Jellico nodded and Mina sensed that though he was frail of body, his mind was keen and vigorous. 'You are of course right that you are being unfairly coerced into complying with his request, but if you were to accuse him of this, there is only your word against his, and I expect that he would deny any such intention. Given his position in society and the regard in which he is held, his word will of course weigh more heavily than yours, and if it came to a dispute you would be in some difficulty. If he should ask to speak to you again, I advise you to ensure that you have a respectable witness to the conversation.'

'That is sound advice. But now I am not sure what to do. On the one hand, I am reluctant to make a statement I know to be untrue, something Mr Hope wishes me to send to the public press, but at the same time I have no wish to place Miss Whinstone in danger. I have given this a great deal of thought, and the only way out I can suggest is for me to prepare and sign a statement for Mr Hope, but somehow find a form of words that would satisfy everyone, although I cannot at present think what they might be.'

'Oh please,' Miss Whinstone exclaimed with unusual energy, 'I beg of you Miss Scarletti – I beg you most earnestly – do not, whatever you do, comply with this horrid man's request. Let them put me in prison if they must!' She started to tremble and Mr Jellico patted her hand.

'They would not put you in prison, I am sure of that,' he reassured her gently.

This was an unexpected turn of events. 'Miss Whinstone,' asked Mina, 'am I to understand that you do not want me to sign any kind of a statement for Mr Hope?'

'Yes. On no account must you do so. You, who have shown others the truth cannot put your name to a lie, even to save me!'

'Miss Whinstone is right,' agreed Mr Jellico, 'and the danger to you, Miss Scarletti, could be far greater than you might imagine. To begin with, I suspect that if you were to agree to make a statement, you might well find that you could not make a free choice of the words. Supposing he provided you with something to sign which stated that it was made of your own free will and for no consideration? That would not be an unusual requirement. Supposing he had it witnessed and then presented it in court in Miss Eustace's defence?'

'But she is not being tried for fraudulent mediumship. That was all the statement was intended to cover.'

'No, but she is accused of extorting money from Miss Whinstone on the basis of false messages communicated during private séances. The nature of those messages cannot be proven, and we only have Miss Whinstone's word that they did not accord with the evidence that was later produced. If we have a statement from you and quite possibly other residents of Brighton that Miss Eustace is genuine, what then becomes of the contention that she told falsehoods? Even if you try to take this middle way you have suggested, agreeing to sign something of your own composition and then later refusing to sign a paper he has drawn up in his own words, just that initial agreement could be held against you and presented in Miss Eustace's favour. As a truthful lady you would not deny it. If there is any doubt at the trial, and her appearance and demeanour excite the sympathy of the jurors, then she might be acquitted.'

Mina could only agree. 'She might, indeed, and if Mr Hope has his way she will be brought to the Pavilion in triumph and produce any number of illustrious ghosts. Of course if she puts on a great show in the manner of a conjuror and entertains the crowds for a few shillings then I have no objection to that. But if she cannot mend her ways she will fleece some of her adherents of their fortunes and they might not be as brave as Miss Whinstone and speak out.'

'Miss Eustace is not the only danger, I am afraid,' said Mr Jellico with a wheezy sigh. 'There have been other séances held in Brighton just lately. We have both been invited to them and refused, of course, despite the promise that Henry VIII and all his wives will appear and take tea with us. All of it is informal for now, no more than an evening's amusement, but the professional mediums will be sure to hear of it and before long they will descend upon the vulnerable like wolves.'

'But you will save us, Miss Scarletti,' said Miss Whinstone, her voice shaking, her eyes bright. 'I know you will.'

Mina returned home with the weight of the world on her aching shoulders.

Thirteen

ater that day, Richard and Mina passed through the southern gate into the grounds of the Royal Pavilion. He had suggested taking a carriage, which would have driven them directly up to the entrance porch, but since the day was fine, Mina, despite the effort it cost her, chose to walk her slow way so as to better see everything around her. Thus they were able to enjoy the luxuriant gardens, which were so well sheltered and tended that trees grew there better than in any part of the town. The lawns were bright with visitors, some of whom were playing croquet. Mina had never played croquet, and no one had ever suggested she try it, since it was a pastime that required the player to swing a large mallet. She was not sure if she would be adept at it, but thought that if she ever took it up, she might at least be able to surprise everyone with her ability to lift the mallet at all, let alone strike a croquet ball.

Mina was not especially well acquainted with the history of the Pavilion; she knew only that it was acquired in the last century by the then Prince of Wales, who later acceded to the throne as George IV, had been remodelled so many times that it no longer resembled the house it had once been, and was now the property of the town. As they approached the domed entrance porch, which itself resembled a palace in miniature, she thought that an entire book could be written about each portion of this astounding building, so detailed and fantastical was the design of every part.

Even though inevitably its apartments were reduced from their once royal grandeur, there was nothing about the Pavilion that could disappoint. Just walking under the first arch was like stepping into another world. Was this, thought Mina, what it would be like to enter paradise – or was it just what the spiritualists hoped it would be like?

The octagonal entrance hall lit by a Chinese lantern had once offered the fashionable visitor to the royal apartments their first real view of the wonders that lay in store in its gilded interior but it now had the humbler duty of an office, where attendants greeted new arrivals and offered to conduct them around the public rooms for the price of sixpence. Mina bought two tickets, and she and Richard joined a party of visitors waiting to embark on a tour. They were soon assigned an attendant, who commenced to point out features of interest. His manner was rather stiff and serious, like an automaton operated by the insertion of a coin, and he did very little to engage his listeners. Mina found herself wondering how many rooms there were in the Pavilion, and how many features each contained, and therefore how long the visit was to take. No wonder the Misses Bland had slipped away to amuse themselves.

The next room, their guide told them, was the vestibule and on entering it Mina found it hard to contain her excitement, since this was without a doubt the Hall of the Worthies, the very room that the Misses Bland had described as the first one they had entered on their great adventure and from where they had escaped their stuffy guide. Mina suspected that theirs had been the same guide. In the centre, and dominating the space, was the statue of the military hero. Greater than life-size it stood high on a plinth, towering several feet above even the tallest visitor. William Henry Cecil George Pechell, said the inscription, of Her Majesty's 77th had died heroically aged just twenty-five at the siege of Sebastopol on 3 September 1855. The son of a Member of Parliament for Brighton, his death had led to a period of public mourning in the town. His statue, depicting him in full uniform, urging on his men with valiantly drawn sword, had been erected by subscription in 1859. Displayed along the sides of the room, and considerably less impressive, were the busts of the notabilities of Brighton, which had been placed there after the building was acquired by the corporation. The whole was lit by an array of hexagonal lanterns embellished by a fantasy of dragons and serpents, while the sage green walls were similarly decorated. Mina at once conceived an idea for a new story in which a visitor to the Pavilion was pursued by mythical beasts which had emerged from the wallpaper. She made a note in her little pocket book, which she now carried everywhere with her. Unfortunately, the attendant, imagining that her note-taking was evidence of her keen interest in what he had to say, was kind enough to describe each of the busts in very great detail.

At this point the attendant mentioned very discreetly that a nearby door lead to an apartment which had once been the King's breakfast room, and was now a cloakroom and retiring room for ladies, while another doorway led to the gentlemen's cloakrooms.

'May I ask a question, please?' Mina interrupted.

'But of course, I will do my best to answer any question you may have about the Pavilion.'

'Would you be able to conduct us to the location where the ghost of the late King George was seen?'

The attendant was too polite to laugh out loud but it was clearly an effort for him not to. 'Oh dear me, I am afraid that all the ladies ask me the same question and it is the very one I cannot answer. There is no room in the Pavilion which matches the description in that – unfortunate book.'

'You have not seen the ghost yourself?'

'I have never in my ten years as an attendant here seen anything of the kind or heard of anything of that sort occurring.'

'Well that is very disappointing,' said Mina.

They proceeded to the Chinese gallery, which, said their guide, was famed for the beauty and delicacy of its design, and was said by those who had seen it in the days of the old King to be one of the most superb apartments that Art and Fancy could produce. While still glorious to the eye, like a visual garden of bamboo and peonies, it contained only a few of the original ornaments since so much had been removed when the Queen had decided to no longer favour the Pavilion with her presence. Later refurbishments carried out at the town's expense had, however, maintained the essential oriental flavour. 'Am I correct,' asked Mina, 'in thinking that there were once, in the time of the late King, life-sized statues standing in the niches clad in Chinese costume?'

The guide paused with a look of surprise. 'That is correct.' This scenario was deliciously rife with potential for a tale of horror and Mina again made a note.

The next wonder they beheld was the enormous banqueting room, dominated by a cut crystal chandelier said to weigh more than a ton. Mina could only worry at the safety of such an item despite the robustness of the gold chains by which it was suspended. When she commented on this, the attendant revealed that Queen Adelaide, the consort of King William IV, had actually had nightmares in which it had fallen, crushing members of the court. This prospect had so terrified her that she had prevailed upon the King to have it removed, and it had not been replaced until the time of the present Queen. Mina again wrote in her notebook: 'Chandelier falling – banquet? ballroom? theatre?' This, she was reminded, was the very room that Mr Hope had said he would hire for the performance of a séance by Miss Eustace. Mina glanced up at the giant chandelier again, but thought it was too much to wish for that it might descend at the very moment that Miss Eustace was underneath it.

The examination of the South Drawing Room, once known as the Green Drawing Room due to the prevailing hue of its draperies, alerted Mina to a passage in *An Encounter* when the ladies had been confused at entering a room they had once thought to be green but now found it had a peculiar blueish coloration. While feeling sure it was the same room, due to its dimensions and the positioning of the columns, they also saw that it was no longer lit by crystal gas standards but a large number of Chinese lanterns. Their account had simply suggested to Mina that since every room in the Pavilion was different in character the ladies had wandered into another room and become confused, but comparing their description with the room she was standing in, she began to wonder.

'These valances are a delightful shade of green,' she commented.

'The only remnant of its former glory,' agreed the attendant with a sigh. 'It was once a very elegant apartment, but little remains to suggest it. Note, however, the fine painting of the ceiling panels, and the beautiful gas lamps and ceiling flowers which were installed by the town authorities and have greatly improved the illumination and ventilation.'

'How was it formerly lit?'

'I believe by oil lanterns as so many of the apartments were.'

'And was it always green?'

'Well, now you mention it, no. It was once known as the 'Blue Drawing Room' but that was very many years ago. This whole suite of rooms has undergone substantial changes mainly dating from the time of King George.'

They moved on through the apartments, and although these were splendid to the eye, the party was assured that what they saw was as nothing to the original beauties of the interior, which had been most dazzling. It had once been the pinnacle of luxury and taste, but with most of the original furniture and decorations having been distributed to other palaces one could only wish that by some magic it might all be restored. Mina was especially curious to see the King's Apartments, assuming that these would be extremely opulent, but discovered that they were no longer so, and the rooms were now available to be hired for private meetings of local societies.

'It all looks rather too grand for me,' said Richard, regretfully. 'A room large enough to hold a play would be an expensive proposition.'

'You may be right,' agreed Mina, but she asked the attendant about hire fees all the same, and he advised her to contact the Pavilion committee.

Their tour done, Mina purchased a slim guidebook, which gave a little of the Pavilion's history and what the modern visitor might expect to see, but she was troubled. She had expected to find that the authors of *An Encounter* had simply described the Pavilion into which they had wandered during their ghostly experience, either as they had seen it, or as it was described in the guidebook, but they had done neither. Nowhere in the guidebook was there mention of the life-size Chinese figures or the South Drawing Room being blue and not green.

Their guide had gone on to greet the next party, one of whom was a very voluble lady with a loud voice. It was impossible not to hear her demanding to be shown the 'ghost room'. The guide was apologetic but told her the same as he had told Mina. 'Are you sure?' bellowed the lady in surprise. 'You have never seen the ghost? But you must have done, surely; my mother told me it is not the first such sighting in the Pavilion, and she is never mistaken about such things.'

Mina looked around.

'Careful my dear,' murmured Richard, 'your ears are waving so much that I will catch a chill in the breeze.'

'Take me for a walk,' said Mina, putting her hand on his arm, and they approached the lady and her group a little closer.

'I assure you, Madam,' the guide was protesting, 'I have been an attendant here for ten years and no such matter has ever been reported.'

'Oh, it was far longer ago than that,' insisted the visitor, 'I believe it was a single lady who saw the Prince. It was the subject of some gossip at the time, but I do not know if she wrote a book about it.'

'There are royal ghosts everywhere in Brighton, just now,' chimed in another lady visitor. 'We held a séance at my house only last night, and Mrs Fitzherbert herself made the table tilt and then she wrote a message on a piece of paper.'

'She peered from behind a curtain in my house,' said another, 'and she looked exactly as she does in the portraits.'

'Oh dear,' sighed Mina. 'Let us go home.'

'You are not about to try and persuade all these people that they are imagining things?' asked Richard.

'No, for I would fail.' As with her earlier conflict with the mediums, Mina knew that she could not save everyone from themselves, and if someone was determined to be duped against every argument there was nothing she could do. 'All I wish to do is prove that the supposed encounter was either a mistake or a fraud. That would calm the concerns of Dr and Miss Hamid and help them with their patients, and knock some of the ground from under Mr Hope's campaign to free Miss Eustace.'

'The ladies said they saw the Prince and his inamorata in the costume of their youth,' said Richard, thoughtfully. 'Was no one performing or rehearsing a play at that time?'

'No, I have studied the newspapers and the only entertainment taking place in the Pavilion which required a special costume of any kind was a series of concerts by the band of the Inniskilling Dragoons.'

'A set of fine fellows no doubt,' said Richard. 'I am sure that many of them could be mistaken for bold young Prinny, and who knows, one or two might even be mistaken for Mrs Fitzherbert.'

Once home Mina began drafting ideas for some new stories, called 'The Golden Dragon', 'A Chinese Mystery' and 'The Crystal Phantom', then, when she was sure she would not be disturbed, she took up the dumbbells and worked until her muscles felt warm and ached pleasantly. She was hoping that as she did so some inspiration would appear and show her a way out of her dilemma, but when at last she rested, she remained unenlightened.

Fourteen

ina was not expecting a second letter from Mr Greville quite so soon, so when one arrived the next morning she opened it with curiosity.

Dear Miss Scarletti

I was not anticipating having to write to you again on the question of the book *An Encounter*, which you mentioned to me recently, but circumstances have changed quite unexpectedly and now it is I who must ask if you know any more of the matter. Mr Worple, the printer who was so very satisfied with the situation only a few days ago, has, in view of the enquiries I made on your behalf, just come to see me in a very anxious state. He has been approached by a Brighton solicitor who demanded to know the real names and address of the authors of *An Encounter*, and refused to believe that he does not have that information or is unable to obtain it. Mr Worple has been given to understand that an action is being contemplated against the Misses Bland for plagiarism. It is beyond him to know what publication it is claimed is being plagiarised and my enquiries have come to nothing. Unfortunately, the solicitor has not chosen to reveal his hand at present.

I should mention that Mr Worple is of the opinion that nothing will come of this action. The book has been extremely successful and, in his experience, when that occurs jealous persons who see some slight similarity between a popular work and one of their own which has not enjoyed the same number of sales make threats of court action hoping to achieve a quick settlement with little trouble and some profit to themselves.

If there is any information you have which might clarify the mystery I would very much appreciate your advising me, assuring you of course of my complete confidentiality.

Mina composed a letter to Mr Greville. She was obliged to tell him that she had no further insights as to the identity of the authors, but had recently learned that Mr Arthur Wallace Hope fervently believed that they were powerful but undeveloped mediums. She also advised him that the Misses Bland's tour of the Pavilion must have taken place on 17 October 1870, giving her reasons behind that opinion. She described her own visit and the fact that an attendant with ten years' service had been adamant that no ghosts had ever been sighted there. Without warning, however, Mina, whose pen seemed to be taking on a life of its own, found herself promising Mr Greville that she would do her best to discover more.

As she sealed the letter Mina reflected on her experience of the Pavilion, and recalled the lady visitor who had been so stridently insistent that the royal ghost had appeared there before. The guide had said he had heard nothing of it in the last ten years, but the lady had countered this argument by declaring that the earlier haunting was longer ago than that, citing her mother as the authority. Mina had thought at the time that this was no more than a piece of town gossip, but now she had to wonder – what if the gossip was based not on mere rumour but an actual publication? If it was, then perhaps this publication was the very same one that had stimulated the legal action?

It was the faintest possible chance that the two events were actually connected but Mina decided to amuse herself by imagining that they were, and considered what she might deduce from that position. First, it meant that the supposedly pirated account had been published more than ten years ago. She doubted that it was written by a noble or royal visitor to the Pavilion during the time it was owned by the Crown. The Queen, she saw in her guidebook, had effectively abandoned the Pavilion in 1845. A book written by a titled individual would have been prominent in the library and widely read – no one would have dared plagiarise it, and the last royal person to write a book about the supernatural was King James I, although his chosen subject was witchcraft. If the author was a member of the public then the work must have been written after 1850, when the building, then in the process of being acquired by Brighton Corporation, was first opened for viewing.

Mina knew that she could not assume that the publication was a book. It might have been a chapter included in a collection of essays, an unbound pamphlet or a contribution to a journal or magazine. It was not an unpublished letter or no action for plagiarism was possible. Nothing had been said about it before now, which suggested that it had not enjoyed a wide distribution, and few if any copies remained. With no title, no date, no author, no place of publication and no guarantee that what she sought even existed, Mina needed more clues. How she wished she had taken more notice of the lady, and would be able to find her again and recognise her, but there had been nothing distinctive about her appearance that she could recall.

Mina wondered if Mr Hope knew about the action for plagiarism, and suspected that he did not. He had had only one meeting with the authors, which must have taken place before the accusation. If neither Mr Worple nor Mr Hope knew the identity of the authors and the plaintiff's solicitor had been unable to trace them, then it was possible that the authors did not know of the action either. The solicitor would have to advertise for the information and employ detectives, and in the meantime Mr Worple, if he had any sense, would print no more copies of *An Encounter*.

That morning's edition of the *Gazette* included a review of Mr Hope's recent lecture, which Mina read with interest, though she did not know how well the newspaper reflected the views of the town. The portion of the lecture describing his adventures in Africa was dealt with very fairly and the writer said many appreciative things about Mr Hope's undoubted courage and spirit of philanthropy. Addresses were provided to enable readers to send donations to the Viscount Hope funds for the relief of Dr Livingstone and assistance for disabled veterans of the Crimea. On the question of spiritualism, however, the writer took a sterner tone. It was to be regretted that the noble explorer had ventured away from matters in which he was undeniably an expert into areas that were still with good reason unpopular in Brighton. Many of those in the audience were shocked to learn that Mr Hope was an advocate of a certain book, which featured unseemly events in the Royal Pavilion, and had even sought to interview its authors. He had also intimated that he planned to give a lecture on spiritualism in the near future, a subject the *Gazette* suggested he would be best advised to leave well alone until a certain trial was concluded.

Mina looked forward to reading what the paper would write when it received news of the action for plagiarism. She had hardly finished reading when Enid came fresh from her morning *toilette* eager for glowing words of her new hero. As she read the *Gazette's* reservations, so her expression of pleasure darkened and finally she threw the paper down saying that the writer didn't know what he was talking about. She made a great performance out of settling to read *African Quest*, which she had been making valiant efforts to enjoy, but it was not to her usual taste and it was hard work for her to conceal the fact that she found it tedious.

✳

Mina decided that the best place for her to seek more information about the previous ghostly sighting was the Royal Pavilion itself. Richard was nowhere to be found, so she decided to venture there alone, posting her letter to Mr Greville on the way. Someone, she hoped, would have more information than the stuffy attendant she had spoken to regarding both the haunting and the publication she sought, and would be more forthcoming. The more she thought about her tour, the more she became convinced that something in the guide's manner suggested that he knew more than he was willing to say.

Fifteen

ina began her enquiries at the Pavilion by spending some time at the bookstall to see if there was anything that recommended itself to her as a possible source of the Misses Bland's story, but all the books and pamphlets had been published in the last ten years, and were either histories of Brighton and the Pavilion or studies of art and design. None of them mentioned a royal spectre. There were, unsurprisingly, no copies of *An Encounter* on display.

'May I assist you?' asked the lady attendant, seeing Mina hesitating over the array of publications. She looked too young to be able to offer advice on old hauntings.

'There are almost too many books to choose from,' said Mina, with a little sigh. 'I will return later to decide which one to purchase.'

'Are you here for a tour?'

'I enjoyed a very interesting tour of the Pavilion quite recently and my guide was very helpful and informative. He told me that he had acted in that capacity for ten years. I suppose he must be the longest serving gentleman here.'

'Very nearly so. But our Mr Merridew has been here rather longer, I believe.'

'Then I would very much like to speak to him. Where can he be found?'

'He should be in the ticket hall if he is not conducting a tour at present. He is very distinguished looking, and you will know him at once by his bald head.'

Mina thanked the lady and returned to the octagonal hall, where she lingered for a while until the gentleman she sought came into view. He was bidding his tour party farewell with extravagantly polite gestures when she approached.

'Mr Merridew?'

He turned to her. She knew how she must look, with her tiny lopsided body, tilted hip, and shoulders at a peculiar angle, but she saw in his eyes neither repulsion nor pity, only welcome. 'That is I,' he announced as if speaking to a great crowd, the voice rich and resonant, 'Marcus Merridew at your service.' He made a dignified obeisance. 'How might I assist you?'

Merridew was, thought Mina, in his fifties, with an elegant carriage and smiling blue eyes. His face was adorned by an iron-grey beard trimmed to a perfect point, and his head was domed, quite hairless, and smooth as an egg. Although he was much taller than she, he did not, as so many tall persons did, try to tower over her in an intimidating fashion, but adjusted his posture so they could converse more comfortably.

'I am very interested in anything I might learn from you concerning the Pavilion, since I have been told that you are the most knowledgeable attendant here.'

'You flatter me, dear lady, but that may well be true, I will not deny it. Some of the gentlemen have only been here a short while, whereas I,' he placed his fingertips to his chest with an expression of quiet pride, 'I was born and bred in Brighton.'

'How long have you been an attendant here?'

'I believe I first trod these royal paths some sixteen years ago. But I have not served here continuously all that time.' He gave her an enquiring look. 'You do not know my name?'

It was clear that he expected her to do so, and Mina feared that her ignorance on that point was in danger of causing him some offence. 'I regret, sir, I do not. But my family has not lived here very long. I have spent much of my time in the service of invalids, and have not therefore been able to move in society.'

He nodded understandingly. 'Ah, of course, that would explain it.'

'Allow me to introduce myself. My name is Mina Scarletti.'

Mr Merridew's eyebrows lifted in surprise. 'Then it seems I have the advantage of you since that name is known to me. Are you by any chance connected with the Scarletti publications company?'

'I am, sir. My father was the manager, Henry Scarletti, who sadly passed away last year.'

'Indeed? May I offer you my deepest condolences for such a sad loss.'

Thank you, sir. I assume you are a great reader?'

'Not – precisely. But the Scarletti company publishes play texts of which I have studied many.'

Mina was not sure how to respond, and he smiled. 'Allow me to enlighten you. I am an actor, a performer on the legitimate stage. Comedies and tragedies are all one to me; Seneca cannot be too heavy nor Plautus too light. I have toured all the major cities of England, from Manchester to Exeter. My Hamlet was the toast of Bolton. But I digress. Please let me know how I might assist you.'

'When I was last here I asked an attendant to direct me to the room where the ghost of the late King George was seen, but he said he knew nothing about such a room, and denied that there had been a sighting. I hoped that you might be able to tell me something.'

He stared at her in astonishment. 'But surely you do not believe in that story? It's all nonsense, you know.'

'I think so too, but I should like to try and prove it.'

'Well now, you *do* interest me. How might you go about it?'

'When I was here last I overheard a lady say that there had been a previous rumour about a royal ghost but it had been many years ago; more than ten. It occurred to me that if such was the case then the book *An Encounter* might simply be a reprinting of an earlier publication, or a retelling of an old story. Do you know anything about this rumour?'

Merridew looked thoughtful. 'Now that you mention it, yes, I do recall something of the sort. When I first became an attendant here someone did tell me of a supposed haunting but it was only in a very general way.'

'So you don't know if the previous haunting was said to have taken place in the same room?'

'I am afraid not.'

'Would you be able to show me the ghost room? I am surprised that the other attendant didn't know of it. I am sure that you do.'

Merridew hesitated, then he offered her his arm and drew her aside so they were not overheard by the other visitors and guides. 'I will let you into a secret. All the attendants here have been asked by their tour parties to be taken to see the ghost room. But we have been expressly instructed by the Pavilion management committee to say that there is no such place. This is not so. The room is, I am sure judging by the description, the King's former breakfast room, the one that has been assigned as a cloakroom for ladies. There is an alcove, but not, nowadays, a long couch as described so very dramatically in the book. After Her Majesty decided not to use the Pavilion as a royal residence, the original furnishings were removed.'

'So the description of the room in *An Encounter* is the interior not as it is today, but as it appeared in the days of the late King George?'

'Precisely, which is why the book is obvious nonsense.'

Mina was reflecting on this information when a man who, from his deportment, appeared to be a senior attendant, approached them. 'Mr Merridew, a tour party is ready for you.'

'Ah, if you will excuse me, I must go about my duties. We will speak later I hope?'

'Oh yes, I will wait here for you. But I wish to study a good book on the history of the Pavilion. What would be your recommendation?'

'*The Royal Pavilion in the Days of King George IV*. You will find it very interesting.'

Mina returned to the shop where she purchased the book in question and then found the ladies' cloakroom, which was a large apartment, graced by slender columns, with a door leading to the usual conveniences. Opposite the windows, which afforded a view of the gardens, there was a long recess, filled by a row of chairs. The most striking feature of the room, however, was the wallpaper, of a pronounced oriental design, in a vibrant shade of red. The authors of *An Encounter* had allowed their imaginations to take hold of them since the dragons and other creatures depicted thereon were noble in aspect and did not appear to be writhing in any pronounced or scandalous fashion. Here, however, with a little embellishment, since there were only a few small paintings and ornaments, and not the costly trappings of King George's day, was undoubtedly the room where the ghosts of the young Prince and his inamorata had supposedly disported themselves.

Mina sat down and studied the book. From time to time, ladies arrived to avail themselves of the facilities, but there were several who made keen studies of the patterned wallpaper, or gazed at the long recess and surreptitiously consulted a publication they kept well hidden from the general gaze.

It soon became clear to Mina that the authors of *An Encounter* had used the very history she had just purchased as the foundation of their description of the interior of the Pavilion in a former age. It even mentioned the warm atmosphere, as the Prince had kept the rooms heated to a degree that many of his visitors found uncomfortable, the large Chinese statues and the formerly blue draperies of the South Drawing Room. Since the book was widely sold, the Misses Bland had not dared to copy actual phrases, but the facts spoke for themselves and Mina, with the eye of an author, could easily spot those fragments of language that had nudged plagiarism without overstepping the mark.

Mina returned to the vestibule and when Mr Merridew had completed his duties he announced himself finished for the day and ready for a pot of tea. They retired to the tearoom, which was filled with thirsty visitors. No places were to be had, but a kind gentleman, seeing Mina approach, picked up his hat and umbrella, rose, bowed, and vacated his table.

'I see you have been making good use of my absence to study that very interesting work,' said Merridew, as the waitress whisked away used chinaware and dusted crumbs from the cloth. Mina ordered tea and scones for two.

'Yes. I believe now that while the ladies who wrote *An Encounter* must have visited the Pavilion, they would have been aware that in the days of the Prince the interior was different to today's, and so used the description in this book to make their tale more convincing.'

He laughed. 'It would have been better for them if they had not. They tried too hard and so exposed their deficiencies.'

Mina sensed a valuable clue. 'What do you mean?'

'Well, to understand that you need to know the history of the young Prince and Mrs Fitzherbert.'

The tea arrived, piping hot, with white, delicately gilded scones like the domes of the Pavilion. Mr Merridew beamed in pleasurable anticipation and helped himself liberally to butter and jam. 'I am all ears,' said Mina.

'When they first met, the Prince was a handsome young gallant, and she an enchantingly beautiful widow. He fell most violently in love with her. Nothing would content him but she must be his; he wept, he stormed, he threatened to stab himself, he *did* stab himself; but all to no avail. His royal father, who was quite sane at the time, would never consent to a marriage since Mrs Fitzherbert was a Catholic. She was also a virtuous lady, and could not be persuaded to become a royal mistress. Finally, the Prince and Mrs Fitzherbert conducted a secret wedding. This satisfied the lady's scruples, but not the law of the land, which stated that the Prince could not marry without the permission of his father. The marriage was strictly no marriage at all.'

There was a brief interlude for the consumption of tea and scones. 'When was this?' asked Mina.

'In the year 1785. Soon after that the Prince took a house in Brighton, which by a number of transformations over time became the extraordinary edifice you see today. Mrs Fitzherbert lived separately but close by, and their connection was an open secret in town. As a gay young Prince holding fashionable assemblies he brought many illustrious and wealthy visitors to Brighton. Trade prospered and he was most popular. For a time the lovers were as merry as could be, but the Prince spent lavishly and without restraint, and his debts increased with each passing day. His had only one means of extricating himself from this predicament. If he married into a royal house, his father would consent to pay his debts.'

Merridew sipped his tea and gave a sad shake of his head before helping himself to another scone. 'Poor Mrs Fitzherbert, imagine her terrible distress when her lover – the man she thought of as her dearest husband – dismissed her; not face-to-face, but with a letter. How cruel! How heartless! How cowardly! The year was then 1794. The Prince married Princess Caroline of Brunswick and his debts were paid, but he was miserably unhappy as his wife was a shameless hussy who did not wash, and he could hardly bear to look at her. They did not live together long. By 1800 the Prince and Mrs Fitzherbert were reconciled. By then neither were the youthful, handsome and relatively slender persons they had once been but they were content. As the years went by, however, the fickle Prince became enamoured of new, younger mistresses and Mrs Fitzherbert, unable to tolerate the many slights she was forced to endure when in his presence, declined to accept any further invitations to his assemblies. It is doubtful that they met again after 1811. She certainly did not visit the Pavilion. He came to the throne as King George IV in 1820. The next time Mrs Fitzherbert entered the Pavilion it was after King George's death and it was so changed that she did not recognise it as the place where she had once been such a frequent guest. Most of the truly elaborate work, the exterior remodelling and the interior decoration, was done after the Prince and Mrs Fitzherbert parted.'

Mina nodded. This was important information. 'The red wallpaper in what is now the ladies' retiring room – was that there in the time of Mrs Fitzherbert's association with the Prince?'

'It was not.'

'I see. So what you are telling me is that the authors of the book tried too hard to make their story convincing by placing youthful ghosts from the last century against a background that is not as the Pavilion is today, but in so doing they made a mistake. They described a room that was not decorated in that style until after the couple had parted, and which therefore they could never have occupied.'

'Exactly!' said Merridew with hearty approval.

'That is a good argument to show up the story as false. Tell me, has anyone tried to hold séances in the Pavilion?'

'No. Several have asked, but all have been refused. The Pavilion management committee will not countenance it, and we are instructed to prevent any such thing occurring. I believe that a number of committee members had their fingers burnt and their pockets emptied during the last eruption of mediums.'

'But I understand that they are happy to allow magicians and other entertainers of a similar kind?'

'Oh yes, but then they are not pretending to be something they are not.'

'Do you remember a Dr Lynn who gave a charity performance here last year? I have heard he is very skilled. Did you see him perform the Japanese butterfly illusion? I should have liked to have seen that.'

'He is very highly regarded and I had hoped to see him, but he gave only the one performance and I was not in town; I had a theatrical engagement that day.'

'And was there not a chess automaton? He was here for at least a week I believe.'

'Oh, who shall ever forget the Wondrous Ajeeb? A Turk in full costume who sat on a kind of pedestal and beat all-comers at chess. It was quite entertaining to see it at work. Mr Mott of the Brighton chess club, who is champion of all Sussex, was so fascinated by it that he came to see it every day.'

'Because it was on the very day that both Dr Lynn and the Wondrous Ajeeb performed here that the authors of *An Encounter* visited, since they mention them both in their book. It was last October. Do you recall any unusual occurrences being reported during that time?'

Merridew thought carefully, not allowing this to hinder his paying diligent attention to the last of the scones. 'No, nothing springs to mind, and I am sure that if any ladies had claimed to have seen a ghost, even as long ago as last October, I would remember it. Several have claimed to have seen ghosts in the last few weeks, but never when they are in the company of another person. I think you understand my meaning.'

Mina was only a little disappointed since she had not anticipated that the visit of the two ladies would have made a mark on anyone's memory at the time, or it would have been the talk of Brighton.

'If you remember anything, you will let me know?' said Mina, handing him her card.

'I will, dear lady, I will!'

'On another subject, do you think the committee would approve the presentation of a play which includes characterisations of the Prince and Mrs Fitzherbert?'

'My goodness, that is adventurous! Is it a new piece?'

'Yes, my brother is writing it, and plans to appear in it with some of his friends.'

'Is it a drama or a comedy?'

'He intends it to be a drama but I fear it might turn out to be a comedy in the performance.'

Merridew laughed heartily. 'Given the subject matter he might be obliged to submit the text to the committee in advance so they can reassure themselves that the play is suitable, even should it receive the approval of the Lord Chamberlain. I would like to meet your brother! I would be able to pass on the benefit of my many years of experience.'

'I will introduce you as long as you make sure not to lend him any money.'

'I promise most faithfully that I will not. Investment in the theatre is an occupation only for the wealthy who have money they can afford to lose.'

'Are you appearing on stage at present? If so I will obtain tickets.'

He drained his teacup. 'Er, no, I am currently between engagements. But you may see me nightly at the Dome where I am employed as an usher. One must do what one can.'

Sixteen

On Mina's return home there was a note waiting for her from Dr Hamid asking her to call and see him as soon as possible. This could only concern his recent interview with Arthur Wallace Hope and such an urgent summons was worrying. The baths were still open and she went there at once, hoping that her anxiety was misplaced. It was clear, however, when she entered Dr Hamid's office that he was a very troubled man.

'I am glad that you were able to come so promptly as I fear that what I have to tell you may involve you directly,' he said, drawing up a comfortable seat for Mina and pouring glasses of his spiced fruit mineral water for them both before slumping heavily back into his chair in most uncharacteristic style. 'Mr Hope came to see me as arranged, and as I am sure you have already observed he is polite and sociable, with a devious manner and a will of iron. He informed me that he has been going about Brighton meeting all the prominent residents who have been clients of Miss Eustace in order to obtain signed statements from them declaring that they believe her to be genuine. I am very glad that you spoke to me on that subject before I met him or I would simply have refused his request and shown him the door. Instead I behaved in a more cautious manner, and as you correctly anticipated, the result was that I learned more of his intentions. I told him that a man in my position needed to give such an undertaking serious thought before it could be performed, and asked him to allow me some time to consider the professional consequences. He seemed easy enough in his mind about that, although he said that it was precisely because of my status as a man of science that he would value my commendation. However —' Mina sipped her drink and waited.

Dr Hamid took a deep breath and continued, 'He then went on to say that he had spoken to you and he was confident that you would agree to sign a similar statement. Given your recent actions your approval is clearly of some importance to him. I did not of course reveal our conversations on the subject.'

Mina was sorry that Mr Hope would stoop to such a deception but found she was unsurprised. 'I neither refused nor agreed, so his confidence is misplaced,' she said. 'However, I can understand that he might have overstated his case in order to persuade you. I wonder how many other people he has visited and what he has told them? We need to be on our guard.'

'I know,' said Hamid, gloomily. 'He could be out and about even now spreading the word that I am a true believer in Miss Eustace. Some people might be swayed into signing papers in the belief that they are joining a general movement. Has he approached you again?'

'No, but it is only a matter of time before he does.'

'Have you spoken to Miss Whinstone?'

'I have, and it might surprise you to know that she has exhorted me in the strongest possible terms not to sign any such paper.'

'She has? You are right, I am surprised.'

'Yes, she has been strengthened in her resolve by her new friend Mr Jellico, who I have found to be a very astute gentleman.' Mina went on to recount Mr Jellico's observations. 'I had imagined that if I was obliged to sign a paper to help Miss Whinstone, then that would be an end of the matter, but he has opened my eyes. It would only be the beginning. And it would be so much worse for you.'

Hamid shook his head, wonderingly. 'An astute man indeed. It amazes me what the legal mind can make of these things. How glad I am that my father put me in for medicine and not the law.'

'I imagine that fraudulent mediumship in general terms is very hard to prove in court without palpable evidence, and the only spiritualistic fraud relevant to this trial is the one practised on Miss Whinstone when only she and Miss Eustace were present. That is why character witnesses are being sought. I can live better with myself if I do not sign a paper for Mr Hope but he strikes me as a man who will not go away if I refuse.'

'No indeed.' Dr Hamid drank deeply of the mineral water. 'In that connection, there is another matter I should tell you about. During the course of my conversation with Mr Hope he evinced a general curiosity about scoliosis. He asked me if I was an expert in the condition and I said I had devoted a great deal of my adult life to its study and treatment. He then went on to ask, since he understood that there were nerves in the spine, whether the condition affected the brain. This is a question I have been asked before, since there are many who believe that the outer presentation of the body is an indication of mental capacity or character. I assured him that those who suffer from scoliosis do not as a result suffer from any mental incapacity. He said he was pleased to hear it, although I have to say I sensed from his manner that he was not. He then asked if such conditions could lead to other complaints such as nervousness or hysteria, or whether persons with scoliosis might be unusually credulous or suggestible. I could see where these questions were tending, so I asked him why he wanted to know and he just brushed it aside and said it was only his curiosity. I told him that as a general principle, my observation of the many patients I have treated suggests that there is no relationship whatsoever between scoliosis and mental affliction or weakness of any kind. As you may imagine, the line of questioning made me feel extremely uncomfortable and it was transparently obvious that he was looking for some way of attacking your view if you did not comply with his wishes.'

Mina was reminded of the doctors who had been consulted when her condition first became apparent, particularly those who had blamed it on the way she habitually stood or walked, or carried things, and refused to accept any denial that upset their favoured theories. Now she had a new battle on her hands. 'I am sure he could easily find doctors who would support his assumptions. One only has to look at the way experts called upon to give evidence at trials can hold completely opposing opinions, when logically one might suppose they ought to agree. I can see that I shall have to be very careful. Your warning is much appreciated. And on the subject of trials, there has been a recent development concerning the book we discussed, *An Encounter.* Since Mr Hope is a champion of this volume and its authors, any doubts about it or the Misses Bland may provide us with a means of opposing him. I trust you will treat this information as confidential?'

'Of course.'

Mina told him of the allegation of plagiarism. He received the news with surprise and not a little pleasure. 'This is far from being determined,' she added cautiously, 'but I wonder what the consequences might be if it was proved?'

'They could be very serious. It is not a criminal offence but it can give rise to substantial damages. Some accused might wish to preserve their reputations by settling the matter out of court by a payment of compensation, but if they decided to refute the charge it would be necessary to take it further. I do recall reading in the newspapers of a case of that sort not so long ago, a work on anthropology I believe. No one has a monopoly on facts but neither does anyone have the right to take another's work and publish it as his own.'

Although all of Mina's work was original, she found the question quite interesting. 'To trouble the law would it have to be the whole of the work that has been copied, or just a portion?'

'Not necessarily the whole, but a material part. If the plaintiff was to succeed, then an order would be made to prevent any future publication of the offending work.'

'But what of the copies previously sold? The culprit would already have profited from them.'

Dr Hamid searched his memory. 'As I recall in that case, the defendant was ordered to pay the plaintiff damages calculated as all the profits made from the sale of the pirated publication as if they had been sales of the plaintiff's original work. He also had to pay all the legal costs. I would not be surprised if the costs in that instance far exceeded any damages, and the plaintiff had mainly to be satisfied with protecting his honour.'

'But that would probably not be so in the case of *An Encounter*. Who knows how many copies have been sold?'

'Sadly, I think a great many. The last time we spoke of this I had hoped that the book would be a foolish fashion, soon gone, but I have been making a few discreet enquiries and also listening more carefully to what my acquaintances and patients have told me and now I fear that may not be the case. The book has been mentioned quite recently in *The Times* editorial column, admittedly in a satirical vein, but that would never stop people from purchasing it, rather the reverse. And I am told that the popular weekly magazines have actually published reviews, while there are engravings of quite a fanciful nature in the illustrated periodicals. It has even been the subject of a cartoon in *Punch*. I don't know what the profits on sales might be but the plaintiff might well think them worth having and the defendant would be loath to hand them over.'

'So as I understand it, this legal action is less a matter of literary pique than money. I am not sure which excites more passion. I suppose that must depend on the individual.'

'Miss Scarletti,' said Dr Hamid, leaning forward on his desk with an intense and serious stare, 'I know that you think of the needs of others before your own, but for once, I beg you to think of yourself. You are being blackmailed into making a declaration that will be used to support a criminal by someone who is prepared to attack you personally if you do not comply. You have warned Miss Whinstone of her danger and now I must warn you. Do not keep this to yourself. You must seek legal advice.'

'I agree I must,' said Mina reluctantly. 'And I know the very man. I shall consult young Mr Phipps.'

An exchange of letters secured for Mina a meeting on the following morning with Mr Ronald Phipps. He was a junior member of a prominent firm of Brighton solicitors, Phipps, Laidlaw and Phipps, although since he was not yet deemed ready for a partnership he was not one of the aforementioned Phippses, who were respectively his uncle and cousin.

He was, as always, meticulously groomed in a manner that must have cost him both considerable time and effort. He doubtless enjoyed a healthy cold bath every morning, wherein he scoured himself to pinkness. He had a chilly stare and formal manner, which could edge from unfriendly tolerance to mildly hostile depending on the matter in hand. Nevertheless, he had proved to be an excellent ally, having been instrumental in providing the information that had led to the arrest of Miss Eustace and her associates for the fraud committed on Miss Whinstone. As a result, he and Mina regarded each other with respect, and he had let it be known that his office door would always be open to her if she ever needed his assistance again.

As Mina described her interviews with Arthur Wallace Hope and the enquiries he had been making about her, Mr Phipps' expression, beginning with a frown of concern, soon developed into alarm, to be followed by frank distaste. He clasped his hands together and gave the question some very solemn thought. 'I am sorry to say this, but you have made an extremely dangerous enemy. I do not think Mr Hope is a wicked man, but he is single-minded and determined. He has influence, wealth and respect. If you challenge him directly you cannot win.

What you have already done – asked for more time to make your decision – was wise, but he will not wait long, especially in view of the impending trial. Mr Hope can and will destroy those in his path, believing it is the right thing to do for his higher purpose. He will sacrifice any man, or woman if need be, in order, as he sees it, to save mankind.'

Young Mr Phipps licked his lips nervously and there was a small flicker of fear in his eyes. Mina knew that it was rumoured that he was not, as was generally said, the nephew of her mother's friend, Mrs Phipps, a lady of advanced years he escorted to many a social gathering. The lady's late husband was so long deceased that no one could recall him, and gossips liked to believe that he had never existed, Mr Ronald being more closely related to the venerable lady than he liked to say. Mina neither knew nor cared if this was the case, but a man like Arthur Wallace Hope had the ability to find out such secrets and no hesitation in making use of them. For a young solicitor aspiring to add a third 'Phipps' to the firm's title, this threat was of some moment. It was unlikely that Hope would discover that Mina was the author of a series of ghost stories under a *nom de plume*, a fact of which he would undoubtedly make much capital, and which would greatly shock her mother, but even if he did, Mina thought she could ride out that particular storm.

'What is your advice?'

'He will undoubtedly approach you again, but this time you should not speak to him without a witness, preferably myself. I will make such enquiries as I can and seek advice from the senior partners. Sign nothing – but then I hardly need to tell you that.' A faint glimmer of a smile played briefly about one side of his mouth and was hastily dismissed. 'If Mr Hope wishes to prove you weak and foolish he will have a hard time of it.'

'Mr Hope may have his own weakness. He has publicly expressed his belief in the Misses Bland and their sensational story, but recently when visiting the Pavilion I overheard a lady say that the ghost had walked before and I could not help wondering if *An Encounter* was simply copied from another lady's experience. Do you know if that is so?'

'I do not,' said Mr Phipps, with narrowed eyes, 'but I should very much like to.'

Seventeen

When Mina returned home, she found the Scarletti household pervaded by a flutter of breathless excitement. The only exception to the general jubilation was Rose, who could see additional work looming before her like a persistent spectre. She did not fear it but viewed it with unspoken bad grace.

The reason for the excitement was a letter Louisa had received from Arthur Wallace Hope. This was no ordinary formal polite missive, expressing how honoured he was to have met the Scarletti family – it did that, of course, in what Louisa declared with a blush to be the most beautiful and gentlemanly language she had ever read, but it ended with a request for her assistance. Mr Hope revealed that he had recently been approached by a respectable and highly regarded entertainer, a conjuror, newly arrived from the continent and anxious to establish his reputation in England. He was hoping to find a substantial drawing room in which to host a magical soiree. Could Mrs Scarletti, asked Mr Hope, with her knowledge of Brighton society, suggest a suitable location?

Louisa could, and while she might simply have provided the information he required in the form of a letter, this was an opportunity not to be missed. Everyone of note in Brighton must know as soon as possible that she had been favoured with the friendship of the famous Arthur Wallace Hope, and there was a general collection of matrons and spinsters whom she could rely upon to carry the news all over town.

It was a vividly glowing Enid who told Mina of this thrilling development, while Louisa busily dashed off notes to her most intimate friends, inviting them to come for tea, saying that they would thereby be regaled with some very interesting news, and replied to Mr Hope promising that she would make enquiries on his behalf.

Mina could not avoid noticing that her mother believed that the gentleman had taken an interest in her. It was in Louisa's mind impossible that he might favour Enid, who was married, and in any case it was she to whom he had chosen to write. Enid, for her part, made her admiration of Mr Hope all too transparent, and Mr Hope, while according her the decorous gallantry appropriate to her married state, had not attempted to conceal that her admiration was returned. Enid clearly thought that the letter to her mother was merely a subterfuge to conceal which lady actually attracted him.

Mina did not know where any of this might lead, but was well aware that it was she who was his object, and her endorsement of Miss Eustace the desired result, his courtship of the good opinion of her mother and sister only a part of his campaign. It was pointless to reveal this to her mother or Enid, although she did suggest mischievously that they might like to invite Mr Hope to the tea party in order for him to make personal enquiries of the ladies. She was greeted by a thunderous look. There was only one widow lady of appropriate age Louisa wished him to take tea with and that was herself.

On the following afternoon a happy and expectant band of ladies assembled in the cosy confines of the Scarletti parlour to be regaled with tea, cake and gossip. Mrs Phipps was one of the number and would have been a useful secret agent to carry intelligence back to her nephew had she not been in the habit of sleeping through most of her visits, waking only when her teacup and plate needed refreshing.

Louisa commanded the room, the wonderful letter in her hand, and talked at a great pace, with the name 'Mr Hope' appearing prominently in every sentence, saying what a charming and attentive gentleman he was, and how her family had been greatly favoured by a visit from him. Now he had been so kind as to make a request and she was sure that someone amongst her dear friends could suggest how his wishes might be accomplished. Mr Hope wished to promote an entertainment for a select gathering of about twenty ladies and gentlemen, and was looking for a suitable drawing room in town. The evening would be offered gratis to all guests, as the object was to confirm his belief that his protégé's displays were to the refined taste of the leading residents of Brighton. If successful then the gentleman intended to take a room at the Pavilion.

Mrs Peasgood, who, in view of her regular musical soirees was the obvious candidate to offer her home, at once demanded to know the name of the gentleman and the nature of the entertainment.

Louisa made a great performance out of consulting Mr Hope's letter, holding it before her face so it was on display to everyone in the room, just in case they had missed it. 'He is called Mystic Stefan. Mr Hope says that he is believed to be the new Monsieur Robert-Houdin, and *he* has performed for the Queen.'

Mrs Peasgood looked unconvinced. 'If this Robert-Houdin is such a wonder, why can *he* not be brought to Brighton?'

'Oh I am sure he is very busily engaged, and Mr Hope would be bound to know this.'

Mina, who had read of the distinguished magician's recent death in the national newspapers, said nothing.

'There was Dr Lynn at the Pavilion, last year,' interposed Mrs Mowbray. 'He gave a performance for charity. So other conjurors can be very respectable, too.'

'How interesting,' said Mina. 'Did you see him?'

'Alas no, but I have heard that he demonstrates the Japanese butterfly illusion, which is said to be a very pretty thing to watch.'

'Mr Hope's friend,' interrupted Louisa, who was starting to see the conversation veer away from her, 'will I am sure be equally as skilled.'

'I am not sure if I wish to see him,' said Miss Whinstone, who was starting to tremble. 'What if this Mystic Stefan proves to be one of those dreadful mediums?'

'Yes, what is it he does?' asked Mrs Bettinson suspiciously. 'I think we ought to be told.'

Louisa looked embarrassed, as well she might since she had obviously not been provided with so much detail and had never, as far as Mina was aware, actually seen a conjuror. 'I suppose he does tricks – he makes things appear – or disappear – but that isn't really important because Mr Hope says he puts on a highly respectable and interesting entertainment.'

'Just as long as he doesn't send us messages from our grand-mothers at five guineas each,' said Mrs Bettinson sourly.

'Or from the ghost of King George,' said Enid, with a titter.

The other ladies tried to pretend they didn't know what she meant by that.

'Do you know, it is a very curious thing,' said Mina in a voice that though gentle, suddenly engaged the attention of the room, 'but I overheard a lady say the other day that the royal ghost which everyone is talking about has appeared in the Pavilion before.'

Louisa frowned. 'Whatever do you mean by that, Mina?' Quickly she held up a warning hand. 'No! Do not tell me, it is almost certainly not a fit topic for you to be concerning your-self with, and I don't want to know about it.'

'Oh, I am not referring to the book which everyone finds so shocking and which no one admits to having read, but nev-ertheless they talk about it all the time; no, this is something different. You know, of course, what I think of people who produce false ghosts by draping themselves in veils, but it does seem from the discussions in the newspapers that there has been a haunting where no such fakery was involved. The ladies had never attended a séance, have no pretensions to be mediums and have not experienced such a thing before. Richard and I visited the Pavilion recently from curiosity but I regret we saw no apparitions, although we looked for them very hard indeed.'

'I would never dare go there in case I was to see one,' said Miss Whinstone, 'even in the company of Mr Jellico.'

For once Louisa did not look jealous of Miss Whinstone for her elderly admirer and was unable to hold back a satisfied smile, the pause giving Mina the chance to pursue her theme.

'While we were there we overheard a lady visitor say that the ghost had appeared before, only it was many years ago, perhaps ten or even twenty. Our family is too recently settled in Brighton to know anything about it, but I wondered if any ladies here have ever heard of such a thing?' Mina glanced at the faces of her mother's guests. Mrs Bettinson, with a mouth full of cake, was unreadable, and Mrs Phipps was asleep. Mrs Peasgood looked pained, Miss Whinstone alarmed, and Mrs Mowbray surly. Whether this was because they knew anything about the subject or simply did not wish to discuss it Mina could not say. All the ladies had once been taken in by the séances of Miss Eustace and might not want to be reminded of this. 'Mr Hope is convinced that the recent sighting was genuine,' she went on.

'Then he must be right,' said Enid, 'for he has travelled so much and has seen so much.'

'I'm not so sure of that,' said Mrs Bettinson. 'How do we even know he went all the way to Africa and back? He could have made it all up.'

'Well he didn't!' exclaimed Enid angrily. 'It was in all the papers, and lots of important people said he was there and did brave things!'

Mrs Bettinson remained unimpressed. 'Wouldn't be much to write about if all he did was go there and walk about and not see anything interesting. I mean, elephants and such like. Not that elephants are all that interesting. If I wanted to see an elephant I could wait for the circus to come again. I don't have to go all the way to Africa.'

'I think we should accept that if Mr Hope says that a thing is so then that alone is sufficient proof that it is,' said Louisa sharply, which made Mina even more relieved that she had not mentioned that gentleman's belief in Miss Eustace. 'As to the strange goings on in the Pavilion, the ladies concerned may have seen something but they most probably had overheated imaginations and did not understand the matter. There, that is all *I* have to say on the subject.'

This effectively put a stop to any discussion about ghosts and over fresh tea and cakes it was agreed that Mrs Peasgood would invite Mystic Stefan to perform his miracles in her drawing room. Mrs Peasgood did not appear entirely happy with the arrangement, but bowed to the majority. She had still not recovered her equilibrium following the extraordinary entertainment of Miss Foxton and her manager Signor Ricardo, and hoped never to see anything like it again.

As the ladies were leaving, Mrs Bettinson hung back, and with a thoughtful look approached Mina for a more private conversation. 'There was something,' she said. 'It was a good while back, but I did hear someone say that there had been a ghost in the Pavilion. I don't know who.'

'Was it ever written about in a book?'

'No, not a book. Not a proper book, just a little pamphlet. I only read part of it, it wasn't all that interesting. Not like —' she stopped and chewed her lip.

'Not like the recent one, I suppose. Well, I can't comment on that. Do you still have it?' added Mina, hopefully.

'I shouldn't think so; I threw out a lot of old rubbish when Mr Bettinson died, and that must have gone with it.'

'Do you remember the name of the pamphlet or the author? Please try.' Mina realised she was sounding a little too eager and tried to restrain the force of her questioning.

Mrs Bettinson squeezed her eyes shut and made the effort, then shook her head. 'No, it was too long ago. It was written by a lady, that's all I can remember.' She gave Mina a searching look. 'Why? What's your interest? After all that bother we had before I can see you're up to something.'

'Perhaps I am.'

'Not that that might be a bad thing, the way the last business turned out. I'd help you if I could, but I don't know much.'

'Can you recall where you obtained the pamphlet? Was it on sale?'

'Not that I remember. I think a friend read it and gave it to me. Don't ask me who, I think it was being passed around.'

A pamphlet, written by a lady; with just those two tiny fragments of clues Mina decided to go to the library.

Eighteen

At the library Mina was soon painfully aware that although she might have more information than previously, it was still hardly adequate to find the item she wanted. She searched the shelves carefully for publications on the subject of Brighton, but even after a diligent examination found nothing to assist her. At last, and realising that she was about to appear very foolish, she approached the desk where a gentleman librarian was seated. He knew her by sight and she him, but she had never needed to ask for assistance before, having preferred to browse the collection for whatever struck her as interesting, since she liked the pleasure of making a discovery.

'I am looking for a pamphlet on the subject of Brighton,' she began, 'but I am sorry to say that I am hampered in my search by not knowing its name, or that of the author. I don't suppose you can suggest where I might look?'

The librarian tried his very best not to look despondent at this request. 'You are sure it was a pamphlet and not a book?'

'Yes.'

'Was this a specific publication? We do have a collection of pamphlets and monographs of Brighton interest, going back many years.'

'It was a specific one, and I believe it was published between ten and twenty years ago. I have been told that the author was a lady.'

The librarian waited in the hope that some more guidance might be forthcoming, but was doomed to be disappointed. 'I'm afraid that we tend to arrange our catalogue of pamphlets by title and not date of publication. In many cases the author does not divulge his or her name.'

'Oh, I see. I suppose there are a great many of them.'

'There are, yes.'

Mina considered this. 'Then I had better start at the letter A.'

Mina took a seat at a table and after a short wait she was brought a box, which, when she opened it, was piled with pamphlets whose titles began with the letters A to C. She hoped for three things; first that the work she sought was held by the library otherwise her search would be in vain; second, that if it was, the ghostly sighting was the main subject and not buried in more general matter; and third that the title started with a letter near the beginning of the alphabet. Several hours and boxes later Mina, still no nearer to her goal, was more thoroughly acquainted with the history, climate, principal buildings and coach roads of Brighton than she could ever have imagined, and she had of course gained a wealth of information on the worthies of the town, the notable visitors, the Royal connection and the Pavilion. Even though Mrs Bettinson thought the pamphlet had been written by a lady Mina did not dismiss without a look any item with a named male author in case that information should prove to be incorrect. She had reached the letter S when she found a ten-page work, the author of which had chosen to remain anonymous, entitled *Some Confidential Observations by a Lady of Quality*. It was dated 1850 and had been privately printed for the author in Brighton.

The author, who described herself as a single lady resident in Brighton, had been interested in the mysterious Pavilion which had been left empty after the Queen had decided not to visit the town again. When it was mooted that the building and its gardens should be purchased by the corporation, tickets had gone on sale so that residents could see it for themselves. She and her father had purchased tickets and made their way there. The interior had impressed them with the dimensions of its magnificent apartments, but all had been emptied of furniture, ornaments and carpets. In some rooms even the wallpaper had been torn down and taken away. The large echoing spaces of the abandoned building gave it the eerie air of a ruined castle.

It was inevitable, thought Mina, that two accounts of a visit to the same place even at twenty years' distance would have some similarities, but as she read on, some uncanny resemblances started to emerge between *Confidential Observations* and *An Encounter*.

As with the Misses Bland, there had been a prior agreement between family members to write separate accounts of the visit. The author in her wanderings had become separated from her father and got lost in the many rooms and corridors. All sounds of the other visitors had faded, but then she, as had the Misses Bland, became aware of the music of a violin and a flute coming from she knew not where, for although she could hear the musicians as if they were very close to her, she could see no one.

Despite making efforts to follow the sound, it remained elusive, the players invisible. Finding herself alone in a magnificent room with a high domed ceiling, she began to wonder what it must have been like in the time of the Kings George and William, when splendid entertainments had been given there. Slowly, she turned in a circle to look all about her, imagining herself in the centre of a glittering company. It was as she completed the turn that she saw the figure of a man standing in the room, a man who had not been there when she had entered. So sudden was the sight that it seemed to her that he had appeared from nowhere while her back had been turned. He was dressed in an elegant costume, which she thought resembled that of a past age, and on seeing her he paused, and bowed in a very respectful and old-fashioned manner, then walked on, passing from the room using the same door through which she had entered. For a moment she stood there mystified by what she had seen, then decided to examine the far doors of the room, the only ones that had not been in her sight when the man arrived, to see if it was possible for them to open silently, but was nonplussed to find them sealed and impossible to open. The only doors that could open were the ones directly opposite, those the man could not have entered by. She decided to follow the figure and speak to him, but on leaving the room she became confused as to her direction and the man was now nowhere to be seen.

The music began again and she followed the sound, eventually arriving at an apartment with red wallpaper much decorated with dragons and serpents, flowers and foliage. There she saw the man again, and this time there was a lady, beautifully dressed in a gown with flowing skirts of golden silk with blue flounces and pink bows, and two musicians, one playing a violin the other a flute. As she observed them, the gentleman took the lady's hand and made a respectful obeisance, then the pair engaged in a courtly dance. She watched them, enraptured with the sight, and when they were done, they bowed to her, and glided from the room. It was a most beautiful scene yet an unexpected one, since she had not been told of any entertainment being provided for visitors. Once again she looked for her father and eventually found him, but neither he nor any of the other visitors had seen anything of the lady and gentleman or the musicians.

She asked the attendant who had been collecting tickets at the door about the surprise diversion, but he said there had been none, neither had he seen any such persons in the Pavilion as she described.

Once they were home, both the author and her father wrote a description of their visit to the Pavilion. Her father had declared himself very impressed and thought the corporation should make every effort to acquire the building for the town as it had wonderful possibilities as a place of entertainment. He had seen no strangely dressed persons and heard no music, although the latter circumstance was not altogether surprising as he was hard of hearing. The author had written of her experience as honestly as possible, even though she knew many would not believe her.

She had tried to describe the appearance of the gentleman as best she could. He was handsome, with curling hair, and she thought he resembled the portraits of King George IV in his youth. The lady had been beautiful with long flowing locks. The author made sketches of the lady and gentleman, along with the musicians and their costumes. Later, while perusing a number of books of fashion, she became convinced that she had seen none other than the late King George IV in his days as the youthful Prince of Wales, and his inamorata, Mrs Fitzherbert. The mystery of the sealed doors was therefore, as far as she was concerned, solved. If they had been in use in the time of the young Prince, then his ghost would simply have passed through them.

As Mina read she felt increasingly sure that the similarities between this work and *An Encounter* were no coincidence. While it was just possible that two similar events might have taken place, some of the expressions and descriptions in the Lady of Quality's account reminded her very strongly of the more recent book. She therefore obtained some sheets of paper and began to make a copy of some of the more memorable portions of the pamphlet, a work that took her some little time. Before she realised it the library was about to close for the day and her body had grown stiff from the prolonged immobility, her back aching as the muscles protested. It was with some difficulty that she rose to her feet and proceeded home.

Comparing her notes with her mother's copy of *An Encounter* Mina saw that the resemblance was, as she had thought, not chance, but blatant and deliberate. The entire incident in the recent work had been copied from the earlier one, in some places with identical words, the main difference being the addition of some sensational material.

Mina accordingly wrote at once to Mr Greville imparting to him the nature of her discovery and supplying some extracts from *Confidential Observations* in support of her argument. She also advised Mr Phipps. Surely, she thought, her work was done.

Nineteen

There was a new burst of excitement in the Scarletti household since Mr Hope was due to call again, and this time he had accepted Louisa's invitation to take dinner with the family. Despite his modest entreaties that they should not go to any great trouble over him, Louisa and Enid were determined to do their utmost to see that their honoured guest was royally entertained, but were uncertain of what such a remarkable man might want to eat. The dilemma was the subject of intense debate.

'Perhaps we should try and make him feel at home,' suggested Enid, 'and give him African food?'

'I doubt that the butcher will be able to supply elephant's foot and even if he could our oven would be quite inadequate to roast it,' said Mina. 'But I believe that when in Africa Mr Hope was obliged to eat what was there, whether or not it was to his taste, and probably pined for the food of his native land. I am sure Mr Inskip would delight in an English beef dinner at this very moment.'

Enid gave her a sour look but said nothing.

Richard, on being given the news, pronounced himself delighted and said he was looking forward to it with keen anticipation. His private comment to Mina was, 'It will be an education to meet the blackguard who threatened my sister.'

In the absence of elephant's foot the gathering around the dinner table was provided with beefsteaks, which was thought to be the most appropriate and manly foodstuff for a bold adventurer, and a bottle of good red wine. Louisa and Enid detested beefsteaks, but pretended to like them and Rose, knowing this, brought the dishes in with the triumphant air of one who hoped there would be good pickings later, if it was not all to be turned into pies and rissoles. Richard and Mr Hope demolished their steaks with hearty appetites, and made free with the wine, which the ladies declined. Mina ate sparingly but that was expected of her.

Mr Hope was all beaming geniality. 'I am most grateful to you Mrs Scarletti for proposing the home of Mrs Peasgood as suitable for Mystic Stefan's demonstration. I have paid her a visit and was delighted with the drawing room, and the lady herself received me with great cordiality and was very obliging.' Louisa smiled thinly, but since Mrs Peasgood was approaching sixty, had long given up any pretensions to beauty, and had never shown any inclination to replace the late and much lamented Mr Peasgood, this was not a serious difficulty. 'I believe she is sending invitations to all the members of her music circle, who will be sure to be as refined an assembly as any in Brighton.'

Mina said nothing, but a thought had occurred to her, one that she determined to pursue.

Louisa, between dainty nibbles from the tip of her fork, was all attention to the visitor. 'Mr Hope, I do beg you to tell us all about Mr Stefan, who has not, I think, been to Brighton before? All my friends are clamouring to know more of him, and I found I could tell them almost nothing.'

Hope speared an extra potato with the dexterity of a hunter. 'He is a native of Hungary, I believe, and this is his first visit to these shores. But he has earned some fame abroad, and thought to come and entertain us here. He speaks very little English, however, and that little he does with an accent so thick that he finds it hard to make himself understood. He cannot therefore perform as other magical gentlemen do, but works in silence.'

'If his illusions please the eye then he hardly needs to speak. They should speak for themselves,' Mina observed.

'I agree,' said Mr Hope wholeheartedly, and Louisa and Enid who had been about to protest, closed their mouths. 'So many of these conjurors rely on taking the audience into their confidence, telling them what they might expect to see and then surprising them. Mystic Stefan needs none of this, and is in my opinion altogether superior.'

'How did you come to meet him?' asked Mina.

'He brought me a letter of introduction from the celebrated Dr Lynn, who has exhibited here before but is currently touring abroad. Did you chance to see Dr Lynn when he was here last year?'

'I am very sorry to say we did not,' said Louisa, with a brave attempt at sincerity.

'Oh he demonstrates with great skill, and has many highly amusing and astounding novelties. His forte is the Japanese butterfly illusion, which few men have truly mastered, but in which Mystic Stefan is also adept.'

Enid had abandoned all attempts at eating her dinner but maintained the pretence by sawing her steak into fine shreds and giving the contents of her plate the occasional stir with her fork. 'I do look forward to seeing that, it sounds so pretty. Can you say what else he will do?'

Hope fastened her with a look implying mystery and deep knowledge. His eyes, which were dark brown, took on the glow of amber and Enid flushed under their warmth. 'As to that it is best that it should come as a pleasant surprise, but there is one thing I do need to advise you of before you see him. Mystic Stefan has a means of answering all questions that anyone in the audience might ask. His replies are just a "yes" or a "no", but I am told that he is wonderfully accurate. So you must have your questions prepared beforehand. You may speak them aloud if you wish, but most persons prefer to write them on slips of paper.'

A faint frown of disquiet troubled Louisa's brow. 'I hope he has not become entangled with spirit mediums? After recent events in Brighton we have learned to distrust such people.'

Hope met the question with a disarming smile, but there was something cold and forced in his expression. 'Mystic Stefan makes no claims one way or another. He seeks only to entertain. We all may have our opinions as to how he performs his miracles, but only he knows the truth.'

'Well, I know what I shall ask him,' said Enid, lowering her eyelashes.

'I think we can all guess your question,' said Richard. 'What we would like to know is what answer you are hoping for.'

'Perhaps since he is so adept, and knows so much, he can conjure up the real names of the ladies who wrote that curious book,' said Mina mischievously. 'It would be interesting to discover how they came to write it.'

'Mina!' her mother snapped with a frown.

Richard finished his second glass of wine and poured another. 'My dear sister is far too modest to admit it, but she is herself an author.'

'Mina writes stories for children,' Enid explained quickly. 'Not at all the same thing as proper books.'

'I should hope not!' said Louisa.

'I have never yet written, but I think I may have a talent for it,' Richard went on, 'so I have determined to write a play, something noble and high-minded, with a monumental subject. It will be like Shakespeare – or – those other fellows who are like Shakespeare.'

'That is an admirable ambition,' said Hope, 'and when it is completed I would like to read it.'

Mina smiled, and he caught the look and returned it in a strange moment of mutual understanding. Both had guessed that the chances of Mr Hope being obliged to meet that promise were slim.

Rose was summoned to clear the plates, and at Louisa's direction moved the wine bottle out of Richard's reach. Mr Hope complimented Louisa on the beefsteaks, saying that a good English dinner was the best in the world, and an excellent butcher a treasure beyond price. Dessert was brought, a moulded blancmange decorated with fruit.

'I would be very interested to learn more of your meeting with the Misses Bland,' said Mina, timing her question at the point when her mother was too preoccupied with dessert to interrupt. 'Was it very recent?'

'Yes, about two or three weeks ago. I was very impressed with how modest they are, and their simple and wholly natural sincerity.'

'If I understand correctly from your lecture, the ladies claim to have seen the ghost of the late King not as he appeared at the time of his passing, but when he was the young Prince of Wales, together with members of his court.'

'Extraordinary, I know, but that is the case,' said Hope. Louisa gave him a worried look, but he did not offer further detail.

'I have recently paid a visit to the Royal Pavilion, and made a study of its history, and I would deduce that the room in which this encounter took place was once the King's breakfast room but is nowadays a select retiring room for lady visitors. The wallpaper is a beautiful shade of red and with a very distinctive pattern. It is part of King George's oriental re-design, the work of Mr Nash, and most probably dates from about 1820.'

'How very interesting,' said Hope politely, but he gave Mina a searching look. Enid and Louisa clearly thought the subject not at all interesting, but since their guest did they said nothing to deter Mina from further observations. Richard smiled the smile he always gave when he knew Mina was up to something.

'But here is the thing that mystified me,' Mina went on, and from the corner of her eye she saw Richard's smile broaden, 'I would have expected that if the ladies had seen ghosts then the figures would have appeared before them in the room as it is now. I hardly ever read ghost stories myself, but when I have that always seems to be the way of things. But in this case it was not, since the furnishings were not the same. Also, in these ghost stories, the figures always appear as they were in their last moments of life, which these did not. Supposing, however, that the figures were not ghosts at all, and the ladies had, as I believe you yourself suggested, looked or even stepped back by some means or other into the days of the King's youth, then they would have seen him and his court in the room as it was then, perhaps in 1790 or thereabouts, before he parted from the lady he loved, but many years before the red wallpaper was placed there. Instead, the figures, which looked as they did in the last century, were in a room furnished as it was some thirty or more years later, a room they could never have occupied. I am afraid that it struck me then that the Misses Bland have done no more than compose a story for their own amusement, basing it on some histories imperfectly studied, and have found against all expectation that their readers believed that they were describing a real incident. If I write a story about a child meeting a pretty fairy, it is no more than a story, and I know it. A young child might believe it to be real, but I do not think an adult would. Adults do not, as a rule, believe in fairies.'

There was a very distinct silence around the dinner table. Louisa was annoyed but clearly did not know how to respond, and Enid was simply bewildered. Mina dared not glance at Richard or she could never have maintained a serious expression.

Mr Hope, however, was obviously well used to having his beliefs questioned, something that amused rather than offended him. He gave Mina's comments only a moment's thought before he smiled indulgently. 'The ways of such events are still a mystery to us, but your concerns do not, as you think, show that the ladies invented the story. On the contrary, it proves to me the very high order of their mediumship, something of which they themselves are quite unaware. Please be assured, Mrs Scarletti,' he went on, turning the heat of his gaze towards Louisa, whose concerns evaporated almost instantly, 'the Misses Bland have no desire to conduct the kind of séances of which you disapprove. They do not seek the admiration of the public.'

He addressed the gathering about the table once more, as sure as a man could be that he had captured his audience. 'Miss Scarletti suggests that what she sees as inconsistencies in the book resulted from imperfect study, but this is not so. The authors informed me that they had never before their remarkable vision visited Brighton or made any study of its history or seen any portraits of the Pavilion's apartments. They knew little about the Pavilion other than that it was very famous and had once been a royal residence. I believe that as they moved about the building they were, without realising it, carried by the influence of spirits to different times in its past. Perhaps a kind of blending of the rooms and the figures took place, created by their own unconscious powers. It is an extraordinary and rare phenomenon, one that is not at all understood, and I hope very much to be able to meet the ladies again and persuade them to submit themselves to scientific study. Just imagine,' he went on with forceful intensity, putting down his spoon to gesture with both hands, 'if we could, as they did, travel into the past. What mysteries we could solve, what wrongs we could make right!'

'Oh, indeed!' breathed Enid, her eyes shining.

Mina could see that whatever objections she made, Mr Hope would somehow turn them about to become proofs of his way of thinking. 'Do you believe that the ladies' experience has revealed a previously unknown branch of science?' she asked, without a change in her expression. Beside her, Richard almost choked on his dessert. It was, as they both recalled, a claim made by those who had once championed Miss Eustace, whose science had consisted of little more than anointing filmy draperies with phosphorised oil.

'I do,' said Hope emphatically, 'and I am so happy that you have hit upon this concept, one that so many of the doubters simply do not understand. They refute anything that does not conform to the way they see the world, and cannot conceive that it can differ in any way from their narrow-minded perception. I compliment you, Miss Scarletti; you are a visionary, you open your mind and in so doing you see into the future.'

Mina wished very much that she could see into the future, but she was less concerned with the world of science or the spirit than the happiness of her family. She pitied Enid, unable to find solace in her children and dreading the return of her husband, and she daily expected to hear that Richard's gadfly adventures had ended with him in a morass of debt, or even under arrest. She was powerless to influence Enid and able only to restrain Richard's wilder exploits. Mr Hope, however, too narrow minded to understand his own position, was a different matter. Once he had taken his leave Mina put her new idea into action and sent a note to her brother's former mistress, the beautiful Nellie, asking if she might pay her a visit.

Twenty

next morning Mina received yet another letter from
Mr Greville.

Dear Miss Scarletti,
Please find enclosed a cheque for the sales of your most
recent publication, *The Tower of Ghost Musicians*.

Mina winced at the title, which she thought clumsily worded
and which she had not approved. She had wanted to call the
story *The Tower of Music* but Mr Greville had pointed out that
one could scarcely have a story about ghosts without the word
'ghost' or 'spectre' in the title, any more than one would publish
a story with a title that promised ghosts but did not provide any.
The letter continued:

Mr Worple wishes me to pass on to you his grateful thanks
for the information you have supplied. As you know, he was
initially of the opinion that the action for plagiarism against
the authors of *An Encounter* was motivated solely by greed
and would quickly prove to have no foundation. Your revelations have convinced him, however, that there is a case to
answer and he has therefore undertaken to co-operate fully
with the plaintiff's solicitors. He has just revealed to me the
outcome, which you might find interesting.

The Misses Bland had recently ordered another printing
of the book, with the usual arrangement that their servant

would arrive to collect the copies. Under the circumstances Mr Worple decided not to carry out the commission; instead he advised the plaintiff's solicitors when the servant might be expected to call, and they came to his office and lay in wait with the appropriate documents. I was not present at that confrontation but Mr Worple was, and I am sure you can imagine the ensuing consternation. The servant was required to reveal the real names and address of her employers and accompany the solicitor to their home to serve the papers. It transpired that the ladies are, as they claim to be, sisters, but they are not called Bland, and the father is not a clergyman, although he is a respectable tradesman who pursues the businesses of undertaker and cabinet maker. He knew nothing of his daughters' adventure in the world of publishing and when he learned of it, it came as a great shock to him. When confronted with the situation, the ladies were sufficiently discomfited that they were unable to say anything on the subject, however, one fact of interest did emerge. Your enquiries showed that the visit to the Pavilion could only have taken place on 17 October last year. Not only have the ladies and their father never been to Brighton, all three were on that date at a family gathering in London, and there are therefore over twenty witnesses to the fact that they could not possibly have been in Brighton on the day in question.

I am not sure what to make of this and neither is Mr Worple, but the ladies have been summoned to Brighton for a formal meeting with the plaintiff's solicitor, should their health permit it, and more information may emerge then.

The only other thing I can tell you is that Mr Worple is quite satisfied that the two ladies are the same two who supplied the original manuscript and who also came to his office for a meeting with Mr Arthur Wallace Hope.

You might be interested in his account of them, and I cannot help wondering as I write these words if they will one day be personated in one of your stories. One sister, who we understand to be the elder of the two, is more retiring than the other owing to some defect about her face, which means that she is always very heavily veiled in public. When Mr Worple and the solicitor came to interview her, she at once threw a shawl over her head and was very distressed at the intrusion. The younger, who appears to be aged about thirty, is altogether the bolder and sharper of the two. She reviled the visitors for upsetting her sister and would speak of nothing else but their impertinence. Mr Worple thought this was no more than a cunning means of avoiding questioning.

Their father has declared most emphatically that the manuscript, which he has been shown, is not in the handwriting of either of his daughters and is prepared to employ an expert to testify to that effect. The case may prove to be more than usually complicated.

Mina could only agree. There were, she thought, several disparate elements in the publication of *An Encounter*; there was the matter copied from the original pamphlet, the facts about the Pavilion drawn from the book she had studied, the details of the events taking place in the Pavilion on 17 October 1870, and finally the indecent gloss on the story. She concluded that the ladies must somehow have obtained a copy of *Some Confidential Observations by a Lady of Quality*, perhaps one that had been passed on by a friend or relation. If they were telling the truth when they claimed never to have visited the Pavilion, they must have been told about its delights and presented with *The Royal Pavilion in the Days of King George IV*, perhaps by a different person to the one who had given them the pamphlet, someone who had visited on the day in question and might not have been aware that the entertainments were unique to that day. Handwriting could be disguised, or they might simply have adopted a clearer copy than their usual for the purposes of the printer.

Why, if the sisters were so modest and retiring, they had introduced matter of an indelicate nature into a story that had not been so in the original she could not say. Perhaps it had been introduced by a third party after the manuscript left the ladies' hands, the only possible object being to make money.

Mina paid another visit to the reading room and was able to study the newspaper record of the day in January 1850 when the public had been able to view the interior of the Pavilion for the first time. There was no note of who had been there on that occasion although it was mentioned that some of the visitors, confused by the unusual layout of the great building, had got lost. Mina thought of what it must have been like to be the very first explorers of that lost and faded grandeur, like finding a sunken wreck on the bed of the sea, and picturing what it had once been in the days of its glory. If she had been there she was sure she would have written about it, too, but it would have been a work of the imagination, and who knows but she might have invented a story of stumbling by chance into the royal court of yesteryear. Could it be, she thought, that *Confidential Observations* had always been and was always intended to be taken as a work of fiction?

The company who had printed *Confidential Observations* might conceivably have assisted her enquiries, but on examining some Brighton directories she found that it was long defunct, the sole manager having passed away several years ago.

By now the news that the authors of *An Encounter* had been accused of plagiarism should by rights have set all of Brighton, if not Great Britain, abuzz with gossip, but somehow it had not. Over the next few days Mina carefully studied both local and national newspapers and listened carefully to conversations, but it was not discussed or even faintly alluded to. She visited

Mr W.J. Smith's bookshop and found that he was no longer selling copies to eager enquirers, but his excuse was that he was waiting for more to be printed. She began to wonder if powerful interests were suppressing the news. She herself was most reluctant to drop the bombshell into conversation as she would then be roundly attacked with demands to know how she had come by the information, and she had no wish to reveal her private correspondence with Mr Greville. If the case did come to court then the truth would be revealed and Mina determined that she would be present when it was, but it could well be many months before any action was heard, if indeed it ever came to court at all. If Mr Hope took an interest in it, which seemed very probable, or the ladies' father had sufficient resources, the whole affair might be quietly settled before the dispute was made public with no one left any the wiser, and all those in the know well-paid to maintain silence.

Mina decided that it was a dreadful shame that so important a case should be in progress without the local press and interested members of the public knowing anything about it. It was one of her wickedest pleasures to place a metaphorical cat into a no less metaphorical flock of pigeons, and so she composed a letter to the editor of the *Gazette* suggesting that he might care to look into the matter.

Twenty-One

The inaugural performance of Mystic Stefan had been set for the following Monday, and Mrs Peasgood's neat little cards distributed to a favoured few. All the Scarletti family was invited, but there was one person above all who Mina most wanted to be present at that event, one with the eye of a professional conjuror, who could see how the illusions were being achieved and comment on the competence or otherwise of Mr Hope's protégé.

The former Nellie Gilden had, before her recent marriage, enjoyed an unusual career. Now aged about twenty-five and admitting to seventeen, she had for some years assisted a Monsieur Baptiste, a highly successful stage magician, and was therefore fully conversant with the secrets of that trade, secrets she would never explicitly divulge. She had also been daubed from head to foot in paint to become the Ethiopian Wonder who could supposedly read minds, danced to near naked madness as Ophelia in a burlesque of *Hamlet*, and appeared on the Brighton stage with Richard as the spirit medium Miss Foxton. Demurely clad Miss Foxton had gone into a trance and by dint of some clever manipulation of her clothing, had transformed via a floating trail of ethereal light into a winged sprite that rose up out of an oriental vase clad in a glowing costume as clinging as a cobweb, a garment that left nothing to the heated imagination of any gentleman in the audience. This brazen attempt to become rich on the fashion for conjuring spirits had failed largely because the expense of Nellie's new gowns had outstripped their income by a substantial margin.

It had been an easy task for a woman of Nellie's unusual and varied talents, arrayed in her best gown and resplendent in paste jewellery, to persuade Miss Eustace that she was the wealthy Lady Finsbury and so lure her into the situation that had exposed the medium as a trickster and a thief.

Richard's association with Nellie had given Mina some disquiet, not because she disapproved of Nellie, who was as charming and clever as she was voluptuously lovely, but because of the explosion that would devastate the Scarletti household should Richard decide to marry her and Louisa discover her origins. In the event, Richard had recognised that Nellie was an expense he could not afford, and they had agreed to be merely good friends. Soon afterwards she had made a marriage that provided her with a respectable position in Brighton society.

Nellie's husband Mr Jordan and his business partner Mr Conroy were purveyors of high-class clothing of every description, Mr Jordan attending to the gentlemen, Mr Conroy to drapery and accessories, and Mrs Conroy to the ladies. Nellie had assured her husband that she was the best possible means of showing off new fashions all about Brighton, thus sending the ladies into a frenzy of jealousy and creating an immediate demand. Since Mrs Conroy resembled a short barrel with tight staves, Mr Jordan took the point. Having the pleasure of escorting his wife to public and private events where he was the envy of every man in the room, he was content to grant her every whim. Earlier that year, during the craze for spirit mediums and the pre-eminence of Miss Eustace in particular, Mr Jordan had made himself most unpopular in Brighton, as an uncompromising sceptic. Since then he had been rather better tolerated, the sudden downfall of Miss Eustace, the company of his delightful wife and her strict admonition that he must never utter the words 'I told you so,' being important aspects of his ascent in the town's estimation. They often attended musical recitals hosted by Mrs Peasgood and, as members of that refined circle, would therefore have been invited to view the continental wonders of Mystic Stefan.

Nellie was not one of those wives who liked to stay at home and manage the household. She and her husband occupied what had once been his bachelor apartments above the shop, but this, she had informed him, was a temporary arrangement. The rooms were quite insufficient to hold fashionable gatherings, there was no suitable boudoir for her personal use, nowhere to decently house a ladies' maid, and far too little space for the wardrobe she wished to acquire. Mr Jordan had been charged with finding a house that would please his wife, and making the profits to pay for it.

Thus Nellie, when not delighting society, was often to be seen riding about the town in her smart little carriage, or taking tea in all the best locations. The weather continued fine and clear, and the little equipage arrived at Montpelier Road where the driver assisted Mina into a seat beside Nellie, who wrapped her in a soft blanket in case the October air was too chill for her fragile bones. Now that Nellie was a travelling advertisement for Parisian fashion, or at least that part of it that came to Brighton, there was something more subtle in her dress. The colours were refined, the taste impeccable, the art used to display her womanly form to its best advantage spoke more of husbandly pride than the theatre, and the jewels were real. Nellie, Mina realised, was the only beautiful woman she knew who had never recoiled from her deformity, but then during her time on the stage she might well have seen worse and stranger sights.

'There is a new teashop open which entices with its lovely aromas and delicate cakes,' said Nellie. 'I have secured a table. We slender ladies must indulge ourselves on mouthfuls of delicious air or lose our waistlines.' They set off at a brisk rate. 'Your brother called on me the other day; has he told you of his grand theatrical scheme?'

'He has, though I am not convinced it will come to anything.'

'I am already appointed to be Mrs Fitzherbert to his Prince of Wales, and he has received a promise from Rolly that once his current engagement is over he will give us his Napoleon. I am pleased to take part as a favour to a friend but Rolly has a less certain existence and if there are to be many performances he will require a fee or a share of the ticket sales. I hope Richard knows this.'

'I doubt that he has given it a thought.'

Nellie's laugh told Mina that she had already reached that conclusion. 'Well, I am sure some arrangement can be made.'

'I hope that you are happy with Mr Jordan,' Mina asked cautiously.

'I am as happy as it is possible to be with Mr Jordan,' smiled Nellie. 'It is a love match. I love his money and he loves *everything* about me.'

'Have you been invited to view the demonstration of Mystic Stefan at Mrs Peasgood's?'

'We have. Is he highly recommended? I have never see him.'

'Nor I, but I would be so grateful if you could attend and let me know what you think of his performance. He is being promoted by Mr Arthur Wallace Hope. I suppose you know that that gentleman has been a caller at our house.'

'All Brighton down to the very last puppy dog cannot fail to know it.'

'It seems that Mystic Stefan is a friend of Dr Lynn who was at the Pavilion last year, and who has recently introduced him to Mr Hope.'

'The name is not familiar, but some theatrical artists change their names if necessary – usually to avoid creditors. Mr Hope, however, has made quite a name for himself amongst conjurors.'

'Oh?'

'Something between a nuisance and a laughing stock. Did you know that he and Dr Lynn are good friends? They dine together when in London, and disagree on almost everything, but that does not seem to affect their regard for each other. Dr Lynn insists that he is a conjuror pure and simple, working with specially prepared apparatus and practised sleight of hand. When Mr Hope refused to believe this Dr Lynn took the unusual step of demonstrating to Mr Hope how some of his illusions are created. He even revealed the secret of the Japanese butterfly trick, but still Mr Hope would not be persuaded. He believes that Dr Lynn is a medium who, without realising it, performs his miracles with the aid of spirits. Mr Hope has been known to openly decry those conjurors who he believes deliberately and knowingly pervert their great spiritual gifts to make money on the popular stage. He has said as much about Monsieur Baptiste, who offered to place Mr Hope in a cabinet and run him through with swords, but he has not taken up the invitation.'

'Perhaps he believes that Mystic Stefan is also a medium.'

'If he is promoting him I have no doubt of it.'

Mina was digesting this observation as their carriage reached the teashop, which had been decorated in a style appropriate to the origins of its tea. She walked in assisted by Nellie, and not for one moment did she feel that her companion was using her as a foil to her own beauty or was displaying her as one might a pet marmoset. Once settled at a table with a cloth that winked white in the sunlight, tea was brought and served in thin cups decorated with peonies, accompanied by tiny meringues dipped in chocolate, and almond-crusted macarons arrayed on a silvery pagoda.

'I can see why Mr Hope is so generous to Mystic Stefan if he believes he is a medium, but I also feel that another purpose is being served with the conjuror as his instrument,' said Mina. She told Nellie of Mr Hope's intention to see Miss Eustace free, his request for a signed paper, and the dangers to herself if she refused. 'Mystic Stefan is a part of Mr Hope's campaign to persuade me to his way of thinking. I had not imagined I was an object worthy of his attention, but it seems that when gossips talk of the exposure of Miss Eustace it is my name that is mentioned. If I was to change my mind about her it would work strongly in her favour. Nothing escapes his attention. He makes eyes at Enid and my mother and has expressed an interest in Richard's play. I should mention that he has heard of Miss Foxton, but so far has not connected her or Lady Finsbury with you.'

Nellie was sufficiently adept at disguise that no one in Brighton had identified her as either the dowdy Miss Foxton or her lustrous sprite, but many of those who had seen the one public appearance of the elegant Lady Finsbury had also met Mrs Jordan, and commented on the resemblance.

'Mr Hope tells me he believes Lady Finsbury does not exist,' Mina continued. 'Part of his action in support of Miss Eustace is a claim that the event hosted by Lady Finsbury which showed Miss Eustace to be a fraud was in itself a fraud. Thus far he has not attempted to discover the lady's true identity, but I am concerned that someone might mention to him that you resemble her.'

Nellie seemed untroubled by this prospect. 'Ah yes, the tangled web of deception. It is true, I am told that I do slightly resemble Lady Finsbury, although I am always at pains to state that we are not related. She and Lord Finsbury are now abroad and will remain there permanently, so comparison will not be possible. Of course when I was Lady Finsbury I did not anticipate becoming Mrs Jordan or even settling in Brighton. Neither did I anticipate the enquiries of a man such as Mr Hope. Mostly, if one looks the part and acts the part, then it is accepted that one is the part. People believe whatever suits them and even pass it on to their friends without troubling themselves to establish if it is true or a lie. I am not sure why that is, but it is a valuable thing to know.'

'What should we do? So far he has not asked me who Lady Finsbury is, but he is sure that it is I who hired her impersonator. He can easily prove that there is no such title, if he has not already done so, so it is useless to have her return to Brighton. It is only because he still hopes that he can persuade or force me into declaring that Miss Eustace is genuine that he does not attack me outright. I am still being assiduously wooed in that respect but I know he is gathering resources to fight me if needs be. If you were obliged to admit the imposture would that not threaten your marriage? How much does your husband know of your past?'

'He knows of my part in Miss Eustace's arrest, and applauds it. I have also confessed my association with Monsieur Baptiste and he has forgiven me everything, but we do not speak of my past and he would not have it broadcast in town. We must bide our time and hope that the truth of Lady Finsbury will not be explored. If it is – well, I know Mr Hope and his kind, they think themselves very clever but the cleverer the man the more easily he is duped.'

'He must guess that I and my family would not willingly go to a séance and so has invited us to one by a subterfuge. Who knows what Mystic Stefan might do? Bring messages from my father, perhaps. But you will come to the performance?'

'I would be quite desolated to miss it, although my husband is currently in Paris, buying silk. I doubt that Mystic Stefan will demonstrate anything new, but even if I could say how his tricks are done, it would be useless to inform Mr Hope. Anyone who does so would simply be added to his growing list of potential converts to spiritualism.'

Mina sighed. 'I feel sorry for Mr Hope. He has had terrible losses in his life, seen so much of senseless slaughter and cruel disease; so many young men sacrificed in vain. I have no wish to take away a belief which obviously brings him comfort, but I will not have that extortionist freed from prison unpunished so she can ruin other lives.'

'Dear Mina,' said Nellie, affectionately. 'Your concern does you credit, as does your generosity to a man who clearly means you no good. Do, I implore you, take care.'

'That is what Dr Hamid says.'

'He is a wise man. Too wise ever to have tempted me, but I admire him as one might admire a finely bound dictionary.'

'I am very fortunate in my friends,' said Mina. 'I could achieve nothing alone.' She was suddenly reminded of a phrenology head showing which parts of the brain were the seats of the various faculties. If the four friends were part of one brain then Dr Hamid would be wisdom, Richard adventurousness, Nellie imitativeness, and Mina imagination. She hoped that together it would be enough.

Twenty-Two

ellie's carriage brought Mina home to her front door. As she turned the key she was greeted by an unexpected sound of laughter, not the little trills that rang out in response to the irresistibly amusing activities of the twins, but fits of helpless merriment. Mina pushed open the parlour door and saw her mother trying unsuccessfully to stifle her peals of mirth with a lace-edged handkerchief, while Enid, also laughing, was being led around the room by Mr Arthur Wallace Hope, his hand tenderly cupping her elbow.

'I do believe you almost have it, Mrs Inskip,' said Hope.

'Yes, yes, you are very near, Enid,' gasped Louisa, dabbing her eyes. 'Oh dear me, I never saw such a thing!'

'There!' said Enid, impulsively, and pointed to a small vase on the mantle shelf. A narrow-waisted confection, like Enid herself, it was as pink as a sweetmeat and decorated with roses. Mina knew that it usually stood as part of a cluster of similar vases, but that morning it had been moved to shelter modestly beside the much larger figure of a porcelain dog.

'Oh, that is well done!' exclaimed Hope, 'a very quick success! You have a singular talent, I congratulate you.'

Enid snatched up the vase, but then seemed uncertain what to do with it and looked about her.

'Allow me,' said Mr Hope and, taking it from her hand, he replaced it on the mantle shelf, very near to where it had been before.

'Whatever is this?' asked Mina.

They had been so wrapped up in the activity that none had seen or heard her enter and all now turned to look at her.

'Why Miss Scarletti, I am delighted you have returned in time for our little diversion,' said Hope. 'We are conducting an exercise in the power of the mind. "The willing game" it is called. And it will be all the more amusing and interesting if there are more players. Please do join us.'

Mina entered the room with some trepidation. Had Mr Hope called expecting to find her home? If he had been disappointed, then he had certainly made good use of his time. Was the willing game an innocent amusement, or did it have another more sinister purpose? Another idea for a story crossed her mind but would have to wait to be committed to paper. 'How is it played?'

'We begin by appointing a game leader.'

'That is Mr Hope!' declared Enid.

'But only for today, as it is the first time of playing,' said Hope, modestly. 'In future games anyone might be appointed. The company generally takes it in turns. Then one of the number is chosen and leaves the room for a few minutes. While that person is absent the other players agree on a task for her to perform. She might be asked to guess an object that is being thought of, or find something that has been hidden, or as you have just observed, moved to a new place. When the chosen person returns to the room, she is told what it is she must do, and then the game leader places a light touch on her arm while the others fill all their thoughts with the agreed task. They "will" her to understand and then complete it.'

And now Mina could see exactly where this was tending. 'So the object of the game is for the idea of the task to flow from the minds of the players into the mind of the person who was absent?'

'Exactly!' said Hope cheerfully. 'How astute you are!'

'But what is the purpose of the game leader?'

'He or she acts as a channel through which the thoughts are conducted.'

'The player might guess the task, of course, without any such communication.'

'That is certainly possible, given enough time and after many false guesses, but if the task is accomplished quickly and easily then we may be sure that some "willing" has taken place. I have always found it goes better and faster when the players are related. This is excellent evidence, which in my opinion amounts to scientific proof, that there has been some transference of thought.'

'Surely if the players know each other well, they will be better able to guess,' Mina pointed out.

Hope gave a slight smile and a casual shrug. 'To guess, or to read thoughts, whatever you prefer to believe. Both are possible.'

'Enid is very adept at the game,' said Louisa, with quiet motherly pride.

'Yes, I nearly always get it right!' Enid exclaimed triumphantly. Mina decided not to cite the pressure of Mr Hope's guiding hand as the most probable reason for this success.

'And you, Mrs Scarletti, have also shown a rare talent for it,' added Hope gallantly.

Louisa simpered, and patted her hair as she always did when enjoying the flattery of a gentleman. The pale blonde waves were still captured in a widow's cap, but it was vanity surely that allowed a lock to escape only to be artfully restrained by a pretty comb. She wore, and would probably wear to the day of her death, an oval locket which housed a greying curl of hair, cut from Henry Scarletti's head as he breathed his last, but she had recently added a small brooch at her throat, silver, decorated with tiny pearls, a treasured gift from Henry on the occasion of their betrothal.

Hope turned to Mina. 'I am sure that you would also be very successful.'

Enid narrowed her eyes and bit her lip.

'Oh, do you think so?' Louisa protested. 'Mina always has her head full of stories and never listens to anything I tell her.'

'I believe that Miss Scarletti listens to you more than you might imagine. A loving daughter always does.' He gazed at Mina imploringly. 'Do try. It would please your mother so.'

Mina felt trapped. She could hardly decline after such a request. Refusal or failure would be an insult to her mother, and if she succeeded in any measure then Hope would use this to try and persuade her that she had mediumistic abilities. For a few moments she considered the advantages of feigning exhaustion, illness or possibly death, but knew that she would not convince Hope that she was doing anything other than avoiding the invitation.

'I am eager to try it,' she said at last. 'Tell me, how long must I remain outside the room?'

'Only a minute or so. I will knock on the door to call you,' said Hope, opening the door for her. It was a courteous gesture, but Mina felt both indulged and subtly controlled. It was not a pleasant sensation.

Standing in the hallway, with the closed door separating her from her family and Mr Hope, Mina was conscious of the whispering that must be happening in the parlour, and wondered what was being planned. How she wished that Richard might arrive at this very moment with his disruptive clatter, but he did not. It occurred to her as she waited that during the turns of the game that had already taken place, Mr Hope had, as a result of the requirement for the brief absence of one player, spent a not insignificant amount of time closeted in the parlour with alternately her mother and her sister, and she wondered what if anything had been said on matters that did not involve setting tasks for the absent player to perform. All too soon Mina was summoned back into the room, to be faced by Louisa and Enid with unreadable expressions, and Mr Hope with the kindly smile she had come to know and distrust.

'What happens now?' she asked. 'What is my task?'

'You must find something that has been hidden,' said Hope. 'Mrs Scarletti and Mrs Inskip must think very hard about the object you must find, and where it may be discovered. They are willing you to find it. You must try to receive their ideas, and solve the mystery.'

Mina was in two minds about knowing what Louisa and Enid were thinking about. On the one hand, she was reluctant to enter into their thoughts and on the other they were all too apparent. It was certainly nothing to do with the task she had been set. Enid and her mother made an effort to look as though they were concentrating, both closing their eyes. Enid had spread her fingers and placed her hands over her face but Mina could see that underneath she was on the verge of giggles.

'Now,' said Mr Hope, taking Mina gently by the elbow, 'let me see if I can transmit to your mind a picture of what is being thought of.'

'Please may I have a few moments to concentrate?'

'But of course.'

Mina glanced quickly about the room. Mr Hope would not have committed to memory the precise manner in which the parlour was arranged and Louisa and Enid were too preoccupied with their own requirements to pay much attention to it. Mina, on the other hand, managed the household and issued instructions to the cook, Rose and the charlady. Nothing seemed to be missing, or out of its usual place, apart from the vase that Mr Hope had replaced and was not quite correct. Mr Hope, she reasoned, wanted her to succeed, so her task would not be too difficult, but on the other hand it would not be so simple that she might easily do it by observation. It was then that she noticed that her mother was no longer wearing the little pearl brooch. Such an item, precious in every sense of the word, would never have been treated with carelessness or disrespect. When her mother was not wearing it, it was on her dressing table in a jewel case that had also been a gift from her father.

'Are you ready to make your guess?' asked Mr Hope. Mina felt a firm pressure on her elbow as his clasp intensified. She was sure that he was about to offer some guidance but she needed none, and if she did accuse him of steering her he would naturally deny it.

'Yes, I am. But I beg of you, Mr Hope, do not try to assist me. It is well meant, I know, but I do not want anyone to imagine that you are directing me, and you might do so by accident.' Hope gave her a cautious glance, and seemed to be on the verge of protesting, but he let go without comment and she crossed the room unaided, stopped at a sidetable adorned with trinkets, took up a small decorative box and opened it, finding inside, as she suspected, the pearl brooch.

'Why I can hardly believe it!' pouted Enid. 'How did you know so quickly? You must have been listening at the door.'

'Surely it is because I can read your mind?' said Mina teasingly. 'Or could there be another reason?'

Hope gazed on Mina with wonder and admiration, like a scientist who had just made a great discovery. 'I doubt it. You are miraculous, Miss Scarletti. I can see that you might have noticed that Mrs Scarletti had removed the brooch, but to know so swiftly and surely exactly where it lay, that is an ability far beyond mere guesswork. I wonder what your secret is? Perhaps you do not know it yourself?'

'I will tell you my secret,' Mina replied. 'I did not need to guess, I did not listen at the door, I did not receive any assistance from another individual and I certainly did not read anyone's mind. This brooch has great sentimental value and I cannot imagine mother treating it other than with respect and tenderness. This box was purchased by my mother and father while on their honeymoon. Where else could such a treasure be?' She limped over to Louisa and gently helped her replace the brooch. As she did so she saw tears glimmer in her mother's eyes.

Hope nodded knowingly. 'Your claim does not surprise me because I have heard such explanations before. I am sure that you imagine that you deduced the answer in the way you have described, but I urge you to entertain the possibility that the idea was placed there by the efforts of your mother and sister to will you into making the discovery.'

'I was trying very hard indeed,' said Enid. 'Mina, did you not feel my thoughts?'

'I felt them very strongly, but only because they were apparent in your expression.'

'You do not believe, Miss Scarletti, because you do not wish to,' sighed Mr Hope, his manner more gentle than accusing, 'but there are many scientific men who share my opinion. Some of them have proposed that there is an organ of sensation, a part of the brain perhaps currently undiscovered, which can enable thoughts to pass from one person to another. But there are others who go still further – they say that the mind can act upon another mind without the need for any bodily organ, and I am inclined to that latter belief.'

Mina understood. 'You speak of the soul or the spirit, and its existence independently of the physical body.'

'I do. Moreover, I think that what is happening here, and indeed in any kind of mental communication, both with the living and the dead, is a force of nature. In a very few years from now, if enough men put their energy into the work, thought transference will be proven and become an accepted scientific fact, and we will laugh at our former ignorance that we ever doubted it. At present, only those with the most sensitive and developed minds can achieve it, but one day, with proper education and guidance, we might all aspire to it, although there will inevitably be classes of persons whose skills in that direction will never be very advanced.'

'I look forward to that time very much,' said Mina warmly. 'Just imagine the world if we were all able to exercise our brains and discover what everyone else thought of us, or learn each other's secrets.'

Louisa looked shocked. 'It would be impossible to live in society!'

Enid said nothing, but her face flushed.

Hope smiled knowingly. 'I know precisely what Miss Scarletti is thinking. She thinks I am a great fool.'

'How very rude!' snapped Enid angrily. 'Mina, how could you?'

'Oh, I am quite used to that,' he said with a laugh. 'When one speaks of new ideas and new discoveries, there are always doubters. Today, Miss Scarletti, you are a doubter, but I will win you over in time, I am quite certain of it.'

No one showed any inclination to continue the game, and Mr Hope did not press the point; he had clearly, thought Mina, achieved what he had come there to do. Soon afterwards he pleaded another engagement that would, to his great regret, oblige him to depart.

When Mr Hope had left them, Enid turned on Mina. 'Why are you so unpleasant to Mr Hope? He is a great man, a brave man, and it is an honour for us to have him come here. If you are not better tempered he might not call again.'

'But don't you see – he wants to convert me to his way of thinking. If I continue to doubt him then he will only come here again and again to repeat his efforts. If you wish him to continue to visit us I think you are quite safe in that respect.'

Enid said nothing and Louisa patted her hair.

Twenty-Three

On the evening of Mystic Stefan's demonstration Mr Hope was kind enough to call on the Scarletti household with a carriage to convey Louisa, Enid, Mina and Richard to Mrs Peasgood's. All three ladies were treated with the same warm courtesy and gallant attention, but as he handed Enid into her place there was something about the glance that passed between them that Mina found worrying. She began to hope for the early return of Mr Inskip and a removal of Enid back to London and out of danger. Richard, who had been out until very late the previous night and then slept through breakfast, was looking uncommonly cheerful, which Mina feared was to do with the absence abroad of Nellie's husband.

'Was there no difficulty about my attending this event?' asked Mina, when they were on their way. 'You know, of course, that after certain incidents I was declared *persona non grata* at séances. Or does Mystic Stefan not know of my reputation for chasing away the spirits?'

Mr Hope chuckled. 'This is not a séance, Miss Scarletti. Mystic Stefan assures me that he does not receive messages from those who have passed, although many of the mysteries he performs are beyond my powers to explain, and quite probably beyond his also. But you are all my very special guests, and while believers in the unexplained are always welcome, doubters are doubly so, for they will one day swell the ranks of the believers.'

Those doubters, Mina knew, would include most members of Mrs Peasgood's select circle. She only hoped that the evening would pass without any upsetting incidents.

Mrs Peasgood was usually the best of hostesses, conducting her gatherings with smooth and practised assurance, but that evening she looked uncomfortable, as if she was already regretting giving in to the entreaties of her friends and nervous about what Mystic Stefan might do. Mrs Mowbray, however, appeared to have no such reservations, although Mina was sure that it was not the presence of the conjuror but of Dr Hamid that largely occupied her thoughts.

Mrs Mowbray was a large but active lady with a prominent bust, which she believed was her best feature, and a substantial amount of whalebone had been employed to ensure that no one could ignore it. Although the doctor had been widowed for only a few months she had convinced herself that all she had to do was wait out a suitable interval of time and he would one day glance in her direction. She had been heard to say that Dr Hamid was the nicest-looking and cleverest man in all Brighton, and no one had sought to contradict her. The fact that Dr Hamid seemed wholly unconscious of the passion he had aroused she doubtless put down to his still missing his late wife, which, in her estimation, only went to show his loving and devoted nature, and his excellent credentials as a husband.

Nellie arrived wearing an extraordinary hat with a silver grey demi-veil that was sure to be all the rage the following day, and such a torrent of lace that it brought gasps of envy from the ladies and looks of terror from their husbands.

As was usual for Mrs Peasgood's soirees, the front portion of the parlour was arranged with rows of comfortable seating for her guests while the rear, which served as a stage for the performance, was occluded by heavy curtains. Mina's interest was in the lighting, since it was the obvious and easiest way to tell if the entertainment was being presented as conjuring or a séance. Conjurors, as Nellie had attested, make much of the fact that they are hiding nothing from the audience. They are, of course, hiding everything of importance and allowing the audience to see only what they wish them to see; that is the art of the conjuror. But they did it in full light, which made their skill all the more remarkable. No one would go to see a conjuror who worked in the dark. Except of course that people did go to see conjurors who worked shrouded in darkness, only those conjurors called themselves spirit mediums and produced glowing spectres and whirling tambourines and brought baskets of fruit from nowhere and claimed that they would die if the lights were turned on. Sometimes someone did turn on the lights, but this had never resulted in the death of the medium, only his or her exposure as a fraud.

The arrivals all mingled cheerfully, especially Mr Hope, who had appointed himself major-domo for the evening, which suited everyone as he was a very commanding and popular presence. A crowd soon gathered around him, the gentlemen wanting to know how dangerous it was to confront an angry elephant, while the ladies, affecting to be terrified by that question, enquired more timorously after the fashionable dress of an African princess. At last all took their seats except for Hope, who stood before the curtains beaming at the assembly. 'My good friends,' he began, 'I am happy to see so many of you here for what I can promise will be a treat for the eyes. For some years the Mystic Stefan has been dazzling audiences on the continent of Europe with his displays, but now, for the very first time in England, he is here in Brighton to show you just some of what he can achieve. Should he meet with your approval it is his intention to take a room at the Pavilion where larger illusions can be presented. As you already know from the invitation, he has little facility with our language, and so will perform without speaking. Some of you will have prepared questions for him on slips of paper, to which he can provide an answer, either yes or no. The means by which he does this will become apparent in due course. When the time comes for that part of the performance he will indicate whose question will be answered and then you will either hold the paper to your forehead, or, if you dare, speak the question out loud.' He paused to allow the listeners to absorb the information.

'Mr Hope?' ventured Mrs Peasgood. 'I trust that the gentleman will not ask for the lights to be extinguished?' She gave a brittle smile. 'If he did, it would be very hard for some of us to see the entertainment.'

Hope bowed in response. 'The lights may remain as they are. Ladies and gentlemen, it is my very great pleasure to present to you the Mystic Stefan!' He drew the curtains aside and returned to his seat.

In the centre of the stage there stood a man. Given his *nom de théâtre*, Mina had half been expecting to see someone in elaborate attire, a long colourful robe perhaps, embroidered with mysterious symbols, and fashioned with deep sleeves, the better for concealment. Instead, the gentleman was clad in a plain black evening dress suit, with a snowy shirt and neat bow tie. It was hard to detect his age, since he wore his whiskers long, with a fine curling moustache and heavy brows, but these and his hair, which was also a little longer than strictly fashionable, were black and glossy, which suggested either that he was a relatively young man or used a great deal of dye. As he stepped forward, however, the ease and lightness of his gait suggested youth. He spread his arms wide, opening his hands so all could see that they were empty, and bowed to the audience. There was polite applause, which he acknowledged with a smile.

The only furniture on the stage was two tables – to one side was a long table on which could be seen in neat array the objects of his art, including a top hat and a wand, and in the centre was a small bare round table with slender legs. Mystic Stefan took up the hat and the wand and showed the inside of the hat to the audience to assure them that it was empty, using the tip of the wand to explore its interior. He then placed the hat brim up on the round table and waved the wand over it. Carefully and with great deliberation, he pushed back the cuffs of his shirt to reveal a few inches of bare forearm, thus demonstrating that there was nothing concealed in his sleeves. Dipping one hand inside the hat, he began to produce from within a rainbow of ribbons, silk handkerchiefs and paper streamers, which, because of their lightness, ascended into the air as he threw them high, and floated down in a colourful cascade, the very volume of these productions suggesting that it was impossible for them all to have been contained in the hat. Just as it seemed that nothing more could be forthcoming, he again put his hand into the hat and this time, brought out a bunch of fresh flowers, which he lifted to his nose to appreciate the perfume. He then proffered them forward, and Mr Hope kindly took them from him and presented them to Mrs Peasgood. That lady had been mollified from her original concern by the nature of the display and took the gift with good grace.

The conjurer, acknowledging a ripple of polite applause, next took a set of large metal rings from the sidetable. He lifted one away from the set and then another to demonstrate to the audience that they were separate, then tapped them smartly together. In an instant they had become magically linked as though the metal had somehow dissolved. He spun one ring around on its fellow to show that there were no gaps, then struck them together with the others, and showed that there were now three linked in the same way. Further taps and clashes continued, too fast for the eye to appreciate, so that more and more of the rings were woven together, forming patterns which he held up for inspection, until he opened them up into a single structure, seven in all, combined. He then closed them up, gave them a final tap and showed that they were free again.

There followed numerous other delights. He cut a rope in half with scissors, showed the cut ends to the audience, tied the two pieces in a knot and then blew on it. The knot was gone, and the rope restored to a single piece. He tore a paper streamer into tiny shreds and then, by blowing on the fragments, made it new again. With a wave of the wand, a vase full of ink became a vase of water, and then wine. He pulled fresh eggs from an empty cloth bag, which he then broke into the top hat, from which he brought out a freshly cooked omelette, a feat that precipitated a round of applause, which redoubled when he showed that the hat was clean inside.

Mr Hope now rose and addressed the audience. 'If a lady or gentleman would be kind enough to lend a ring for the next demonstration. I promise it will be returned quite unharmed.' Mrs Peasgood looked doubtful, but Nellie very charmingly removed a glittering token of her husband's adoration from her finger, and instead of handing it to Mr Hope, as that gentleman clearly anticipated, she approached the stage and put it directly into the open palm of Mystic Stefan, who inclined his head in thanks. When both Nellie and Mr Hope were seated again, the ring was placed in a casket, the lid snapped shut and a key turned. Mystic Stefan then produced an orange out of thin air and tossed it to Mr Hope, who caught it deftly and gave it to Enid to hold. There was now much waving of the wand over the casket, and a light tap, before it was opened and shown to be empty. Nellie obligingly gave an affecting performance lamenting the disappearance of her ring. All was not lost, however, as Mr Hope returned the orange to Mystic Stefan, and was prevailed upon to cut it open. The ring was duly discovered buried in the fruit, and after some polishing with a silk handkerchief, restored to its delighted owner.

Stefan bowed again, but in a manner that suggested he had only just begun to show what he could do. Taking a walking cane, he made passes over it with one hand, then, letting go of it, showed that not only could it stand by itself, but with more passes it could be made to dance, swaying from side to side on its point as he moved first one hand then the other in the air around it. He next took one of the metal rings and placed it over his head so that it rested on his shoulders. Some of the colourful paper streamers he crumpled into a ball, which he placed on the palm of his left hand. He then made circular passes over the paper ball with his right hand and it rose slowly into the air, wobbling a little, and floated gently between his palms without touching either. He smiled at the audience as if to say 'I know what you are thinking, you believe the paper ball is suspended by a hidden thread'. He took the metal ring from around his neck and passed it back and forth around the ball, showing that it was unsupported. Putting the ring back around his neck, he made further movements above and below the ball with both hands, then with a snap of his fingers it dropped into one palm, and he stepped forward and tossed it into the audience. Enid caught it and showed it to Louisa, who agreed that it was merely crushed tissue paper. The metal ring was handed to Mr Hope, who passed it around so it could be seen that it was quite solid and unbroken.

Stefan then brought forward what appeared to be a kind of nest made of many folded sheets of paper and placed it on the round table. Mr Hope rose to face the audience once more.

'Ladies and gentlemen, you have all been asked to think of a question you wish to address to the magical divination device of Mystic Stefan. All questions must be capable of being answered by either a "yes" or a "no". You may choose to ask your question aloud, or by writing it on a slip of paper and holding it to your forehead. The answer will be revealed on a paper within the device. So, I wonder, who dares ask their question first?'

There was the usual reluctance of individuals to be the first to venture. Heads were turned to see who might be brave enough, but no one was.

'Now please don't be shy, I can assure you that no secrets will be revealed.'

'I have a question,' said Mina. In fact, she did not have a question, but was impatient to start this portion of the demonstration.

'Please let me have some paper and I will write it down.' Paper and pencil were provided and Mina tore off a piece, made some meaningless scribbles and folded it.

'You will receive your answer on this paper,' said Hope, showing Mina a blank square. He turned it over so everyone could see that it was clean and unmarked on both sides, then handed it to Stefan, who opened out the nest like a flower and dropped the little slip into its deepest recesses. Quickly and dexterously the papers were turned in on each other until the result was a tight round package. This he handed to Mr Hope who gave it to Mina. 'Just place it on your lap, hold the paper with the question to your forehead, and the answer will be revealed.'

Mina obeyed, and saw that Nellie was looking at the package with a smile. Stefan took up the wand once more and made some elaborate passes in Mina's general direction with an expression of the most profound concentration. Something in his manner told Mina that everything else that had gone before was just a preparation for this moment. Had there been music provided it would have been mysterious, soft and evocative of strange things occurring.

Hope then brought the package back to Stefan, who unwrapped it, extracted the previously blank paper and held it up to show that on it was written 'No'. Mrs Peasgood and Mrs Mowbray glanced at Mina with expressions of great pity. They had doubtless assumed that she had asked if she would ever be cured, a question Mina had no need to ask as she already knew the answer.

Mrs Mowbray, with a sly glance at Dr Hamid, her slip of paper already written, raised her hand. 'I have a question.' Another blank paper was provided and the elaborate process repeated.

Mrs Peasgood was beginning to look worried. 'Mr Hope, might I ask where the replies are coming from?'

'Ah, that is a very great question, and one to which I am sure none of us here has the answer.' Mr Hope seemed very satisfied with his own reply, which was more than Mrs Peasgood was.

Mrs Mowbray's paper read 'No', a response that she received with very ill grace.

Mrs Peasgood declined to ask a question, so Nellie was next, receiving the answer 'Yes.'

Now that others had dared, Enid volunteered that she would like to ask a question, and also received the answer 'Yes', which she clearly found disappointing.

Mr Hope rose to his feet. 'I have a question,' he announced, 'a very important one, which I do not hesitate to ask aloud. Is Dr Livingstone alive?'

There was a buzz of whispers around the room as he took the paper package into his hands and Mystic Stefan made his magical passes over it. When the package was unwrapped the slip of paper said 'Yes'.

Hope gave a little gasp of joy. 'Oh then we may breathe again because the dear brave good man is alive and may yet be found and relieved! God and the spirits grant that this great work may be done!'

Mystic Stefan, holding the paper nest, suddenly looked astonished, held it to his ear and shook it as if there was something new inside. Replacing it on the table, he folded back the inner petals, dipped his hand inside and took something out, not a paper but a small colourful object, which he offered to Hope. Mr Hope reached out and the object was dropped into his cupped hands. He stared momentarily dumbstruck at what lay before him. It was a cylindrical blue glass bead, of a similar kind to the ones Mina had seen on display at the Town Hall.

When Hope regained his powers of speech there was an unmistakable sob in his voice. 'Why, this is extraordinary! Miraculous! Not only is Livingstone alive but he has sent me this to say – what is it he can be saying? That he needs supplies, succour? Yes, that is it! Oh how I wish I could send it to him now! Food, medicines! The poor fellow must be in sore need.'

Mina watched him carefully but if he was pretending he was doing it very well.

Mystic Stefan merely smiled and stepped back. He took up his top hat, twirled it between his fingers by the brim and put it on, then with an expression of mock surprise, lifted it to reveal a cake. He put the cake on the table, then bowed to the audience and drew the curtains so they met in the middle.

The audience applauded as vigorously as was thought polite.

Mrs Peasgood rose to her feet. 'I assume the performance is at an end?' she asked, but Hope was clutching the bead in his fist with an expression of fierce determination. 'Mr Hope?'

He started. 'Oh, yes, forgive me. It is over.'

Mrs Peasgood rang for the maid. 'Ladies and gentlemen, the evening's entertainment is now complete and I am sure we would all like to thank Mr Hope for arranging it. Refreshments will be served in ten minutes.'

While Enid and Louisa were concerned with Mr Hope and the bead, Richard took Mina by the arm and they went to talk to Nellie, who had risen and was making a tour of the room to show off her gown to the best advantage.

'What do you think of Mystic Stefan?' asked Mina.

'He is a conjuror of some ability, but none of his tricks were new, and he was clearly working with little apparatus. Monsieur Baptiste could perform all of what we saw, but with more drama. Of course much of his work was more suitable for a stage than a drawing room. The rope trick for example, cutting in it half and then joining it up, he did that with a live chicken, removing its head and then restoring it whole.'

'A live chicken? How can one do that?' Richard exclaimed.

Nellie smiled enigmatically. 'Well, the secret is to start with two chickens.'

'It is obvious to me that the device that answers questions is simply another conjuring trick,' said Mina. 'He must have the answers already hidden inside.'

'Of course,' agreed Nellie, 'its method of operation lies in its construction and the way the papers are folded and unfolded.'

'Do the answers appear by chance? Or does Mystic Stefan decide if they are yes or no?'

'The operator decides. Usually the questions are personal and secret so no one dares to say if the answers are right or wrong. In any case most people don't know the right answer, because they ask about the future or the unknown. The general way of proceeding is to give the answer "yes" to any lady who is young and beautiful, since she always asks about romance, usually whether her admirer truly loves her and will be faithful.'

'And if she is not young and beautiful?'

'Then the answer is "no", for the same reason. A gentleman generally asks about business and the answer given depends on how he is dressed.'

'Enid was most unhappy with her answer,' Mina observed. 'She must have asked if Mr Inskip was alive and well. What was your question?'

'I asked if Mystic Stefan was wearing a false beard,' confided Nellie and they all laughed.

'What about the bead he produced and gave to Mr Hope?'

'Was that what it was? I did wonder.'

'Yes, I think it was an African bead, they are used as currency there. I saw some displayed at the lecture.'

Nellie nodded thoughtfully. 'A sop to his patron perhaps. The bead was never in the paper of course, he palmed it and made it look as if it came from there.'

'Is it unusual to pretend contact with the living?' asked Richard.

'Not at all, I have known mediums do as much when the person being enquired about is far away, especially as in this case, when they are in danger.'

'I am very glad that we had no ghosts appear,' said Mina. 'I expect Mr Hope was too well acquainted with Mrs Peasgood's opinions on that subject to risk giving offence and losing her good will. I was prepared for an event of some kind designed to turn me into a fervent spiritualist, but there was nothing of that description apart from the Livingstone message, which we can hardly treat as evidence unless the man is found and confirms sending it. But Mr Hope is a subtle man – he may simply be paving the way for wonders to come.' She worried about it all the way home.

Twenty-Four

There was good news for Mina when she opened the next edition of the *Gazette* and saw that her letter had had the desired effect.

'AN ENCOUNTER': IS IT PLAGIARISED? asked the editor in a bold headline.

All Brighton has been talking about this controversial book, indeed we might say all England. Just as we thought there was no more that could be said on the subject, we have a brand new sensation. When we first heard the news, we could hardly believe it but our enquiries have shown it to be true. We can now inform our readers that an action is being taken by a Brighton lady for damages against the authors of *An Encounter*. From what we have been able to discover, the lady, whose name is being carefully withheld, wrote a pamphlet many years ago about a ghostly sighting in the Royal Pavilion. Without commenting on the likelihood of such an event, we must point out that the lady in question is highly respectable, and of a pure and elevated character. Her work contained none of the questionable passages that have made *An Encounter* so notorious, and describes only seeing the shades of the Prince of Wales' royal assembly and an entertainment consisting of music and a genteel and decorous dance. Nevertheless, the lady alleges that the authors of *An Encounter* have copied a material part of her publication, representing it as their own while adding the other less savoury portions which are quite unsuitable to be described in the press. Her legal representatives are demanding the immediate withdrawal and destruction of all copies of *An Encounter*, together with damages not only for the profits they have already made on it, but also to recompense their client for the great distress this situation has caused. The original book was created by a lady of refined and delicate taste, but she fears that those of her intimates who know of it may be under the impression that she is also the author of the subsequent volume. This anxiety has caused her much suffering, and she has asked not only for a public apology but substantial damages for the attack on her reputation. We do not know, but rumour has it that some thousands of pounds may be involved.

Louisa read the article and gave a sharp snort of a laugh. 'I knew it! These Bland sisters are wicked conniving women. Mr Hope was wrong to trust them.'

'I am sure there is some mistake,' said Enid, sulkily. 'In any case, you can't blame Mr Hope for being kind-hearted. He is very chivalrous towards ladies and likes to think of himself as their champion. He believes Miss Eustace is innocent and he means to prove it too.'

'What nonsense!' Louisa retorted. 'Enid, you can know nothing of the matter. You were not in Brighton when she was here and have never met the woman.'

'But —'

'No! I forbid you to speak of it!'

'You won't forbid Mina,' Enid went on, with a stubborn pout. 'She thinks so too but won't admit it.'

Louisa turned to Mina, wide-eyed in astonishment. 'Mina! Is this true?'

Mina made an effort to remain calm. 'It is not. Mr Hope would like it to be true, and I am afraid he has been carried away into telling people it is.'

Louisa gave the newspaper an angry shake. 'I trust you have undeceived him.'

'I have tried, but it doesn't take. Mr Hope believes he is right and encourages others in that view. Some more than most. He thinks it is only a matter of time before everyone agrees with him. One might as well tell the tide not to come in as expect him to change his mind.'

Louisa's expression hardened with new determination. 'I see that I shall have to have a very firm word with him. He is an excellent man in many respects, but overconfidence is something he must learn to curb.'

It was time for Mina to go for her steam bath and massage, which were more needed than ever as she had been both active and anxious of late. As she left the house she saw Enid and Anderson with the twins in their perambulator, marching down Montpelier Road towards the sea.

Mina did not know what herbs Dr Hamid used in his therapeutic steam baths, only that there were several recipes depending on the condition being treated, and all of them were secret. Her treatment began when wrapped only in a sheet, she sat at rest in the tiled steam room, and as the hot mist enveloped her she closed her eyes and beads of scented moisture rolled down her face and body. Sometimes Mina drifted into a light sleep, in which her sore back and shoulders eased most deliciously, but today she was too concerned about the pressure being placed upon her to become fully relaxed. She wondered when Mr Hope had told Enid that she believed in Miss Eustace, and supposed it had been confided during the 'willing game' when they were alone together in the parlour. What else had he said? She didn't like to think.

Anna, of course, at once detected Mina's tension during the massage that followed. She had not yet read the article in the

Gazette, although her brother had and she was extremely gratified to learn from him that the disgusting book was to be withdrawn. 'But as I understand it the earlier book was all about ghosts, too,' she said. 'So my ladies will protest that there is truth in it after all.' She worked firmly and diligently at the knots in Mina's muscles. 'Sometimes I wish I could massage their brains for them.'

Her treatment concluded, Mina, feeling somewhat restored, went to see Dr Hamid, who admitted that he had found the article in the *Gazette* highly amusing.

'Where the *Brighton Gazette* leads so the London daily papers will follow,' she assured him, 'not to mention *Reynolds* and *Lloyds*, and all the others that like a good scandal.'

'I wonder how the *Gazette* came to hear of it?' It was a question to which he seemed to neither need nor expect a reply. 'Do you think the respectable lady author would approve of this article? I am not sure that she intended to have her private business advertised in the press.'

'She seems to be biding her time but will, I think, be happy to admit to the first publication when she has received an apology about the second. I, however, am very curious to know what Mr Hope will make of it, since he believes in the Misses Bland's experience. Knowing his ways, I fear he will find some method of dismissing any truth that threatens to upset his beliefs. This plagiarism case has, however, come as something of a relief to me. Mr Hope has been pressing me to make this declaration, sometimes outright and sometimes more subtly, but however he does it I know what he is about. Now that it is public knowledge I can make use of it. It will give me an excuse to delay any decision.'

Mina's way home took her along the Marine Parade, and with the wind from the sea coming in cool and blustery, she decided to hire a cab. There were some days when high gusts threatened to carry her up into the air, skirts flapping, like a witch who had lost her broomstick, and consequently she could not leave the house unaccompanied, but that day she just needed to be careful. Most of the regular Brighton cab drivers knew her by sight and she never had to wait long to secure a vehicle. Within minutes a cab had drawn up beside her, and she was about to board it when she chanced to see Anderson and the twins on the other side of the road. There was no mistaking the unusual double perambulator, but Enid was not with them. Anderson looked dull and bored as usual, although she took her duties seriously, and made sure to give the twins equal attention. The babies, she had told the approving grandmother, were extraordinarily well behaved, and Mina had to agree that they were remarkably content and placid. Neither had yet threatened to produce a tooth, although that event was undoubtedly imminent, so the situation could well change. Louisa had given orders that her grandchildren were not to be pampered, and then proceeded to pamper them mercilessly.

Mina took her seat in the cab, but told the driver not to move off until directed and part drew the window curtain so she could peer out unnoticed. Had Anderson been waiting outside a shop selling confectionery or novels or millinery, Mina would have been able to guess where Enid was, but the nursemaid was exercising her charges around the gardens of the Old Steine. Enid could surely not be far away, but there were few locations in the immediate vicinity to tempt her. The area was, however, much populated by the surgeries of doctors and dentists and Mina wondered if Enid had arranged a medical consultation that she did not wish to reveal to her family. It was a worry, although Enid, she reflected, had not complained of her teeth, or any indisposition, and her husband had been absent too long for her to be in a delicate condition that was not yet apparent.

Anderson walked on slowly, but then paused, leaned over the twins, made a great show of ensuring that they were warmly wrapped, turned about and walked back the way she had come.

There was one other possibility, thought Mina with a horrible pang of dread; they were very close to the stately pile of the Royal Albion Hotel. Mina continued to keep watch for some minutes, and saw Anderson's performance repeated a number of times. Finally, she ordered the cab home, wondering what to do.

'Is Enid not yet home?' said Mina lightly, as she joined her mother, who was toasting her toes before a crackling fire in the parlour. 'Surely she isn't shopping again? Does she not have enough ribbon?'

'Enid has taken very well to the climate here,' said Louisa. She was amusing herself with a dish of sugared almonds and a volume by the famed Brightonian master of literature Mr Tainsh, although she was quick to cast the book aside as soon as Mina entered. Even Louisa found so much noble virtue grating after a while. 'She says it is good for the complexion, as the air is pure and the breeze stimulates the skin if there is not too much sun, and it is beneficial for the twins, too. They are still out for their walk, and may stop for refreshments before they return.'

Mina said nothing. There was nothing she could decently say. She could hardly make an accusation without proof. She might almost wish she was able to divine thoughts as Mr Hope believed she could. Retiring to her room, she looked amongst her papers and found the card Mr Hope's manservant had given her, showing that his master was staying at the Royal Albion Hotel. Had Enid really gone in to meet him there? Mina fervently hoped that nothing had occurred beyond smiles across a tea table. Even that was highly indiscreet. If they had spoken, the main subject of their conversation, once they had briefly revisited Enid's great love of Africa, Mr Hope's concerns about the safety of Dr Livingstone, and the new science of mind-reading, would almost certainly have been Mina's intransigent attitude to Miss Eustace. Hope could not parade Miss Eustace in front of Mina and ask her to change her mind, so, thought Mina, he was using the Misses Bland and Mystic Stefan as lesser weapons of persuasion, and engaging both Enid and Louisa as agents and spies in her home.

When Enid finally returned an hour later she announced that the walk had done her a great deal of good, and she did appear undeniably cheerful.

'I hope you did not find the Marine Parade too blustery,' said Mina.

'Why no, the air was most invigorating.' Enid gave a little frown. 'How do you know where we walked?'

'I attended Dr Hamid's establishment – do you know it? It is close by the Royal Albion Hotel. I chanced to see you and Anderson with the twins. At least, I saw Anderson, so I assume that you were shopping nearby, or perhaps sheltering from the breeze. It is a pleasant location, but when the wind blows too fiercely it may be hazardous.'

A variety of emotions flitted across Enid's face.

'I would not wish you to expose yourself to any possible dangers,' Mina went on.

Enid's lips trembled then she threw back her head in defiance. 'I thank you for your concern. Yes, the wind is fierce, but I can endure it.'

Twenty-Five

The day passed without a visit from Mr Hope. Mina suspected that the public revelation of the plagiarism action had, in view of his pronouncements about *An Encounter*, required some urgent investigation. He had probably tried to arrange another meeting with the Bland sisters to discover what they had to say on the matter. Mr Hope, she realised, the man who could stare a charging elephant in the face without flinching, did have one fear – of being made to look a fool.

Next morning, Enid and her mother went out in each other's company together with Anderson, to show off the twins to one of the few notable residents of Brighton who had not yet been privileged to view them, and Richard left the house for an unknown destination almost as soon as he had breakfasted.

Mina was busy completing her new story about the man pursued by demons. The narrative had changed somewhat since its original conception. When she had started to write, the demons had been real and hounded the sinful victim to his grave, where he discovered that even this gave him no respite from their torments. Now the story ended with the revelation that the demons only existed in his overheated brain. Mina was in two minds as to whether death would bring an end to his sufferings or not. Did one lifetime of sin really deserve an eternity of punishment? She supposed it must depend on the sin. Looking back on the earlier pages she saw that she had only alluded to the man's many foul deeds without describing them, leaving the reader to colour in the picture. She hardly felt qualified to insert more frankness, which in any case would result in an unpublishable manuscript.

Instead, Mina delved into her stock of adjectives. A few examples of 'unspeakable', 'heinous' and 'loathsome' would suffice.

She was still debating with herself how to end the narrative when she heard the doorbell. Hoping that the visitor was merely a messenger, or an importunate tradesman, a situation that only required Rose to send him away with a snarl, she took no notice until Rose knocked at her door. 'It's Mr Hope,' she said. 'He is asking for you most particularly.'

Mina sighed. She might have asked that he be told to leave, but there would be no use in that, as he would only keep returning until satisfied, and in the light of recent developments she was extremely curious to know what he would say. 'Very well, ask him to wait in the parlour. I will come down and speak to him, but you are to remain in the room throughout. Do not leave us alone together for even a moment.'

Rose gave Mina a surprised look, and a spate of questions trembled on her lips but remained unspoken. 'Yes, Miss.'

As she descended the stairs, Mina reflected on the fact that her visitor had appeared at a time when she was almost alone in the house. Was this mere coincidence, or had he been informed by Enid as to when this might be possible?

Mr Hope looked friendly enough, as he always did, but wore a look of underlying concern. His discomfiture deepened when Rose, instead of dutifully removing herself from the room, as he must have anticipated, went to stand in a corner and remained there like a statue, her gaze fixed firmly on the carpet.

'Miss Scarletti, I apologise for calling on you without notification,' he began.

Mina did not sit but merely placed a hand on the back of a chair for support, neither did she offer Mr Hope a seat. It was the clearest possible indication that their interview was not to be a long one. For his part, Hope looked too distracted to want to sit. 'I am sure you would not have done so without good reason,' she replied.

Hope glanced at Rose. 'I could not trouble you for a glass of water?' he asked.

'Oh we can do better than that. Rose, please pour a glass of that lovely mineral water for Mr Hope.'

There was a bottle of Dr Hamid's spiced berry water and some glasses in the room, and Rose obeyed. Hope, who had quite clearly not noticed the presence of the beverage, and had made the request anticipating that Rose would be obliged to leave the parlour to enable him to interview Mina alone, attempted unsuccessfully to conceal his disappointment. He took the glass, but was still too agitated to think of sitting down.

'I assume that refreshment was not the sole object of your visit?' said Mina.

He glanced at Rose again. 'The purpose of my visit is such that I would prefer to speak with you in private.'

'Maybe so, but I am afraid that will not be possible. When we last spoke alone my mother discovered it, and delivered a substantial scolding to me afterwards. She is very strict about these things and thought it most improper. People do gossip. At least let me know your subject. If you wish to make me a proposal of marriage you will need to speak to mother first.'

Mr Hope looked understandably alarmed, and for a few moments was unable to make a coherent reply. 'But I am sure that is not the purpose of your visit,' Mina continued. 'Let me reassure you that Rose is the soul of discretion and will not discuss your business.' Rose favoured Mr Hope with an unsmiling glance, which he did not appear to find encouraging.

At length he sighed and gave in. He drained the glass and set it down. 'Very well. I have just been advised of the date that Miss Eustace's trial begins, it is only four weeks from now. That might seem like a long time but it is very little when one considers how much information is still to be gathered, and the number of witnesses to be found and statements assembled. Can you reassure me that you will be providing the signed document we discussed earlier? I was wondering if it would help you to make your decision if you were to pay a visit to Miss Eustace and have some conversation with her. I would be happy to arrange it.'

Mr Hope was a tall man, a broad man. He towered over Mina, he overshadowed her like a leviathan come up from the deep, while she, a tiny frail sprat had only moments to see her doom before she was swallowed.

Mina faced him boldly. He was no charging elephant, but he was just as dangerous. 'I have no intention of seeing Miss Eustace again until she appears in the dock at the Lewes Assizes. Neither can I presently see my way to providing you with the statement you require. In fact, I am unable to discuss this matter with you at all. I have been ordered by my solicitor to do no such thing except in his presence. It follows, of course, that anything we say here without him as a witness has no legal force.'

'I don't understand,' said Hope, with a grim expression.

Mina smiled, a sweet innocent smile. 'Neither do I. The law is such a curious thing, is it not? But I am told that that is the case. What I suggest to you, Mr Hope, is that you make an appointment to see my solicitor and then we may conduct this conversation properly in his presence.'

'Who is your solicitor?'

'Mr Phipps.'

'Of Phipps, Laidlaw and Phipps? Which one is he?'

'Neither, he is Mr Ronald Phipps.'

Hope uttered a groan of despair. 'He is a bad choice. I am sorry to hear it.'

'In the meantime, I suggest you peruse the most recent edition of the *Gazette*, which has some interesting information regarding the authors of *An Encounter*. If you continue to support their cause I can hardly support you.'

He gave a scornful grunt. 'I have seen the article. It was almost to be expected. The newspapers are unfailingly inimical to the world of the spirit. They cannot see the great truth – they only know how to deride it so they may sell more copies to the ignorant and the bigoted. It may interest you to know that the Misses Bland are even now in Brighton; in fact, I have already had a meeting with them. They have a perfect defence to the charge, and in time their extraordinary abilities will become apparent to the world.'

'A perfect defence? What can it be?'

It was his turn to smile, and it was not a pleasant sight. 'Oh I couldn't possibly discuss that with you. It is a legal question.'

'I would very much like to meet these ladies.'

'So would many people, and you may do so in time, but for now they are reluctant to conduct any private interviews. It is my intention to introduce them gradually into society in small select gatherings, in which the people of Brighton can properly appreciate them. Their book is just a beginning. The Misses Bland are destined to achieve great fame. They will be celebrated all over the world. Jealous people who accuse them of dishonesty will find their efforts rebound upon them and do great harm.'

'Have you read the work which was copied?'

'I dispute the word "copied",' he said quickly.

'But what else could it be, if not copied?'

'That will be apparent in due course.' He offered no further clues, but Mina suddenly saw it all, including, chillingly, the reason why he had involved her and her family in the 'willing game'.

'I think our discussion must end there,' she said. 'Rose, please show Mr Hope out.'

'I can see all his plan,' Mina told Richard later. 'I cannot discuss it with mother, who would not listen in any case, and Enid is half in love with the man.'

'She is entirely in love with him,' said Richard. 'Her husband is a poor forgotten creature, and if he ever comes home she will stamp on him like a rat. But Mr Hope's plan?'

'The Misses Bland have been accused of plagiarism. They deny copying the original work, yet the similarities are too great to plead coincidence. I think they mean to say that they read it from the mind of the writer or something very like it, and wrote it down in all innocence thinking it was their own.'

'Will such a defence help them?'

'I doubt that a judge will be convinced. But what Mr Hope is trying to do now is create witnesses who will attest to their abilities. He wants to introduce the ladies into society where they will no doubt perform the "willing game" with great success in front of the best citizens of Brighton. These people will then all be called upon to add some weight to the claims. He has already tried to convince me, and mother and Enid. If the dispute comes to court and there are men of spiritualist persuasion there, the Misses Bland could be given the benefit of the doubt.'

'What about Mystic Stefan? What is his place in Mr Hope's schemes? I thought Hope was using him to bring you onto the side of the spiritualists but if that is the case he has made a poor effort of it so far.'

'Mystic Stefan claims to be no more than a conjuror. But he is very skilled. Perhaps in return for Mr Hope's sponsorship he is willing to testify that what Miss Eustace and the Misses Bland do cannot be accounted for by stage trickery.'

It was a reasonable enough explanation but Mina felt sure that there was something else staring her in the face, something important which she was just not seeing.

Twenty-Six

The public revelation of the plagiarism case and Mr Hope's visit gave Mina an ideal excuse to see Mr Phipps again. She was also anxious to know if he had discovered anything of value. Young Mr Phipps was with a client when she arrived, but he was willing to conclude his business quickly in order to see Mina and she did not have long to wait.

'Are you acting for the plaintiff?' she asked him, showing him the newspaper.

'Not personally; Mr Laidlaw is undertaking that, and of course I am not at liberty to divulge the identity of the author.'

'But can you tell me if what the newspapers say is correct?'

He paused. 'I do not know where they got their information but they have done their work well.'

'Do you know who is acting for the defendants?'

'They have engaged a London man. One of the best.'

'And therefore the most expensive?'

'Indeed. No man of reputation would defend such a case unless he was very well paid.'

'I am not sure if the Misses Bland have revealed this, but I think I know what their defence will be. The sisters will claim to be mediums and say that they obtained the manuscript through the spirits, or by mind-reading, or some such device.'

'Surely not!' exclaimed Phipps derisively.

'Mr Hope visited me unexpectedly this morning. I made sure there was a witness to the conversation but in any case refused to discuss Miss Eustace. But he has been trying to convince me and my family that mind-reading is a fact. He would not, of course, tell me what the Misses Bland's defence will be, but if the two works are sufficiently similar, so as not to support a claim of coincidence, then I think that it can hardly be anything else.'

'That will not be favourably received in court.'

'Mr Hope also told me that he intends to introduce the ladies to Brighton society. He must be trying to convert respectable citizens by having them observe the sisters reading minds, and thus create witnesses as to their abilities.'

'He might try. But I understand your concern. He is a very influential and respected man, and money is no object to him. I suggest, however, Miss Scarletti, that you can safely leave this question in our hands. I will, of course, pass all your observations to Mr Laidlaw.'

Mina acquiesced. 'During my conversation with Mr Hope he actually suggested that I visit Miss Eustace in prison.'

Mr Phipps looked startled. 'I sincerely hope you did not agree!'

'I did not, and told him that if he wishes to discuss her forthcoming trial with me, he should do so in your presence. I expect you may be hearing from him soon.'

Mr Phipps winced, indicating how little he was looking forward to this.

'I fear that the case against her will rest solely on what passed at her private sittings with Miss Whinstone. Can she not be tried for fraudulent mediumship? There is abundant evidence of that.'

'There is no law specifically against it, unless one wishes to charge her with pretending to summon spirits under the Witchcraft Act of 1735.'

'And the penalty?' asked Mina hopefully.

'Burning is no longer an option. In fact, such cases rarely end in a custodial sentence.'

'I can see why the more serious charge was preferred,' said Mina, imagining Miss Eustace tied to a ducking stool. She made another note in her pocketbook. 'But she might well escape if Mr Hope has his way.'

Mr Phipps, more than usually glum, could only agree. 'Does the man have no weaknesses?'

'None that I have been able to discover. There is his fanatical devotion to spiritualism, which, since it is apparently well-meaning, is tolerated, and attracts many adherents.'

'I cannot believe he is such a paragon. All men have secrets, and whatever Mr Hope's may be, I will find it out.'

Mina was aware of one of Mr Hope's secrets, but the last thing she wanted was for any indiscretions involving her sister to be exposed to the ruinous air of publicity. From Mr Phipps' comments she deduced that he had been trying to find some way of arming himself against Mr Hope. For all she knew he was having him followed by detectives. She hoped that her warning conversation with Enid had proved sufficient to ensure that no further assignations took place.

Next morning, Mina, Enid and Louisa were discussing Mr Hope's forthcoming talk on the subject of spiritualism, which was due to take place in three days. Enid demanded that they all go, and said that she could hardly wait to hear what Mr Hope would say while Mina, more reserved in her anticipation, thought she ought to go as she might learn something of interest. Louisa, however, was adamant that she did not wish to be seen at such an event, and declared that poor Mr Hope was a very misguided man and it was a pity he did not have a sensible wife who could explain things to him properly.

'Mr Hope says that everyone should go as he has an important message we must all hear,' said Enid. 'He says people who won't listen to him have closed their minds to the truth. Even Mina is going, and Mina is only just beginning to believe.'

'Is that true?' queried Louisa.

'I neither believe nor disbelieve,' said Mina. 'All I can say is that I do not believe in anything I have seen so far. I very much doubt that being exhorted by Mr Hope will change that position.'

'Well at least you are going to hear him,' said Enid, sulkily.

Mina did not say so but she rather wished that Mr Hope might prove to be his own worst enemy, and, carried away by his great enthusiasm, make claims that would invite ridicule and so weaken his influence. If so, she would like to be there to witness it.

The conversation was interrupted by the delivery of a note from Mrs Peasgood, announcing that she wished to call. Her handwriting was not as elegant as usual, suggesting unusual haste in the composition, and there was hardly a decent gap of time between the arrival of the card and its sender. Rose showed Mrs Peasgood into the parlour and it was obvious that the visitor was very upset. There was a moment of hesitation as she saw all three women there together.

'Why, what can have brought you here so urgently?' said Louisa. 'I do hope it is not bad news. Do you wish to speak to me alone?'

Mrs Peasgood dabbed her temples with a cologned handkerchief and shook her head. Louisa gestured her to a seat, and told Rose to pour a glass of mineral water and then leave.

Once refreshed, Mrs Peasgood began to speak.

'I know that Mr Hope is a very important man, and he has such a charming way with him, so he always gets what he wants, but I am afraid that this time he has gone too far. He has just paid me a visit asking if he can hold a drawing room at my house and introduce the Misses Bland to all my friends.' She pressed the cool glass to her forehead. 'Is it true that he is a Viscount?' she asked, faintly.

Louisa and Enid looked at each other and it was left to Mina to say, 'He is, but he does not make a great show of it.'

Mrs Peasgood uttered a sigh that almost became a groan. 'That makes things so much harder! I would like to oblige him in any reasonable request, but I do not want to have the authors of that disgusting book in my home.'

'But you were at his lecture,' protested Enid. 'Surely you must remember – Mr Hope assured us that the authors composed it in all innocence, and cannot be blamed for how others might interpret it.'

'They did not compose it all!' snapped Mrs Peasgood. 'Have you seen the *Gazette*?'

'We have,' said Louisa, 'and it does appear that Mr Hope has been misled.'

'Well *I* don't believe it,' said Enid stubbornly. 'It is a well-known fact that not everything in the newspapers is true. Sometimes they just make it all up.'

'In this case,' said Mina, 'I am inclined to believe the *Gazette*. Such a serious action would never have been taken without some proof. There must be an earlier publication which the Misses Bland copied.'

'Well, even if they did, it wasn't deliberate,' argued Enid. 'You'll see; there will never be a court case and they won't have to pay a penny piece.'

'I don't see how that could be at all,' objected Mrs Peasgood. 'And even if they simply forgot that they had read the other book, the one they have shamelessly stolen – one which I understand was wholly above reproach, to which they have added their own offensive insinuations – they have still committed plagiarism and will have to pay the price!'

'But they did not read it and never have!' exclaimed Enid.

Mrs Peasgood stared at her suspiciously. 'How do you know that? You seem to be unusually well-informed.'

Enid blushed. 'Mr Hope told me. I chanced to meet him in the street when I was out walking with Anderson and the twins, and we conversed on the matter. I mentioned the *Gazette* article and he said to take no notice of it as the accusation would be shown to be all lies.'

'But how could they have copied a book they have never read?' asked Mina.

'Because it came to them in a dream. They have always shared their dreams and one night they found they had both dreamt the same thing, so they wrote it down. Dreams are very important things and we should always pay attention to them.'

Louisa looked misty eyed. 'I often dream of Henry as if he were still alive,' she sighed. 'He was a dear man.'

'I can well understand that you would dream of father,' said Mina, soothingly. 'I dream of him, too, and the wonderful conversations we used to have. But I do not see how anyone could dream of the words of another person's book.'

'Perhaps the person who wrote it dreamed about it?' suggested Enid.

'That is not impossible,' Mina agreed, 'but can one person's dreams enter the head of another?'

'I trust they cannot,' said Louisa, looking alarmed.

'Did Mr Hope, in your fascinating conversation with him, elaborate on how it occurred?' Mina enquired of Enid.

'Not exactly, and I am sure it is a very strange matter which I would not be able to understand. But I suppose the Misses Bland have special brains, which allow it to happen. You must know about it, Mina, you divined where mother hid her brooch just from her thoughts.'

'I guessed where it was, and explained afterwards exactly how I did so. I can assure you I cannot read minds, whatever Mr Hope might like to imply.'

'Well, he says you can, only you do not like to admit it.'

'Mr Hope places a great deal of reliance on what was no more than a simple parlour game,' Mina explained to Mrs Peasgood.

'But you only think that because your mind is closed to the truth!' said Enid accusingly.

'*I* think,' said Louisa, 'that Mina may have a better appreciation of the truth than you do. No arguments, please.'

Enid frowned hard.

'The fact remains,' went on Mrs Peasgood, 'that nothing will persuade me to have those women in my house, and neither will I enter any house they may be visiting. I have so informed Mr Hope. Anyone with the slightest pretensions to respectability will, I am sure, feel the same and do the same. I believe I make my meaning clear?'

'Abundantly,' said Louisa.

'All of my dear friends are bound to agree with me. Which reminds me, I will be holding a musical and poetry evening a week next Wednesday. I shall very shortly be distributing invitations.'

With that singular threat, Mrs Peasgood departed.

'What a perfectly horrid person that Mrs Peasgood is,' said Enid. 'She thinks herself so grand that she can order other people who they might invite into their homes and where they can visit.'

'I regret to say that she does hold some power in Brighton society,' said Louisa, 'if only because she has a drawing room ideally suited for entertainment and chooses to use it so. But she has had a great horror of anything that might be deemed suspect ever since she allowed that dreadful Miss Foxton to perform there. I am very pleased that I did not attend that event. I am told that she produced an apparition that was quite naked. Fortunately for the morals of the town, the woman has left Brighton. But our way is clear, I am afraid. If Mr Hope wishes to bring the Misses Bland here, they cannot come.'

It crossed Mina's mind that Mr Hope was not above using a subterfuge, and introducing the sisters under another name. She further realised, although she did not say it, that she had the advantage of almost everyone in Brighton since from her correspondence with Mr Greville she knew something of the appearance and character of the sisters. More importantly, no one else, least of all Mr Hope, knew that she had this information.

Twenty-Seven

Later that day, at a conference held by Dr Hamid's cosy fireside where Anna was wielding a toasting fork, he told Mina that Mr Hope had called on him once again. 'It is rather like being haunted, only by a living man. I am sure there are ghosts that give far less trouble.'

'He keeps trying to charm me with flattery,' said Anna, 'he thinks he can charm all ladies.' Her expression showed that Mr Hope's efforts had been met with icy distaste. She stabbed a crumpet with more than the usual force.

'Perhaps you could have him exorcised?' Mina suggested with a smile.

'I wish I could, but I am not sure how Reverend Godden would take such a request,' said Dr Hamid. 'It is still a matter of surprise to him that we attend church.' He glanced fondly at a portrait of his parents, the Bengali father and Scottish mother who had raised their children in the Christian faith.

'I assume that Mr Hope is still trying to obtain a statement from you?'

'He is, but at your suggestion I am using the controversy over the Misses Bland to put him off. Of course no sooner had I mentioned them then Mr Hope, who is quite shameless in his espousal of every halfway plausible charlatan, asked if I would host a small gathering to introduce the Misses Bland to my friends. That, I refused outright. I felt quite safe in doing so, citing the alleged indecency of the book and the accusations of plagiarism, and pointing out that a doctor has to be above reproach. I think no more will be said on that subject. Is it true that they are already in Brighton?'

'It is, and under Mr Hope's protection. But I have some information about them, which Mr Hope does not know I have. I will tell you this in the strictest confidence as I would not want anyone outside this room to know it, but you may need it for your own protection in case he tries to introduce you to them by some subterfuge. I have discovered that one of the ladies in question suffers from a defect in her countenance, such that she will only appear in public if she is heavily veiled. I do not think it is simple modesty or a veil for protection against chills. There is some compelling reason why she does not wish her face to be seen.'

To her surprise Dr Hamid and Anna looked very uncomfortable at this news and glanced sharply at each other.

Mina understood at once. 'Has this lady been to the baths for treatment?'

Anna hesitated, then nodded. 'She has, although she did not use the name Bland and I did not know it was she. I cannot, of course, discuss with you the nature of the medical condition or the treatment she received.'

'I would not embarrass you by asking,' said Mina. 'I would very much like to speak to her. Will she return, do you think?'

'It is very possible that she may do so since she felt some benefit from the treatment.'

'Then I may well chance to see her here. Will you be attending Mr Hope's talk on Monday?'

'We will not,' said Anna, before her brother could speak. 'Given the subject matter it would be very unwise.' Dr Hamid nodded agreement.

'My sister is intent on going and I will accompany her,' said Mina. 'I will let you know if I learn anything of note.'

The audience at the Town Hall for Mr Hope's address on spiritualism was not only far smaller than had assembled for the lecture on Africa, but was differently composed. Many of the worthies of Brighton and their wives who had previously crowded to see the great man were notable by their absence. Louisa had, despite Enid's entreaties, remained firm in her resolve not to attend but had asked Mina to let her know if the man showed any signs of coming to his senses. She, Miss Whinstone and Mrs Bettinson were going to a recital at the Dome. There was a scattering of young men present, some of whom were probably from the newspapers, while others looked as though they were happy to attend any kind of entertainment that did not include the warblings of a mature soprano. The bulk of the audience was made up of ladies of all ages and classes, many of them veiled, some of them in the company of embarrassed-looking husbands. By some dexterous manipulation, there was a goodly gathering of invalids in bathchairs, or accompanied by medical attendants. Mr Ronald Phipps was there, as was another gentleman with whom he exchanged some words, and who Mina felt sure must be the senior partner interesting himself in the Bland case, Mr Laidlaw. He was accompanied by a plumply pretty lady who, she guessed, was Mrs Laidlaw.

Mina looked about to see if there was any lady in the audience with a more than usually heavy veil, but there was not. Enid was glowing, as if her unspoken happiness was enough to make her rise up and float above the company like an apparition. Even if her meetings with the commanding Mr Hope had been wholly innocent, a reputation could be destroyed in a few whispered words and more than ever Mina wished there was some way she could remove his influence from their lives.

Hope took the platform and acknowledged the applause, his eyes moving carefully over the audience, nodding and smiling at those he recognised. Always an impressive-looking man, there was something especially compelling about him that night. His hair, dark with flecks of grey, was shaped like wings to frame a countenance that promised nobility, courage and strength.

Everything about him inspired confidence, the very shape of his head implied the possession of a powerful mind, and told the audience even before he spoke that here was a man to be listened to, trusted and followed.

'My dear friends,' he began. 'I am happy to see so many of you here tonight. We live in an extraordinary world where almost daily great discoveries are being made which will benefit mankind, and our understanding of the mysteries that surround us is growing faster than we can appreciate. We are emerging from the darkness of ignorance and superstition into a great and glorious light. We have machines that do the work of men, devices that capture light to create pictures, cures for disease. If a hundred years ago you had predicted that we might speak to men on other continents by means of a cable, you would have been derided as a fool, yet now the electrical telegraph beneath the Atlantic Ocean is a fact. What a wealth of knowledge we have, and who knows what marvels the future might bring. But science is only one kind of progress. How empty we would be without spiritual awakening. The good news for you is that we are at this time in a period of intense spiritual advance that has been unknown since the lifetime of Jesus Christ. And just as Christ was initially derided and rejected by all but a blessed few so the spiritualists who are ushering in this new movement are being attacked and ridiculed, when we should be hanging on their every word. Sad to say those men of science who have pronounced on phenomena that have been proven again and again to be real, have with a few notable exceptions done so from a stance of blind scepticism in which they ignore all the evidence that does not suit them, and then assert that everything is a fraud. Truly, I pity them. The subject on which I wish to speak is too great to cover in one evening, so I will proceed to tell you very briefly something of the history of the movement and its principal exponents.'

Mr Hope then went on to describe the careers of those individuals who had ushered in the new age of spiritual enlightenment.

Many of the names were known to Mina from her recent reading. Some of these men and women were undoubtedly sincere – visionaries whose value to mankind would only become apparent with time and who for the present were either viewed as prophets or delusional depending on the preconceived notions of the listener. Hope reminded his audience of how the great prophets of the Bible had been received in their lifetimes and contrasted this with the way that they were now revered. Other individuals he named as the current leaders of the movement were, however, table-tippers or producers of raps and clicks, who Mina felt were less worthy of consideration.

'There is a lady,' he went on, 'whose name I cannot mention, since there is a court case shortly to be determined.' There was a stir of discomfort in the audience, some raised eyebrows, and a few frowns. 'I see that some of you here are gentlemen of the press if your busy pencils are anything to judge by, and you may well have been present at an event which took place in Brighton a few months ago, which I am certain will soon prove to have been a monstrous misunderstanding. Prepare yourselves, in only a few weeks from now, for some miraculous revelations. That is all I have to say at present on that subject.

'And now I come to the celebrated Misses Bland. I am sorry to say that many in this town have misjudged them on account of a circumstance that in my opinion only goes to prove their innocence. To the pure, all things are pure and it was beyond their imagination that anything they wrote could be seen in an indelicate light. I appeal to you on their behalf to receive them into your homes at small select gatherings and then you may make your own informed judgment.' Mina glanced about her but saw little enthusiasm for this proposal amongst any but the newspapermen.

He paused. 'Ladies and gentlemen. Let us consider what the message is I am bringing to you. What is my name – my name is Hope and hope is what I bring. Over the years our religious leaders have given us little insight into the world of the spirit.

For true knowledge and certainty we must turn to men and women of advanced intelligence who have been graced with the rare ability to see the wonders that lie in store for us.

'In your earthly lives you may have worked diligently, been virtuous, treated others with consideration, honoured your families, and yet you have suffered reverses which were wholly undeserved, and failed to find the love, the respect and the advancement that are surely due to you. Why this is so, I cannot say; it may be evil influences or unkind chance. What I can tell you is that in the spirit world, all injustices will be mended.'

Mr Hope now had the whole attention of his audience, who were listening to him with increasing interest. 'Those who pass from this earthly life aged, infirm of body, suffering the ravages of disease, will in the world of the spirit be whole again – young, strong, comely, in the perfection of health. They will live in fine houses, reunited with their loved ones who have gone before. Married couples who have not lived harmoniously on earth will be permitted to part and they will then be able to make new spiritual unions, a form of marriage that will lead to eternal happiness. Those who have not met with earthly success will find all that they need to develop their minds and gratify their highest senses, so they will achieve recognition. Children who have passed before their parents will be carefully nurtured until they are reunited with their mothers. But what of the wicked, I hear you ask? Will they not be cast into damnation? No, they will be met with compassion, not burning fire, and will be guided to the ways of righteousness, so, having done their penance and found a true path, they too will be admitted to the world of blessed spirits. Is this not wonderful?'

All around her Mina saw the enthralled expressions of those who had been offered a miracle, and were eased of man's oldest fear – death. Many of those present were elderly, and several had the grey shrunken countenances of declining health. There were couples whose postures of formality told of marriages endured but not enjoyed, and humbly garbed young men who had been disappointed in their ambitions. In the wonderful world of the spirit, all wrongs would be righted. And then there was Mina herself, bowed but not broken, cheated of the most fundamental desires of womankind, every day a battle against strain and frustration. She did not know if this world described by the great seers was real or not, but she had no desire to hurry towards her death to find out.

On the way home Enid's eyes were bright with happiness, and Mina did not care to enquire why. Here was proof, if Enid had ever needed it, that her union with Mr Inskip was not a blessed one, but a temporary affair, and that her beloved in eternity would be another. 'I expect you will be a disciple of Mr Hope now!' said Enid. 'He is such a clever man; it quite makes my head spin when he speaks.'

'Mine also,' said Mina.

'Oh please do say you will sign a paper for him! It is such a small thing to do.'

Mina had no wish to argue with her sister. 'It is a serious matter and I have asked the advice of my solicitor. I can do nothing until I hear from him further.'

'Not that dreadful Mr Phipps. I have heard some very unfortunate things about him. I would not go to him on any matter!'

'If Mr Phipps is being slandered then he really ought to know what is being said and who is saying it. Can you enlighten me?'

Even Enid had the sense to say no more.

Twenty-Eight

ext morning, as Enid excitedly regaled her family across the breakfast table with the wonders revealed by Mr Hope, a set of beautifully printed invitations arrived, addressed to Louisa. 'They are for all the family,' she said, waving a hand at Enid to stop her chattering, 'for an exhibition at the Royal Pavilion. The Mystic Stefan invites us to a demonstration of conjuring promising never-before-seen mysteries. All ladies will receive a present.'

'Which room has been hired?' asked Richard.

'The banqueting room. He must be expecting a large crowd.'

Richard looked unusually mournful at this prospect, and took the first opportunity of speaking to Mina alone in her room, flinging himself down on her bed in an altogether casual fashion which he would never have displayed before their mother, while Mina sat at her desk with her little wedge of a cushion supporting her hip.

'Dare I ask why you are so despondent?' asked Mina.

'Well, here is Mr Hope taking the banqueting room which may hold hundreds, and I find even the smaller suites are far beyond my means. Do you know, the Pavilion committee actually wants money in advance! That is most unfair since we have not yet performed the play or sold any tickets. I asked them if they could wait for their money but they absolutely refused. Is that how people run an enterprise nowadays?'

'But surely that should not pose any difficulty to you as you have just borrowed some money from mother.'

'Yes, but I have had expenses.'

This theme was all too familiar to Mina. 'Please don't tell me you have already spent it!'

'I couldn't help it, there was just one thing after another. You know how it is.' He sat up. 'Mina – I don't suppose —'

'No, Richard, this time I must put my foot down. I have lent you money before, paid your bills, and seen you fritter it all away and waste opportunities. Where is the play? Can I see it? Is it written yet?'

'Not yet, but it will be.'

'Good. When you have it complete, show it to me, and if I think it worthy to be performed and not likely to bring shame and ruin to our family, I will reconsider, but not until then.'

Richard gazed on her with his most imploring look, but she remained adamant. He rested his chin in his hands gloomily. 'Also the Pavilion committee has told me it needs to be submitted to the Lord Chamberlain for his approval. Something about preserving good manners, decorum, and the public peace. What has any of that to do with a play?'

'Well at least you now know what is expected. If that is all you have to say, I think both of us have some writing to do.'

'Can't I sit here and write?'

'No, because you would be forever interrupting me and then neither of us would finish anything.'

He looked so downhearted that she took pity on him and, getting down from her chair, went to his side and hugged him warmly. 'Richard, I love you dearly, but my best advice for you is to forget all about this play, go back to London, take up Edward's offer and try to make a success of it.' It was not what he wanted to hear.

Once Richard had left her Mina tried to settle to her writing. The story involved a young girl visiting a museum and being enthralled by oriental figures in magnificent costumes, which came alive and acted out a drama of the past. Later the girl discovered that what she had seen solved an ancient mystery of a missing princess. Mina managed to construct the framework of the story but so preoccupied was she with Mr Hope's talk and its effect on the listeners that the detail eluded her, and finally after a struggle, she laid aside her pen. More than anything else she was struck by the ease with which he had swayed his audience, and she could only feel helpless at the thought. She might resist him, and so would Dr Hamid, but that was not enough. She needed more facts, more ammunition.

Some months ago, when Mina had been gathering the information which had resulted in Miss Eustace and her coterie finding themselves behind bars, she had obtained through Mr Greville an advance copy of a report made following an enquiry carried out by the erudite men and women of the Dialectical Society into the claims made by devotees of spiritualism. Mina once again turned to its four hundred or so pages, hoping to find something she might use to oppose Mr Hope.

Mina had first been alerted to the dangers of trust in mediums by the activities of a Mr D.D. Home. This Scottish-born American spiritualist had very nearly succeeded in defrauding a seventy-five-year-old widow, Mrs Lyon, of her entire fortune – some £30,000 – by persuading her that he had received messages from her late husband who wished him to have it. Fortunately, a court action had seen through his villainy, cancelled what he had intended to be irrevocable deeds, and obliged him to restore the lady's property. Extraordinarily to Mina's way of thinking, the egregious criminal had not been cast into prison as he richly deserved or even put on the first ship back to his adopted homeland, but remained free to perform his mediumistic tricks, and had even participated in the Dialectical Society's enquiry. Mina had never met Mr D.D. Home, but often rehearsed exactly what she would say to him if she ever did.

The Society's report had ultimately been inconclusive, although some members of the committee had strongly suspected that the manifestations produced by the mediums they had witnessed were solely the result of trickery designed to deceive credulous onlookers, and said so. The Davenport brothers, famed American mediums who had made a triumphant tour of England, had been subjected to a close examination by one of the Society's members and been caught out in a blatant deception, disguising a prepared drawing to look like a blank sheet with the object of claiming when the picture was revealed later that it was the work of spirits. Their best-known performances, however, were those in which they had been securely bound with ropes inside a large wooden cabinet, which they had had specially constructed for their purposes, and from which they were able to produce spirit sounds, wave spirit arms through apertures, and cause musical instruments to fly through the air. Nellie had explained to Mina that none of this was very amazing if one only assumed that like the good conjurors they indubitably were, the brothers had some method of freeing their hands, and then re-tying themselves so they would appear to have been bound all along.

Inevitably, the Society's objections were vigorously opposed by champions of the spiritualists, including a Mr Samuel Guppy, a gentleman of advanced years and strong opinions. Mr Guppy's wife was a famed medium who claimed to be endowed with more than the usual abilities. Her speciality was making all manner of produce appear on the séance table. She had conjured up a basket of fresh flowers and shrubs at a séance attended by a sceptic from the Society, who was sure that it had come from no further than the nearby sideboard, an easy enough deception to manage in darkness. Mrs Guppy naturally claimed that she had brought them from a distance, and she had assured her enthralled devotees that flowers could travel bodily through walls or window panes or shutters, just as easily as a bird flew through the air. Mina was reminded that at the séance conducted by poor Eliza Hamid, a little posy had appeared on the table, which had surely flown from no further distance than Mr Clee's pocket.

Mrs Guppy had more than one trick, since she had, it was reported, been seen by witnesses at séances actually rising into the air, lifted by some unseen agency that placed her on the table around which the guests were seated. Mina found this unimpressive as evidence of spirit activity, since she had already seen Richard produce exactly the same effect with Nellie using nothing more ghostly than a roll of opaque black fabric. Having said that, Nellie was no great weight and Mrs Guppy was reputed to be a lady of generous dimensions, which suggested that she required not one but two confederates in the room.

To dispel any lingering doubts as to her close relationship with the spirits, Mrs Guppy, when holding subsequent séances, was happy to agree that the doors of the room should be locked and windows fastened. She then allowed herself to be searched by a lady, and when seated at the table her hands were securely held. Despite these precautions, the sitters were still greeted by cascades of fresh scented flowers.

Last July, however, several newspapers had reported an even more sensational achievement by the miraculous Mrs Guppy and Mina, out of curiosity, had made a study of the various accounts, which had afforded her a great deal of amusement. A Mr Benjamin Coleman had launched the story by advising a journal called *The Spiritualist* that 'living human bodies may be transported from place to place' and that Mrs Guppy, although 'one of the largest and heaviest women of his acquaintance', had been carried a distance of three miles by some invisible agency 'in an instant of time' to be dropped with a heavy thump on a table around which clustered a number of people seated shoulder to shoulder in a dark séance. The doors of the room in which they sat were locked, the windows fastened, and the fireplace covered in, although, given the size of the lady in question, Mina wondered why Mr Coleman had thought it necessary to add this last fact. So unexpected was this journey to the lady that she arrived without bonnet, shawl or shoes, and holding a memorandum book in one hand and a pen, still with the ink wet, in the other. When Mrs Guppy, who appeared to have been in a state of trance, recovered from her ordeal, she said that she had been at her home three miles away writing up her household expenses in the company of a Miss Neyland, when she had suddenly lost consciousness and knew nothing more until she found herself at the centre of the circle.

Mrs Guppy returned home by more conventional means, accompanied by a party of interested gentlemen who questioned Miss Neyland. She confirmed that she had been in the company of Mrs Guppy, who was writing up her household accounts. Miss Neyland had been reading a newspaper, and when she looked up found that the lady had simply vanished. A search had confirmed that Mrs Guppy was not in the house. Miss Neyland naturally informed Mr Guppy of his wife's disappearance, but he seemed not to be troubled by this, and after consulting the spirits to satisfy himself that she was safe, went to have his dinner. This curious lack of concern was explained by the fact that he was not a stranger to such incidents, since a gentleman of his acquaintance, a Mr Hearne, had quite literally dropped in on him one evening by descending from the ceiling after being snatched up by the spirits while out taking a walk. Careful reading, however, told Mina that this event had only been witnessed by Mrs Guppy, who had uttered a loud scream, and when her husband came to see what the matter was, told him that their unexpected visitor had fallen from the ceiling like a large black bundle.

Mr Coleman advised his readers of other wonders, too. The most extraordinary items would arrive on the table at séances conducted by Mrs Guppy as soon as asked for – seawater, snow and ice, even lobsters. The readers of *The Spiritualist* were presumably delighted by these tricks, although other newspapers took a heavily satirical tone, suggesting that if spirit transport of individuals was possible, as suggested, then this would do away with the necessity for railways, the only problem remaining to be resolved being that of arriving in the place one wanted to go. There was a danger that the traveller might end up somewhere quite different, such as an income tax office, or the Court of Chancery.

Following a certain amount of press ridicule, Mr Guppy issued a bold challenge, wagering his wife's diamonds against the Crown Jewels. His wife, he offered, after an examination strict enough to satisfy a jury of matrons, would go either to 'the inmost recesses of the Bank of England' or 'the deepest dungeon of the Tower' and there, behind locked and guarded doors, she would bring to her by spiritualistic means, something she did not take in with her. This item might only be flowers or fruit, but it might also be a dog or cat, or even a lion or tiger or elephant from the Zoological gardens. Mr Guppy asserted that just as an engineer could send a ball through an iron plate leaving a hole where it passed, so spirit power could convey a living organism, whether plant or animal, though iron doors and stone walls, without leaving a mark of its passage.

The press was quick to observe that a wager against the Crown Jewels would never be accepted, and thus Mr Guppy could feel perfectly safe that his suggestion would never be taken up. A more moderate stake, however, hinted the newspapers, would surely be possible, and Mr Guppy's response was awaited with interest. One journal, with tongue very firmly in cheek, suggested that Mrs Guppy be taken to the 'inmost recesses' of the nearest lunatic asylum. If Mr Guppy was also there to participate in his wife's joys then it might, it was suggested, do him a great deal of good.

Mina had been unsurprised to discover that Mr Hearne, who had made such a dramatic and unexpected visit to the Guppys, was himself a medium, but it further transpired that both he and another medium of their acquaintance had been at the séance table when Mrs Guppy made her unexpected appearance, and that Miss Neyland was herself being developed as a medium. All of Mrs Guppy's mysteries, which would have been hard for her to achieve alone, would have been simplicity itself with a few confederates and a willing audience.

That, of course, was the difficulty concerning Mr Hope, Mina realised. He did not simply believe, he *needed* to believe. If a medium was comprehensively proven to be a fraud he could easily persuade himself that they had resorted to fakery on just the one occasion to please their needy audience, but were otherwise genuine. If a medium confessed to fraud then Hope would put it down to illness, or alcohol, or insanity, or the harsh pressure and even bribery of those dreadful bigoted unbelievers, and he would trumpet his joy when the confession was retracted. In the remote likelihood that it was possible to prove that a medium was and had always been a fake, then there were numerous others he would be certain were genuine. Mr Hope believed in Miss Eustace, and since he was a man used to getting his own way, it seemed that the more Mina refused to approve her, the more his determination to exonerate the fraudster hardened.

Twenty-Nine

The banqueting room of the Pavilion, the one with the great chandelier that had so alarmed William IV's consort, Queen Adelaide, was a spacious apartment, much used for public events such as balls and concerts. There was easily room enough for rows of seating to accommodate a substantial crowd. Mina suspected that young Mr Phipps would not be one of the recipients of Mr Hope's free tickets and since she very much wanted him to be there, she had made sure that Phipps, Laidlaw and Phipps knew about the event, as tickets would be bound to be available for paying patrons. While Mr Hope might fail to extend his favour to Mr Phipps, he was, thought Mina, unlikely to cause a disturbance by refusing him admission at the door, and so it proved. Mr Phipps, in any case, arrived in the company of his elderly aunt, who leaned heavily on his arm and required his constant attention. Any intolerance of his presence would therefore have been a gross solecism. The gentleman who Mina had previously surmised was Mr Laidlaw was also present with his lady wife, and the two solicitors sat side by side. They glanced at each other once, and thereafter remained carefully silent.

Mina had thought of a new plan but it was one she could not carry out herself, and required the assistance of Richard. He had promised to attend but when the carriage came to take her family to the Pavilion, he was not at home, so they were obliged to go without him, Louisa commenting that her son must have been delayed by business. On their arrival, Mina saw that Nellie too had chosen not to join the assembly, and she had little doubt that the two were together. She hoped against hope that Nellie was simply helping her brother write his play.

Neither Mrs Peasgood nor Mrs Mowbray were there, but Mina saw other Brightonian notables, including the Mayor and one of the aldermen who had attended the lecture on Africa, and they introduced Mr Hope to three couples whom she did not recognise but ascertained from what she overheard that they were members of the Pavilion committee and their wives. Louisa and Enid, seeing an opportunity, decided to lurk about that distinguished group in the hope of obtaining an introduction. When Mina pleaded weariness and took a seat they did not dissuade her. Mina's object was to place herself where she might best observe the audience, and she would not be able to do this on the front row where her mother and sister intended to be.

Dr Hamid arrived and greeted Mina, saying that Anna was busy with her patients, but that in any case she did not find such entertainments to her taste. For his part, he did not either, but felt he should be there if only to discover what Mr Hope was up to.

'I agree,' said Mina, 'and I am very glad to see you here as there is something I would like you to do for me.'

'Ah,' said Dr Hamid, looking apprehensive.

'Would you be able to follow Mystic Stefan after the performance and discover where he is lodging? There is something about him I find very strange and I would like to learn as much about him as I can. You must be sure not to be seen.'

He glanced quickly about the room. 'Is your brother not on hand to undertake your private detective work?'

'No, he has other calls on his time.'

Dr Hamid gave her a sceptical look, as well he might. 'Do you think this is suitable behaviour for a medical practitioner? What would happen if my quarry realised I was following him and stopped to ask me my business?'

'I am confident that you will be able to think of some excuse,' said Mina. 'I would do it myself only I cannot go quickly enough to be sure of getting a cab in good time.'

'Let me consider it,' he said, but with a lack of enthusiasm that suggested that even she would not be able to persuade him.

The end wall of the room had been prepared as a stage for the performance. Screens had been brought in to create a three-sided enclosed space and they were draped with dense dark fabric, which fell into sufficiently voluminous folds that there could well have been room for something or someone to be concealed behind them. The demonstration promised to be more extensive than the one in Mrs Peasgood's parlour, since a long sidetable was very generously loaded with the para-phernalia of a magician. At the centre back more screens had been arranged to form a curtained recess in which there stood a square table, and there was a smaller table at the front. Mina looked about her, hoping to ascertain if the Misses Bland were there, but while there were some ladies she did not recognise, none of them was heavily veiled.

When the expectant audience was settled Mr Hope addressed the company and introduced Mystic Stefan, who stepped out lightly from behind the screens and bowed. He was clad as before in full evening dress, with the addition of a short dark cloak. He performed an elegant pirouette, his cloak lifting gently to swirl about him, then, as he faced the audience once more, it was seen that in each hand he held a small glass bowl in which goldfish swam. There were gasps and applause, which he acknowledged with a smile.

The bowls were placed on the sidetable and he took a tray with a dark bottle, a jug of water and six glasses, and brought it to the front. With grace in every elaborate gesture, he poured water from the jug into the bottle, then poured it back again. Upending the bottle, he shook it to show that it was empty before replacing it on the tray. He now produced as if from nowhere a magic wand and waved it over the bottle. Taking up the supposedly empty bottle once more he used it to fill the glasses, but even more miraculously, the colour of the liquid in each was different, so that one appeared to be white wine, another red, and the next four pale sherry, milk, whisky and crème de menthe. As if this was not enough he then gave the bottle several smart taps with the wand, which broke it in half, and removed the base, from which he pulled a dry white handkerchief.

The next trick required three identical goblets. Into one he poured water, the next he filled with sweets, and the third was left empty. The goblets were then covered with a large scarlet silk handkerchief. After a tap with the wand the handkerchief was whisked away to show that the water was now in the formerly empty goblet and the sweets too had changed places. Once again the goblets were covered and after another tap with the wand the contents had rearranged themselves.

The amazing Stefan now brought forward a carved box of oriental design from which, after demonstrating that it was empty, he drew a host of items which it could never have contained, little parcels of sweetmeats which an attendant distributed to the ladies, coloured balls, streamers, and a whole host of paper lanterns.

His next demonstration required a Japanese fan, with which he had all the dexterity of a juggler, opening and closing it with a deft flick of the wrist, throwing it up so it rotated in the air, and catching it one-handed. He brought a porcelain bowl, and showed that it was filled with nothing more than multi-coloured pieces of torn tissue paper. With the bowl in one hand and the fan in the other he began to fan the papers. By rights they should have been scattered about the room in disarray, but instead they rose together in a cloud, and the fluttering of the delicate papers made them resemble a swarm of exotic butterflies. Stefan now moved about the stage fanning gently as he went, and he was followed by the paper butterflies, which first rose high, then sank low. Sometimes the delicate shreds were only a little apart from each other, sometimes the distance was as much as two feet but all throughout they formed a moving garland about his head. The effect could not fail to both mystify and enchant the audience, who uttered little sighs of appreciation. Mina noticed that Mr Hope was leaning forward and paying special attention to this trick, which was the forte of his friend Dr Lynn. Finally the butterflies gathered themselves into a small cluster and subsided back neatly into their pretty bowl.

Stefan next brought forward a large shallow silver dish and cast into it some powders, causing a brief flash of fire from which a smoky haze arose. Mr Hope rose to his feet and addressed the audience. 'In this next demonstration, Mystic Stefan requests that members of the audience provide items to be cast into the bowl. If they do so, they will see an image of the person or place or object they are thinking of. Be assured that nothing will come to any harm and all your property will be returned to you safely.' To avoid the usual hesitation in such matters, Mr Hope moved amongst the audience with his most ingratiating smile and collected the items. Many of the onlookers, including Enid, were too embarrassed to have their secret thoughts exposed, and Mr Hope understood this and did not press the unwilling. Neither Mina nor Dr Hamid participated, and Mr Hope moved so quickly past Mr Phipps and his party that they could not have taken part even if they had wanted to.

Louisa provided a lace handkerchief and it was dropped into the bowl, whereupon a cloud of white smoke was seen to arise, and in it appeared the face of a man, which had some passing resemblance to Henry Scarletti. Louisa pressed her fingers to her eyes and Enid was obliged to lend her mother her own handkerchief. One of the ladies supplied a locket, and was shown a face she recognised as her late grandfather. One by one, items were dropped into the bowl, which obligingly provided whatever was expected, a child, a church, a Bible, a ring. At last it was Mr Hope's turn, and his contribution was the African trade bead he had received at Mystic Stefan's previous demonstration. The image that arose peering through a greenish mist was recognisably that of Dr Livingstone.

There was no suggestion that the demonstration was anything more than a conjuring trick or that the images were other than pictures, especially since the one of Dr Livingstone was a copy of the well-known portrait Mina had already seen in the window of Mr Smith's bookshop. It was no great surprise to anyone that Mr Hope might be thinking of the man who was his friend and whom he desperately wanted to rescue. Nevertheless, Hope was undoubtedly moved by the occurrence. If Mystic Stefan intended to strengthen his reputation with his promoter then, thought Mina, he was surely succeeding.

Stefan then brought a new item from the sidetable, a square board bearing an article more than a foot in height, mysteriously draped in black cloth. This he placed on the small table in the curtained recess at the back. On carefully removing the cloth a very strange-looking object was revealed, a white arm and hand, very delicate like that of a lady, rising up out of a shallow plinth, and resembling a model made of wax. Stefan made some elaborate passes with the wand, and the arm began to move, swaying gracefully, the fingers opening and closing, undulating as if stroking the keys of a piano.

There were little gasps from around the room, and a few people even leaned forward for a closer look, as if unable to believe their eyes. Mina, supposing the arm to be a contrivance like the Wondrous Ajeeb or the chess-playing Turk of old, decided to look about the room to see the reactions of those around her. Stefan, of course, was smiling enigmatically from behind his luxuriant beard, and most other persons were staring fixedly at the display, looking amazed or even frightened, but there was one lady in the room who wore the same superior smile as Stefan. She was not one of the Pavilion committee party and Mina could not recall ever having seen her before. There was nothing unusual about the lady or her dress, and she was aged about thirty, but she had a sharp face and a knowing expression.

Stefan, after making some more passes over the disembodied hand, brought a pen, which, after dipping it in ink, he placed in the pale fingers. He next brought a sheet of paper, which he first showed was blank on both sides, and laid it on the table within reach of the pen. As the enthralled onlookers watched, the hand began to write, and so quiet was the room, with all breaths held, that the sound of the scratching nib was clearly heard.

After a few moments the hand lifted, and Stefan picked up the paper and showed it to the audience. The words were unclear, but words there were, and he offered the paper to Mr Hope, who seemed no less astonished than anyone else. Hope darted forward out of his seat and took up the paper, then read aloud: 'Blessings and good fortune'!

There was a relieved murmur, as if the message could have been motivated by anything other than pious goodwill. Such openly or quasi-religious messages were, Mina knew, an essential feature of the work of mediums, used to convince doubters of the godliness and purity of their work. She was reminded of the words of Reverend Vaughan, Vicar of Christchurch in Montpelier Road, whose sermons often warned the unwary of false prophets, assuring his congregation that the Devil could cite scripture when it suited him. Not that Mystic Stefan was a fiend, but there was something about him she did not trust.

The hand was impatient to write more. Putting down the pen it tapped on the table, as if demanding another paper. Stefan smiled, produced what was required and re-dipped the pen. The hand began to write again, but this time it moved very rapidly, speeding over the sheet. On and on it wrote, until at last it stopped, dropped the pen and seemed to droop with exhaustion.

Stefan lifted the paper and this time it was his turn to look astonished. He passed it to Mr Hope.

Hope, in an increasingly faltering voice, read aloud: 'Food gone, medicines stolen, companions dead, sustained by prayer, God have mercy on me, the sun burns my eyes, I am wounded and ill … D L.' Hope's hands trembled. 'What is this? Is it for me? Can it be – surely not —' His eyes suddenly blazed. 'It must write more! Make it write again!'

Stefan made a helpless gesture and then turned to indicate the white hand, which still drooped as if all its energy was spent. He took the black cloth and covered the hand, then picked up the tray and replaced it on the sidetable. Hope went to approach it but Stefan stood with palms out, preventing him and solemnly shook his head. Hope sighed and turned back to his seat with the paper in his hand, his face deeply pained.

Stefan came to the front of the stage area and made a respectful bow. The audience understood that this was the end of the performance and applauded. He then summoned an attendant, who helped move his tables and equipment behind the black curtain, and finally made another bow and himself disappeared behind the drapery.

There was a hum of conversation in the room as the guests rose to leave, although Hope remained in his seat.

Dr Hamid looked grim. 'I will secure a cab at once,' he told Mina, and left hurriedly.

Thirty

ina went to examine the paper in Mr Hope's hand, something he was more than willing for her to do. 'Can you doubt the spirits now?' he demanded. 'The poor dear good man! How he suffers!'

'You think this is a message from Dr Livingstone?' Mina asked.

'It can be none other! Who else would send me such a message! Imagine him, alone and ill, without succour, in the most terrible danger, probably dying!'

'May I see the first message?'

He thrust it at her distractedly and she was able to compare them. She did not say it, but saw that the handwriting on the second message was very much better than the first. Now that she thought about it, before the first message was written by the white hand, Stefan had shown both sides of the blank paper to the audience, but he had omitted to do so for the second one. While he had apparently dipped the pen in ink again, it was possible for him to have made the motion without actually wetting the pen. He might even have employed a second clean pen and provided a paper with the pre-written message, much like the trickery of the Davenport brothers. To the man who had made water transport itself between goblets, and produced a dry kerchief from a bottle of multi-coloured fluids, all things were possible. How clever, also, thought Mina, to engage with the question of the fate of Dr Livingstone, a matter that was constantly in the newspapers and therefore known to everyone, and about which it was impossible for anyone to check the veracity of the message.

All these objections, she thought, would make no difference to the fixed opinions of Arthur Wallace Hope.

Mina looked about her and saw again the sharp-faced lady with her secret smile, turning to leave.

'Oh poor Mr Hope!' said Enid, almost elbowing Mina out of the way in her eagerness to comfort the stricken explorer. 'What a terrible thing! How you must suffer! And poor Dr Livingstone who is such a very saintly man. How brave he is! I promise to pray for him, I will pray very hard indeed!' Enid did not have a large bosom, but what there was of it heaved mightily.

'That is very much appreciated, Mrs Inskip,' said Hope gratefully. 'I too shall pray; indeed, I shall make an appeal to all the gentlemen of the church to include Dr Livingstone in their prayers this Sunday, to grant him the strength to go on until help can reach him.' He rose to his feet, looking unusually weary. 'Will you too include the good doctor in your prayers, Miss Scarletti?'

'Of course I will. I pray for all the afflicted and unfortunate in this world.'

Mina and her mother and sister returned home, Mina wondering whether there would be any result from Dr Hamid's expedition. Now that she gave it some thought, she could not help but feel guilty about asking him to do something so dangerous to his reputation. Without knowing how long his adventure might take she was obliged to wait impatiently for a note, which she felt sure would merely be a request for a visit. He was a cautious man and given the nature of his errand, nothing of any significance would be committed to paper. The following morning, after receiving the expected summons, Mina departed early for the baths, where she found Dr Hamid in his office.

She began by apologising to him for asking him to act in such an unprofessional manner but he waved it aside. 'The request was yours, but the choice was mine, and after what I saw I knew that something had to be done. I know it is not the kind of thing I ought to be undertaking, but I appear to be acquiring new skills in that department, and I am confident that I was not seen. I went as far as I could by cab but the roads are so narrow in the centre of town I found it easier to abandon it and travel on foot. It was not the most salubrious area. However, I can now tell you that the Mystic Stefan is lodging in rooms above a public house in Trafalgar Street. At any rate he went in through the side entrance avoiding the saloon bar entirely. I did look inside and there are stairs leading up to the next floor. That was where I believe he went. He was carrying two large bags, which must have held the materials he used in the performance. I remained in the street for a short while, pretending to be a traveller who had lost his way, in case he went out again, but he did not. However —' he took a deep breath, 'while I was there I saw a closed cab stop at the end of the street and a lady stepped down and began to walk towards where I stood. She wore a veil, but it was not Miss Bland, nevertheless I recognised her from her garments as a lady we both know, and I had to hide round the corner like a footpad in case she saw me. It was not the most edifying experience and I am reluctant to do anything like it again. Then, to my amazement, she entered the building through the same door Mystic Stefan had used, and I saw her ascend the stairs. I decided it would be highly unwise to remain and see how long she stayed there in case I attracted attention or encountered anyone else who knew me, so I went home.'

'Who was the lady?' asked Mina.

'Mrs Mowbray.'

'Really!' Mina exclaimed.

'Of course there is no means of knowing if she was actually there to see the man. But what her purpose might otherwise have been I really couldn't say. It is not a place a respectable single lady ought to go unaccompanied, even a lady of matronly aspect like Mrs Mowbray. Had it been a female of another sort – well —' he let the implication hang.

'We could have drawn the obvious conclusion,' finished Mina. 'But I think we may absolve Mrs Mowbray of having an illicit liaison of the romantic kind with the Mystic Stefan.'

'And it is improbable that he is a relative if he is Hungarian and a stranger to England. Unless of course he is some distant connection she does not wish to acknowledge openly.'

'Well I for one cannot believe he is Hungarian at all,' Mina declared. 'That is all part of the cloak of concealment these conjurors like to draw around themselves. I suspect that most of the Chinese magicians in this country have never been east of Margate. It is all costume and wigs and an air of mystery. That is why Mystic Stefan doesn't speak, he wants to preserve the illusion. If I was to step on his toe we would find him very fluent in English.'

Dr Hamid looked worried. 'Are you planning to step on his toe?'

'If the opportunity presents itself. But I can see his value to Mr Hope. He is the instrument Mr Hope is using to try and draw me into a belief in mediums so I can join his campaign to exonerate Miss Eustace. And of course a patron like Mr Hope is a valuable commodity to a performer, so Mystic Stefan provides Mr Hope with what he wants – messages from Dr Livingstone.'

'I agree. Which leaves us with the worrying question of Mrs Mowbray. I have given this a great deal of thought but am afraid that there is nothing we can do for her. We cannot warn her, or tell her sister what I observed; if confronted she would only deny everything.'

'Perhaps,' wondered Mina, 'Mystic Stefan holds private séances or tells fortunes. That could be the purpose of the visit. Unwise, of course, but less worrying than other possibilities. Mrs Mowbray is not a wealthy woman, so she has no fortune to tempt an adventurer, which may in this case be a good thing. She would not wish him to come to the house for such sittings, since her sister would undoubtedly disapprove.'

Dr Hamid nodded thoughtfully at this new, less scandalous interpretation of events. 'I think you may be right. But Mrs Mowbray is surely content with her lot since she lives with her sister most comfortably, and I never observed her wanting to contact her late husband, who left her so dependent on the family affection of Mrs Peasgood. What can she possibly wish for?'

'What indeed? Oh, I meant to ask you, there was a lady at the performance last night, aged about thirty with sharp features. I have not seen her before. Do you know who she is?'

'There were several people there not known to me. Why are you interested in that lady in particular?'

'Because she was the only person not surprised by what she saw. If any member of the audience was a confederate of Mystic Stefan, it was she.'

Dr Hamid was unable to offer any insight, and Mina determined that if she was to see the lady again she would do her best to study her further.

As Mina was leaving she saw an unfamiliar figure walking towards the entrance to the bathhouse, and suspected at once who she might be, since she was so heavily veiled that no outline of her features was visible. If Mina's guess was correct this was the elder Miss Bland, come for her treatment. Mina was tempted to follow her, but it would look suspicious to turn back into the premises as she had only that moment emerged, also to do so would reveal that she knew that the elder Miss Bland wore a veil to conceal some defect, something she was not at present supposed to know. Mina resolved to do nothing for the moment except observe, and carefully slowed her pace to give her more time to do so. However, an unexpected thing happened. As the lady approached the building she saw Mina and stopped in her tracks, clearly startled. Mina pretended not to notice this, and the lady, after her hesitation, collected herself and moved on, passing swiftly through the doors. Had Miss

Bland – if indeed it was she – merely been taken aback at Mina's appearance? It was not unknown for people to recoil from her. Or was there something more? It was almost as if she was being deliberately avoided.

There was one person who would be able to explain some of the mysteries of the Mystic Stefan's performance. Mina sent an urgent message to Nellie, who indicated by a scented note that she would call on her that afternoon, and convey them both to where they could enjoy light refreshments in the tea room of the Grand Hotel. There, surrounded by elegant glamour with service deferential to a fault and where comestibles appeared on tables in the blink of an eye, Mina told Nellie in as much detail as she could recall of the magic of the strange Hungarian.

'How interesting,' said Nellie, sipping from a pale china tea cup and nibbling bread and butter so thin it was almost transparent. 'It confirms my original opinion that Mystic Stefan is no novice. I have been making some enquiries of my own and I can tell you that none of my friends have heard of a conjuror of that name, from which we must assume that he has previously performed under another.'

'I assume the production of images required a simple apparatus combined with actual portraits?'

'Indeed. In such conditions the portraits need not be very distinct as people tend to see what they expect to see, and the same male or female pictures will be identified many times over by different persons as deceased relatives. Either that or the portrait, as in the case of the one of Dr Livingstone, will be that of a public figure who is well known and held in esteem.'

'I was hoping you would be able to enlighten me as to how the mysterious hand was effected. Of course I know that you are bound by secrecy and cannot describe exactly how it was done, but you might be able to guide me in some way to coming to my own conclusion.'

Nellie gave one of her inscrutable smiles. 'I am sure you have a theory of your own.'

'Yes, I think it was one of those clockwork automatons, and the machinery had been specially made to actually write the first message we were given. Then for the second message, Mystic Stefan simply substituted a dry pen and a paper that had already been written on. But the arm was so graceful in its movements, I have never seen anything like it. I am familiar with mechanical toys and have seen sideshow exhibits that move so stiffly, one would never imagine that they were anything more than what they are. But this – there was no sound of any machinery and I could see no obvious joints. I could almost be persuaded that it was a real, living but somehow disembodied arm moving of its own volition. Of course that was the intention of the trick. I believe from the reactions of the audience that I was not alone in this.'

Nellie poured more tea and added just a whisper of milk to her cup. 'The arm, you say, was resting on a table?'

'Yes, it was carried there from another table on a board covered by a cloth.'

'But you did not know it was an arm until the cloth was taken away?'

'No.' Mina thought about this. 'So what was under the cloth and taken to the table might have been something else, perhaps just a wire or rod that he could have removed. The secret is in the second table.'

'I assume that there was room for someone to hide under the table and put an arm through an aperture?'

'There was room, yes, but the lower part of the table was not hidden from view. We could see right through it to the curtain at the back. There was nothing there.'

Nellie took one of her little calling cards from her reticule, and held it up before Mina's eyes. With a deft gesture it vanished,

and then, just as suddenly, it reappeared in her hand. She uttered
a little laugh at Mina's gasp of astonishment. 'Oh I may only
have been Monsieur Baptiste's assistant but I took care to learn
a trick or two. Consider this. Your senses tell your mind what
you are observing, but sometimes those senses can play you false.
You know that a card cannot disappear but that is still what
you see. You see darkness under a table and assume that you are
looking through an empty space at a curtain. People thought
that Miss Foxton's heavenly sprite rose up out of a vase in a
cloud of smoke and floated through the air, whereas of course
she did no such thing.'

'I think I understand,' said Mina. 'You are saying that the arm
was actually that of a real person, and there was a confederate
there – from the shape and whiteness of the arm, a lady – only
somehow our eyes were tricked into seeing just the arm, and no
more.'

'Exactly. It is all a trick. Everything you see on stage or at a
séance is a trick. This one is really quite simple. I have seen the
same thing done with the head of a Sphinx which sits in a box
and answers the questions put to it by the audience.'

'I wonder who the confederate could have been?'

'Magicians who do not work with assistants will often
hire individuals for simple tasks and pay them a trifle for the
performance.'

Mina wondered if the confederate could have been
Mrs Mowbray, and that had been the subject of the secret meeting. But was there room for a lady of her proportions to hide
under the square table? Were her hand and arm so white and
delicate? She could hardly be so desperate for a few pennies that
she could be inveigled into doing something quite so vulgar as
crouching under a table and putting her arm though an aperture,
even if it was possible for her to adopt such a position and then
manage to rise from it unaided. One mystery had been solved
only to be replaced by another.

Thirty-One

Richard's current state of despondency was a rare one for him, a mood that normally only lasted for the short while it took for him to dream up another alarming scheme to make money. Even knowing this, Mina was unprepared for the exuberance of his manner next morning. Breakfast was over, Louisa and Enid were out visiting, and Mina was planning a new tale about a witch undergoing horrible punishments when there was a brisk knock on her door and Richard's cheerfully smiling face peered around it.

'The play will take place after all!' he announced, waving a sheet of paper. 'I have received a letter from the Pavilion committee saying that they have reconsidered their decision and will let me have the music room gallery at no charge.'

'At no charge?' Mina glanced at the letter but there was no mistake. 'I wonder how that come about?'

He shrugged. 'Does it matter? I must seize the chance. I trust the printer will not require a stiff advance for the tickets.'

Mina recalled the room in question from her tour of the Pavilion, a pleasant apartment usually employed for recitals before small audiences. Had there been an unexpected cancellation by another hirer, or – and the more she thought about it the more she felt she was right – had Mr Hope paid for it and used his influence on the committee as another means of winning the support of her family?

'What about the requirements of the Lord Chamberlain?'

'Well I must get around that one somehow, and very soon, or the fashion will fade before the play can go on. For some reason the rule applies to all plays where one charges for tickets. I can do as I please if I charge nothing, but where is the point in that? Why is the law so inconvenient?'

'It is even more inconvenient if you mean to flout it.' Mina saw that she would get no work done that day and put down her pen. 'I have a suggestion. Why not come with me to the Pavilion and I will introduce you to Mr Merridew who is one of the guides there. He is an actor with many years' experience, and is sure to offer good advice.'

'What a wonderful idea! Mina, you are the darlingest sister in the world! Let us go at once.'

Due to the inclement weather Mina hired a cab and they rattled off together in good humour.

'So you still mean to be Prinny?' enquired Mina. 'I think you are admirably suited to the role.'

'I do indeed, and I have written to Rolly offering him Napoleon.'

'Nellie tells me she will be happy to portray Mrs Fitzherbert.'

'Ah yes,' said Richard with an expression of great satisfaction, 'the absence of her husband abroad has been *very* convenient.'

It was a comment Mina decided not to explore, although she knew that Richard and Nellie had been playing at Prinny and his wife long before the play had ever been thought of. At least, she thought, one of the pair was adept at the art of concealment. 'I hope that the play text is now complete?'

'Well – not exactly.'

She looked at him accusingly. 'Have you started it?'

He crumpled a little under her gaze. 'Er —'

'Obviously not.'

'I have been very occupied with – with —'

'Richard, I don't wish to know. At any rate, as you have already told me that a play is no more than idle chatter, you ought to be able to write it in no time. I expect to see it finished by this evening. Ideally it should take at least an hour to perform; anything less and the public will feel cheated.'

Richard looked startled. 'An hour? I thought fifteen minutes would be more than enough. After all, how many people do you know who can speak for longer than that without repeating themselves and boring everyone.'

'I think it will need to be of some appreciable length if you expect people to pay for tickets.'

'But an hour would be – oh I don't know – hundreds of words.'

'Thousands, I expect. But you told me yourself it was easy.'

'And what about the actors – how can they be expected to remember so much?'

'You should ask that of Mr Merridew. He is famed for his Hamlet.'

Richard was lost in thought as they arrived at the Pavilion. They had to wait a while in the entrance hall until Marcus Merridew was free from his duties. Seeing Mina from afar he hurried towards her and took her hand. 'Dear lady, how delightful to see you again!'

'I am likewise delighted. Allow me to introduce you to my brother, Richard, who is writing a play which will shortly be performed here.'

'It is always a very great pleasure to meet a lover of the theatre. What is the subject of the piece?'

'It will be about the great romance of the Prince of Wales and Mrs Fitzherbert, set against the magnificent backdrop of the war with Napoleon.'

'Oh my word! How very exciting! Then there will be a large cast required.'

'Er no, this is my first play so it will be quite a modest production. I will be the Prince of Wales, and the other two roles will be taken by friends of mine. I have very little in the way of funds, or we might have had more actors.'

'That is always the way,' said Merridew, nodding regretfully.

'The main feature of the piece will be a splendid sword fight between the Prince and Napoleon. The Prince will win, of course.'

'Well that sounds most promising! Are you an accomplished swordsman?'

Richard hesitated. 'I expect to be. I might need to learn. Is it hard?'

Merridew considered the question. 'If you like, I can give you some instruction in the art. In my youth I was considered very adept with the rapier. How many performances will there be?'

'To be determined when we know how much interest there is,' said Richard.

'There is still much to be determined,' added Mina.

'I see. Well, with your permission I would be quite fascinated to see a copy of the play script.'

'That is one of the things still to be determined,' muttered Richard.

To Mina's relief, Merridew laughed heartily. 'Ah, the theatre! I do miss it!'

At that moment Mina chanced to notice a familiar figure in the vestibule. 'Why, that is Mr Arthur Wallace Hope.'

'I see him here quite often,' said Merridew. 'A friend of yours, so I have heard. He occasionally takes a tour, but seems mainly to be fascinated by the statue of Captain Pechell. He likes to stand and gaze at it.'

'Understandably, since they were comrades in arms. He comes here to convene with the Captain's spirit.'

'But you don't believe in all that?' asked Merridew. 'If there was a ghost in the Pavilion I think I would have seen one by now.'

'I am not a convert to spiritualism, although Mr Hope has been doing his best to convince me.'

A new tour party was ready to depart and Merridew was obliged to join them. It was quickly decided that he, Mina, Richard and Nellie would all meet up to dine in two days' time to discuss the forthcoming play, and he bid a cheerful farewell.

'I have had a thought,' said Richard. 'Perhaps I don't need to write anything at all.'

'Your play would be a dumbshow, you mean?'

'No, there would be words, but if the actors are simply told the story, then they could just make up the speeches as they go along.'

'Is that a good idea?'

'It's a wonderful idea! Then we will finish with the sword fight, and that could go on for quite some time. And – here is the clever thing – if there is no play text then it is not a play at all. I will call it a diversion and I need not trouble the Lord Chamberlain with it as there will be nothing to send him. So all difficulties are solved.'

'I suppose you will not need as many rehearsals,' Mina admitted.

'Rehearsals?'

'I believe they are usual.'

'Really? Well, we'll see.' Richard patted his stomach. 'Time for some refreshment, I think. Shall we return home?'

Mina hesitated. 'I would rather like to speak to Mr Hope, as it is always instructive to know what he is thinking, but I have been warned not to do so without a reliable witness.'

'I can be reliable,' Richard declared, 'and I should like to have a far closer acquaintance with Mr Hope. Perhaps when Mr Merridew has instructed me in the art of the rapier I will be able to persuade him to treat you with more respect.'

'I trust that we may find a better way,' Mina said, taking his arm. Together they approached the great statue. Hope stood before it, gazing up at the sandstone face, absorbed in his thoughts.

'Is it a good likeness?' Mina asked.

He turned to her, startled. 'Miss Scarletti! Mr Scarletti! What a pleasure to see you both again. Yes, the statue is a fine likeness, so noble and courageous, although nothing; no words, no image, can capture the essential goodness of the man I knew.'

'I can see that you are very drawn to it.'

He sighed. 'I am not a son of Brighton as he was, but if I had been then by rights it would be my statue there and Pechell, an ornament to his family and the town, would be standing here in my place, feeling keen sadness at the cruel death of a friend.'

'Why by rights? Surely his death was a chance of war?'

'In a sense it was, as so much is chance, but I am sorry to say that I must bear some of the blame. The day before, being young and foolhardy, I took too many risks, and against all pleading, placed myself in danger and received a leg wound. Had I not done so I could well have been where Pechell was and been killed in his stead while he was on another part of the field. He and all the men with him were torn apart by a fusillade.' He breathed a deep sigh, and Mina saw tears start in his eyes. 'This place, yes you are right, I am drawn to it – I can feel Pechell's spirit demanding that I come here – it is such a powerful focus of energy. Dr Lynn, so I have been told, was here on the very day of the extraordinary encounter, and he too attracts spiritual energy, though he does not know it; indeed, he continues to deny it against all the evidence. Mystic Stefan undoubtedly has psychic abilities, too, and he may prove to be, if anything, a more powerful medium than Dr Lynn. The butterfly illusion you saw is almost unique in that form and elegance to the performances of Dr Lynn but Mystic Stefan does it equally as well. If I could only draw together all the things that brought so much energy into one place at the same moment then we might even divine the secret of what the Misses Bland experienced. I thought it might have been possible when Stefan made his wonderful demonstration, but it was not. Perhaps something is missing?'

Mina smiled. 'There was the chess automaton, the Wondrous Ajeeb, but I would not attribute any special powers to what is after all only a child's plaything built large.'

Hope stared at her, his jaw dropping as if seeing a vision appear before his eyes. 'Of course! That is it! The Wondrous Ajeeb! I am so grateful to you, Miss Scarletti. Why did I not think of it!'

'Because it is just a machine, Mr Hope,' she reminded him gently.

'Oh no, he cannot be. He is surely imbued with the spirit of the great Turk, the one who has gone before but whose outer form has sadly perished. But Ajeeb is no longer here in Brighton, I believe?'

'No, I think he must be back at the Crystal Palace where he continues to exhibit.'

'Then he must return,' said Hope, clenching his fists with a look of unshakable determination. 'And we must be prepared for wonderful things.' He laid his hand on the arm of the statue. 'Pechell, you are here, I can feel it. And I hope that you can forgive me.' He turned to Richard with a more benign look. 'I gather that the Pavilion committee has smoothed the way for your play to be performed?'

'They have,' said Richard. Realisation dawned. 'Was that your influence?'

Hope smiled. 'Oh one just needs to know whose ear to whisper into. I look forward very much to seeing it. I shall take ten tickets and recommend it to all my friends in Brighton.'

'I owe you my thanks,' murmured Richard awkwardly.

'You owe me nothing,' replied Hope. He glanced at Mina. 'Have you given further thought to my request for a statement? Please say that you have.'

'Now you know we cannot discuss that here. I am under strict orders from Mr Phipps.'

Hope made a gesture of frustration. 'I cannot understand why you fail to see a truth that is so very clear to others and has been proved again and again. Is it because you do not want to? I do so hope you are not secretly one of those materialists who believe in nothing at all and can have no comfort in life. They seem to me to be the saddest of creatures. Some of them even deny God; they certainly deny the spirit, the existence of the immortal soul of mankind. What a terrible empty world they must live in! You have said that you go to church and pray, but I cannot help but wonder if that is only a matter of form.'

'I pray often and most earnestly,' replied Mina. 'But whatever I might believe in my heart, it will not change the truth, a truth I cannot yet know.'

'And are you not hungry for the truth? Do you not seek it?'

'The truth is the truth whether I seek it or not. I am content to apply my energies such as they are to living this life as best I can.'

He sighed. 'That is the difference between us. I know that the truth is out there, in the great wide world we inhabit. I need to seize it, and lead others to it.' He stared at her, a deep imploring look. 'I want to lead you to it.'

'But I do not wish to be led. Whatever is there I must see and recognise it for myself, not have it forced on me. But to be blunt with you, the truth that you believe in is one I do not recognise. Miss Eustace and her friends only succeeded in demonstrating to me that the works of spirit mediums are a fraud. Some are merely entertainers, some do bring real comfort to the bereaved, but there are also those who are thieves and must be punished. There may be genuine mediums, but I do not know of any. I have read about the trickery of the Davenport brothers, the supposed flight of Mrs Guppy and the crimes of Mr D.D. Home, and all I have learned supports my original impression. I ask to see the Misses Bland and they are strangely reluctant to see me. What do they have to hide? Are they afraid I will unmask them as cheats? I think they are.'

'Not a bit of it, but you do have a reputation as someone with a profound negative influence on the delicate constitution of spirit mediums.'

'Well that is a very convenient excuse, is it not? The perfect reason to avoid me and thus avoid the danger of exposure.'

'That is not the reason they are unwilling to meet you. They are very private persons, timid even, and do not go about in society. Their new powers they find very disturbing and are afraid for their health if they exert them too much or encounter anyone such as yourself while they are still in the process of development.'

'I think that is nonsense. If they are genuine, and as power-ful as you say, they should hardly be afraid of me. They should want to meet me, in order to convince me that they are genuine. This avoidance further convinces me that they are tricksters.'

Hope frowned thoughtfully. 'If I could arrange a meeting, would you agree to sign the document regarding Miss Eustace?'

'You know we cannot discuss that here.'

'I only wish I could persuade you to attend a séance conducted by some of the leading practitioners of that art. The Davenports have returned to America, but there are others.'

'Mr Home or Mrs Guppy I suppose?'

'Yes. I have attended their séances, which you have not, and can heartily recommend them both. You would see won-ders beyond imagining, and I can promise that you would be received into the fold of believers with great happiness.'

'I would rather not meet Mr Home for fear that he would make an attempt to fleece me of my property.' Hope opened his mouth to protest but Mina waved him to silence. 'Do not try to defend him, the Lyon case is a matter of court record. And as for Mrs Guppy —' Mina was suddenly struck by a new thought. 'Do you really believe that she can fly through the air and pass through walls?'

'Yes I do! There are many competent witnesses who say she can. Educated men and women of the most impeccable reputation were present at that extraordinary event and have signed affidavits to confirm what they saw. Oh I know the men of the press have greeted the news with insults and ridicule, but they were not there. Had they been, they too would have been convinced.'

'If this lady can really do what she claims, and I for one cannot believe that anyone can fly through walls, but if she and other spiritualists can do this, then why, pray, are men risking their lives going to Africa? Why are they marching through lands infested by flies and deadly disease, facing starvation and wild animals, dangerous rapids and murderous attacks; why are they doing this and suffering and dying? I can see the importance of finding trade routes but it comes at such a price – the lives of brave men. Why do the spirits not take pity on us and send a medium to find the source of the Nile and then come back and tell us where it is? Why do they not find Dr Livingstone and rescue him and bring him home, if he is alive, or carry his body back for burial if he is no more?'

'I do believe you are mocking me,' said Hope.

'I am afraid that you open yourself to mockery by telling me that you believe a lady, who I understand is of somewhat generous dimensions, can fly through the air and pass through walls without leaving a sizeable hole.'

'Yet you refuse to see her and witness it for yourself.'

'Not at all. But I am a negative influence. More to the point I am not a credulous believer, and it would be known that I was looking for fraud. I would never be admitted, and even if I were, there would be no wonders to behold that day, as my mere presence drains away whatever powers the medium claims to be using. Everyone would be disappointed, and it would all be my fault.'

Hope sighed and shook his head. 'I am so sorry that your mind is closed to these wonders. I do wish you would reconsider. Please, allow me at least to send you the paper I wish you to sign. Read it through and let me know if you can oblige.'

'I will receive it only if you send a copy to my solicitor.'

'Very well, I will. And since we may not discuss the issue except before him, then I will with some reluctance ask him to arrange a time when that can take place. Good day.'

As Hope bowed and walked away Richard stared after him. 'What a very dangerous man,' he said.

As they stood there contemplating the conversation that had passed, a gentleman, very plainly dressed, who had been paying careful attention to the row of busts of the Brighton worthies, noticed that Hope was leaving the Pavilion and discreetly followed him.

Thirty-Two

Next day Mina received a note from Mr Ronald Phipps, saying that he had been supplied with a document by Mr Hope and wished to arrange a meeting at his office at a time convenient to all parties. Mina had also received the document that Hope wanted her to sign, and it was everything she feared. It read:

To whom it may concern

This is to certify that I, Mina Scarletti, have attended séances conducted by the spirit medium Miss Eustace, and declare that I am convinced of the genuineness of the manifestations and materialisations she has produced in my presence. I also renounce all statements I have made in the past which might suggest that I do not believe that Miss Eustace is wholly genuine and apologise for any distress my words and actions may have caused her.

My signature is appended below in order to establish the truth of my beliefs and I confirm that I have not been offered any inducement of whatever nature to secure that signature.

Mina felt she needed to discuss the document with someone who was already conversant with the circumstances, but Richard was absent once more and Dr Hamid and Anna were busy with patients, so Mina took the paper to the one person she would be sure would advise her – Miss Whinstone.

'Oh my dear,' said that lady, perusing the document, 'you cannot, must not, sign such a thing.'

Mina had hoped that the report in the *Gazette* of Mr Hope's recent talk on spiritualism would strengthen her case and weaken his but following the previous adverse comment this new review was more muted in tone, and while not actually praising the speaker, neither did it take a contrary point of view. Mr Hope's address, said the correspondent, had been 'interesting' and 'informative' and suggested that 'further study of the subject might be necessary'. Mina felt that a support had been knocked away from under her, and Enid was jubilant.

She had been giving some thought to her last conversation with Mr Hope in which the Wondrous Ajeeb had been mentioned, and accordingly sent a note to Mr Merridew asking if he would be kind enough to let her know if the great automaton should make a future appearance at the Pavilion. He replied quickly, promising to inform her the instant he had any news, and also, if she was interested, to introduce her to Mr Mott the chess champion, who might be able to provide some fascinating information as to the working of the mechanism.

Mina arrived at the office of Phipps, Laidlaw and Phipps a few minutes before the time appointed for the meeting and asked if she could be admitted to speak to the young solicitor before Mr Hope was there. She was conducted to Mr Phipps' faultlessly neat domain, where he was already studying his copy of the document. They took the precaution of comparing his copy with the one in Mina's possession and established that they were identical.

'I do not trust Mr Hope at all,' commented Mr Phipps. 'One must take every precaution.'

'He is not a wicked man,' said Mina, 'but he is driven by the need to be correct. I recently encountered him at the Pavilion when I was accompanied by my brother, who was a witness to our conversation, and Mr Hope revealed that he feels some personal guilt concerning the death of Captain Pechell, which may be one of the keys to his obsession. I do not think the guilt is justified as the Captain's death was a tragedy of war, but Hope clearly thinks that had circumstances been different he and not the Captain would have died that day. His belief in spiritualism is a means of comforting himself, and we can never shake it. But there was one other thing I observed – when Mr Hope left the Pavilion another man who was standing nearby followed him. I wondered if that man was a detective, and if so, whether he had been sent by you.'

Mr Phipps went slightly pink in the face. 'It seemed like a wise precaution. For all we know he could be undertaking some unlawful action in the pursuit of his ends, but so far it seems he has not. I know he has met with some members of the Pavilion committee, and he has hired and paid for three apartments, the banqueting room, where we saw the performance by the Mystic Stefan, the chess club room, where he means to exhibit an automaton, and the music room gallery, although I am not sure what that is for.'

'That is on behalf of my brother who means to perform a play there. He did so unasked, and I am sure we understand his purpose.'

'Indeed we do. He is also paying for the Misses Bland to occupy lodgings very near to the Royal Albion Hotel, and he does meet them from time to time, but he is never alone with either. The only thing that I have been able to establish is that he might be conducting an intrigue with another lady. My man has been instructed to discover her identity, as the secrecy of their meetings suggests that she might well be married.'

Mina did not know what to say without giving away what she knew. 'Surely you do not intend to drag a lady's name through the mud in order to attack the character of Mr Hope?'

'That ought not to be necessary, but it could well be a bargaining counter. I am sure he has no wish to be named in an action for divorce.'

'No indeed,' said Mina, appalled at the effect that this would have on her family.

Phipps looked at her anxiously. 'Are you quite well, Miss Scarletti? I hope the journey has not fatigued you.'

She laid a palm against her forehead. 'I may have caught a slight chill, that is all.'

He nodded understandingly. 'Well we will conduct the meeting as quickly as possible so that you may return home and take care of yourself,' he said with unexpected gentleness.

A clerk knocked on the door and announced the arrival of Mr Hope, who was ushered in. He looked annoyed to see Mina already there, and although he did not voice his suspicions that they were plotting against him, it was obvious from his demeanour.

He sat down, his body tense like a lion about to spring, his deep chest thrust forward aggressively. Mr Phipps was not a large man and the presence of Mr Hope made him seem smaller than he was. It was an uncomfortable meeting since Hope and Phipps clearly disliked each other, and each man eyed the other like two contestants about to fight a duel, not actually wanting to meet, but recognising that the safest place to have one's enemy was where you could actually see him. Phipps looked unusually apprehensive and Mina realised that neither he nor she really knew how low Mr Hope might stoop in the pursuit of his obsession. Mr Hope might be risking his reputation by his own actions, but Mr Phipps could well be suffering from a sense of shame over something – his true parentage – that was in no way his fault.

'I come here,' began Hope, 'in a spirit of peace and reconciliation. I wish to be good friends with Miss Scarletti. Few ladies of my acquaintance rank higher in my estimation, few have earned so much of my respect in so short a time. It pains me therefore to find that Miss Scarletti is so opposed in every way to Miss Eustace, who is a lady of exceptional talents, and it is my greatest wish to bring them together in harmony and friendship. I should mention that I am here only on behalf of Miss Eustace and have nothing to do with the gentlemen currently under arrest. She has been most dreadfully led astray by others and cannot be held to account for any doubtful proceedings, for which she is entirely blameless. It is this misunderstanding that has led to Miss Scarletti attributing to Miss Eustace the iniquity of her former associates. My mission is to see that matters are put right.'

'Miss Scarletti, would you like to comment?' asked Mr Phipps.

'I would. With respect to Miss Eustace's claims to be a spirit medium and Mr Hope's request that I sign a statement, I had wondered if it was possible to arrive at a form of words that would satisfy all parties, but now that Mr Hope has presented me with this document I can see that we are very far from that. All the evidence of my senses has proved to me beyond any doubt that Miss Eustace's supposed mediumship is a fraud. I cannot therefore sign a paper to attest to any other point of view, and neither will I retract any of my past statements on that subject or apologise to Miss Eustace for any of my words or actions. If a paper such as this one should emerge in the future which has my signature on it then I declare it now to be a forgery.' Mr Hope's expression was severe. 'There is one more thing. I am supposed to declare that I have not been offered any inducement. This is untrue. It has been suggested to me by Mr Hope that Miss Eustace intends to accuse Miss Whinstone of committing perjury; a very serious matter. Mr Hope intimated to me in a private conversation that if I would sign a paper sympathetic to Miss Eustace then she would be willing to abandon that defence and propose only that Miss Whinstone had been mistaken and confused.'

'I deny that, of course!' thundered Hope indignantly.

'Mr Hope has recently been trying to persuade other residents of Brighton to sign similar testimonials by telling them that I have already agreed to do so.'

'I deny that also!'

'I will not sign this paper and I confess that at present I am unable to see what Mr Hope could ask me to sign that I would find acceptable.'

'I believe you have your answer,' said Mr Phipps, 'and given Miss Scarletti's opinions on the issue I would strongly advise her not to sign, even if she had any inclination to do so, which clearly she does not.'

Hope stared at the paper and was deep in thought. 'Very well,' he growled. 'I can see I will get no further with this. You are set against Miss Eustace and you are also set against other celebrated mediums who you have never even met.'

'Including the Misses Bland who refuse to meet me.'

'Are they mediums?' asked Phipps.

'They purport to be. I feel sure that their defence against the charge of plagiarism will be that they dreamed the book or it was dictated to them by a spirit, or, since the writing is not theirs, that a ghost actually appeared and wrote it all down for them. Maybe Mystic Stefan's disembodied hand wrote it after visiting them by flying through a wall. They will find such claims impossible to prove; in fact, it will be hard for them not to be laughed out of court.'

'Such things do happen!' Hope insisted. 'They do! I know it! You should not ridicule what you do not understand!'

'A court of law will take a very materialistic view of the matter,' said Phipps drily.

Mr Hope was displeased but pensive. 'Supposing,' he said suddenly, 'that the Misses Bland were to agree to meet privately with Miss Scarletti. Supposing they were to offer convincing proof that they receive information from the spirit world?' He turned to Mina. 'What do you say? Is your mind closed to that possibility?'

'Not closed, of course not. Let them meet me and prove it, and I will say I am convinced.'

'Then that is decided,' said Hope, rising to his feet. 'I have nothing more to say until this event has taken place. I wish you both good day.' He departed at once and there the meeting ended.

Mina was left considering how she might best warn Enid of her danger without also warning Mr Hope, since anything the detective might achieve could do some good if it did not involve her sister.

'Enid,' she said, when they were next alone, 'please reassure me that you are not meeting with Mr Hope in a situation which might be misconstrued.'

'What is it to you what friends I have or where I meet them?' said Enid, with a frown of annoyance.

'Well, you know what the gossips are like. However innocent it might be, if you choose to take tea with a man they will make it into something it is not. Think of what that would do to mother. I am not saying you cannot speak to him, only it might be best if you did not do so unaccompanied.'

Enid laughed. 'Do you know mother thinks he admires her? He doesn't at all, but he is kind to her because of me.'

'At least mother is single. Have you considered what Mr Inskip might think?'

'Oh bother Mr Inskip! May he be eaten by wolves and an end of him!' Enid flounced out of the room.

Thirty-Three

'Well,' said Richard as he, Mina, Marcus Merridew and Nellie were seated around a table in a private booth at one of Brighton's smartest restaurants, 'here is another setback. I am now missing a performer. Rolly Rollason has written to say that he cannot after all be Napoleon in my play! He has been ornamenting the London stage to very great acclaim, where it appears that he is the only man in England, and quite possibly the world, who can play the bagpipes while riding a velocipede. The crowds have been roused to madness at the sight of him in a kilt and he has been engaged for the remainder of the season.'

The waiter arrived and Nellie ordered champagne with a nod to the company to indicate that the expense would be on her account, or to be more accurate, her husband's. 'Can he not recommend another man?'

'There is a difficulty about that, too, since those he had in mind all require to know how many performances they are to be engaged for and require fees enough to cover the train fare to Brighton and board and lodgings.'

'It is a sad fact that actors need to eat in order to perform, or the business of theatrical management would be so much simpler,' said Merridew.

'I don't suppose you could attempt it, Mina?' pleaded Richard.

'No I could not! I think it will be quite enough of a shock for mother to see you on stage without having me appear in a breeches part. And the sword fight you plan would be very brief.'

'Might I make a suggestion?' said Mr Merridew. 'As you are all aware I am a professional actor of many years' experience. I would be willing, in return for a share in the ticket price, to perform in your play. Indeed, I do flatter myself that my name on the playbill will create some interest. You might even make a profit on the enterprise. It is not unknown.'

'Oh that is a very kind offer and of course I accept!' said Richard, eagerly. The champagne arrived, as did a dish of savoury tartlets, and toasts were drunk to theatrical success.

'I also have some items of costume and wigs I could lend to you to improve the appearance of the piece – they have had some use but will look perfectly splendid from a distance – and some blunted stage swords for the fight. Many years ago I toured with a company that performed *King Lear* in the style of the court of George III and still retain some of the ensembles, which will suit the setting of the Pavilion perfectly. The play had of course been banned from public performance during His Majesty's unfortunate affliction, but in later years it enjoyed a considerable revival. I was Edgar. It was very affecting.'

Nellie smiled. 'I know that our work on the stage is different but yours is a name known and held in great respect by all in the theatre. In fact, I have heard you spoken of as the handsomest man who ever trod the boards.'

'Oh my dear,' said Merridew with a little gasp of pleasure, 'how happy it is to be remembered. Yes, I was terribly good looking as a youth. My hair, my poor long-gone hair, was the most delicate shade of auburn and fell almost to my shoulders in ringlets. It sparkled like gold in the footlights and all the ladies sighed to see it. And oh, the many little gifts I received, the sweetmeats and nosegays, not to mention the love notes, it is astonishing that my head was not turned by the admiration.'

A large platter arrived, the very best fruits of the sea, prettily garnished, and they all fell to. More champagne was ordered, and while the ladies sipped theirs with decorum the gentlemen more than made up for their restraint. The gentlemen drank to the ladies, the ladies replied to the gentlemen and they all raised their glasses to William Shakespeare.

'There is just one little condition, if I might mention it,' said Merridew, when the platter and a third bottle of champagne were both empty. 'While I would be exceedingly happy to act in the play, I believe I would be better suited to play the Prince. I have a costume that would do very well and even with the advance of years it fits me to perfection. And of course my admirers do expect me to take the leading role.'

Richard looked a little disappointed for a moment, then quickly rallied. 'Well, why not? I am sure I could be Napoleon. I can speak a lot of nonsense in French.'

'In any language,' said Mina.

'After all,' said Marcus Merridew with a smile as the iced desserts were served, 'the play's the thing.'

Mina had received a note from Mr Hope confirming that she could meet the Bland sisters in a private room at the Royal Albion Hotel. She met the news with keen anticipation, but this was tinged with concern. Mr Hope knew that Lady Finsbury had been portrayed by an actress. It was not beyond his guile to present her with two impostors, ladies who were professional mediums of his acquaintance, adept in the art of illusion. Mr Hope, however, did not know that she had some useful information concerning the appearance of the sisters.

Mina arrived in good time, and after making enquiries at the reception desk, was directed to a smartly appointed meeting room. Smelling strongly of polish, it was furnished with comfortable seating and a side table held a vase of fresh flowers, a tray of glasses and a carafe of water. She took a seat and waited. After a few minutes there was a knock at the door and

Mr Hope entered accompanied by two ladies. Mina rose to her feet and studied the ladies carefully. Neither was of uncommon size, although one was a little taller and more slender than the other, and both had good figures giving the impression that they were not very aged. They were well dressed, although not extravagantly so, with neat lace gloves and light bonnets, but both wore their veils forward.

'Good day to you,' said Mr Hope in a very formal manner approaching coolness. 'Allow me to introduce Miss Ada Bland,' here the taller lady inclined her head, 'and Miss Bertha Bland.' The shorter lady greeted Mina in the same fashion. 'Ladies, I would be delighted for you to make the acquaintance of Miss Mina Scarletti.' Despite his words, he looked far from delighted.

'It is my very great pleasure to meet you at last,' said Mina. She sat down and the ladies were seated side-by-side facing her. Mr Hope took a seat to one side where he could observe all of them. Mina had not anticipated that he would remain and would have preferred it had he not been present, but felt that as he had made all the arrangements, she could hardly insist that he withdraw.

Mina tried to see if there was anything about the Misses Bland she could recognise. Was Miss Ada, the taller of the two, the same lady she had seen outside the baths and who had fled from a meeting with her? It was possible. Mina noticed that Ada wore a thicker veil than her sister, plain and very dark so that no feature of her face could be seen. Miss Bertha's veil, however, was lace, worn more for modesty than outright concealment, although it still served to obscure her features. Unless a gross falsehood was being practised – and Mina still thought that under the circumstances it was very possible – these were the Bland sisters and the lady with the heavier veil was the one who habitually wore it to conceal some defect in her appearance.

'The purpose of this meeting, as I understand it,' said Miss Bertha Bland, 'is to enable us to make a demonstration of our small abilities. You must excuse us as we are far from being developed in that way, but we believe that with time we may become better.' The quality of her voice and pronunciation were that of an educated young woman, but although her words were modest there was a hardness in the tone which suggested that she could not easily be confused or swayed.

'How would you describe these abilities?' asked Mina.

'We can read minds. Not all minds, but we can certainly see into each other's as we are sisters. This is something we have been able to do from a very early age. When we were children we thought nothing of it, as I suppose in our innocence we thought that all sisters could do the same. In our family it was treated as a parlour trick and we often performed it for the amusement of visitors. It was only later that we discovered that it was something quite out of the common way.'

'Would it be possible for you to provide me with a demonstration?' said Mina. 'You would not find that my presence hinders the operation of your powers?'

'We are stronger when we read each other. If you could open your mind to the idea that we can do this, quell all negative thoughts, dismiss your doubts, then I think we can be assured of success.'

'I will do my best,' Mina promised. She glanced at Ada, who remained silent and motionless, then at Mr Hope, who was watching closely.

Miss Bertha drew a small packet from her reticule. 'It is usually done with playing cards. Please examine them. You will see that this is a normal set of cards.'

She rose to bring the cards to Mina, and as she bent to hand them over, her proximity enabled Mina to see some of the outline of the face beneath the veil. In a flash of recognition, Mina felt sure that Miss Bertha Bland was the sharp-featured lady who had attended Mystic Stefan's demonstration and been the one person in the audience not astounded by his tricks.

What, wondered Mina, was the connection? Were the two related in some way – confederates – or merely friends? Or was she simply there as a guest of Mr Hope, her reaction that of someone in the same business – the art of illusion?

Mina slid the cards from their packet and examined them. Having been assured that they were normal cards she had to wonder what an abnormal set might be. Was there some trick by which a magician might be able to read the face of a card from a secret marking on the back? What signs should she be looking for? As far as she was able to see it was the usual full deck with all the suits, but she also glanced at the backs and saw nothing out of the ordinary. Her fingers found both sides smooth to the touch. She went to hand them back, but the lady, who had returned to her seat, declined.

'Now, Miss Scarletti, you must draw a card from the pack, but hold it close, making quite sure that I cannot see it. I will turn my back so you can be certain that I do not know which card you drew. Remember which card it is, then hand it and the pack to my sister, who will memorise and replace it. I will then read my sister's mind and tell you which card it was.'

'Very well,' said Mina. Miss Bertha rose and moved to the side of the room, her back turned so that she faced away from both her sister and Mina. There were no mirrors in the room, but all the same Mina, to be quite sure, also rose and turned away. She was especially careful that Mr Hope should not see what she did, as she would not put it past him to be their confederate, her attention so focussed on preventing the Misses Bland from seeing the card that she did not take his presence into account. When she was satisfied that she could not be overlooked, she drew a card – the six of diamonds – laid it carefully on top of the pack, then, still ensuring that Hope could not see the card, approached Miss Ada Bland, who had also risen to her feet. Mina handed her the cards and she held them close to her veil the better to see, nodded, and replaced the exposed card in the pack. Although Mina was close to the lady, the veil was so thick that the wearer's features could not be seen through it.

'There,' said Mina, 'it is done.'

Miss Bertha turned to face her sister and pressed her fingers to her forehead. There were a few moments of silence, during which she appeared to be making a great effort, then she said, 'I believe I am beginning to see it. Yes, it is a red card – I am sure I am right.' No one spoke and Mina tried not to give anything away by her expression. There was another pause. 'I can see the suit, now – it is – diamonds. And now the number – yes, I can see it all, it is the six. Am I correct?'

'You are,' said Mina.

'Do you wish for another demonstration?'

'If that would not be too much trouble.'

The trick was repeated and once again Miss Bertha identified the card.

'I suppose you would like to know how it is done. It is really quite simple – at least it is to us. My sister thinks about the card and I then look into her thoughts, and the card appears to me as if I was seeing it myself.'

'Can you read things other than cards?' asked Mina. 'Supposing I drew a picture of something in my notebook and showed it to Miss Ada – would you be able to tell what it was? Could you draw a copy of it?'

Mr Hope leaned forward and was about to speak, but Mina held up her hand. 'If you please, I wish only Miss Bland to answer that question.' Hope looked displeased but said nothing.

'As I have said,' replied Bertha, 'our powers are not yet fully developed. I could not guarantee success.'

'I suppose that would be a far harder thing to achieve.'

'It would.'

Mina turned to Miss Ada Bland. 'Forgive me, but I am concerned that you have been silent so far.'

'Please do not ask her to speak,' said Bertha quickly. 'I say all for both of us.'

Mina looked back at Ada, who nodded her head.

'Might I ask the reason for this?'

'My dear sister has a defect in her speech. Please spare her. If she objected to anything I have said for us both so far she would have made it known.'

Ada nodded again.

'Very well,' said Mina, addressing Bertha once more. 'Can you tell me how you came to write *An Encounter*? Was it through mind-reading?'

'I do not think it was intended that you should broach that subject at this meeting,' interrupted Mr Hope.

'No?' said Mina. 'I don't recall any such agreement. In any case, I was given to understand that the purpose of this interview was for me to be presented with proof of mind-reading.'

'And have you not seen proof enough?' demanded Hope.

'I will give that question some consideration. But further information will assist me.'

'I have no objection to answering,' said Bertha. 'There is still much about that incident that we do not understand. We both dreamed about the book before the words came to us. It was as if we were there ourselves, in that extraordinary palace, which neither of us had ever visited. We always talk about our dreams, and wonder what they might mean, but we have never before experienced the identical dream on the same night. We knew at once that this must mean something, but we could not tell what it might be. We decided that in future as soon as we awoke we should write down everything we remembered of our dreams as quickly as we could. When we dreamed again, a voice came to us, asking us to listen to it and write down what it said. We didn't know what to make of it, but next day, when we were both quite wide awake, we were both suddenly seized with the desire to write, and so we did. Imagine our amazement when our pens travelled across the paper, quite undirected by either of us, and the words just came. Not only that but the writing was not in the usual hand of either of us. At last we compared notes and found that although we had not written the same thing, when we put the pages in order we had a single book.'

'Did you show it to anyone?'

'No. It was so strange we didn't know what anyone might make of it – or indeed, us.'

'Why did you decide to have it published?'

'It seemed to be the right thing to do. Why else would the story have come to us? Surely it was not intended for my sister and I alone, but for the world?'

'Despite the passages that are held to be indecent?'

'You must believe me, neither of us know which those passages might be. We have been told that there are some portions which might be read in that way, but we prefer not to enquire further.'

'How can you explain the charge of plagiarism?'

'I think you have gone far enough!' said Hope, rising to his feet.

'Mr Hope, I was afraid when you remained here that you would object to my questions, but can't you see that all these matters are part and parcel of the same thing?'

'I do not!'

'We cannot explain the charges at all,' said Bertha. 'We have no knowledge of any other book describing a similar event. As far as we are aware we have copied nothing.'

'And this is to be your defence if the case goes to court?' asked Mina.

'I doubt that it will go so far. We expect that all will be settled quietly without recourse to a public airing.'

'That is as well since you will not be able to prove you received the book through a dream.'

'No one can prove we ever went to the Royal Pavilion or saw a similar book.'

'I think,' broke in Mr Hope firmly, rising to his feet, 'it would be advisable to end this interview now.'

'As you wish,' said Mina.

'You must be aware that the time is fast approaching when I must press you for a decision on the document. You have two days. That is all.' He conducted the Misses Bland from the room, his words ringing in Mina's ears like a declaration of war.

Thirty-Four

Next morning, once breakfast was done, Louisa and Enid went out on one of their shopping expeditions to which Mina was never invited, since it went without saying that she would inevitably hinder their progress, spoil their enjoyment and was in any case deemed to have no interest in fashion. The twins were left in the care of Anderson, and Richard had just risen sleepily from his bed and was exploring the kitchen for leftovers of the family breakfast. Mina tried to settle to her writing, but her thoughts kept straying to the demonstration by the Misses Bland. While she could not by her own efforts devise how they had performed their mind-reading trick she recalled that Nellie, in the guise of the Ethiopian Wonder, had achieved something very similar when assisting Monsieur Baptiste, and determined to place the question before her.

Mina had not expected Mr Hope to call so soon after the meeting for a private discussion, and was therefore surprised when the doorbell rang and Rose came to announce the visitor.

'Yes, admit him to the parlour and fetch my brother to me,' said Mina, hoping that his call meant that something at least might be resolved.

Rose looked relieved that she was not to stand duty as witness again. There was some delay while Richard, devouring a toasted muffin into which he had thrust a cold fried egg and some bacon, was apprised of the situation, carelessly flung on some halfway respectable clothes and conducted Mina to the parlour, where Mr Hope awaited them.

'Thank you for agreeing to see me,' said Hope, in a milder tone than he had adopted the day before. 'I feel I should apologise for becoming a little overwrought at the interview with the Misses Bland. It is hard when one can see so clearly the great shining light of an eternal truth and find that others who are far from ignorant and worthy of respect cannot see it and refuse even to make the attempt. Have you arrived at a conclusion?'

'All I saw was a very pretty trick with cards. It reminded me of nothing more than the mind-reading acts of stage magicians.'

'Then I hope you found it impressive? They and the stage magicians you mention are all adept at that skill. It is really quite marvellous!'

Richard was lounging in an armchair, toying with his cigar case. Mina gave him a warning look, as their mother would never permit him to smoke in the parlour, and he returned it to his pocket. 'Have you ever witnessed the Ethiopian Wonder?' he asked.

'Indeed I have,' said Hope, enthusiastically, 'I take an interest in all practitioners of that nature. She has the most extraordinary perception. If I could only persuade her to hold a séance I feel sure the results would be astounding!'

'You see I have spoken to the lady, in fact I know her very well and she has taken me into her confidence. She has admitted to me that she has no psychic abilities and her act was all down to a clever feat of memory. Her partner, Monsieur Baptiste,' Richard explained to Mina, 'first blindfolded her, then he took items from the pockets of members of the audience and asked her to identify them. Every time, she was able to describe what object he was holding.'

'Exactly,' said Hope, 'how could she have guessed?'

'Quite easily with a little preparation. There is only a limited selection of things one might have in one's pockets, and there was a secret form of words for each. I am sure the Misses Bland have their own method of passing messages to each other.'

Hope chuckled. 'I am sorry to say that so many of our conjurors claim their work is only a trick. Some cannot recognise their abilities, which they undoubtedly have, and so they go on performing their acts and forever denying what God has given them. A few, unhappily, know exactly what it is they do and yet prefer to perform for their own advantage rather than use their gifts as they were intended to. The Misses Bland may not understand their powers but I am pleased to say they do not deny them.'

'What about Dr Lynn, who introduced you to Mystic Stefan, is he also deluding himself?'

'Lynn is a friend, and a splendid fellow in many respects. I know that in time he will come to see the true way. He thinks he knows how he performs his wonders, but what he achieves is quite impossible without the intervention of spirits. Miss Scarletti, can you now believe on the evidence of your own eyes that the Misses Bland are genuine? Would you be prepared to certify that? You may word the certificate in any way you please.'

'My eyes told me that I saw an interesting trick, but I certainly cannot attest on that basis that I believe the Misses Bland to have spiritualistic abilities. I am also concerned that if I signed any such document it would be used to defend them against the charge of plagiarism. It might even be used in the defence of Miss Eustace in an attempt to show that I have changed my mind on the subject.'

Hope's sudden hard frown told Mina that her last surmise had hit home.

'Why do you champion that woman – she is such a transparent fraud!' demanded Richard.

Mr Hope shook his head very emphatically. 'She is no fraud! I know it! Oh I accept that spirit mediums attract the derision of the ignorant and blinkered, and they have learned to ignore such ill-judged criticism, but to threaten a virtuous lady with prison only for practising her skills for the common good is outrageous. I wish to see her freed and achieve the recognition she deserves.'

'And you will achieve this by bringing her to Brighton to conduct a séance in the Pavilion?' asked Mina.

'That is my intention.'

'You are aware, are you not, that even if Miss Eustace was acquitted, she would not be allowed to hold a séance in the Pavilion? The committee are quite against such demonstrations.'

'They cannot be, since they allowed both Dr Lynn and Mystic Stefan to demonstrate there.'

'They are not mediums, they are conjurors.'

'I beg to differ. In any case,' Hope smiled confidently, 'I think I can persuade the committee to change their minds. It is my intention to bring the Misses Bland to the Pavilion, together with Mystic Stefan and the Wondrous Ajeeb. They and the spirit of Captain Pechell will create such a confluence of power that it will no longer be denied! Right will prevail. It is only a matter of time.'

He prepared to take his leave. 'Mr Scarletti, I wish you well with your play, which promises to be the first of many successes. Perhaps when I have departed you and your sister might discuss what I have said and with a little thought I am sure you will reconsider your position. Miss Scarletti, I am sorry to press you, but I must have your decision very soon. Please let your solicitor have the statement in writing by tomorrow.'

'Well,' said Richard, when their visitor had left, 'the Bland sisters, Mystic Stefan and the Wondrous Ajeeb, I should like to have tickets for that performance! It sounds like the playbill of a music hall. This business must be costing Mr Hope a pretty penny.'

'He is undoubtedly paying Miss Eustace's law costs, as well.'

'Yet he says he takes no profit from his books or lectures. All goes to the fund to rescue Dr Livingstone. Is he very rich?'

'You know who he is?'

'Er — no.'

'He prefers to go by plain "Mr" but he is actually Viscount Hope, owner of a substantial estate in Middlesex, and from what I have heard he is not one of those impoverished noblemen barely able to maintain appearances but a very wealthy man. His standing in society, his resources and his history, which cannot be denied, make him powerfully placed to overcome any opposition.' Mina refreshed herself with some mineral water, though Richard looked as though he wanted something stronger and she could hardly blame him. 'I am doing my best to fight him, but I don't know how much longer I can go on. I am constantly under attack, first on behalf of Miss Eustace, then on behalf of the Misses Bland and next thing I will be asked to stand up in court and say that the Mystic Stefan is a medium and the Wondrous Ajeeb works through the power of the spirits.' Mina had deliberately not told Richard what she suspected about Enid and dreaded the prospect that Mr Hope might use the potential for a damaging scandal to blackmail her. 'Mr Phipps is trying to discover some weakness of Mr Hope's with which we can arm ourselves.'

'We all have weaknesses,' argued Richard, fingering the cigar case once more. 'Apart from mother who has none. I have a great many, I know, though I try not to let it worry me. Enid is vain, Edward is serious, you think too much, Mr Hope is gullible and Miss Eustace and her like are interested in nothing but money.'

'In that case I really can't see why Miss Eustace means to return to Brighton. She could never become rich here. Too many people remember her; she has a bad name. No one of any note would receive her and she certainly would not be allowed to hold a séance in the Pavilion.'

'I agree. Once she is free, and whatever happens at the trial she will be sooner or later, she would be far better advised to avoid Brighton altogether and make a new start with new victims somewhere else.'

'Then why come here? Whatever she is, Miss Eustace is not a fool.'

Richard laughed. 'No, if there is any fool, it is Mr Hope.'

'So maybe she has another purpose, another target, perhaps one that Mr Hope does not know about. Oh of course!' said

Mina with a sudden gasp of realisation. 'Why did I not see it! The real target is Mr Hope and his fortune. I have been too preoccupied with seeing him as the enemy to recognise that he is actually the victim. I am simply an instrument. He is the mark.'

Richard mused on this. 'I think you may be right. Of course, it would be useless to warn him.'

'Poor Mr Hope, I almost feel sorry for him, he is such an easy dupe. She works on his sympathy, presents herself as the injured party and not a criminal, and he buys her the best lawyers in the land. Once she is freed she will leech off his generosity for life. That is her scheme. Well he will learn his lesson the hard way.'

'If he ever learns it at all. But what do you mean to do?'

Mina knew she had to take a gamble that however misguided Mr Hope might be he was not actually wicked, and if necessary she could appeal to his better nature to preserve Enid's reputation. 'I will be true to myself. Mr Hope will never have a statement from me.'

Richard hugged her.

Thirty-Five

The following morning Mina received a note from Marcus Merridew stating that it might interest her to know that the Wondrous Ajeeb had arrived in Brighton and was currently in the process of being installed in the Pavilion where, at the express behest of Mr Hope, he would perform for a few days only. Mina, as Mr Merridew's special guest, might like to come and enjoy a private viewing. Mina was eager to see the famed automaton and presented herself at the Pavilion without delay. Mr Merridew greeted her in exuberant style and conducted her to the room usually hired for meetings of the Brighton Chess Club, where the Wondrous Ajeeb was to hold court.

As Mina was ushered into the room, leaning on Mr Merridew's arm, an attendant, who was bustling about making all the arrangements, looked up in surprise. He was a tidy-looking man with a deft fussy manner, his glossy dark hair straight to the point of perfection, and combed back over his scalp as if painted on with a wide brush.

'Mr Franklin,' said Merridew, 'I would like you to meet Miss Mina Scarletti, my very particular friend, who has come to satisfy her curiosity as to the Wondrous Ajeeb.'

'Delighted, and you are very welcome,' said Mr Franklin, who seemed from a change in expression to have made the assumption that Mina required this individual visit because she was too frail to mingle in a crowd. He stepped back so that she could enjoy a better view. The apartment was decorated in light green, and was less opulent than the other rooms of the Pavilion, quieter and more subtle. As a result the display stood out even more dramatically than it might have done in a more elaborate setting.

A screen had been arranged at the back of the room and lavishly draped with multi-coloured oriental fabrics to form a suitably exotic backdrop to the figure of the Wondrous Ajeeb. 'Is he not a great marvel?' enthused Mr Franklin. 'Have you ever seen the like?'

'Never,' said Mina. She did not ask if she might move closer, but did so, knowing that she would not be prevented. She had not expected such a large piece of machinery. The apparatus towered far above her head and must have been in all some ten feet in height. Its base was a square wooden cabinet mounted on castors, on top of which was an octagonal plinth covered in figured velvet in a rich shade of burgundy, beautifully fringed. There, sitting cross-legged upon a tasselled cushion, was the figure of Ajeeb, fully life-size, perhaps even greater. He was, to all appearances, a Turk, since his countenance, which bore a mild expression, suggesting wisdom and concentration, was burnished brown and his long beard was fashioned somewhat exotically in a double point. He wore wide silk scarlet trousers and soft slippers of the same shade, with vividly striped stockings and a loose chemise of pale blue, over which was a voluminous dark red coat. His turban and the brocade sash about his waist were gold. The hands and face looked as though they were made of carved painted wood, but the right hand, its fingers curled inwards, was hinged so that the thumb might be brought to the fingers to grasp objects.

As Mina took in every detail of this extraordinary machine, Mr Franklin placed the other parts of the display in place. A hookah was positioned to the figure's left and the tube with its mouthpiece put into the wooden hand. A pedestal with a circular top was placed to its right and on this rested a chessboard. On a side table was a basket of chess pieces, and another with draughts, while a third was filled with small white counters.

Mina gazed up into the enigmatic face of the Wondrous Ajeeb and he, through heavily lidded eyes, appeared to be staring down at her. 'I don't suppose I could ask how he is operated?' she asked. 'I understand he is very adept at chess.'

'Many people ask me that,' smiled Mr Franklin, 'but it is of course a great secret.'

'Why surely there is a man hidden inside,' exclaimed Merridew. 'He must be underneath, in the cabinet.'

'Not at all,' said Franklin, who, from his air had heard this suggestion many times. He stepped up to the figure and opened a door in the front of the cabinet. Mina and Mr Merridew peered inside, and Merridew even got down on his knees for a closer look, but the interior was filled with a profusion of rods, cords, pulleys and wheels. There was no room for a human operator.

'Then there is a man inside the figure itself,' said Merridew, getting back to his feet. 'It is large enough!'

Franklin merely smiled again and showed that part of the chemise concealed a door in the figure's chest. This he opened to reveal that inside the breast of the great Turk was still more machinery. Another door opened in the figure's back and it was possible to see all the way through.

Merridew took a tour about the figure, looking for some method by which a man might enter it. 'Perhaps the man is not yet inside. Ah, I know, the old theatrical trick, a trapdoor, he comes in from below.' He winked at Mina. 'The Pavilion is full of surprises.'

Mr Franklin, with some effort, moved the figure about on its castors, showing that the carpet below was entire. 'As you see, there are no trapdoors. All that is needed is this.' He took from his pocket a key of the kind used to wind up a very large clock. After returning the figure to its former position, and closing the doors in the cabinet and torso, he inserted the key into a keyhole that was hidden by the fringing of the plinth and proceeded to wind the mechanism, which made a loud grinding and clicking. 'Do you play chess?' he asked Mina.

'I am afraid I have never learnt the game,' Mina confessed.

Franklin stopped winding and stepped back, dropping the key into his pocket. 'I am sorry to hear it.' There was a creaking like the movement of hinges and metal joints, and slowly the Wondrous Ajeeb shook his wooden head from side to side. This action of the otherwise impassive figure created a strange effect, as if he was both alive and not alive at the same time. 'I think Ajeeb is sorry, too. It is the finest game in the world and an excellent occupation for the mind.' The metallic noise ground out again as this time Ajeeb nodded his head, sagely.

Mina looked at Mr Franklin, but he was too far from the Turk to have created the movements. 'I hope that Ajeeb does not pretend to bring messages from the spirits,' she said. 'There has been too much of that in Brighton recently.'

'No, he only plays chess and draughts. Let him show you what he can do.'

Franklin fetched the basket of chess pieces but instead of setting them out for a game, he placed only one piece on the board, a white knight, which he put in a square in the row nearest the Turk. 'The chess knight has an unusual move, unlike that of any other piece. He goes in the shape of a letter L, two squares one way, and then one at an angle, like so.' He demonstrated. 'It is possible to move the knight all about the board but going to a different square each time, so that he visits every square on the board once and once only. Sixty-four squares and sixty-three moves.' Franklin placed the knight back on its starting square and stepped away. 'Wondrous Ajeeb I beg you to demonstrate the knight's tour.'

Ajeeb obligingly leaned forward from the waist, an action accompanied by the sound of rotating cogwheels, and stretched out his arm. Then, grasping the knight in his right hand, he lifted it and placed it on another square. Franklin had picked up the basket of white counters, and now he came forward and placed one on the square just vacated. This sequence of actions was repeated, move-by-move, and as Mina and Merridew watched, the board began to fill with white counters, each one on a different square, until finally the knight reached the last unoccupied square and the board was full.

'Oh bravo!' exclaimed Merridew. 'I can't say how it is done, but it is a wonder.'

Ajeeb favoured him with a polite bow, then lifted the hookah pipe to his mouth as if to say that his work was complete.

'How marvellous!' Mina agreed. 'Whether done by man or machine it is very impressive. And does Ajeeb win every game he undertakes?'

'Very nearly,' said Franklin, 'but he is gracious in defeat. The only thing that angers him is an opponent who breaks the rules or tries to cheat. I have seen Ajeeb put an end to such games by sweeping all the pieces from the board.'

'Does he speak?'

'Alas, no, he expresses himself only through gesture.'

'Will Ajeeb be performing for the public? I have seen nothing advertised.'

'He has been brought here at very short notice so there has not been time to advertise his visit in the newspapers. But some placards have been prepared which will be placed in the vestibule. He will entertain the paying public this evening and tomorrow afternoon, and then tomorrow evening there will be a private performance for the Mayor and aldermen and other specially invited guests.'

'My thanks to you good sir for the demonstration,' said Merridew. He glanced about him. 'Would you be so kind as to tell me where we might find Mr Mott of the Brighton Chess Club? I know he is in the Pavilion today as I saw him arrive earlier and rather fancied I might find him here.'

Franklin gave an innocent smile. 'I can't say, I am afraid. Perhaps he is having tea.'

'Or smoking a pipe,' suggested Merridew. 'Well, Miss Scarletti and I will retire to the tea room for now. I am sure we will have the opportunity of speaking to Mr Mott later. He may well join us there.'

'So you think Mr Mott was inside Ajeeb?' asked Mina once she and Merridew were on their way back to the vestibule.

'I think this is how all these things work if they do anything out of the ordinary that cannot be achieved by mere clockwork, otherwise why is it so very large? The original Turk was only a figure of a man from the waist up, and no one could have fitted inside, but it rested on a very much bigger cabinet.'

'But we looked inside the cabinet and the figure and saw only machinery.'

'Oh, I expect a great deal can be achieved with false doors and mirrors. Did you ever see the head of the Sphinx?'

'No, but I have heard of it.'

'It was a disembodied head sitting on a table, telling fortunes. Of course there was a living man underneath, putting his head through a hole in the table-top, but his body could not be seen as there were mirrors under the table so placed that they deceived the audience into thinking they could see right through to the back of the stage.'

'Both simple and clever,' observed Mina, thinking of Mystic Stefan's miraculous disembodied arm.

'All the best tricks are.'

'Do you happen to know what kind of entertainment Mr Hope is planning to give the Mayor and aldermen? I know he has brought Ajeeb to the Pavilion with the idea of having in one place all the elements that resulted in the visions said to have happened here. On that day, as described in *An Encounter*, there was Ajeeb and Dr Lynn the conjuror – who Mr Hope insists is a medium – demonstrating his Japanese butterfly illusion. The Mystic Stefan who performs the same miracle will be a suitable substitute for Dr Lynn. Then there is Mr Hope's former comrade Captain Pechell, whose presence he senses hovering over the statue and who he seems to think of as a spirit guide. He is also bringing the Misses Bland who do a kind of parlour trick, a mind-reading game with cards. Surely he can't imagine that the sisters might have another curious experience. Well, when I say "another" it is probable that they did not have one in the first place.'

'Did they not copy their book from another's work? That's what the newspapers say.'

'I think they did, but that is for a court to decide. Mr Hope would find it better to invite the person who wrote the plagiarised book, but no one knows who he or she is.'

'Well, the public events are not of his doing, they are under the auspices of the Pavilion. It is only the last display where he is overseeing the arrangements.'

'And I think I suspect what he might be doing. I can't prove it, of course, but it is possible that he is intending to hold a private séance under the guise of an entertainment. He has invited the Mayor and aldermen so they can witness the miracles performed, his intention being that they would then be prepared to give evidence in favour of the Misses Bland. Of course he will not have dared to describe the event as a séance or the committee would have objected, but that is what it will be, and if Mystic Stefan is the conjuror I think he is, he will be able to produce some very convincing illusions.'

'Has he not invited you?'

'I am afraid not.'

'But you said he has been trying to convince you of spiritualism.'

'He has. And that can only lead me to one conclusion. He is deliberately excluding me in case my presence exerts a negative influence and the spirits are unable to perform. That means that he has finally given up all attempts to convert me to his way of thinking and from now on I must consider him an enemy.'

Merridew looked dismayed. 'Well, we must do something!'

'I wish I knew what. I could try and gain entry to the event and observe it, but attempting to disrupt the séance by seizing the apparitions would not be the answer.'

'I should think not!' said Merridew with a gentle smile.

'I tried doing that before with Miss Eustace and it didn't work.'

'Oh, I see.'

'And such a desperate action would be playing right into Mr Hope's hands. He has already been making enquiries to try and prove that I am mad or hysterical.'

'But nothing could be further from the truth!'

'It will look very like the truth if I create a disturbance in front of the Mayor and aldermen. Mr Hope might be half wishing I will do so, and then I would be taken away in a strait-waistcoat before I knew it.'

'Well,' said Mr Merridew, thoughtfully, 'let us have a cup of tea and make a plan. And I feel sure that we do not need to search for Mr Mott. He will know where to find us.'

Thirty-Six

'It is a pity we do not know who wrote the original piece, the one that has been plagiarised,' said Mr Merridew, as he and Mina refreshed themselves with tea. 'I have not read it myself, but from what the *Gazette* says it was beyond reproach.'

'My feeling is that it was a story rather than a history,' said Mina, thoughtfully. 'Part of it is true. A lady visited the Pavilion in the days before there were guides and as she explored it alone, she got lost. But then, enthralled by its air of mystery and romance, she thought what an amusing adventure it would be if she met its royal owner.'

'It is very easy to become lost and confused without a guide,' said Merridew, knowingly. 'When one thinks of the number of times the Pavilion has been enlarged and altered, and then there are doors which are not actually doors at all, and real doors that don't look like doors, and long passages that run secretly alongside the main apartments to enable servants to walk about discreetly without bothering their masters.'

'You must show me them. That might well inspire me to write a ghost story myself.'

Mr Mott appeared soon afterwards, looking a little warm, as if he had been exerting himself, and joined Mina and Mr Merridew at the tea table. He was a small man, not a great deal over five feet in height, with a narrow body and the kind of whiskers that suggested he would be better advised to be clean shaven. If he was trying to look older and more authoritative by growing whiskers then he had, thought Mina, made an all-too-common error. Nevertheless, he was pleasant and polite and greeted Mina warmly when they were introduced, saying that he was charmed to meet any intimate friend of Mr Merridew.

'I am told that you entertain a great fascination for the Wondrous Ajeeb and have seen him play chess often,' said Mina.

'Oh, yes,' exclaimed Mott with all the eagerness of a devotee, 'I have lost no opportunity to watch and learn.'

'Have you formed an opinion as to how the mechanism is able to play chess so well without the assistance of a human operator?' asked Mina, signalling the waiter to bring a fresh pot of tea.

Mott paused and licked his lips nervously. 'Ah, well, I really couldn't say. I know nothing of clockwork devices, they are a mystery to me. My expertise, such as it is, lies in the art of chess.'

'I have been told by Mr Franklin, who I am sure you must know, that there will be a special demonstration given before the Mayor and aldermen tomorrow evening. Will you be in attendance?'

Mott's expression continued to be wary and anxious. 'I think,' he ventured carefully, 'that it is very probable that I will be there, yes.'

'In that case, since I am not one of Mr Hope's guests, I must entreat your assistance in a matter of some difficulty.'

'Oh, but surely you will be there? It is all over town that Mr Hope is a very particular friend of your family.'

'The town does not know everything. I have not received an invitation and suspect that if I asked to attend it would not be permitted. I must let you into a secret, Mr Mott. I am concerned – very much concerned – that Mr Hope, who is the guiding light behind this private display, will be attempting, quite against the rules and wishes of the Pavilion committee, to hold a séance. I have said nothing, as I have no proof, only suspicions, but if you are there I would like you to observe what happens and then report back to me. Would you be prepared to do that?'

Mott looked surprised, then he became thoughtful. 'That explains a great deal,' he said at last. 'I have noticed that ever since Ajeeb arrived there have been preparations in hand for the private event, which were markedly different from the public displays and those at his last appearance here. The conjuror Mystic Stefan has been involved in the arrangements, although I am not sure how, and a large trunk has been delivered which is locked and guarded from general view. I have also heard that Mr Hope actually asked the committee if the statue of Captain Pechell could be moved to the room where the event is to take place, but he has been told it is not possible due to its weight and the danger of damage. Instead it is agreed that a portrait of the Captain will be hung there. What all this has to do with chess I am not sure, but he is very clearly not about to present the usual demonstration.'

'None of it has anything to do with chess I am afraid,' said Mina, and explained to Mr Mott what she thought Mr Hope's intentions were.

'He believes that Ajeeb is operated by disembodied spirits?' said Mott, incredulously.

'I am afraid he does.'

'Well now I have heard everything. There are very few persons who know precisely how the Wondrous Ajeeb performs, but all are sworn to secrecy and cannot enlighten him.'

'I doubt that he would believe them, in any case.'

The teapot arrived with a plate of scones that Mina could not recall ordering. 'My treat,' said Merridew with a wink.

Mr Mott was too troubled to eat. 'And you say that Mr Hope actually champions the Misses Bland? How could he? My sister read their dreadful book in all innocence and was so upset that she has been under treatment from her doctor ever since. And didn't they copy the work of another? They should be in prison!'

'If Mr Hope has his way they will be exonerated of all blame and will reap the financial rewards of their deceit,' said Mina.

'Well, we can't have that,' declared Mott. 'Miss Scarletti, I am extremely grateful for your warning. I shall alert the committee at once.'

'Do you think they would put a stop to the event?' asked Merridew. 'The man is a Viscount, after all. And as Miss Scarletti has said we have no actual proof of what he intends to do. If challenged, he might simply say that he is providing an entertainment to honour the memory of his late comrade in arms. Since the Misses Bland are friends of his then it would not be a matter of surprise if they were invited.'

'And I would be made to seem like a hysteric,' added Mina. 'I am far from hysterical but Mr Hope would like to prove that I am in order to assist in the defence of Miss Eustace, who he also champions.'

Mott was horrified. 'That conniving woman! I am ashamed to admit that I actually attended one of her séances, mainly because my mother insisted I go. It was all a great deal of nonsense of course, and I was not at all surprised when she was arrested. She comes from a whole family of conjurors, you know. In fact, she was the only visitor to the Pavilion who saw at once how Ajeeb performed his feats.'

'Ah, the trained eye of the illusionist,' said Merridew.

'I suggest,' advised Mina, 'that we do not try to prevent the private demonstration from occurring. I might be wrong about it, but if I am right I would hope that the Mayor and aldermen, being men of common sense, will not be deceived. If you could simply observe and let me know what actually takes place, I would be very grateful. Then I will consider the position and think again.'

'Very well, I agree,' said Mott.

The scones were finally finished and tea-time service was ending for the day. Waiters were darting about busily sweeping dishes from the tables and Mr Merridew peered hopefully into the teapot to see if one last cup might remain to round things off. Mr Mott rose to depart, saying that he was going to make a close observation of that evening's public performance of the Wondrous Ajeeb. It was as he walked away that a realisation struck Mina. 'Mr Mott,' she called, leaving her seat as fast as she could and limping after him, 'pray Mr Mott, do come back – I have something very important to ask you!'

He stopped and looked back at her with some surprise, as if the suggestion of hysteria was not after all so very wide of the mark, and Mr Merridew quickly appeared by her side and carefully took her arm for support.

'I may have misheard you of course,' Mina continued, 'but did you just say that Miss Eustace was the only visitor to the Pavilion who realised how Ajeeb worked?'

'Yes, that is correct.'

'But Ajeeb has not been here since last October – or has he?'

'No, you are quite right, Miss Eustace saw him when he was here last year.'

This was a surprise to Mina. 'I had been under the impression that her arrival in the summer of this year was her first time in Brighton. Of course I can see that she might well have made a preliminary visit to gather information about the residents to provide material for her séances and carefully concealed that fact. But you are quite sure it was she?'

'I am, yes.' Mott hesitated and looked about him but no one was close enough to overhear. 'I cannot say too much about the location I was in at the time that I observed her, only that I was in a position to see her but she was unable to see me.'

Mina nodded. 'I understand. You need say no more on that subject.'

'When she viewed the Wondrous Ajeeb she was very amused by him, and actually said that she could see how he performed his feats. I think she may have been accompanied by a gentleman, but I am not sure. Later that day I went to see Dr Lynn's demonstration of conjuring. He was giving an exhibition for charity and the same lady was there, I recognised her, and given her earlier comment I paid some attention to her demeanour. She watched all that Dr Lynn did with very keen attention, but not as someone might have done for the mere purpose of entertainment. She was studying him with the eye of one whose family profession was in that field. When Dr Lynn's performance was over she approached him and they had a conversation. I heard her say that her father was in that line of work, and he had a business providing materials and equipment to conjurors. She gave Dr Lynn a card. I thought, earlier this year, when Miss Eustace held her séances, that it was the same lady, but I couldn't be sure, so I said nothing at the time, but then when she was arrested it was in the newspapers and mention was made of her father's business, so I knew I must be right.'

'Mr Mott, I hope you won't be offended, but have you read *An Encounter*?'

He blushed. 'I – no – when I saw how upset my sister was I threw it on the fire.'

'Without reading it?'

'Naturally.'

'Like you, I have never read the book, but I understand from those who have, that the vision seen by the sisters was supposed to have taken place on the very day that you describe, the one day that Dr Lynn and the great Ajeeb were both at the Pavilion.'

'What can that mean?' asked Mr Merridew.

'I wish I knew. Mr Mott, please could you gather for me all the information at your disposal concerning what is planned to take place before the Mayor and aldermen, and then we will meet again.'

✳

Mina wrote to Mr Phipps to advise him of Mr Hope's ultimatum, saying that she would not under any circumstances comply. He replied stating that he agreed with her position and was watching the case for her. He had attempted to obtain an appointment with Mr Hope to try and reach an amicable agreement, but that gentleman was currently too busy with the arrangements for the event to be held at the Pavilion to be able to attend. Mina realised to her relief that she had a short breathing space, but she knew she was in danger and would need every ounce of her limited strength for the battle to come.

On her next visit to the baths she undertook her callisthenics class under the watchful supervision of Anna Hamid. Anna sensed a new, grimmer determination and had to quell Mina's need to push her efforts too far into areas that would harm rather than develop her. 'You are making good progress,' she said, 'but you must not go too fast. I can see that the muscles in your back and shoulders are offering improved support for your spine, and your arms are far stronger. The walking you do will also, with care, strengthen your limbs and reduce the strain of movement.' As Mina rested from her efforts Anna explored with her fingers the areas of tension in her patient's back. 'You are very troubled, I can feel it. Is this still concerning Mr Hope and those dreadful women?'

'Yes. I see I can hide nothing from you. I was recently permitted an interview with the Misses Bland, but it was very strange indeed, and Mr Hope sat and watched and interrupted if he thought my questions too searching. They performed a parlour trick with cards to try and convince me that they had the power to read minds. I am sure they could not have read my mind on that occasion, which held far from flattering thoughts, although I did make it clear that I was not converted to their cause. Throughout the interview only one of the sisters, the shorter of the two who calls herself Bertha, spoke for both of them. Miss Ada was heavily veiled and said nothing at all. If I could only conduct a private interview with her, I think I would learn a great deal.'

Anna said nothing, but simply massaged Mina's back.

'Have you received an invitation to Mr Hope's demonstration at the Pavilion tomorrow?' Mina asked.

'We have but we are not inclined to go.'

'I would take it as a very great favour if you could both be present and observe the proceedings. I have not been invited and I fear that is no accident.'

Anna paused. 'Very well, I will speak to my brother about it.'

'Only I think Mr Hope has some strange plans afoot.'

'Strange in what way?'

Mina sensed that much as Anna felt she wanted nothing to do with Mr Hope and his mystical demonstrations, some interest had been aroused. She explained her concerns about the proposed event, and as she did so a new idea emerged. Mr Hope was not the only person who could make strange plans.

Once Mina was dressed and about to leave, Anna, after a struggle with her conscience, said, very quietly, 'The elder Miss Bland has an appointment with me tomorrow morning at ten o'clock. My brother will be seeing patients all day and will not be in his private office when she departs, so you may sit there. I did not tell you this.'

Thirty-Seven

Next morning, and with the Pavilion event due to take place later that evening, Mina presented herself at the baths and settled herself comfortably in the ladies' salon. Miss Ada Bland arrived for her appointment punctually at ten. Mina, partly hidden from her view in the depths of a large armchair, peeped out from behind a periodical and saw the distinctive figure pass quickly by. After that, it was just a matter of waiting. Mina, who had had another interview with Mr Mott only an hour before, had a great deal to think about. The all Sussex chess champion had been very diligent following their first meeting. Given his close involvement in the planned event, a certain amount of prying had not aroused any suspicion in either Mr Hope or Mystic Stefan. Mott had told Mina that he had overheard a conference between the two in which the conjuror had reassured his patron that he could sense that the spiritual forces were very powerful in the Pavilion, and promised to produce some remarkable manifestations. The one thing that they were both agreed upon very emphatically was that on no account must Mina be admitted. If she attempted to take a place amongst the company, she would be politely but firmly removed. If she caused a disturbance, however, then other arrangements would have to be made and she could well find herself placed under the care of doctors.

Mina knew approximately how long Miss Bland's appointment might take, and once it came near to the time, she listened for each creak of a door. Finally she was rewarded, went to the entrance of the salon, and, seeing her quarry, emerged to accost her in the corridor. There was an audible intake of breath as Miss Bland stopped, then tried to move around and past Mina.

Fortunately the passage was narrow enough for Mina to be able to interpose her slight form in the lady's path, trusting that she might be reluctant to push her over in her desperation to leave. 'Miss Bland, please don't be afraid of me. I only want to talk to you.' Miss Bland paused for a moment, then turned her thickly veiled face away and shook her head. Once again, she made to try and move on, but Mina quickly reached out and took her by the wrist. There was a slight gasp of surprise from behind the veil. Slim little fingers used to wielding dumbbells made for a sharp grip.

'We must speak. I insist on it. For both our sakes. Let us not fight each other. There is a private room here. We will not be overheard or interrupted. Please.' Firm and insistent, Mina drew Miss Bland to Dr Hamid's office. The lady was reluctant, but as another patient appeared in the corridor, she capitulated rather than make a scene. They both entered the office and were seated facing each other uncomfortably across the desk.

'I do hope that we can be open and completely truthful with each other,' Mina began. 'I do not know what it is that afflicts you, but all the same I think we two might understand each other better than most. I cannot and do not attempt to hide what I am, neither do I conceal myself from the world. My life is a good one and I am my own woman. I speak my mind; I do not allow others to speak it for me.'

Miss Bland uttered a miserable sigh. 'It is ... hard for me to speak,' she said in a slurred breathy whisper.

'For both of us, each day is one of testing and tribulation, but we must meet it and make the best of it.'

'Your body is your burden. Mine ... is different.' Miss Bland paused. 'I would not show this to everyone.' Slowly, hesitantly, she raised her veil.

One side of her face was almost no face at all. It was without shape and the surface was scarred, furrowed and reddened. Tight folds of flesh hung over one eye so that she could barely see through it, the nose was flattened and twisted cords of skin pulled at one side of her mouth, further distorting her appearance. The other side was quite normal and not unattractive. 'I was a child when it happened,' she said with an effort, through tightened, constricted lips. 'I fainted and fell with my face against a hot stove. I was burned almost to the bone. I nearly died. Sometimes I wish I had.'

'My spine is twisted,' said Mina, 'pulled first one way and then the other. It reduces me to the size and shape you see. Too much movement can pain me. I live with the danger that my own skeleton may one day crush my heart and lungs. I will probably not have a long life. I will never marry or bear children. But we must both of us make what we can of our lives. There are respectable paths of fulfilment. I beg you, do not seek it by condoning a lie!'

The good side of the damaged mouth rose in a travesty of a smile. 'Then I am more fortunate than you. I am fulfilled in ways you can never be. I am married. And there is no reason why, God willing, I cannot in time become a mother.'

Mina found it impossible to hide her surprise at this revelation. 'My congratulations,' said Mina at last. 'I had been given to understand that you and your sister led very retiring lives. Who is your husband? How did you meet him?'

'He is – a man of business – a customer of my father's.'

Mina recalled what she had been told of the Bland sisters' father, information she was not supposed to know, and also what had been printed in *An Encounter*. 'Oh? That is a strange way of putting it. According to your infamous book your father is a clergyman. Clergymen do not, as a rule, have customers. But I have heard it rumoured that your father is an undertaker and cabinet maker. Is that true?'

Miss Bland was aware that she had made a slip. 'It is,' she said defensively. 'We were obliged to provide a *nom de plume* and a false history in order to preserve our anonymity.'

'And also provide your efforts with a gloss of respectability. How long have you been married?'

'Just three months, but he has been courting me these two years. Oh, I assure you, nothing has been hidden from him. He has seen past the veil and he does not recoil. He is young – handsome – he finds beauty in my soul. He kisses my hands.' She raised her hands, which were very white, like those of a marble statue. She wore dainty lace mittens and the fingers that peeped from them were long, slender and delicate. In a life dominated by her disfigurement, Miss Ada Bland was clearly very proud of her sole claim to womanly beauty. Seeing Mina's fascinated glance she performed a kind of ballet with the arms, which curved like the necks of two swans in a tender embrace.

Mina was powerfully reminded of another arm she had seen, one equally as white and graceful. 'Was it you – the disembodied hand at the Pavilion? Of course! I see it now. Your sister was there in the audience, but you were not because you were assisting the conjuror! And – Mystic Stefan, or whatever his real name is – is he your husband?'

The-one sided smile again, and a soft throaty laugh. 'I will not deny it.'

'And now I think I understand the connection. It is not the undertaker's but the cabinet maker's services he employs. Is part of your father's business the construction of the kind of special cabinets used by stage magicians? Like the one the Davenport brothers take on their travels?'

Miss Bland said nothing but she didn't need to.

Mina thought again. The father of both Miss Eustace and her acolyte the dreadful Mr Clee was in the business of supplying equipment for the stage. There were few enough businesses of that kind in London. Were the Misses Bland a part of the Clee family or friends with them? 'Is your father a Mr Benjamin Clee or a relative of his?' Mina demanded. 'Is Mr James Clee your brother or cousin?'

Miss Bland was undeniably shocked. 'No, he is – no!'

'But you know him, do you not?'

Miss Bland was silent, but she put her veil back in place and rose to her feet. 'That is enough. I regret that I agreed to this.'

'I have never met Mr Benjamin Clee, who may be a perfectly respectable gentleman for all I know, but I have encountered his son, who is an unmitigated scoundrel.'

Miss Bland was about to make for the door but turned back to face Mina with a little gasp of anger. 'That is not true! How dare you!'

'Then what is he to you that you defend him?'

Miss Bland did not reply but the fingertips of her right hand touched the knuckle of her left. From under the lace there was the thin soft gleam of a ring.

'Heaven help you woman, do not say that he is your husband!' Mina paused. 'But no, that can't be so – James Clee cannot be masquerading as Mystic Stefan, he is in prison awaiting trial. Unless of course he can fly through walls like Mrs Guppy. That is just as well for you, for had you married him you would still be single and he a bigamist.'

'What do you mean?' said Miss Bland faintly.

'Mr Clee made a scandalous marriage here last June.'

'June?' There was a long silence. 'You are lying to me.'

'Why would I do such a thing? If you don't believe me you have only to go to the Town Hall and see the evidence for yourself.'

'But …' Miss Bland suddenly sat down again, rather more heavily than she had done before.

'Yes?'

'Are you … certain of it?'

'Quite certain. They parted soon afterwards under circumstances that were reported in the newspapers. You can check that for yourself, too. There has not been time for him to regain his freedom to marry again.'

Miss Bland uttered a sob. She took a handkerchief from her reticule and applied it under the veil.

Mina took pity on her, poured a glass of the restorative water from the supply that Dr Hamid always had to hand and limped around the desk, proffering it to the unhappy woman. Gradually, in small sips then great anguished gulps, the liquid disappeared. Mina removed the empty glass and took Ada's hand in her own. 'Tell me the truth, please. I am very much afraid that you and your sister have been led astray by a criminal.'

It was some time before Miss Bland could speak. 'He did say at first that there was an obstacle to our marrying, but when I insisted, he said that he thought he could remove it, and only a day later he told me that by some quirk in the law he was free and we could be united.' She wiped her face with an increasingly damp handkerchief. 'Very well, I will tell you all, but if you have lied to me, Mr Hope will hear of it.'

'Mr Hope will hear of this very soon in any case.' There was a crucifix on the wall behind Dr Hamid's chair and Mina crossed the room to place her hand on it. 'I swear by all that is most holy that I am telling you the truth.'

Ada nodded. 'My husband is Mr James Clee. After his arrest last summer he was refused bail, but I begged my father to stand surety for him. He applied again and this time it was granted.'

Mina understood. 'And somehow that later hearing was never reported in the newspapers, so I wasn't aware of his release. When were you married?'

'July,' she sighed.

'Oh dear. So Mr Clee, who we all thought was safely in gaol, has been a free man these three months.'

'But he does love me!' Miss Bland insisted. 'He has been true to me! If he parted from that other woman, he cannot love her at all.'

'I am quite sure he does not,' said Mina, a comment that the unhappy Miss Bland appeared to find comforting. 'I suppose – I don't mean to be cruel – but before your marriage you had money of your own?'

'Some, but not a very great fortune as you seem to imagine. Of course it is now his, as a husband's right – except – he may not be my husband at all, and I —' she sobbed again.

Mina gave her some time to recover. 'Miss Bland – who wrote *An Encounter*? It wasn't you or your sister. Was it Mr Clee?'

'I don't know. I don't think so. James brought us the manuscript. He didn't say who had written it, but it wasn't in his hand, only he said he needed it printed to make some money. What with the fraud case the family had a lot of expenses and a stop had been placed on their finances, which were assumed to be the profits of crime and which might have to be restored. Many of their possessions were in the hands of the police to be used in evidence at the trial. So my sister and I agreed to act for him. He wanted to borrow the money from me to pay for the work but I put my foot down. I said he could have the money not as a creditor but as the rightful property of a husband. And so we were married. After all, as a wife I would have the benefit of his protection.' She shook her head in disbelief. 'I feel sure that there has been some mistake! Perhaps he has been led astray by others. James is no criminal; he has always sought to earn a living by legitimate means. The book and the conjuring are not his only business ventures.'

'Really?' queried Mina trying to keep the frank scepticism from her voice. 'What other businesses does he have?'

'He is in the export trade. And before you ask, he needed no funds from me to launch it. I suppose he used the profits from the book. In the last weeks it has been very lucrative, far more so than his other businesses, it brings in a great deal of money.'

'You surprise me. What is the name of this business? Where is his office?

'I – don't know. I don't really trouble myself with matters of commerce. That is his affair.'

'Has he visited his office in all the time he has been in Brighton?'

'I don't think so.'

'What does he export?'

'All manner of things.'

'Where to?'

'I don't know – or at least – I did ask him once and he said he mainly sends goods to Africa only I don't know if that was really the case or just his joke.'

'I think it was a joke,' said Mina, 'and I can guess who the butt of it was. I suppose he ordered you to have nothing to do with me?'

'Yes, and I can see why.' Her voice trembled and she applied the handkerchief to her face again. 'I can't help thinking that this is all a mistake. Perhaps James really thought he was free to marry me. The law is such a strange thing. Perhaps once he is properly free we can be married in church. I must see him.' She rose to leave.

'Miss Bland, please take my advice. First satisfy yourself that everything I have said is true. You will see that he is a villain beyond redemption and nothing can excuse his actions. Then consult a solicitor.'

'I suppose you mean to see James convicted?' she said accusingly.

'That will take care of itself. I have another matter in hand.'

Thirty-Eight

It was a fine but gusty evening as the Lord Mayor of Brighton, his aldermen and their wives arrived at the Pavilion for Mr Hope's special demonstration. Mr Hope himself conducted them into the chess room, promising them a very remarkable entertainment. The screens, with their delicate oriental traceries, were draped even more lavishly than before in brightly coloured silken shawls and in front of them, the Wondrous Ajeeb's devoted attendant Mr Franklin was fussing about the towering figure of the automaton, ensuring that it was beautifully presented, the chess board fully laid out ready for a game. On the wall there hung an engraved portrait of the statue of Captain Pechell, and a photograph of the man himself on the battlefield together with some of his men of the 77th Foot. In addition, and what the visitors might have found slightly more interesting, a side table had been furnished with bottles of wine and glasses, with water for the more abstemiously inclined. A lady, demurely dressed, was standing near the table, eyeing the refreshments with anticipation.

'Before we begin,' announced Mr Hope to the assembled notables, 'there is someone I would very much like you to meet, a lady who I believe will one day be feted worldwide as a great visionary and seeker after the truth. Allow me to introduce Miss Bertha Bland.' Mr Hope offered his hand to the demurely dressed lady and brought her forward to present her to the distinguished company.

The Lord Mayor, aldermen and their wives were understandably startled to be confronted by so controversial a figure, but after a moment's hesitation, made the best of it so as not to offend their host or his guest. Cool greetings were exchanged.

'As you know,' continued Mr Hope cheerfully, 'Miss Bland and her sister have been the object of some unwarranted publicity and vile allegations which have no foundation whatsoever in fact. Proof of this will be provided very soon and their accusers will live to regret their words. One day we will all feel most privileged to have made the acquaintance of the Misses Bland.'

The Lord Mayor, aldermen and most especially their wives looked unconvinced, but did not comment.

'I am afraid,' Hope went on, 'that I must apologise for the absence of Miss Ada Bland, who is unfortunately indisposed. But have no fear, Miss Bertha Bland reassures me that such is the intimacy of her mind's connection with that of her beloved sister that she can achieve all that is necessary during tonight's entertainment through her very remarkable skills.'

'I hope there will be none of this psychic trickery,' said the Mayor, with a worried look.

'There will be no trickery at all,' Mr Hope reassured him.

Dr Hamid and Anna arrived, both looking rather uncomfortable at being there, and Mr Hope, leaving the dignitaries to further acquaint themselves with Miss Bland, went to greet them. Anna, after the briefest possible acknowledgement of their host, excused herself and went to pour a glass of water. 'My dear Doctor,' said Hope, unabashed, 'it is always a pleasure to see a respected man of science at my gatherings. I believe that most of the eminent men of Brighton are now present in this very room!'

'But not all of the eminent ladies,' Dr Hamid observed. 'I would have expected you to invite Miss Scarletti.'

Hope had the good grace to look slightly embarrassed at this question and did not try to evade it. 'To be perfectly honest, Dr Hamid, I believe that Miss Scarletti's presence here would not assist in the success of the demonstration. It was my choice that she should not be invited, and if she attempts to gain entry she will not be admitted. In fact, I have increasingly suspected of late that she might not be altogether in her right mind. I have consulted a London specialist on the subject, who agrees with me.'

'What is the name of this specialist?'

Hope smiled. 'We must talk about this on another occasion.'

'Indeed we must,' said Dr Hamid with a frown. Mr Hope returned to the side of Miss Bland, who was eagerly telling an alderman's wife about her wonderful ability to read what was in her sister's thoughts and know exactly where she was at all times. At present her dear Ada had a slight cold and cough, and, claimed Bertha, she could actually see the poor invalid in her mind's eye, resting before a warm fire, with a bottle of physic by her side, reading an improving and moral volume by that wonderful Brightonian author Mr Tainsh.

The Lord Mayor was standing before the figure of the mighty Turk, gazing up at the calm wooden face. 'I came here to see him demonstrate last year and even challenged him to a game,' he told one of the aldermen. 'I was most soundly beaten, though I am no beginner at chess. But Mr Hope promises we will see something even more extraordinary tonight.'

There was a metallic grinding sound and very slowly the wondrous Ajeeb bowed his head. The Mayor was disconcerted for a moment, then chuckled. 'He is certainly a respectful fellow. One might almost imagine him to be alive.' He turned to Mr Franklin. 'How does he work?'

'By clockwork, sir,' said Franklin, with a worried look, 'although I don't remember winding the key this evening.' Ajeeb turned his head creakily to look at him and nodded.

The Mayor laughed, 'Well it seems you did and forgot.'

Mr Franklin did not laugh.

'If you will kindly take your seats, ladies and gentlemen,' announced Mr Hope, 'the demonstration is about to begin.' Everyone complied and Hope surveyed the distinguished company with great satisfaction. 'I would like to start with a short prayer. Let us give thanks for the lives of those noted citizens of Brighton who have gone before us across the great veil. I most especially pray for eternal blessings on the soul of Captain Pechell whose portraits grace this apartment. He was my comrade and my friend, a brave soldier and a fine example to all who knew him.'

With the brief homily done, Hope turned to Mr Franklin. 'It is time to turn the key so we may view the great mysteries of the Wondrous Ajeeb.'

'I am not sure, sir, if he has not already been wound,' said Franklin, but he tried the key and found it turned easily, which further puzzled him. He continued to wind until the mechanism was fully primed. 'We are ready now, sir. Ajeeb will be pleased to challenge any gentleman present to a game of chess.'

To his astonishment, however, Ajeeb shook his head and the onlookers laughed. 'Is he too tired to play chess today?' joked one of the aldermen. 'That is a fine thing from a machine.'

'Ajeeb, will you not play chess?' asked Franklin, mystified. Once again the wooden head indicated he would not. 'Would you prefer draughts? I will put the pieces in place.' Franklin hurried to get the basket of draughts, but again Ajeeb declined.

'What is happening?' asked Hope.

'I don't know, sir, I don't understand it, he has never done this before.'

Hope gave a grunt of impatience, which was not improved by the amusement of the audience.

'Your Turk is misbehaving tonight,' chortled the Mayor.

Hope faced the giant figure. 'Ajeeb!' he cried commandingly, 'I order you to play chess for the Lord Mayor and aldermen of Brighton!'

Ajeeb's reply was swift. With a sweep of his arm the chess pieces were knocked from the board and tumbled across the floor. 'Franklin, deal with this!' demanded Hope.

'I'm really very sorry, sir,' said Franklin, with growing concern. He picked up the chess pieces and tried to replace them on the board, but the insistent Turk merely swept them away again, and he had to back away to avoid being struck by the mechanical hand.

'Is there nothing you can do, man?'

'I don't know,' said Franklin helplessly. 'Once it has been wound I cannot unwind it, one must just let the clockwork run down and that could take several hours, but then I didn't think it was wound before and it still moved.'

'Well if this is all a part of the show it is very entertaining,' said the Mayor. 'I must say we had not expected a comedy.'

Franklin tried to approach his charge once more, but was defeated as Ajeeb's body began turning from side to side, both his wooden arms waving with increasing wildness. It almost looked as if the giant form was preparing to leave his plinth and wreak havoc amongst the onlookers, whose exclamations started to tell more of alarm than amusement.

'This has gone far enough,' said one of the aldermen at last, getting to his feet. 'Your machine is frightening the ladies! Make it stop!'

Franklin ran his hands through his hair distractedly. 'Mr Mott! Mr Mott!' he cried. 'Stop this at once, I beg of you!'

At the back of the room Mr Mott rose to his feet. 'Might I assist you, Mr Franklin?'

Franklin turned and stared aghast at the chess champion of all Sussex. 'But, but – who – I mean how —'

'Stop the thing now!' shouted Hope, coming forward and receiving a blow on the forehead from a thrashing mechanical hand.

'It's alive, it's alive!' wailed Franklin, his hair in a state of unaccustomed dishevelment, flopping alarmingly over his forehead.

'It is possessed!' cried Miss Bland dramatically, rising to her feet.

As if in response Ajeeb turned and, making a large gesture with one arm, struck the draped screen, which teetered and collapsed in folds, revealing the figure of Mystic Stefan crouching behind it. He was clearly unprepared for this exposure, since he was holding some images of the Prince Regent and

Mrs Fitzherbert, which had been fastened to poles and draped in transparent veils.

All the invited dignities now roared with laughter.

Stefan quickly dropped the poles on the floor and rushed to tackle the Turk, which struck him across the face. As he stood dazed and surprised, Ajeeb seized hold of the dark wig and tugged it off, revealing a more natural looking set of Byronic curls. The conjuror clapped his hands to his head in dismay, then tried to retrieve the wig, which was being waved in the air like a dead rat, but the mechanical arm flung the hairpiece across the room and, turning back, began tugging at the false beard, which led the previously mute magician to cry 'Ouch! Stop!' in a very un-Hungarian accent.

'Wait – I recognise that scoundrel!' exclaimed an alderman. 'He is Mr Clee, who was arrested here only a matter of months ago, and a most contemptible fellow. I thought he was in prison.'

Clee, his beard now half hanging from his face, looked wildly about him, then quickly pushed Mr Franklin out of his path and made a rush for the door, where Mr Mott and Dr Hamid barred his way and smartly apprehended him.

The Mayor turned to a thunderstruck Hope. 'What is the meaning of this? I am shocked and amazed that you have anything to do with this villain, and have the effrontery to invite us and our lady wives here to see some fakery which you have no doubt cooked up between you. This is the grossest possible insult. Gentlemen, ladies, we will see no more of this farrago.'

The Mayor, aldermen and their wives all prepared to depart in a body, with Hope vainly begging them to remain, protesting that there had been a terrible misunderstanding, but before they could reach the door it burst open and Miss Ada Bland marched in accompanied by two constables and waving some documents. She pointed to Mr Clee, who was being held very firmly by the arms. 'There! That is the monster who deceived me, the vile criminal who took my honour and my money too. I see you have been unmasked at last you horrid fiend,' she shrieked. 'I wish I could mark you as I am marked so you could never again work your wiles on a trusting woman.' For a moment it looked as though she might launch herself at him and make good her threat, but her sister hurried to her side and embraced her and she dissolved into sobs of anguish.

'Disgraceful!' said the Mayor's wife as the dignitaries all left. Mr Hope, speechless, sank into a chair and buried his face in his hands as the constables took Mr Clee away and the Bland sisters quickly departed.

'Well done, Miss Scarletti,' said Mr Mott, 'you astonish me, you really do.'

Mr Hope's head jerked up. He turned around and saw an unexpected tableau – the towering figure of the wondrous Ajeeb, now stilled, the maniacally giggling Mr Franklin, and beside them, the unmistakable diminutive, lopsided form of Mina. Anna Hamid had already run forward to envelop her patient in a cloak since Mina had no desire to appear in public wearing her callisthenics costume. 'But – how can that be? Where did you come from?'

'Really, Mr Hope; use your intelligence; where do you *think* I came from?' Mina gasped from exertion and dabbed her brow with a handkerchief. Anna quickly assisted her into a seat and Dr Hamid brought her a glass of water.

'I see the exercises have been of benefit,' he said dryly, 'but now I insist you rest.'

Hope, with the obvious staring him in the face, stood and turned about as if searching for another way into the room. 'But that is impossible unless – unless Miss Scarletti is a second Mrs Guppy. Of course! I knew it! I always knew it!'

'No, Mr Hope,' sighed Mina. 'I am no medium, no psychic, no seer, and I cannot fly through the air or pass through walls. All I have is common sense. You have been duped by a clever trickster, who seeks out the gullible and the credulous. You are not a fool; you are just too willing to believe. Does Mr Clee claim to be able to move objects through the ether? Has he told you that he is sending needful supplies to Africa for the succour of Dr Livingstone?'

'How could you possibly know that?' demanded Hope, turning pale.

'Well it wasn't by reading minds. I didn't need to. Clee and his accomplice in crime Miss Eustace see people's weaknesses and use them to extort money. I won't ask how much he has taken from you. If this scheme is ever revealed in court you would, I am afraid, become a public laughing stock. Perhaps, Mr Hope, from now on no more will be said of my having to sign any papers, neither will you pay some London doctor to declare me insane, or work your wiles on my family. Do I have your promise before these witnesses?'

Confronted by Dr Hamid, Anna and the all Sussex chess champion, none of whom from their expressions looked inclined to accept a refusal, Mr Hope promised.

Thirty-Nine

Against all Mina's expectations, Richard's play had survived its many setbacks and was due to be performed in the Pavilion as planned. The fracas at Ajeeb's demonstration, which might have prevented it by the loss of Mr Hope's sponsorship, had not done so. The cost of the room hire, which, Mina suspected, Hope would have withdrawn had he been able to, had already been paid and could not be unpaid. Whether he had ever made good on his promise to buy ten tickets she did not know. Even had he chosen to raise an objection to the performance, his protests would not have been listened to, since the Lord Mayor, aldermen of Brighton and the Pavilion management committee were of one mind on the subject of Mr Hope. Like the fabled Emperor who had paraded in supposedly invisible garments that only the wise were able to see, he had been revealed in his naked obsession and was now acknowledged to be a well-meaning but sadly flawed man. Worse still, an ugly rumour was busily circulating in town that Mr Hope had, during his residence, been conducting an intrigue with a married woman. This last allegation was too much for Enid and Louisa, both of whom emphatically refused to believe it. Mina was anxious to know what Mr Phipps had discovered, but dared not show her hand by questioning him. Word had it that the tainted hero was preparing to leave Brighton and might already have left.

One of the fruits of Mr Hope's patronage was a set of nicely printed handbills, which Mr Merridew had volunteered to design. Decorated with a pretty border, they read:

The Famed Exponent of Shakespeare
Who has appeared before Royalty
MR MARCUS MERRIDEW
Will grace the Pavilion in a leading role
in
THE COURTLY PRINCE
a diversion
by
Richard Scarletti

On seeing the handbills, Richard had been slightly taken aback by the fact that it was the actor and not the writer who was so prominently featured. However, Mr Merridew explained to him that the audience always came to see the actors and never took any note of the author, and that his wording would undoubtedly sell more tickets. So it was to prove.

Louisa was impressed to learn that Richard had penned a play that was to be performed by a famed professional actor, but she had not appreciated and had certainly not been informed that he also planned to appear in it. She was aware that her dear Henry had written some of the stories he published, and then there were Mina's little homilies for children, and of course the late Mr Dickens had been a good and charitable person by all accounts, and very rich. Louisa had therefore convinced herself that the business of playwrighting was a good one, and perfectly respectable as long as the writer did not have anything to do with the performers. This entertainment, she felt assured, was only the start of Richard's new career, which would lead to fortune and fame. She had been busy calling on all her friends insisting that they buy tickets and accepting no refusals. Several, who recalled Marcus Merridew in his heyday as the darling of the ladies, needed no persuasion. As a result, the performance, which was to take place before a potential audience of some fifty persons, which was as much seating as the apartment could accommodate, was quickly sold out.

The space available for the actors was not large and there was no furniture or properties of any sort, but Mr Merridew had taken great care in arranging the room, and it looked very elegant. Two of the ornate pillars – delicate looking yet strong – which supported the roof of the music room gallery, served to mark the boundary of the acting space, framing it like the feet of a gilded proscenium arch in a London theatre, while the deep drapery of the window curtains formed an opulent backdrop. Chinese screens had been placed discreetly to the right and the left to act as wings.

Mina anticipated the event with some apprehension, but felt that she ought to be there if only to deal with any upset that might result. She made sure to carry a good supply of hand-kerchiefs and a smelling bottle. All the seats were filled, with the Scarletti family accorded places on the front row. Louisa was proud and excited but Enid still wore the sour expression that had been her most prominent feature since Mr Hope's fall from popularity. As they waited for the production to begin, still more ladies crammed into the room, chattering with excitement at having bought last-minute tickets for standing room only, almost doubling the size of the audience. Most of them, Mina noticed, were of her mother's age or older, and many were holding little posies.

The tinkling of a bell announced the start of the performance and the audience, after the last trills of laughter and excitement had died down, fell silent. After a certain amount of whispering from behind one of the screens, there burst upon the stage an alarming figure. It was Richard, wearing a blue frockcoat too large for him, with ragged epaulettes very much tarnished, and an enormous bicorne hat that threatened to fall over his eyes. He was waving what Mina knew to be a blunt sword but which looked dangerously real.

'Aha!' he exclaimed, striding to the front of the space and striking a fierce pose, one hand on his hip, the other pointing the sword skywards, chest thrust out. 'Aha, aha!' he added, either for greater effect or to give himself time to think. 'I am ze great Emperor Napoleon! *Mais oui, ma foi, zut alors, sacre bleu!*' He made some wild passes with the sword, which caused the ladies in the front row to sway back in alarm. 'And my greatest enemy is George, Prince of Wales, regent of England! 'e is tall, 'e is 'andsome, and 'e has everysing I most desire! *Comme il faut! Consommé du jour!*' Richard strode about the stage waving the sword. Mina glanced quickly at her mother, who had clapped a palm over her mouth, her eyes wide open.

Richard took up his heroic pose again. 'Yes, 'e has ze srone of England, but 'e also 'as ze 'and of ze lady I love! Ze incomparable, ze beautiful Mrs Fitz'erbert. *Mon cœur! La choucroute farci!* I am determined! It is farewell to Josephine! None but Maria will be my Empress!'

There were a few titters from the audience. Undismayed, Richard paraded about in a circle once more before facing the increasingly amused assembly.

'Ah, you English, you sink that I, Napoleon, am not a tall man. But it is ze madness of love that 'as brought me low!' Here Richard fell to his knees, and his hat slipped over his eyes, requiring him to make some adjustment. 'I 'ear you ask, *quelle horreur!* What will I do to achieve my desires. I will tell you! I dare all! I will invade England wiz all of my navy. *En avance, mes amis! A l'eau, ces't l'heure!*' Richard made another circle about the stage only this time on his knees, an art which he had not sufficiently practised. If his intention was to make the former French Emperor appear ridiculous, he was succeeding.

'And now 'ere I am en Angleterre, ze land I mean to rule! But where oh where is my great love, *ah mon ange! Mon petit poisson! Chacun a son gout!* My 'eart beats only for Maria Fitz'erbert. Where is she?' He placed a hand behind one ear. 'Wait, I 'ear 'er dainty feet approach, I will 'ide and learn if she returns my love.'

As Richard shuffled behind a screen, Mina braved another look at her mother. Louisa now had her face buried in her handkerchief but whether she was laughing, crying or simply hiding, it was hard to tell.

There was a brief pause, carefully studied so as to produce the maximum anticipation in the audience, then Nellie made her entrance. Magnificently gowned in the fashion of the day, her hair shining, her skin aglow, her eyes bright and beguiling, there was no mystery as to why an Emperor should invade another country to make her his own.

She approached the front of the little stage, smiling with the knowledge that every eye was upon her. 'Ladies, gentlemen, all, I beg you not to blame me for my unusual mode of life,' she said, allowing a lacy fan to flutter modestly. 'I was an honourable widow when I first became acquainted with the Prince of Wales, and he fell most passionately in love with me. For years he pursued me to attain his heart's desire, but I am a respectable lady and would never consent to an improper connection, even at the entreaties of a Prince. At last we were married, and though the law of the land will not recognise me as his true wife, I am content that our love has been sanctified by God. My dear Prince, beloved husband, my own darling George, how can I not love you and be true forever to you and you alone!'

Nellie took an elegant tour about the stage so that everyone could feast their eyes on her ensemble. As she passed by one of the side screens, Richard, still on his knees, made a lunge, probably to try and kiss the hem of her garment, and fell flat on his face, his hat tumbling off and rolling across the stage. He stood up, dusted off his knees, retrieved the hat and jammed it firmly back on his head.

'Aha!' he exclaimed. 'It is ze beautiful Maria, ze angel 'oo rules my 'eart! *Veuve Clicqot! Coup de foudre!* Oh mon amour, say you will be mine; be my bride and I will make you Empress of la belle France!'

'But sir,' said Nellie, turning away bashfully, 'that cannot be, I am the wife of George, Prince of Wales, and he alone has my heart.'

'*Tonnere!* Zen I will slay 'im!' Richard waved the sword about his head in a manner that probably endangered himself more than anyone else. 'Where is my 'ated rival? I will seek 'im out and take 'is life, zen England and Mrs Fitz'erbert will both be mine!'

He rushed back behind a screen and Nellie took the audience into her confidence. 'Little does the Frenchman know that my husband is as brave as he is handsome. He will not fear to fight, either for his country, or for me!' She moved aside in a swirl of silk and waited by the screen, her fan beating like a dove's wing, her eyes gazing from above the snowy lace.

Marcus Merridew now made his appearance. He glided rather than walked, advancing in true dignified fashion, elegant of gesture and precise of step. By the art of the actor he had turned back time, and though Mina knew he was near her mother's years, everything about him suggested a man hardly more than thirty. He was clad after the style of Beau Brummell in breeches and boots, with a buttoned long-tailed coat, and the wig he wore framed his face in a cluster of golden brown curls. Those ladies in the audience who had seen him shine as Hamlet many years ago were not disappointed, and there were many sighs of appreciation and some enthusiastic clapping of mittened hands.

Mr Merridew greeted his admirers with a gracious smile and, advancing to the fore, bowed to them several times before taking up a position, one hand pressed passionately to his heart. The audience quickly hushed with anticipation and when he spoke, his voice was rich and mellow, effortlessly filling the room. 'Ah what a rogue and peasant slave is that Napoleon who seeks to rob me of my love! But I will defy him, take arms against a sea of troubles, and by opposing, end them. I have had word from my dear wife that the tyrant is even now on our shores and seeks to murder me. What will it be, will he, like

the coward he is, pour poison into the porches of mine ears as
I sleep, or stab me with a bare bodkin? But I mean to face him
like a man, I will be as Hyperion to a satyr.' He looked to the
side and saw Nellie. 'Soft you now, the fair Maria. How I wish
to make her my lawful bride and my Queen, but the King my
father would never condone it. My will is not my own, I am
subject to my birth.'

He crossed the space to Nellie, who advanced to meet him.
'My dearest Maria, my eternal love, the wife of my heart.' He
reached out his hand and gently clasped her fingers, then made
an extravagantly stylish obeisance.

There was a strangled cry from the audience. Mrs Peasgood,
in a state of great agitation, had risen to her feet. 'I can be silent
no longer! It is he, or his spirit, the very he who appeared before
me, he whose ghost walked through the wall dressed just so and
bowed to me, he who danced with the lady in the room with
the red wallpaper. Is he a ghost or a demon?'

Mrs Mowbray rose up and tried to comfort her sister, who was
trembling violently. 'Oh my dear, please sit down and calm yourself!'

'How can I when a spirit walks in the shape of a man? What
does it mean?'

Several ladies waved at Mrs Peasgood and urged her to keep
quiet.

Merridew turned to the gathering with an arched eyebrow.
'The lady doth protest too much methinks.'

It was left to Mrs Mowbray to remove her almost hysterical
sister from the room, which, with profuse apologies, she did.
The most likely place to console her was the ladies' retiring
room, and Mina feared that the sight of the red dragon wallpaper would bring on another more serious fit, but there was little
she could do.

After this interruption order was restored and the play
proceeded. Marcus and Nellie conducted a courtly dance
of matchless elegance and refinement after which the Prince,

on bended knee, declared his undying love for his Maria. Richard rushed back on stage and exhausted his entire fund of repeatable French phrases, and a few others that ought never to have been uttered. Finally there was the sword fight, which was conducted with more dash than skill by Richard and with consummate skill by Mr Merridew. Napoleon duly met his Waterloo on the point of the Prince's sword and spent ten minutes expiring noisily, clawing the carpet. There was rapturous applause after which Mr Merridew was prevailed upon, an exercise that took barely moments to achieve, to entertain his admiring public with some of the great classical speeches in his repertoire, after which he was lavishly pelted with flowers by weeping matrons.

By the time it was all over Mrs Peasgood and Mrs Mowbray had long departed, and Louisa took her daughters and the entire cast for dinner. Since Mrs Peasgood's outburst had been highly embarrassing, no one chose to mention it.

The wine was poured and hors d'oeuvres brought to the table. 'It was a perfectly splendid evening,' said Louisa, raising her glass, 'but Richard —'

'Yes, mother?'

'You must never do that again.'

'No, mother.'

'Mr Merridew, I must compliment you on your costume,' said Mina.

'Thank you dear lady; it is the very one I wore when appearing in the Regency gloss on *King Lear*. As you saw,' he added modestly, 'it still fits me to perfection.'

'Have you ever worn it in the Pavilion before?'

'As a matter of fact I have, but not for a performance. When the Pavilion was first opened for inspection some of our little troupe made the tour in costume – it was amusing and we hoped to attract some interest in our play.'

'Do you recall if you entered the music room on your tour?'

'I expect so, but it is hard to remember exactly where we went. We did march along what I now know to be the servants' corridors and then we executed a pretty little dance.' He looked suddenly thoughtful. 'You don't think that could have anything to do with —' he shook his head, 'but no, that cannot be, it was over twenty years ago and it was all in the best possible taste.'

When Mina was home once more she again studied her guidebook to the Pavilion, and was now quite sure of the train of events. She sent a note to Mrs Peasgood, saying she hoped very much that she was well, and wished to speak to her on a matter that she felt sure would set her mind at rest.

Forty

ina was not at all sure if Mrs Peasgood would consent to see her and half expected to receive either no reply or a letter from Mrs Mowbray with a polite refusal. To her surprise, however, a note was delivered inviting her to call. Neither Louisa nor Enid were disposed to visit Mrs Peasgood until they felt reassured that her sudden malady was not catching, and it was only to Richard, who was still exuberant from his theatrical triumph, that Mina revealed the true reason for her proposed visit.

'Mrs Peasgood knows you too well, Mina,' said Richard, 'you would have secured an interview with her sooner or later and she has decided to accept the inevitable.'

'I hope I can bring her some peace. Poor lady, it has been a long time coming.'

In Mrs Peasgood's quiet parlour Mina was greeted by the lady herself, who seemed to have recovered much of her accustomed composure and now appeared merely sad. She was attended with care and sympathy by Mrs Mowbray.

'I think,' said Mrs Peasgood, once refreshments were brought and the maid had departed, 'that you and possibly you alone, apart from my sister, understand some of the reasons for my agitation yesterday.'

'I do,' said Mina, 'and that is mainly because I was probably the only person present at my brother's play who had made a recent study of *Some Confidential Observations by a Lady of Quality*, the pamphlet you wrote in 1850.'

Mrs Peasgood's hand trembled and her sister rescued a teacup from potential disaster. 'How, pray, did you obtain a copy?'

'It was in the library. It is a part of their collection of works on the history of Brighton.'

Mrs Peasgood frowned. 'I sincerely hope it is not on open display.'

'No, it is stored in a box with a host of other pamphlets.'

'Then I don't understand. Was it just by chance that you found it?'

Mina explained how she had searched for the pamphlet when all she had was a clue that it might exist at all.

'Well that is quite astonishing,' said Mrs Peasgood. 'I compliment you on your insight and diligence.'

'I have also read an account in the *Gazette* of the occasion when the Pavilion was first opened for viewing by the public, the time you must have gone there with your father. There were no official guides as there are now, people simply walked from room to room, and given the nature of the building, and how many times it has been altered and enlarged, some visitors did get lost and confused. I expect that that is what happened to you.'

'Yes, I do recall that. But I wrote a true and honest account of my visit, not the despicable and indecent invention of that horrid book.'

'Then it was not, as I had initially supposed, intended to be a work of fiction?'

'No, not at all.'

'I take it that you have not visited the Pavilion since then?'

'I dared not! I wanted no repetition of that experience. Before last night I had not stepped through its doors in over twenty years. It was only with the passage of time, and your mother being so insistent, that I consented to go again.'

'Mr Merridew, the actor who played the Prince of Wales, has been an attendant at the Pavilion for many years, and knows the building well. He told me that he and a theatrical troupe, which included some musicians, had in 1850 been performing a play costumed in the style of the court of King George III. They decided, for their amusement and also to stimulate interest in the play, to visit the Pavilion in costume. I believe that it was they you saw.'

'Are you sure? I heard the music very distinctly before I even saw them; it seemed to come through the walls.'

'It did come through the walls. There are long corridors for the use of servants which run alongside the main rooms. The musicians walked along them with violin and flute.'

'But how did the gentleman come into the room when the doors could not be opened?'

Mina opened the guidebook and showed Mrs Peasgood the page describing the music room. 'I think this is where you were standing when you saw him. The music room has four doors but two of them are false to give the appearance of symmetry. There is, however, another door for the use of servants covered in the same paper as the walls. The room was ill-lit when you were there and you would not have noticed it. I think that is how Mr Merridew entered when your back was turned.'

Mrs Peasgood took the guidebook and spent several minutes studying it. 'So there was not, after all, a ghost,' she said at last.

'There was not.'

'I confess that that is something of a relief to me.'

'Knowing this, and being able to connect your pamphlet with the recent sensational volume, will greatly strengthen the plagiarism case.'

'I am sure it will,' said Mrs Peasgood, but she did not seem comfortable with the prospect.

'There is nothing to give offence in your pamphlet, and it is very nicely written. You could have it printed again, as a story, rather than a history. I think it would do very well.'

'Really? Well I am not sure about that.' Nevertheless she looked flattered.

'I have my suspicions as to who wrote *An Encounter*, but there are some pieces of the puzzle I am missing, although I think you might be able to enlighten me.'

The two sisters exchanged glances and Mrs Peasgood patted Mrs Mowbray's hand. 'Caroline has confessed all to me and I have forgiven her. Miss Scarletti, I am grateful to you for all you have done, and I am therefore prepared to tell you all I know.'

'I too,' said Mrs Mowbray, 'although I have much to be ashamed of. It was at one of those séances with Miss Eustace, last summer. Mr Clee was there, only none of us knew at the time that he was in league with her. There was some conversation afterwards and he was asking if there were any legends in Brighton about hauntings, so —' she uttered a despondent sigh, 'I regret to say that I mentioned the business in the Pavilion. I know I shouldn't have but it just seemed to come out. I'd never told anyone else before or since.'

Mrs Peasgood gave a faint smile. 'The young gentleman was very persuasive. After my marriage, which took place in 1851, I decided to put all that business behind me and Caroline promised to say nothing. Truth to tell I wished it had never happened at all, as I thought it made me appear rather foolish. I was not eager for it to be broadcast, and most especially I did not wish Mr Peasgood to know.'

'As soon as I told Mr Clee about it I regretted my betrayal,' Mrs Mowbray continued, 'but he kept on and on, asking me more about it. He was very charming, as you know, and so I told him it was in a book, and then of course he wanted to know where he could get a copy. I didn't know there was one in the library.'

'Nor I,' said Mrs Peasgood. 'I suppose the printers must have sent them one.'

'Well in the end I lent him mine, thinking that would put an end to the matter. But then he said he wanted to meet the lady who had written it so I told him the lady was dead long ago and had no family. I'm so sorry, Mattie, I didn't want you to know I'd broken my promise.'

'So of course he then believed that there was no one who might notice the pirating of the work, and thought he could copy it with impunity,' said Mina. 'I doubt that he was expecting it to be such a sensation.'

'That was quite a shock,' said Mrs Mowbray, 'especially after what he had done with it. It was disgusting. When he came back to Brighton recently he asked to see me, saying that he had found out that the writer was alive. We met in secret a number of times, but he never wore that disguise when I saw him. He was very insistent that I tell him who the author was – I think he suspected that it was really me – he kept on asking, but I wouldn't say. He told me I must tell no one that I had given him the book and I promised him I wouldn't. He even offered to share some of the profits of *An Encounter* if I could get the action for plagiarism stopped. Do you think it will all come out in court? I will look like such a silly woman.'

'Not as silly as I will look,' said Mrs Peasgood grimly. 'I do hope that with good advice we can settle it without recourse to a public hearing. Who knows if the culprits can even pay the damages? I fear that after my public outburst it may become common knowledge but if it does not feature in a trial which is reported in the newspapers it may, I hope, be more quickly and quietly forgotten.'

'I promise that I will not reveal the confidences you have granted me today,' said Mina. 'I do, however, have one request.'

'Oh?'

'As the matter proceeds through the usual legal channels you will undoubtedly learn more, and I should very much like, for my own curiosity, to hear the whole story.'

Mr Peasgood did not hesitate. 'You deserve no less. I agree.'

Forty-One

Mrs Peasgood was true to her word. During the next few weeks the full sequence of events was uncovered and Mina was in receipt of much confidential information that she promised not to reveal. The plagiarism case against the Misses Bland had initially been pursued by Mr Laidlaw, of Phipps, Laidlaw and Phipps, but then, quite abruptly, he decided to retire from practice, and he and his wife left Brighton to reside in a small Scottish estate owned by his family. The reasons for his decision and the suddenness of it were never disclosed, although there was a suspicion that pretty Mrs Laidlaw and Mr Arthur Wallace Hope, as well as a certain private detective, could, had they wished, have solved the mystery. Young Mr Ronald Phipps swiftly and smoothly took up the reins of the enquiry and it was thought that the date on which a third Phipps would be added to the partnership had been considerably advanced.

Mr Phipps had established beyond doubt that *An Encounter* had been written by Miss Eustace during her summer residence in Brighton. It had been composed with the intention not only of making money but also of creating more interest in her séances. The text, based on Mrs Peasgood's pamphlet, a history of the Pavilion, the author's recollection of her own visit, and a lurid imagination, had been completed shortly before she and her accomplices were arrested. With legal expenses mounting and the proceeds of their fraudulent activities having been seized, when Mr Clee was released on bail it was decided to use the book to raise funds. He had known the Misses Bland's family for some years and was well aware of the stricken older sister's attraction to him. He had made use of her weakness before to borrow money when business had not been successful, and approached her once again for a loan to pay the printer, only to find that he had gone to the well once too often. This time, her price had been marriage.

Thereafter he had stayed in touch with his 'wife' by letter in order that she could send him the profits of the enterprise. When Mr Hope, a wealthy and influential spiritualist, had come to Brighton to lecture, Mr Clee had spotted a chance. The friendship of Hope and Dr Lynn was common knowledge amongst magicians, and Lynn, after receiving the business card of Benjamin Clee, purveyor of theatrical supplies, from Miss Eustace, had become a customer. Letters from Dr Lynn placing orders had provided enough examples of his writing to enable Clee to forge a convincing letter of introduction to Mr Hope and launch a new career as Mystic Stefan.

All was going well for Mr Clee until the shock accusation of plagiarism. The Misses Bland, equally unprepared for the allegation and the predicament they found themselves in, had fled to Brighton to confront him. He had been alarmed to see them at first as he did not want his real identity revealed, but also saw that their presence in Brighton could be made to work to his advantage. He told the sisters that as far as he was aware the author of *Confidential Observations* was deceased and that they should if challenged say that they had received the book through the spirits. He also instructed that on no account should they tell anyone of his masquerade as Mystic Stefan, and above all they must not speak to Miss Scarletti the crippled lady, as she was his enemy and the reason he was in his current difficulty.

Clee had strongly recommended that the Misses Bland approach Mr Hope for assistance as he would undoubtedly be sympathetic. The sisters were very adept at the 'willing game' as they had since childhood employed a system of secret signals to communicate the answers, and Clee believed that this would easily fool Mr Hope into accepting them as mediums and earn his loyalty to their cause. As predicted, when the sisters came to Mr Hope with their story and performed their mind-reading trick, he was delighted with it and became a fervent believer. Hope had told the Misses Bland that while he could not personally intervene in the plagiarism case at present, he could help promote them in Brighton as psychics, which would assist in their defence. Clee had also become aware of Hope's obsession with finding Dr Livingstone, and was able to convince him that while lacking sufficient power to transport the good doctor home, he could through the energy of the spirits send the beleaguered explorer comforting messages and much-needed food and medicines. It was a service that came at a price, but it was a price that Mr Hope could afford and was willing to pay.

Mr Clee's one remaining difficulty was Mrs Mowbray and he had done everything short of promising marriage to extract more information from her, but the situation had finally concluded with an uneasy truce in which both parties had agreed to be silent about their involvement.

The trial of Miss Eustace and her confederates duly took place at Lewes Assizes and Mina made sure to be present. A statement was read from Dr Lynn who was currently away on tour, saying that he had never met Mr Clee or Mystic Stefan, and had not written either of them a letter of introduction to Mr Hope. It was also revealed that Miss Eustace had never intended to return to Brighton and appear at the Pavilion. Mr Clee, anticipating an acquittal, had been making plans for them to leave for America and had secured the services of an agent there who would obtain bookings for séances and theatrical performances.

Miss Whinstone gave her evidence with as much courage as she could summon, and Mr Jellico, with tears of pride in his eyes, sat urging her on with smiles and nods. She barely faltered. Miss Eustace's counsel offered the defence that Miss Whinstone had lied to the magistrates and was now lying to judge and jury, but in view of the other revelations this rang hollow and was in itself a further proof of the scurrilous depths to which the prisoners would sink.

The accused were duly found guilty of obtaining money by deception, and in view of the substantial sums involved, the suggestion that there were numerous victims, and a previous conviction for the same offence, they were sentenced to terms of five years in prison. Mr Clee, in a separate hearing, was found guilty on an additional charge of bigamy. As he was removed to the cells, Clee loudly derided Mr Hope as a fool, saying that he had never duped anyone as easily. Hope, he said, had even been taken in by a tawdry glass bead that came from a theatrical costume shop. Mina surmised from this outburst that the Viscount, who was not in court, had withdrawn all financial assistance from the conspirators.

Mr Hope was long gone from Brighton by that time, but Mina did hear that he still believed in the Misses Bland, who had been absolved of all blame concerning the plagiarism, and was launching them on a career as mediums and mindreaders. There was a newspaper report that he had asked Mrs Guppy to apport Dr Livingstone to one of her séances. So far she had not been successful.

Richard had decided to abandon the stage as a career. He said that he had enjoyed the experience enormously and had even made money on the ticket sales, but thought that it was too much hard work to be a regular thing. Mina was obliged to remind him that his profit had mainly resulted from the fact that the venue and advertising had all been paid for by Mr Hope, which was not a source he could rely upon in future, and Richard was obliged to admit that this was true. His early return to London was precipitated by the fact that both the twins had started teething. Before he left he promised Mina to accept their brother Edward's offer of a position as a clerk. She implored him to try and make a success of it, but was concerned that it would not keep him out of trouble for long.

Following his magnificent success in *The Courtly Prince*, Mr Marcus Merridew enjoyed a well-deserved revival of his theatrical career. While continuing his work at the Pavilion, which he would never have given up as he found it very pleasurable, he was able to combine this with a sudden demand for his services as an actor and raconteur. He was soon engaged for a series of public lectures on the history of the legitimate theatre and readings from Shakespeare, and was positively begged by Brighton Theatre's stock company to ornament their stage in the leading role of his choice.

Meanwhile, fashion in Brighton changed with the wind, and there was no more talk of ghosts in the Pavilion, although there were visitors aplenty.

Enid continued to pine for the company of Mr Hope and sat wanly at meals, eating very little and making the occasional suggestion that it would be charming to visit Middlesex as there were so many fine country estates there. She seemed unable to accept that Mr Hope's attentions had not been genuine. One morning she was absent from the breakfast table and Mina was worried that she might have fled to join her admirer.

'Enid is in her room,' Louisa explained. 'She received a letter this morning from Mr Inskip. It seems that his business with the Carpathian Count has been completed earlier than expected and he should be home before winter if the weather holds. Enid was quite overcome by the news and has been bilious ever since.'

✳ End ✳

Historical Note

The principal inspiration for this book was *An Adventure*, first published in 1911 by Miss Charlotte Anne Elizabeth Moberly and her companion Miss Eleanor Frances Jourdain, under the pseudonyms Elizabeth Morison and Frances Lamont. The ladies had visited Versailles in 1901 and, after comparing notes and conducting extensive research, became convinced that while there they had entered a time-slip and seen Marie Antoinette and members of her court.

In the summer of 1871 the sensation of Brighton was Christiana Edmunds, a spinster who had attempted to poison the wife of a Dr Beard, for whom she had an obsessive admiration. She tried to deflect suspicion from herself by distributing poisoned food, resulting in the death of a four-year-old child. The police issued a warning notice and newspapers reported that people were talking of the 'days of the Borgias' returning. At her later trial she was declared insane and sent to Broadmoor.

Dr Hamid must have read about the plagiarism case of Pike *v.* Nicholas, which was reported in *The Times* on 25 May and 25 November 1869.

Wondrous Ajeeb the chess automaton was built in 1865 by Charles Hopper, a Bristol cabinet maker. Ajeeb would have been inspired by Wolfgang von Kempelen's more famous Turk, which was destroyed in a fire in 1854. Ajeeb, like the Turk, was controlled by a hidden operator. From 1868 to 1876 it was exhibited at London's Crystal Palace, but performed at the Royal Pavilion in October 1870. It was later taken to the United States, where it was destroyed by a fire in 1929.

Captain William Henry Cecil George Pechell was the son of Vice-Admiral Sir George Brooke Pechell, Bt, Member of Parliament for Brighton. Pechell, a Captain in Her Majesty's 77th Middlesex Regiment of Foot, was twenty-five when he was killed at the siege of Sebastopol on 3 September 1855. A statue was commissioned by public subscription and placed in the vestibule of the Royal Pavilion in 1859. It remained there until about 1940 when it was placed in Brighton's Stanmer Park, where it stood neglected until 2015. It was rescued and at the time of writing it stands near No. 22 Waterloo Street, Hove, and can be viewed on Google street view.

An article about the public viewing of the Royal Pavilion can be found on p. 5 of the *Brighton Gazette* of 24 January 1850. No one seems to have reported seeing any ghosts.

The 'willing game' was a popular Victorian parlour game played as described in these pages.

Hugh Washington Simmons (1831–1899) was a stage magician who toured the world performing under the name Dr H.S. Lynn. One of his specialities was the Japanese butterfly illusion, which he claimed to have seen in Japan and first introduced it to the West in 1864. On 17 October 1870 he gave a performance in the Royal Pavilion, Brighton for the benefit of the families of the men lost on HMS *Captain* that sank on 7 September with the loss of about 480 lives. This performance is described on p. 5 of the *Brighton Gazette* of 20 October.

Edward Campbell Tainsh (1835–1919) was a Professor of Literature and author of morally uplifting novels, who disapproved strongly of sensational fiction.

A paper device that answers 'yes' or 'no' is described in *Houdini's Paper Magic*, by Harry Houdini, (E.P. Dutton, New York, 1922). Mystic Stefan must have used an earlier version.

The 'floating arm' and Sphinx's head were both Victorian stage illusions.

Dr Livingstone was discovered by Henry Morton Stanley in November 1871, although the news did not reach Britain until the following year.

William John Smith, bookseller, traded from Nos 41–43 North Street from 1865 to 1913.

Mrs Guppy did indeed claim to have flown through a wall as described. For more information see *Mrs Guppy Takes a Flight* by Molly Whittington-Egan (Neil Wilson Publishing, Castle Douglas, 2015).

Mr Arthur Wallace Hope is a fictional character but his beliefs as described in this book were held by many educated men and women of his day and have not been exaggerated for the purpose of fiction.

About the Author

Linda Stratmann is a former chemist's dispenser and civil servant who now writes full-time. She lives in Walthamstow, London.

Website www.lindastratmann.com
Twitter @LindaStratmann
Facebook www.facebook.com/Books-by-Linda-Stratmann-270261905489/

In the Mina Scarletti Series

Mr Scarletti's Ghost: A Mina Scarletti Mystery

Also by the Author

Chloroform: The Quest for Oblivion
Cruel Deeds and Dreadful Calamities: The Illustrated Police News 1864–1938
Essex Murders
Gloucestershire Murders
Greater London Murders: 33 True Stories of Revenge, Jealousy, Greed & Lust
Kent Murders
Middlesex Murders
More Essex Murders
Notorious Blasted Rascal: Colonel Charteris and the Servant Girl's Revenge
Fraudsters and Charlatans: A Peek at Some of History's Greatest Rogues
The Marquess of Queensberry: Wilde's Nemesis
The Secret Poisoner: A Century of Murder
Whiteley's Folly: The Life and Death of a Salesman

In the Frances Doughty Mystery Series

Praise for the Frances Doughty Mystery Series

'If Jane Austen had lived a few decades longer,
and spent her twilight years writing detective stories,
they might have read something like this one'

Sharon Bolton, bestselling author of the Lacey Flint series

'A gripping and intriguing mystery with an
atmosphere Dickens would be proud of'

Leigh Russell, bestselling author of the Geraldine Steel novels

'I feel that I am walking down the street in Frances' company and seeing the people and houses around me with clarity'

Jennifer S. Palmer, Mystery Women

'Every novelist needs her USP: Stratmann's is her intimate knowledge of both pharmacy and true-life Victorian crime'

Shots Magazine

'The atmosphere and picture of Victorian London is vivid and beautifully portrayed'

www.crimesquad.com

'Vivid details and convincing period dialogue bring to life Victorian England during the early days of the women's suffrage movement, which increasingly appeals to Frances even as she strives for acceptance from the male-dominated society of the time. Historical mystery fans will be hooked'

Publishers Weekly

'[Frances'] adventures as a detective, and the slowly unravelling evidence of multiple crimes in a murky Victorian setting, make for a gripping read'

Historical Novel Review

'The historical background is impeccable'

Mystery People

Lightning Source UK Ltd.
Milton Keynes UK
UKOW06f0958240616

276982UK00002B/27/P